Whatever Happened to Madeline Stone?

www.penguin.co.uk

Also by Louise O'Neill

For Young Adults
Only Ever Yours
Asking For It
The Surface Breaks

For Adults
Almost Love
After the Silence
Idol

Whatever Happened to Madeline Stone?

LOUISE O'NEILL

bantam

TRANSWORLD PUBLISHERS

UK | USA | Canada | Ireland | Australia
India | New Zealand | South Africa

Transworld is part of the Penguin Random House group of companies whose addresses can be found at global.penguinrandomhouse.com.

Penguin Random House UK, One Embassy Gardens, 8 Viaduct Gardens, London SW11 7BW

penguin.co.uk

First published in Great Britain in 2026 by Bantam
an imprint of Transworld Publishers

001

Copyright © Daughter of Eve 2026

The moral right of the author has been asserted.

This book is a work of fiction and, except in the case of historical fact, any resemblance to actual persons, living or dead, is purely coincidental.

Every effort has been made to obtain the necessary permissions with reference to copyright material, both illustrative and quoted. We apologize for any omissions in this respect and will be pleased to make the appropriate acknowledgements in any future edition.

Penguin Random House values and supports copyright. Copyright fuels creativity, encourages diverse voices, promotes freedom of expression and supports a vibrant culture. Thank you for purchasing an authorized edition of this book and for respecting intellectual property laws by not reproducing, scanning or distributing any part of it by any means without permission. You are supporting authors and enabling Penguin Random House to continue to publish books for everyone. No part of this book may be used or reproduced in any manner for the purpose of training artificial intelligence technologies or systems. In accordance with Article 4(3) of the DSM Directive 2019/790, Penguin Random House expressly reserves this work from the text and data mining exception.

Typeset in 12.5/15.25 pt Dante MT Std by Falcon Oast Graphic Art Ltd
Printed and bound in Great Britain by Clays Ltd, Elcograf S.p.A.

The authorized representative in the EEA is Penguin Random House Ireland,
Morrison Chambers, 32 Nassau Street, Dublin D02 YH68

A CIP catalogue record for this book is available from the British Library.

ISBNs:
9781787635357 (cased)
9781787635364 (tpb)

To Grace O'Sullivan –
for every letter you wrote to me x

Prologue

1988

It had been unusually warm that day, even for Nevada in June. That was what Erin told people later, when the story became legend, part of the Stone Sisters' mythology. The twins were only two years of age when she'd buckled them into the back seat of the car, crying that the worn pleather fabric was too hot, it was burning their skin, but she had told them to shush, this wouldn't take long. Then she drove with the windows down and the music loud, singing along to 'Dirty Diana' on the radio, glancing at her daughters every so often in the rear-view mirror to make sure they were okay. They were all she had now.

The real deal: that was what her boss had said about the psychic. Almost spooky, the woman had added, with a shiver. She knew things she had no business knowing. And although Erin could barely afford the gas money it would take to drive to see the fortune-teller, let alone pay her fee, Erin knew she would go anyway. All she wanted to know was that her husband was coming back: he'd realized he'd made a mistake and was sorry. He missed her, he missed the girls, he couldn't live without them. That was what he would say as he walked through the front door. They would be a family again, and maybe then Erin would be able to sleep, without thinking, *thinking, thinking* about where she was going to find the money for the rent and the electricity bill and food for the babies. The fear crept up her spine and wrapped a hand around her neck, until she thought she might choke on it.

She pulled into the trailer park, a cloud of dust swirling around the car as she screeched to a halt. The girls were drowsy, half asleep, but it was too hot to leave them in the car, even with the window open. She put her right hand on one girl's knee, her left on the other, and gently shook them awake. 'It's okay,' she said, when they began to fuss. 'Be good, now.'

She carried one of her daughters on her hip, holding the other by the hand, and they walked slowly towards the trailer. She rapped on the front door, waited until she heard the psychic call, 'Come in!' Erin climbed up the steps, and it was dark inside, the plastic blinds closed to keep the heat out. It smelt like a hospital, like the whole trailer had been bleached that morning, and the woman sitting at the table with a deck of cards in front of her was not what Erin was expecting. She was so ordinary-looking, her dark curly hair tied in a messy ponytail, wearing a navy-blue polo shirt and khaki shorts. 'Cute,' the fortune-teller cooed, peering to look at the girls. 'Twins?'

'Yes.'

'Identical?'

'Yes.'

She told Erin to sit down, to settle herself. There was nothing to be scared of, she said. Then the woman had taken Erin's hand in hers and stared at her palm. She didn't tell Erin anything about her missing husband, and neither did she foretell a tall, dark stranger coming to Erin's rescue and falling wildly in love with her. All she wanted to talk about was the twins.

'Your daughters will be famous,' she told Erin, 'and beautiful. One will become the most celebrated woman of her generation. She will know fame that you can only dream of, wealth, success . . . but heavy is the head that wears the crown. For in her victory, her sister must die.' The psychic coughed, spluttering, and she closed her eyes as if the vision hurt her. 'Only one will see their thirtieth year,' she whispered.

'Which one?' Erin asked, looking at her two girls, identical in every way.

'I do not know,' the woman said. 'The stars have not aligned yet. But you shall see, in time. When the prophecy has come to pass, you shall see.'

I.

2025

Chelsea sat up, pushing off the quilt. Like everything else in the house, the bed was custom-made and enormous. When Nick was at home, he was so far away from her that she could barely hear him breathing, but she didn't mind. It meant that when she woke, sweating, from yet another nightmare in which her twin sister was begging Chelsea to find her, her husband couldn't hear that either.

There was a knock on the door, soft. 'Mrs Bennett,' a voice called. Conchita, the housekeeper. 'I'm sorry to disturb you but it's past ten p.m.' The woman was apologetic, nervous. She was new and still seemed afraid of her, no matter how nice Chelsea tried to be. 'I'm gonna head home now, if that's all right?'

'Of course! Drive safely! I hope—' Fuck, what was her son's name again? Juan? '—I hope Juan does well in his math test. See you in the morning.' Chelsea squinted at her iPad. She hadn't realized it was so late. She had been using her favourite method of dissociating: online shopping, putting dozens of designer dresses, shoes and handbags into her cart. She liked to see how much she could pretend to spend before she got bored – a million dollars was her previous record. If the public knew about it, they would be revolted and rightly so. It was obscene. She usually X-ed out without buying anything but sometimes, if she was especially annoyed with her husband, she ordered the lot. Dozens of boxes arriving at their estate, carried in from the front gate by the security guard, carefully piled up in the guesthouse.

Chelsea would ask one of the housekeepers to unpack it all, hanging each item in her walk-in wardrobe, and she would forget about them until months later when she would find something with its tag still on, an evening gown, perhaps, or a Le Smoking tuxedo. She would try it on, staring at her reflection in the mirror, wondering why she felt even emptier than she had before. *Why do you do it?* her therapist had asked her, when Chelsea explained this little habit she had. She couldn't tell Kelly about it: her friend would just take it as more evidence of how spoiled and out of touch Chelsea had become, and Nya would want to talk it out, as if Chelsea was one of her clients rather than her best friend, and Chelsea wasn't sure what to say in response. *Because I'm rich? Because I can? Because it stops me, just for one evening, going on the message boards to read what people think really happened to Madeline Stone?*

The electric blinds were still up. It was a full moon and Chelsea liked to watch its dappled reflection on the sea's surface from her window. How beautiful it was, this view of hers. Another luxury reserved for the rich, spoils that would not be shared. *Chel,* she could almost hear her sister say, a suppressed eye-roll in her voice, *you married the man. Own your choices.* Maddie had never had much time for self-pity, even in Chelsea, no matter how much she loved her. What would her sister have thought of Nick? She pictured her husband, sprawled on the velvet chaise longue in their bedroom, reading passages aloud from a book on parallel universes, and she could only imagine Maddie's reaction. *What's happening here, Chel? Does he think he's giving a lecture?* Nick sometimes forgot that Chelsea was not one of the sycophants who worked for him, those eager young men and women who hung on his every word, open-mouthed, hoping to swallow his voice whole as if they could absorb his genius for their own. *It's about the theory of the multiverse,* he'd said, waving the book at her, and Chelsea had pretended to listen. Sometimes she thought that was what marriage was, pretending to be interested when the other person was talking and hoping they would do the same for you in turn. And they had tried, she and Nick. They'd tried so hard, in the beginning, to be what the other needed.

Parallel lives, matter, energy, time and space, expanding for ever and ever, Nick had said, and Chelsea had felt a shiver run through her. She thought of another reality, running alongside this one, invisible and unseen. A world in which her father had stayed and her mother had never had her fortune told. The prophecy left unspoken. Where she and her sister remained ordinary, unexceptional. A life in which fame had not come for them. What would that have been like? Would Maddie still be alive?

Her phone beeped. She reached for it on the nightstand, unplugging it. The message was from Kelly, the only person who would text her past ten p.m. on a weekday. *Phone me as soon as you get this,* the message said, and it sounded urgent: there were no exclamation marks, no emojis. *I'm sure she's fine,* Chelsea told herself, the same way she did every time she got a text from Kelly, even though usually the other woman was *not* fine. She needed Chelsea's help, which meant she needed Chelsea's money. Nick's money, if Chelsea was being honest, which she tried to be as little as possible. She had far too many secrets for that.

She pressed call, holding her breath as she waited for the answer. 'Hey, boo,' Kelly said. 'This is late for you. Wild night planned?' Her voice sounded steady, no slur at the edges or any hint of speediness, like she was trying to get the words out of her mouth as quickly as possible.

'Oh, the wildest.' Chelsea hesitated. She didn't want to seem like she was monitoring her friend but she couldn't help herself. 'You good?'

'Of course! Just wanted to check in with my girl.'

Chelsea wished she didn't feel surprised. She wished her automatic response to a phone call from Kelly was not to count the months since her friend's last relapse, and make an educated guess as to when the next was due. 'I know you want to help her,' Nick had said, when they'd dropped Kelly off at rehab during the summer, leaving Nick's credit-card details on file yet again. 'But we're enabling her behaviour at this point. She needs to stand on her own two feet.' Chelsea had agreed, even though they both knew she didn't mean it. Kelly was more than a former co-star – she was family, and Chelsea would do whatever it took to keep her friend alive. She had lost enough as it was.

'So . . .' Kelly let the sentence draw out '. . . I have some news.'

'Really?' Chelsea waited for her friend to tell her about a job she'd booked, or maybe she'd met someone. A nice, stable man who would take Chelsea aside and tell her that her work was done, that he would take care of Kelly now. 'What's happened?'

'It's Nya. She's agreed to do the reunion.'

Nya had been the third star of *Vigilante Queens*, the show that had been *Charlie's Angels* for a new generation. That was what everyone had said, anyway. It had transformed the landscape of teen drama in the early noughties, and saved AtomicKids from extinction, finally making the network a contender against its competitors, Disney and Nickelodeon. More importantly, it had made bona-fide stars of the three of them – Chelsea, Nya and Kelly – and, to a lesser degree, the actor who played Frank, the boss of their crime-fighting agency. And, as every interview with him liked to point out, *Vigilante Queens* had been where The Director had cut his teeth. Would the world have discovered his genius otherwise?

'Oh,' Chelsea said. Why would Nya tell Kelly about this and not her? She put her friend on speakerphone and scrolled down to Nya's name in iMessage. There were several unanswered texts, and she instantly felt guilty. *Hey, girl, can you phone me when you get this?* and *Chel, I need to talk to you!* and *Hey, I know you're super busy but could we just hop on a call for, like, two secs? Xo* It had been a busy few days, trying to get the kids settled back into school after the Christmas holidays, and she had completely ignored Nya's messages.

'I'm surprised to hear that,' Chelsea said, putting the phone back to her ear. 'I didn't think she'd go for it, not an official reunion anyway.'

Nya had played Walker, tough, fierce, borderline terrifying. 'The angry Black woman,' Nya used to complain, when they got their weekly scripts and her character was, yet again, beating a man to a pulp for daring to look sideways at her. At the time Chelsea hadn't understood what her co-star had meant, thinking Nya was too sensitive, something she felt embarrassed about now. On the other side, there had been Kelly. She had played Wren, the scrappy, straight-talking blonde bombshell, the 'tits of the operation', as a popular men's magazine had described her when Kelly was barely seventeen. She was the one they all wanted to fuck but she wasn't, like, girlfriend material. *She looks . . . dirty*, Chelsea had seen someone comment about Kelly on the RumorMill blog once and, shamefully, Chelsea had agreed. And then there was Willow Gray, Chelsea's role, the heroine of the show. The girl next door. Beautiful, of course, but she had never realized how gorgeous she was. ('Bullshit,' Nya used to say whenever she heard the character described like this in the scripts, arguing that beautiful women were never allowed the luxury of forgetting what they looked like. 'Does Willow own a mirror?' she would say. 'Is she, like, legally blind?') Willow Gray was the one the boys wanted to date, and the girls wanted as their best friend. Willow was kind and sweet and oh-so-perfect, and the problem was that everyone assumed Chelsea must be perfect too.

Kelly took a beat, waiting for the news to sink in. 'The author isn't doing it, but that woman hasn't left her house in, like, twenty years so the fans won't expect her to be there. So it's me, Nya and . . .' She cleared her throat. 'Well, that's all of us signed up. Everyone except you.'

'It's hard to believe it's been twenty years since the show aired,' Chelsea said, trying to play for time. 'It's crazy.'

'I know,' Kelly said. 'And even longer since you first set eyes on me and decided you couldn't live another minute without being best friends.'

They laughed, although Chelsea knew there was an element of truth in it. That first day of filming in North Carolina, she'd been so nervous, she'd thought she might be sick. The Director had explained how much was resting on her shoulders, and she couldn't let him down. After everything she had done to get the role, it *had* to work. Kelly, however, had rocked up to set late and a little hung-over, young and beautiful and completely fearless. That was before the tabloids had taken hold of her friend. Before they'd decided to destroy her for sport.

'Twenty years,' Kelly repeated. 'It's a big deal, Chel.'

There had been a smaller reunion during the pandemic, when every famous person seemed to haunt Instagram Live, singing a cappella versions of iconic songs and complaining about music festivals being cancelled, desperate for any attention from their fans. Some of the biggest celebrities in the world had taken to Zoom, doing table reads of their old scripts, pretending it was for charity and not for the validation, and the cast of *Vigilante Queens* had been no different. It was just Kelly and Nya that time. The actress who had played Winter, Willow Gray's baby sister on the show, had filled in for Chelsea. The reaction had been instantaneous and, to Chelsea's mind, oversized. It was covered in all the trades, the blogs and magazines breathlessly recounting every second, and the fans had gone wild. There was still such an appetite for the Queens, no matter how long the show had been off air. Agents began reaching out, making plans for a more formal arrangement, something they could properly monetize. Chelsea was the only hold-out from the original cast – they could do it without her, as they'd done in 2020, but they knew it wouldn't be the same.

'I . . .' Chelsea didn't have any intention of taking part in that show. Nick wouldn't like it, for one thing, not when he was considering running for mayor of LA next year. Her husband would probably support her if she decided to do it: they were a team, as he kept reminding her, but it was so clearly a team in which he was the leader. And anyway, Chelsea had spent her entire adult life trying to separate herself from the character of Willow, why would she want to go back? When she allowed herself to think of what it would be like, the bright-hot glow of the spotlight on her again after all these years, being asked questions about her sister's death, her breathing became shallow. She didn't want people looking too closely at her and her family. What might they find if they did? Better to keep quiet, unknowable, a blank image they could project their fantasies on rather than open her mouth and ruin it all.

'I'll think about it,' she said weakly, hating herself when Kelly gasped in delight. Why was she giving her friend hope? Didn't Chelsea, of all people, know how dangerous hope could be?

'Oh, my God,' Kelly said. 'This is amazing. You, me and Nya. The gang back together!'

'I said I'd think about it, please, I didn't—'

'It's what the people want.' Her friend cut across her, talking about wardrobe and how she'd have to go on a strict diet, she needed to be camera ready, and did Chelsea think she should dye her hair even blonder, the way it used to be when they were on the show? Chelsea tuned her out, *hmm*ing whenever there was a pause in the conversation.

It's what the people want. But hadn't Chelsea given those people enough? She'd given them her childhood. She'd given them her sister, too. What more did they want from her?

2.

2025

Chelsea hadn't spoken to the media directly in almost two decades. She left that to Nick's people – they were so good at it: the manipulation, the spin, the creation of the perfect family image – but still she found herself mentally narrating her morning routine as if she was giving an interview to a glossy magazine. *I wake up at 4.45 a.m.*, she imagined saying, *and after pulling with organic coconut oil, I drink a litre of filtered water. Then I head down to our home gym to meet my personal trainer for a workout* – the former actress lives on a sprawling estate in Montecito, the article would say, where she brushes elbows with celebrities and royalty alike at the local farmers' market. She loves Reformer Pilates, which explains her lithe frame, of course. She hasn't gained a pound since her days as a teen sensation! *Afterwards, I take a cold plunge, and I try to meditate for thirty minutes before getting dressed.* Would she allow an accompanying photo in her dressing room, Chelsea wondered, as she changed into white cigarette jeans and a cashmere sweater, slipping her feet into Chanel ballet flats, or would that seem ostentatious? So many people out there wanted to 'eat the rich', these days. Did Chelsea really need to give them another reason to hate her? *I'm ready by 6.45 a.m.*, she continued silently. *That's when I wake the kids up. It's important to me that we have breakfast together, no matter how hectic life gets*, the former child star and mother of two (Grayson, ten, and Ivy, four) says. *It's pretty normal, to be honest. We're just like any other family.*

'Good morning, loves,' Chelsea said, as she walked into the kitchen. She had renovated it last year and it was possibly her favourite room in the house. Airy and bright, with floor-to-ceiling glass, the interior design team had placed a large farmhouse table with bench seating in front of the slate-grey bi-fold doors leading out into the pool area. The range was in the centre of the room, cut into the island, and the cabinets surrounding it were grey and glass with silver door pulls, displaying the antique china.

Her children were sitting at the table. Grayson still looked half asleep, his eyes drooping, and Ivy, her surprise baby, a human ray of sunshine, was sipping her juice and chatting brightly to Poppy, the day-time nanny. 'Yum,' Chelsea said, checking their plates. 'That looks good.' Organic eggs, kale, and avocado on Ezekiel bread, and green smoothies, just as she'd requested. It was so important they had adequate sustenance before their school day.

When she was a child, her mother used to cut a grapefruit in two, hand one half to Maddie, the other to Chelsea. 'Is this all we're getting?' Maddie had once asked, holding the fruit. Their mother's mouth set, the way it always did when Maddie challenged her – sometimes it was hard to tell which one was the kid.

'We're leaving in five minutes,' Erin had said. 'You'd better be ready, both of you.' She'd left the room then, and Maddie turned to Chelsea, giving her the other half of the grapefruit.

'I have snacks from Craft Services hidden in my bag,' Maddie had whispered. 'And, besides, I don't want you going hungry.'

Chelsea took a seat between her son and daughter, pretending to wriggle her butt into the bench to make Ivy laugh. 'Okay,' she said to Grayson. 'Why does a certain somebody look so tired this morning?' She stroked her chin. 'Could it be because he was awake all night, reading his new book?'

'I just wanted to—'

'You just wanted to finish it even though you promised you'd go to sleep?' She'd gone into Grayson's room the night before, sat with him as he outlined the plot of the novel in great detail, then kissed him goodnight, turning off the light. When she'd checked again an hour later, he had been snoring but he must have been faking. Her daughter might have looked more like Maddie, with her pouty mouth and her dark blonde hair, but Grayson's wilfulness, as well as his love for reading, reminded her so much of her sister that it gave Chelsea an ache in her chest. 'What am I going to do with you, Gray-Gray?'

She turned to Ivy, smoothing her daughter's blunt bangs back. 'Tell me, Ivy. What do you think is the best way to deal with your brother?' she asked. 'You're so wise.' The little girl laughed, spilling some of her green juice. 'It's okay,' Chelsea said, as the nanny stood up. 'I've got it.' She dipped her napkin into a glass of water, dabbing at the stains on her daughter's shirt. 'We might have to change this, sweetie,' she said, and Ivy whinged a little. She had to wear this top, she said, she and Aurora had promised to wear matching outfits today. Grayson snorted and Chelsea raised an eyebrow at him. 'Enough of the attitude, please,' she said lightly. 'Just because you have a pop quiz in English today does not mean you can be snarky with your baby sister.'

'Sorry, Ivy,' Grayson said, and the little girl beamed at him. 'And it's social studies, actually,' her son continued. 'Dakota and I made flash cards and she said I'm going to smash it.'

'Well, Dakota would know.' Chelsea cut her eyes to the nanny; *Dakota?* The young woman checked the kids weren't looking and mouthed, *New tutor*, back at her. Chelsea nodded. She felt ridiculous enough as it was, having a full fleet of staff to run her household – the maids, the gardeners, the security guards, the chef, the nannies, the tutors, the drivers. The very least she could do was remember their names. *All those people in your home,* her therapist had said. *Does it bother you?* Chelsea hadn't known what to say to that. She'd been working since she was four years old; she'd grown up with a team of people around her – the makeup artists and hair stylists, wardrobe, her agent, the directors and show-runners. All she had ever known was *people*. When she'd finally left the business at twenty-three, she discovered almost immediately that she didn't know how to take care of herself. Without someone to remind her, Chelsea would forget to brush her teeth in the morning, or to comb her hair. She didn't know how to balance a cheque book or put an outfit together without a stylist telling her what worked. She had been a mess by the time she'd met Nick at twenty-four, desperate, multiple cavities in her teeth that needed filling but she was too ashamed and too broke to go to the dentist. Her husband had saved her, she knew that. The problem was so did he.

'Time to get going,' she said, checking her watch. She kissed Ivy and Grayson, telling them to get their coats, it was chilly outside, for California anyway. 'Wait a second,' she said, grabbing Grayson's school bag and pulling him back gently. 'Good luck in the quiz,' she said. 'You're so smart, G, and you work so hard. That's all we can ask for.'

'Dad said . . .' He trailed off, a frown creasing his forehead.

'I know.' Chelsea could only imagine what Nick had said to him. Her husband had been a gifted child and Valedictorian at high school and college. He had made it perfectly clear that he expected academic excellence from both children, especially Grayson. 'But ultimately all your dad and I want is for you to do your best, okay?'

'Sure,' he said, but he didn't look convinced. 'I've got to go. I don't want to be late.' He called over his shoulder as he left the kitchen, 'Love you, Mom.'

Chelsea stood by the dining table, her hands hanging by her sides. For a moment, she didn't move. She didn't like it when her children were worried, even if it was just over a pop quiz. That wasn't what she had worked so hard for. She wanted Grayson and Ivy to move through their childhoods with ease, with the comfort of knowing they could never truly fuck up. With their resources, every mistake could and would be easily fixed. She looked at Ivy sometimes, four years old, the same age as she and Maddie had been when they'd got their first TV role, and she could hardly believe how young her daughter was. Ivy with her lisp, Ivy who couldn't sleep without her blankie. She was an entirely different prospect from the Stone sisters. Chelsea had felt so grown-up when she was a kid but, then, she'd had so many responsibilities. She'd had to be professional both on and off the set. She'd had to make good choices because they didn't just impact her, she had been told countless times. The livelihoods of dozens of people depended on her and Maddie. The crew had families to feed, mortgages to pay, and it all rested on the twins' shoulders.

'It's funny,' Chelsea had said to her therapist. 'When I look at Grayson and Ivy, the thought of putting them to work to pay my rent . . .' She'd laughed: it seemed so ridiculous. 'They're just *babies*.' The therapist had looked at her, maintaining a neutral expression. (Is that what they teach you at therapy school, she would ask Nya, how not to react? And her friend would reply, Yes, bitch. Obviously.)

'And what about you and your sister?' the therapist had asked. 'Were you babies? Or . . .' The woman took a long pause. 'Were you ever given the freedom to just be a child?'

She heard the front door opening, a voice calling, 'Hey! It's me.' The click-clack of heeled boots on the marble floor, a whiff of Baccarat Rouge 540 as Hannah marched in – that was the only word to describe how Hannah moved through the world, she *marched*, stomping through every obstacle with remarkable confidence – still staring at her phone screen as she raised a hand in hello. Hannah had been Chelsea's PA since she'd graduated from Barnard College almost ten years previously. A born and bred New Yorker, Hannah smoked fifteen cigarettes a day, refused to vape ('And, what, look like Leonardo DiCaprio at Coachella? No thanks'), dressed exclusively in black, and made complaints about California's lack of public transport, weather and culture her entire personality. She was also terrifyingly bright. She was so competent that, within six months, Chelsea was utterly dependent on her. Hannah was far too brilliant to be an assistant for the rest of her life, something she and Chelsea were both aware of, but every time she hinted that she was considering leaving, Chelsea gave her yet another pay rise. Hannah was probably the best paid PA in California at this point, and worth every cent.

'Coffee?' Chelsea asked.

'Obvs,' Hannah answered. 'Oh, my God, this girl is, like, obsessed with me.' She turned her phone around so Chelsea could see the screen. There were paragraphs of text from the other person, followed by Hannah's one-line answers. 'It's giving stalker.'

'Brianna?' Chelsea turned her mouth down. 'I liked her. She seemed sweet.'

'Brianna asked what animal turkey came from while *eating a turkey sandwich*.' Chelsea snort-laughed as Hannah continued, 'Is that what you want for me? A hot little dummy? Anyway, Brianna could barely spell her own name, let alone send these kinds of essays. This is Hailey, she's a ballet-barre instructor.' She clicked into a dating app, showing Chelsea a photo of a tall, toned Black woman with loose braids. 'Isn't she fab?'

'She's gorgeous,' Chelsea confirmed, although that was

nothing new. All of Hannah's girlfriends were beautiful. 'When do I get to meet her?'

'Never.'

'Hannah!'

'No! You get too attached. You're worse than my mother.'

'But I got you that reservation at Plume,' Chelsea protested. 'The place is impossible to get into. You owe me.'

'With that argument, I owe Nick,' her assistant said firmly. 'Or Nick's vineyard, to be precise.' He had bought the property in France five years ago. *I didn't know you were interested in wine*, Chelsea had said, confused, and he'd laughed and said he wasn't. *But owning a vineyard means I'll be able to get a table at any restaurant in the world, no reservation needed*, he'd said, and she wondered how he had discovered that. Was there a Rich Man Conference at which they shared tips on how best to cheat the system? 'Now,' her assistant said, 'on to business. Did you get a chance to look through the Google doc I sent you?'

Chelsea was standing in front of the fancy coffee machine Nick had insisted upon installing, frowning. 'Erm,' she said, taking an educated guess and pressing a random button, startling as the machine made an unpleasant noise.

Hannah sighed and walked to her, moving Chelsea out of the way so she could take over. 'Stop looking at me like I'm the Second Coming of Christ,' Hannah said. 'This is not hard, you're just spoiled.' Chelsea staggered back, clutching at her chest like she'd been shot and Hannah rolled her eyes. The younger woman leaned against the gleaming counter top, sipping her coffee. 'Now. The Google doc?'

'I haven't had a chance to look at it yet,' Chelsea said. 'I try to stay off my phone until ten a.m. The research says that—'

'Hmm.' She and Hannah often disagreed about phone usage. Chelsea thought her assistant was addicted to technology, but Hannah was impossible to argue with. She would listen, nod, then just do things her own way. 'Let's go through your schedule now,' Hannah said, holding her phone in her left hand, espresso cup in the right. 'Dr Shulman is coming to the house at ten fifteen for your biannual bloodwork. There's a meeting with the committee about the LACMA fundraiser at the same time but I told them you had a medical appointment. Barbara Jackson's PA is fucking terrifying by the way, and that's coming from *me*. But it's the second meeting you've missed this month so you have to attend the next or there'll be an uprising, it doesn't matter how much money Nick is donating.'

Having to buy friends again, are we, Chel? That was what Kelly had said in the group chat when she heard about the committee. Kelly protested it was just a joke when Nya had told her, tersely, that it was a bullshit thing to say. *You get it, don't you, Chelsea?* Kelly had said, and Chelsea, always anxious to keep the peace between the three of them, said it was fine, it didn't matter. Later that night, Nya had texted her. *I love Kelly,* she wrote, *but you don't need to put up with this, Chel. You do know that, right?*

'I'll make the next one,' Chelsea promised.

'You also need to confirm that Thursday works for the photo shoot,' Hannah continued. 'I've been liaising with your mother and the glam squad and they're holding that day. I've freed up your schedule, so I just need you to—'

'I know,' Chelsea replied, sharper than she intended, then felt guilty. She shouldn't speak to Hannah like that. 'Sorry,' she added.

'I know it's tough,' Hannah said, unfazed. 'But we do need those pics before your birthday in April, and this is the only day that works for everyone.'

'I know. Sorry. Thursday will be fine.'

'Do you want me to come with you? I can deal with your mom if she steps out of line. You know Erin's scared of me.'

'Everyone's scared of you,' Chelsea said fondly.

'And that's how you like it,' Hannah said, pretending to check her manicure and they laughed. 'Okay, so you've got a Zoom session with Dr Ursula at eleven thirty. She's sent the invite link through already and –' Chelsea's therapist was on a book tour in Europe that month and was taking her sessions via video call rather than her usual house visit '– then you've got a hair appointment with Chris McMillan. Are you sure you want to go into the salon? I mean, it's fine and they said they'll order a salad from Goop Kitchen for your lunch but . . .' She trailed off when she saw her boss's face. Chelsea had made it clear that she didn't want to become a recluse, barely leaving her house because of security concerns. It was important the kids saw her living her life with some semblance of normality. 'Sure thing, it's up to you. After that, you—'

'I'm going to visit Linda,' Chelsea cut in. 'I haven't seen her in two weeks, I feel bad.'

'Do they know at the care home you're coming? It's not your usual day.'

'No, I just thought . . .' Chelsea was aware of how stupid that sounded. She couldn't just 'pop' in anywhere unannounced.

The PA nodded briskly. 'I'll take care of it,' Hannah said, like she always did.

'I'll drive myself.' Chelsea opened the fridge and found a glass cup of green juice waiting for her. She took the straw into her mouth, a shiver at how cold it was. 'Tell Afi he can have the day off. Did you know his wife just had a hysterectomy?'

'Yeah, I sent her flowers, like you asked. But won't Nick need him?' Hannah asked. Chelsea's husband, who had been raised in Montana, had an acute aversion to LA's freeways. That was why he'd hired Afi full time. If Nick had to get stuck in traffic, he wanted to be able to work in the back of the car. He used to take his plane more until he was named as one of the top ten offenders by Celebrity Private Jets and he had been paranoid about helicopters since Kobe's death in 2020. So, chauffeured car it was.

'Nick is in Sedona again,' Chelsea said. On yet another ayahuasca retreat, but she didn't tell Hannah that. *Why can't he just do molly, like a normal person?* she'd asked, the last time Nick took plant medicine, and Chelsea had felt disloyal for laughing. 'You can tell Terry to make something easy tonight,' she said. 'Vegetarian, even.'

'I'm sure Terry will be excited to hear that,' Hannah murmured. Chelsea knew that Hannah found her husband ridiculous, with his intermittent fasting and his raw-meat diet, his hyperbaric and cryotherapy chambers, his cold plunges and infrared saunas, his obsession with 'longevity'. She was sure that Hannah would go to the chef and they would make jokes about Terry being allowed to cook something with *fucking salt*, for once.

'Oh, and Nancy Taylor called. Again.' Hannah drained her coffee cup, rinsed it and put it into the dishwasher.

'About the—'

'Of course it was about the reunion.' Hannah ran her fingers through her long, glossy black hair, pulling it up into a high ponytail, rummaging in her jeans pocket for an elastic band. 'That's the only thing Nancy Taylor wants to talk about, no matter how many times I tell her you're not interested.' She half laughed. 'The woman is determined, I'll give her that.'

Everyone still called her by her full name, Nancy Taylor of Nancy Taylor Management. The most famous agent in LA for child stars, bar none. Any time one of those listicles was released online, a round-up of the most beloved kid actors of all time, Nancy was behind every name except Judy Garland and Shirley Temple. Every Nickelodeon, Disney or AtomicKids superstar over the last thirty years had been a part of the NTM family. The Stone Sisters had been the jewel in her crown, and the only two clients she had continued to represent into adulthood. The producers of the reunion show couldn't get to Chelsea directly – she was too rich for that now, too well protected – so they were going through Nancy Taylor, like it was the old days. As if that woman had any control over Chelsea's life any more.

Chelsea sat at the dining table, slumping until she remembered what her Pilates instructor had told her, and straightened her spine. 'Hannah,' she turned to look at her, 'do you think I should do it?'

Chelsea presumed her assistant would give a measured, thoughtful response, as she always did, so she watched in astonishment as Hannah actually *blushed*, the tips of her ears and cheekbones turning pink. 'I . . .' Hannah's voice sounded younger, childlike. How had Chelsea not realized before? Hannah might be impossibly chic and put-together but she was also thirty-two. Which meant she would have been twelve when *Vigilante Queens* first aired. Meaning that beneath her shiny, intimidating surface, Hannah was just a fan girl at heart. 'That's not my place to say,' Hannah said, picking up her satchel and pretending to rifle through it until her skin returned to its normal pallor. 'But,' her assistant cleared her throat, 'I know that you doing the show would mean a lot to a whole generation of young women out there. Girls who were raised on Willow Gray.'

That was what Chelsea always heard until she married Nick and he used his money to protect her from the baying masses. She would be stopped in the drug store, on the street or at the park when she was walking her dog. Those young girls with bright eyes and metal braces, telling her they loved her, they loved her so much, but Chelsea knew they meant that they loved Willow Gray. Beautiful, kind, *good* Willow Gray, whose moral compass was set at true north. She was nothing like Chelsea, and the things she had done to survive. The people she had hurt.

'Tell Nancy Taylor—' For a second, Chelsea felt the overwhelming urge to say yes. She was so used to saying whatever would make the person standing in front of her happy. It was an automatic reflex. But then she imagined herself in that room, with those people, talking about that time of her life. With *him*. 'No,' she said. 'I can't. Tell Nancy Taylor I'm sorry, but I just can't do this.'

3.

2025

'You look tired, babe.' Her husband frowned at her through the laptop screen. Nick had finished the plant medicine retreat in Sedona – 'Transformative!' he said. 'I'm going to bring the entire Foto team here for our summer Think Week in June' – and he was now recuperating at the nearby Amangiri resort, brainstorming ways to make his social-media site bigger. Foto was currently ranked just above X in popularity but still below TikTok, let alone Instagram and Facebook, and it was driving Nick crazy. He always needed to be the best. 'Have you been sleeping okay?' he asked. 'You know Dr Breus says that—'

'I'm fine,' Chelsea said before her husband could lecture her on the specifics of the latest studies he had read. Sleep is so important for rejuvenation, he kept telling her, it keeps us young, and he would look at Chelsea in the way that made her either want to get thirty units of Botox in her forehead immediately or stop her injections altogether, just to spite him. 'I was restless last night,' she said.

It wasn't her fault. She had done what she was told to yesterday: she'd followed the schedule Hannah had laid out for her. She'd had her bloodwork done, smiling at the doctor, telling him, yes, she was taking all of her supplements and, yes, she had upped her protein intake. Yes, she knew it was so important coming into her forties. She'd had a therapy session in which she didn't mention her dead sister or the reunion show or her marriage. Instead, she discussed her body image, as if any woman, famous or not, could have survived the early noughties without developing issues with food. She went to the hair salon where she chatted a lot but said very little, a trick she had perfected over the years, then left a tip so extravagantly large that the staff would say she was the nicest client they had.

She'd driven back to the estate afterwards, making small-talk with the security guard, waiting for the kids to come home. When they did, she'd asked them about school, about what their teachers had said that day, how their friends were doing. She'd given Ivy a bath and talked to Grayson about his pop quiz and the boy in his class who had received a higher grade than him – Grayson had inherited his father's competitiveness, she noted – and when the kids were asleep and the day staff had gone, she'd taken a bottle of very good wine upstairs to her bedroom. She'd drunk a glass, and another, and then she'd crawled into bed, her phone in hand, and she went looking.

'What's the *need* behind this behaviour? How is it serving you?' her therapist asked, when Chelsea told her about searching for the Stone Sisters online, poking around the darkest holes of the internet. It didn't matter how hurtful the threads on the message boards were – Madeline had always been the prettier, more talented sister, they said, and Chelsea wished she could reply and say, *Yes, she was. I agree with you* – or how dehumanizing it was to read strangers swapping conspiracy theories about what had happened that night, but she couldn't seem to stop herself.

Where was Madeline Stone? There was no way she had died, the commentators agreed. Maddie's car might have been abandoned at Pismo Beach, but a body was never found. They posted old photos of Chelsea, noting how the tiny scar across her hairline had disappeared – the result of a childhood fall in the playground, it had been the only way their mother had been able to tell the twins apart until Chelsea had had intensive laser treatment to remove it – speculating that maybe Maddie and Chelsea had switched places years ago. That would explain Chelsea's almost miraculous improvement as an actress in her late teens, wouldn't it?

They shared snippets of Maddie's infamous interview with *GQ* magazine, the one that had tanked her career, and screenshots of old posts from RumorMill, each one breathtaking in its cruelty. *How hasn't Milo James been cancelled for this shit yet?* someone commented, and someone else replied, *Bitch, we been trying. That man is like a cockroach: he'll survive a nuclear war.* And then there were the sightings – one commentator had seen 'Madeline' in a thrift store on Venice Beach or waiting at the DMV in Michigan; another had seen her in a crowded bar in Nashville; yet another spotted her hiking the Pacific Crest Trail. It infuriated Chelsea that these people would make up stories just for entertainment. Her sister was dead. Would she never be allowed some peace?

'Why were you restless?' her husband asked now. 'Were you . . .' He didn't finish his sentence. They both knew what he meant. She had told him about this little habit of hers years ago, when they were still close, and he didn't like it. It made him worry about her, he said, and Nick didn't like to be worried.

'I . . .' She tried to think. 'I went to see Linda yesterday and I was feeling down, you know.'

'We've talked about this, baby. You can't let it get to you. Linda isn't your mother and—'

'I'm very well aware of who my mother is, Nick.'

'I know.' He raised an eyebrow at her tone. 'I didn't mean it like that. I'm just concerned that your energy gets depleted and I need you to stay positive for Grayson and Ivy. We're already paying for the nursing home. You've gone above and beyond in taking care of Linda.' He took a beat. 'Between her and Kelly, I think we've got most of your former co-stars covered.'

Chelsea curled her hands into fists, out of sight of the computer screen, then took a breath to calm herself. 'Kelly has had a hard time.'

'I know that, too. But sometimes you have to let a person take responsibility for their own destiny. You're a very giving person, Chel, and I love that about you, but you need to have boundaries. That's why I keep telling you to drink Mother with me,' he said. If there was anything more annoying than hearing someone describe their ayahuasca experience as 'Mother', Chelsea wasn't sure what it was. 'It would be so healing given everything you've been through.'

'Maybe,' she replied, although she knew she would never do it. She had spent years being so disciplined, keeping an iron-clad grip on anything to do with her body, her diet, her exercise, and the mere thought of taking ayahuasca – the vomiting and the diarrhoea and the loss of control – made her feel nauseated. And what if she started spilling her secrets too? She had kept them clutched so tightly to her for such a long time, she couldn't risk it. 'I'd better go,' she said, when her phone lit up. 'Kelly's calling.'

'Leave it,' he said. 'Let's talk some more.'

'But it might be important.'

'Babe, come on. She's calling about the show.'

'Well . . . she really wants me to do it.'

'Of course, Kelly wants you to do it. Kelly doesn't have a career any more. She *needs* this show.' Chelsea winced at this ruthless analysis but Nick wasn't wrong. 'And Kelly knows as well as I do,' Nick continued, 'that a *Vigilante Queens* reunion won't work without the *numero-uno* queen. They can try, but no one's gonna watch if Chelsea Stone isn't there.'

That was the problem. She couldn't refuse to take part

without disappointing everybody. *Who the fuck does Chelsea Stone think she is?* the fans were already saying online. The Director was doing it, and he had two Oscars! He didn't need to do the reunion. If there was anyone this was 'beneath', it was him. But The Director understood how important the show was to the fans. He cared about them – he was so humble, so down to earth. *Chelsea Stone was just a Beverly Hills Housewife, a washed-up has-been, the fucking bitch.*

It was funny how, until now, her early retirement and decision to focus on her husband and children had been seen as classy, a sign that Chelsea was in her 'feminine energy'. How quickly people turned once they wanted something from her. But why was she surprised? She had seen first-hand what they had done to Maddie, how easily they had destroyed her sister once they'd decided she was a difficult woman.

'Nancy Taylor won't stop calling either,' Chelsea said, and at the mention of her former agent's name, her husband made a face, then stopped himself. Their couples' therapist had told him it came across as condescending when he did such things while Chelsea was speaking. Nick tried his best to take that on board. That was the thing about her husband: he really tried to make her happy, in his own way. But it wasn't enough, not since . . . 'And she sent through another proposal for the reunion,' Chelsea said, attempting to distract herself from that dangerous thought. She couldn't go there, not now. As Maddie would say, she had made her choices and she had to live with them. 'I can veto the interviewer, and they'll give me question approval.'

'That's interesting. And would we get that in writing?' Her husband tilted his head back, thinking. 'Would it be a pre-record?'

'No. They said it has to be live.'

'Fuck that.' Nick was definite. 'It doesn't matter if you

approve the questions beforehand if it's live. They can just claim the conversation naturally went to . . .' He stumbled. He never brought up Maddie if he could help it. 'And then you'll be on live TV, trying to get out of a black hole.' He ran his fingers across his freshly shaved face. 'Look, babe, I've talked it over with the team. We thought there might be a nostalgic factor that could play well with younger voters but they're not exactly a reliable demographic. I'm not telling you what to do,' he said, and Chelsea had to fight the urge to beg him to do so. That was what she was used to, it was how she was raised – being told what to say, how to behave to make people love her. She didn't know any other way. 'If I'm gonna run next year,' Nick said, 'I can't afford any unnecessary drama. And this show? It's gonna be a circus.' He peered at her through the screen. 'Is that okay?'

'Sure,' she said, pretending she wasn't dizzy with relief. This was the perfect excuse. Nick, and his campaign to become mayor in 2026. The city had its problems, he said, with the homelessness and addiction and the fires and the riots, of course. It needed a strong voice to fix it. No one could argue with that, not even her mother. 'Whatever you want, darling.'

After they'd said their goodbyes, Chelsea changed out of her sweats and walked down to the spa area. Her phone flashed again.

Nya: Call me when you get this

She tapped out a text – *I'm just going for a quick swim, will call afterwards. I've been useless this week, sorry!! love you xoxo* – stuffed her cell into the pocket of her robe and hung it on a brass hook, stepping into the plunge pool. Her breath shortened to a hiss, but she kept going until she was submerged in the icy water up to her neck. When Nick had read a research paper on the benefits of cold-water submersion, he'd insisted on building a fully functioning spa on the estate. A cold plunge, a steam room and sauna, a rain shower. Hand-made mosaic tiles in forest green and cream, his favourite colours, the same ones he'd used when creating his social-media site all those years ago. *You're still going to die*, Chelsea wanted to say, like she always did when Nick told her about a new bio-hack he'd discovered that guaranteed longevity. *We all are*. Yet it was Chelsea who continued to use this pool every morning. It was so cold that, for a minute, she forgot who she was. All the questions about her life, her marriage, her sister – they simply dissolved.

The phone started to ring, echoing against the tiled walls. *Anyone who doesn't put their phone on silent is either a boomer or a sociopath*, she imagined her assistant saying. Chelsea focused on her breathing, trying to ignore the noise. The call stopped, then started again, and again, until she cursed and climbed out, almost slipping on the wet floor as she reached for her robe. She sighed when she saw the name on the screen, answering, 'Yes?'

'Hey,' Kelly replied. 'It's me. Have you seen—'

'No,' Chelsea said, like she had practised with her therapist. Dr Ursula said she needed to have better boundaries with Kelly, establish a more appropriate relationship – 'She's a former colleague, Chelsea, not your si—' and trailed off, but they both knew what she was going to say. Dr Ursula thought Chelsea couldn't say no to Kelly because of some sort of misguided guilt over what had happened to Maddie, that it was an attempt to make good on the sins of the past. What she didn't understand was that Maddie had been the one person Chelsea *had* felt comfortable saying no to, because she was the only person in Chelsea's life whose love she had never doubted. What a gift that had been, and how little she had appreciated it until it was gone.

'We've talked about this a million times,' Chelsea said. 'I know this is a big deal for you, and I wish I could help. But I can't do the show. I'm sorry, Kel. But you have to understand why, surely.'

'No, babe.' Kelly was gentle, which was unnerving because that wasn't how their friendship worked. Chelsea was the one who comforted Kelly, not the other way around. 'I'm not phoning about the reunion. It's . . .' she hesitated '. . . it's about Maddie.'

4.

2025

'I'm very upset,' Nick said, holding the printouts gingerly between his fingers as if afraid they might burn him. 'My wife has been through enough without someone pulling this kind of cruel prank on her. We need this shut down *immediately*.'

Nick had taken his private jet back as soon as he'd heard, landing in the airfield near their estate by midnight, summoning a small team to the house by twelve thirty. Pete, Foto's best tech guy, had been dispatched to work his magic, and now Nick was berating his lawyer, a man so old that his spine had begun to curve and he could barely stand up straight, hunched over, like he was permanently trying to tie his shoelaces. They were in Nick's home-office, which had been stripped of all technology for this meeting. No laptops, no computers – Chelsea wasn't even allowed to bring her phone in here. This website was making her husband anxious, and when Nick was anxious, he became paranoid.

'Yes, it's terrible,' the lawyer said. What was his name again? The firm was called Cohen & Ashforth, and Chelsea could never remember which partner was which. Not that she had much to do with either of them. The first and only time she had been in their office was in 2010, just before the wedding, when she was signing the pre-nup. *All done*, Cohen/Ashforth said as she set down the pen, and she thought she saw a flash of pity in his eyes, as if he could hardly believe she was agreeing to the draconian terms he had dreamed up for her. But

Chelsea had been so young then, and she had just wanted to be married. She had wanted to be *safe*.

'We haven't found the location yet. But here is what we do know,' the lawyer said. 'It looks like there was a storage locker your sister used before her . . .' He hesitated, never sure of the right terminology when it came to Maddie. Missing person, presumed dead: that was what the cops said.

'Her death,' Chelsea filled in for him.

'Yes,' he said gratefully. 'I'm guessing she'd paid for it up to a certain point, and when the money stopped coming, the company put the goods on sale.' Chelsea started to speak but he cut across her. 'As I said, we haven't sourced the location yet but we should have it soon. And as for the website, they are, as your colleague Peter said, using, eh,' he looked at his notes, 'Virtual Private Networks to disguise their locations.' Chelsea swallowed a smile. Somehow, she doubted Cohen/Ashforth knew how to operate an iPhone, let alone what a VPN was. 'Peter said he suspects they're working from an internet café,' he finished.

'An internet café.' Nick was scornful. 'I didn't know they still existed.'

'I think it's just poor people who use them, these days,' the lawyer replied, and he smiled at Chelsea, as if waiting for her to laugh. She looked down at her perfectly manicured hands resting in her lap, and clasped them together so tightly the knuckles went white. Was that how she came across, like an out-of-touch dilettante in a ten-thousand-dollar camel-hair coat? She opened her mouth to say something, then closed it again.

When Kelly had rung her earlier, telling her about this website – she'd called out the letters one by one as Chelsea typed them into her iPad with trembling fingers – her friend had said that it was already going viral. It was all over every social-media platform, including Foto. It had been seventeen years since Maddie's death and everyone was still obsessed with the Stone Sisters. The website had loaded slowly, the images appearing on the screen inch by inch. It was scraps of pages torn out from a notebook, diary entries. There was a to-do list – *organize house, stop eating junk food, go to NA meetings twice a week, no matter what* – and, she couldn't help it, Chelsea gasped when she saw her sister's handwriting. She had burned all of Maddie's letters after she'd died, the postcards her sister had sent from vacation – *missing you more than liiiiife!!! Antigua is MAGIC. Why didn't you come again?!!!!* – the scribbled notes, the birthday and Christmas cards. The Director had told her it would be better that way. Maddie had made her decision: she had left Chelsea behind, and now it was time that Chelsea did the same, he said. He had lit the fire and she had fed it with her memories. All of Maddie's words, consumed by flames, as Chelsea stood and watched and did nothing. Her sister had needed her and she had done *nothing*.

'Chelsea.' Nick waved a hand in front of her face. 'Are you okay?'

'Sorry,' she said, still clutching the paper.

'What do you think this person means, there's more to come?' His blue eyes were narrowed and Chelsea had a sudden flash of fear. Whoever was behind this, they couldn't possibly know about— *No*. This was about Maddie, not her.

'I'm not sure,' she replied, and her husband gave a deep sigh. Nick had done so much for her – he had stopped her mother giving tasteless interviews about life with the Stone Sisters, he had paid for rehab stays and care homes and anything else she asked for. But in return Chelsea had her own role to play. She was supposed to love their children and deal with the household staff, maintain her figure, be beautiful and ageless for ever. After that, she was to sprinkle a little stardust at company events and charity fundraisers from time to time. She was still Chelsea Stone, after all. She was not supposed to create any problems for Nick. That wasn't part of the deal.

'Okay,' he said. 'Pete will find out what he can. We'll manage this.' He took a look at his watch. 'Have you spoken to your mother?' he asked, and Chelsea froze. *Shit.* Had Erin seen it yet?

5.

2025

Afi glanced at her in the rear-view mirror, reddening when they made eye contact. The driver looked away quickly, keeping his gaze on the road ahead. He always seemed nervous around her, clambering to his feet when Chelsea walked into the garage earlier, straightening his already perfectly straight tie. 'I was just . . .' he'd started to say, guiltily, as if it was a crime to be found sitting during the work day, no matter how many times she told him to relax.

'It's fine,' Chelsea said, before he could finish. 'But I need you to drive me to Calabasas, if you have time?'

She was staring out of the window at the sea and the sky, both a faded blue in the January light, when her phone lit up, a text from Nick: *Are you on the way to see her yet?* and then, almost immediately afterwards, a message from Nya. *I'm serious, Chel,* her friend wrote. *I'll get the first flight to LA, Marcus can take care of the girls. I just want to see you.* Chelsea started recording a voice message back: 'Hey, Nee Nee,' she said. 'I love you so much for offering. You are the fucking best, do you know that? But, um, it's good. I promise. Nick has his best guy at Foto taking care of it. It's shit but we've been through worse, haven't we? . . . Okay, I love you so much. I'll give you a call later? Give the girls a kiss from me. Bye, my love,' and she pressed send. They both knew it wasn't easy to rearrange Nya's life, her husband and kids, and her busy practice. She would never ask Nya to do that but there was comfort in knowing her friend was willing, all the same.

Since the website had gone live, Chelsea had been inundated with messages, people 'Just checking in', saying, 'Hope you're okay!' when, really, all they wanted were the gory details. It was *everywhere*, this story about Madeline Stone and the storage unit full of her most personal possessions. What was coming next? they wondered.

Chelsea usually drove herself to her mother's house – it was only an hour and a half's trip from Montecito to Calabasas. She preferred to be distracted by the traffic and a podcast so she could keep at bay the anxiety she always felt before spending an afternoon with Erin. But today she wanted to look at the website yet again, and the photos. A scrap of paper from a yellow legal pad, Maddie's writing almost intelligible. *Yesterday I ate a quart of Ben & Jerry's*, it said, *a carton of Milk Duds, and Sour Patch kids, then chocolate chip cookies with milk. I am SO GROSS. I had to throw up, what else could I do??? BUT NO MORE!!! Today is a new day. I'm going to eat fruit for breakfast, a salad for lunch, and a smoothie for dinner and THAT'S IT.*

Chelsea put the phone face down on the seat next to her, closing her eyes. Maddie had had an eating disorder, and Chelsea hadn't known about it? She'd thought the two of them had always been so close, except for those last few months, but she didn't like to think about that. Maddie had been more than her twin: she had been her best friend. If Maddie was capable of keeping this from her, what else did Chelsea not know? She pulled up a photo on her camera roll of the two of them, and she looked from one girl to the other, comparing their bodies. She tried not to do this any more – comparison is the thief of joy, her therapist would say – but today, she couldn't resist the temptation.

Chelsea had always envied her sister's ability to eat whatever she wanted and maintain her figure. The twins had the same build – five foot six and slim – but they carried any extra weight in their lower bodies. If they wanted to keep their legs thin for the requisite skinny jeans and cut-off shorts of their heyday, their arms and chests became skeletal, the clavicle bones so sharp they almost pierced the magazine covers they were splashed across.

When Chelsea finally got her period at fifteen, she went into her mother's room to tell her, adding desperately, 'I'm sorry, Mom.'

'Don't be silly,' Erin said. 'We'll just have to be a little more careful going forward, won't we? No more sneaking snacks from Craft Services!' That was when Erin had stood Chelsea on the scales, and said, *From now on, that's the number you need to be at if you want to look your best on screen.* The magic number: that was what Erin had called it. Chelsea had struggled to maintain that weight, and she had envied how easy it seemed for Maddie. How easy everything had seemed for Maddie back then.

'We're here,' Afi said, as they drove up to the gated community in which her mother lived. She took three deep breaths to steady her nerves as the guard at the security gate looked at Afi's ID, checked the list in front of him and nodded. It was a collection of thirty houses, each made of stone and slate, the eaves painted white, with a small, neat lawn in front. *Four million dollars apiece to cosplay a 1960s suburb*, Nick had said, when Erin told them where she wanted to live, but he'd bought it for her anyway. Her mother was standing at the front door in cropped jeans, her feet bare, her blonde hair loose and her lips painted bright red. Erin Stone – she had reverted to her married name when Maddie and Chelsea became famous, for 'continuity', she said, even though that made no sense – was still the kind of beautiful that would cause heads to turn, even at fifty-eight, even in a town like LA, where the person pumping your gas could easily be the best-looking person you'd ever seen in real life. *Jesus*, Nick had said the first time they'd met, when Chelsea was sure of him and felt he wouldn't scare easily. *At least I know the genes are good*, and Erin had swatted his shoulder and told him he was 'so bad', although it was clear she loved it. Their mother had always needed male validation to feel seen.

'Darling!' Erin cried, hugging her closely. Chelsea stiffened as her mother's hands ran down the sides of her ribcage, as if checking to see if Chelsea had gained weight, but Erin released her without saying anything. She looked past Chelsea towards the car. 'Where are the kids?'

'I didn't bring them today.'

Erin frowned, a tiny crease in her forehead. Whoever was doing her Botox was an artist. 'What?' she said. 'But I haven't seen them in months, and I'm their only maternal grandparent—' She looked to the side and muttered under her breath, 'The only one worth mentioning, anyway.'

'I'm sorry, Mom, but they had school.'

'Ivy is in pre-K. You could have taken her out.'

'I'm . . .' Chelsea could feel herself faltering. 'I'm sorry, I . . .' This was why she didn't spend time with her mother, why she left it to Hannah to deal with Erin as much as possible. Chelsea was a thirty-nine-year-old mother of two and she still couldn't say no to her mommy. 'I didn't think it was appropriate for the kids to be here today,' she said. 'I don't want to talk about the website in front of them.'

'The website?' Erin said, going into the baby voice she used when she thought she was in trouble and wanted to wheedle her way out of it.

Chelsea gritted her teeth. 'Let's just go in, okay, Mom?'

Inside the house, it was frenzied with people. Two racks of clothes – one for Chelsea and one for her mother, although Erin always stole a look from Chelsea's rack anyway, just to prove she could still fit into the same outfits as her daughter – and the assistants were testing the lights, rearranging the furniture.

Chelsea kissed the photographer and the stylist, asked about their partners, cooed over the photos of babies and dogs that were duly produced. They always used the same team: it was easier in terms of logistics, the lawyer said, by which Cohen/Ashforth meant they didn't have to draw up yet another set of contracts and non-disclosure agreements. Chelsea's birthday was six months away but they would need official pics to share on Foto. She didn't have any other social-media presence, something Nick had asked of her from the beginning. He needed *some* advantage over Instagram, he said. They were supposed to get these shots alongside the Thanksgiving and Christmas images in early November, but by five p.m. that day, Chelsea had spent as much time with her mother as she could tolerate.

'This for the first shot?' The stylist held up a silver maxi skirt and blazer in crushed velvet.

Chelsea made a face. 'It's cool but it's pretty low-key,' she said. 'It's supposed to be my fortieth birthday party. What about that one?' She pointed at a sky-blue dress with a daringly low cut-out detail at the back.

'Perfect,' the stylist said. 'Bottega Veneta, me looooves.'

'It just doesn't make any sense,' her mother muttered. 'Why would we have your birthday party without the kids?'

Chelsea could feel a headache forming behind her eyes. 'Because,' she said, 'they're at school. Besides, you know how I feel about the kids being on social media.' It always made her uneasy when people used their children for content online. The performed cuteness, the bright smiles, how at ease the kids seemed in front of the camera, it felt far too familiar. She had watched as a guest star from *Vigilante Queens*, an actress turned Mommy Blogger, had used her daughter's first period for sponsored content with a tampon brand and it had turned Chelsea's stomach. She didn't want that for Grayson and

Ivy. 'I'll get the team to put something in the caption about mother–daughter bonding, okay?'

Erin pursed her mouth, far from mollified. Chelsea wished that her mother was keen to see her grandchildren because she genuinely missed them, but they both knew the real reason was that photos with the kids – even if they just showed the back of their heads or had an emoji covering their faces – guaranteed more engagement on the app. That was Erin's love language, after all, attention. Even after Maddie had died, her mother would regularly give interviews about the twins, recording a true-crime podcast called *Whatever Happened to Madeline Stone?* and selling an online course called *How To Make Your Child Famous!*, all of which Nick had promptly put an end to, much to Chelsea's relief. Whatever he'd had to pay to buy Erin's silence, it had been worth it.

'Ladies! Let's get this party started!' the hair stylist called. He and the rest of the glam squad had set up in the kitchen, and were waiting for them.

'Just a minute,' Chelsea said, grabbing her mother's elbow. 'Mom, the website,' she said, as quietly as she could but the older woman's face was deliberately blank. *Could it be . . .* Nick had asked her that morning and he hadn't needed to finish the sentence. Chelsea had had the same suspicion as soon as she had seen the website, and it made her so sad that it was even a consideration. *No*, she'd replied. *She wouldn't risk her allowance*, and her husband had smiled ruefully. They both knew that was far more likely to deter Erin from exposing her daughters' secrets than any kind of family loyalty. But, still, Chelsea had resolved to ask her mother about it today, just in case. Now that she was here, though, with Erin standing in front of her, she felt the old fear arising. 'I – I . . .' she stuttered. 'Come on, Mom. The blog about Maddie?'

Erin must have seen it: her mother was more online than

Chelsea was, not that such a thing would be hard. Besides Chelsea's anonymous trawling of the message boards, she generally stayed off social media as much as she could. The post had been up for less than forty-eight hours and it was everywhere – E!, Pop Crave, Just Jared, Deux Moi, and RumorMill, of course. Milo James could never resist the opportunity to write about her and Maddie.

'Did you know that . . .' Chelsea couldn't say her sister's name '. . . she had bulimia?'

Her mother's face was still but Chelsea knew Erin's tells off by heart. A half-swallow, her eyes flicking ever so slightly down, then meeting her daughter's gaze again, defiant. 'You did,' Chelsea said slowly. 'You knew? And you didn't—'

'Oh my God, don't start this again,' her mother interrupted. 'I did my best for you girls no matter what you'd like to believe. I was alone, remember? Your father was no help, was he? It's easy for you, Chelsea, with your husband and your money and your perfect little life. What was *I* supposed to do? Should I have let you and your sister starve to death?'

You could have got a job, Chelsea thought, but she didn't say it. She never said what she wanted to her mother, yet another difference between her and Maddie. But her sister had always been the favourite, the daughter Erin loved most, no matter what Maddie said or did. It was easy to be brave when you knew you couldn't lose.

'Who do you think is behind it?' she asked instead. That was the question she had been obsessing over since she had seen the blog. Who was it and what did they want? 'I thought it might be Milo James – this kind of online shit-stirring is right up his alley – but how would he have found the storage unit in the first place? And wouldn't he want credit? Surely he'd have it all over RumorMill if it was him.'

'I have no idea,' Erin said.

'Okay, but you do think it's legit, right? I mean, it looks like Maddie's handwriting.'

'I don't know why you're asking me. Your sister never told me anything. The two of you were always doing your twin thing and excluding me.' Erin's eyes were glistening, tears fast approaching, and Chelsea couldn't have her mother ruining her makeup, or refusing to do the photos today because she was too upset. Nick didn't ask much of her, but he needed this content for the app.

'It's okay,' Chelsea soothed her, as this woman had trained her to do since birth. 'Let's get our hair done. We want to look our best, don't we?'

'Hmm,' her mother said, pretending to resist Chelsea's attempts to placate her but her shoulders dropped a little. 'I hope I look all right. I need a top-up of my Botox.' She waited for Chelsea to tell her she was being silly, that she looked great, younger than ever. Erin had been gunning for a neck lift for ages now, kept saying she wanted it done, but they were 'so expensive . . . for me anyway'. Chelsea thought about the blood money Nick paid her mother every year, yet it was still not enough.

'You know,' Erin said, putting her arm through Chelsea's, 'this could really help you with the show.'

'What?'

'The reunion,' Erin explained, as if Chelsea was being silly. 'Don't you think this would help in the negotiations?'

'What are you talking about? The blog has nothing to do with *Vigilante Queens*.'

'Yes, but all publicity is good publicity. It could help you get an even bigger deal.'

Sometimes Chelsea's therapist would say it was unlikely Erin was as callous as Chelsea perceived her to be. Maddie was still her child, she was still missing, presumed dead. That wasn't something a mother could easily shake off, even one with narcissistic tendencies. Chelsea wished she could record conversations like this and send them back to Dr Ursula as proof. *See?* she would say. *Look what I have to deal with.*

'Stop it,' Chelsea pulled her arm away. 'I'm tired of this. I don't want to do the reunion. Between you and Kelly and Nancy and—' She stopped but it was too late. Her mother knew Chelsea's tells too.

'He's doing it, of course,' Erin said, her face thoughtful. 'Well, whatever else you say about Robbie, he was always smart when it came to this stuff.'

'I can't do it,' Chelsea said. Why didn't her mother, of all people, get that? Erin had lost Maddie too.

'Ladies, we gotta roll if we want to keep the light.' The photographer clapped his hands and they hurried into the kitchen, taking their seats in the fold-up director's chairs.

The hairdresser loosened Chelsea's curls, raking his fingers through them. 'Remember,' he warned her. 'No drastic changes between now and your actual birthday if we want these pics to look authentic. Can't have pap photos of you with, like, a cunty little bob or something.'

Chelsea was about to answer when she heard a sharp intake of breath. 'What?' she said, turning to her mother. Erin was staring at her phone, her face pale beneath her false tan, and she handed it to Chelsea wordlessly. It was the same website, maddiestonestorage.com, but there was something else there now. White text on a black screen. Her vision blurred and she made herself focus, so she could read it properly.

I know everything. I know what you did.
And I'm ready to tell your secrets.
Yes, Chelsea. Even that one.

6.

1998

'That's the last of it,' Erin said, slamming the trunk door. It didn't quite close, the strap of an old duffel bag getting caught, and Chelsea dashed forward to fix it before her mother noticed, tucking the bag in carefully. It was squashed between refuse sacks full of clothes and shoes, mementoes they'd taken from their final day on the *Heartstrings* set, the stacks of magazines their mother had insisted on saving over the years, any time the show or the twins' character had been mentioned, a cardboard box of bed linen and towels, another of kitchenware, and that was it. It was surprising, really, how little they had after eight years at Cedar City.

Erin stood at the kerb, staring up at the sprawling complex of apartments, a renowned haven for aspiring child actors and their families who moved to LA from out of town. The whitewashed building, the small balconies overlooking a pool where tanned, thin mothers lay on rainbow-coloured loungers, one hand shading their eyes from the sun as they called to their kids in the water. 'Be careful of your hair, Amber,' Chelsea heard one of them say. 'The chlorine will turn it green and you need to look your best for your audition tomorrow.' So many mothers packed into those square, blandly furnished rooms, so many kids always and for ever just on the verge of their big break.

No fathers, but that wasn't because all men were as useless as *their* dad, Erin had explained to the twins. These fathers hadn't abandoned their wives and children, like Ed Stone had. They hadn't absconded from their responsibilities without so much as a goodbye note. No, these fathers were back home in their small towns in Georgia and Louisiana, in Ohio and Wyoming, working as hard as they could to pay for Cedar City, and to cover the costs of the headshots, the acting coaches, the extensive dental work, sending pay check after pay check so their children could achieve their dreams. *Not like us*, Erin told the twins. *We're alone, girls. Don't ever forget that.*

'Erin!' A southern accent, drawling. When Chelsea turned, she could see Delilah Banks, a heavyset woman with teased blonde hair and frosted lipstick, getting out of her old Chevy. Right beside her, as ever, was her daughter Birdie, in a strappy dress and flip-flops, her pale skin flushed from the midday heat. They had moved into Cedar City on the same day as the Stones, their apartments next door to one another. Delilah pulled Erin into a hug, saying, 'I can't believe you're moving! I'm gonna miss y'all so much.'

'I'll miss you too,' Erin said, and Chelsea and Maddie glanced at each other. Their mother had never been shy about her feelings for Delilah and Birdie, once describing them as 'that pushy cow and her loser daughter' after a couple of margaritas.

'Girls,' Erin said, stepping out of the other woman's embrace. 'Say goodbye to Delilah and Birdie.'

Chelsea did as she was told, smiling as she hugged them both, but Maddie leaned against the car, giving a mock salute. Erin's jaw tightened but she didn't say anything. 'Thank you for being the best of neighbours,' their mother said, tucking her hair behind her ears. 'And I hope Birdie books something soon. I can't imagine how difficult it must be for—'

'Don't you worry about Birdie. The casting agent today said she's one of the most *interesting* girls he's seen in a long time. She's doing just great.' Delilah wrapped an arm around

Birdie's shoulders and the girl's face went blank, the way it always did when her mother talked about her acting career. 'Aren't you, Birdie?'

'Yes, ma'am,' the girl replied, her voice monotone. She didn't make eye contact with any of them, just stared at the ground. *I don't wanna be mean,* Chelsea had overheard Erin saying to one of the other Cedar City moms after a particularly disastrous talent show in which Birdie had performed an off-key rendition of 'Kiss From A Rose', her eyes closed for the duration, *but do you think there could be something . . . you know . . . wrong with her?*

A high-pitched squeal from across the parking lot saved Birdie from further interrogation, a blur of khaki and denim as a body rushed towards them. 'Oh, my gosh, oh, my gosh!' It was a white middle-aged woman with tight corkscrew curls and baby pink lipstick. She shoved a notebook in the direction of the twins and they looked at it for a second, neither moving.

'Girls,' Erin said sharply – she had taught them better than this – and Chelsea stepped forward to take the notepad. She scribbled a quick note, signing her name with a flourish. She handed it to Maddie, who sighed heavily but took it all the same.

'Oh, gosh, I am just the biggest fan of *Heartstrings*! I think it's the best show on television,' the woman said. It was always people like this who approached them, and it had started almost immediately after the show aired. *Heartstrings* was a faith-based drama about a family of seven daughters going through typical teenage-girl scrapes, each one neatly resolved by the end of the twenty-five minutes.

Chelsea and Maddie shared the role of Charity, the precocious youngest daughter with insight beyond her years, the moral compass of the show. Strangers would hug the girls upon meeting them, or they would cry, weeping as the twins stood awkwardly, wondering what they could say to make it stop. The fans would say they had watched the show while they were going through a divorce or when their husband cheated on them, while they were getting chemo, after they had miscarried alone in a bathroom stall at work or their teenage son died in a drunk-driving accident. *You got me through it*, they would tell Maddie and Chelsea. *Thank you. Can I have an autograph? Can I have a photograph for my sister? She's your biggest fan. Can you come with me to this pay phone? We have to ring my grandma or she won't believe I met you. I need proof! It's her birthday! It's Christmas! It's Hanukkah! She's like, dying, she's in the hospice, and this would mean a lot to her, it'll only take two minutes, you have two minutes, don't you?*

And then, as they hit their pre-teen years, there were the men in their late forties and fifties, standing a little too close, their fingers drifting higher on the twins' chests when they posed together for photographs. *Say cheese!* Erin would yell, and Chelsea wondered if her mother ever felt unsettled by these men the way she did, if Erin noticed the hands, the heavy breathing, or if Chelsea was just being paranoid. *You have to be nice to the fans*, Erin would tell them afterwards. *They can make or break your career. And it's just a photograph. It's just an autograph. Can't you see how much it means to them? Don't you know how lucky you are?*

'I cannot believe I ran into you like this,' the woman said, flapping her hands at her face, fanning herself. 'Here you are, Jason Simmons's daughter!'

'Well,' Maddie said, 'he's an actor. It's a television show.' She spoke slowly, like she was explaining the concept of TV to a toddler, and Chelsea had to turn a snort of laughter into a cough so she wouldn't seem rude. 'Which means he's not our actual father.'

'Maddie.'

Erin's teeth were gritted but the woman didn't even notice. She was looking between Maddie and Chelsea, frowning. 'Wait. There's two of you? But on the show, it's only—'

'Child labour laws!' Delilah cut in. She handed a set of house keys to her daughter and Birdie scurried away towards the complex without saying goodbye. 'Erin is so lucky. It's much easier to cast twins.' She blew a kiss at their mother, and followed Birdie into Cedar City. *We'll never see you again*, Chelsea thought, and she knew it was true. She could feel it in her bones.

'Is that right?' the woman asked Erin, and their mother cleared her throat, saying something about legally, yes, having twins helped, but the girls were so magnetic, so special, she had known they were different from the moment they were born. 'Do you know,' Erin said, leaning in conspiratorially, 'I went to see a psychic when they were toddlers.' Chelsea resisted the urge to roll her eyes, the same as she always did when her mother talked about the prophecy. 'And she told me they would be more beautiful than I could ever imagine,' Erin continued. 'As well as the most famous girls of their generation.'

That wasn't the whole prophecy but Erin never did repeat the second part. The whole prophecy said that only one of the twins would be famous, and the other would die before her thirtieth birthday. It had been Maddie who had made that discovery a couple of years ago, when she'd found a stack of their mother's letters to their grandmother, all stamped with RETURN TO SENDER across the front. 'I went to see a fortune-teller today,' Maddie had recited aloud from one. 'And you'll never *believe* what she told me.' Chelsea laughed but she was nervous too, listening to make sure her mother wasn't coming through the front door, finally persuading Maddie to put the letters back where she'd found them. 'And one shall DIE,' Maddie had intoned later that night, just as they were falling asleep, and both girls had broken down in giggles. It was so Erin, they agreed, to decide that one part of the prophecy would come true and the other would not.

The woman gulped, visibly impressed. 'I know,' Erin said. 'And it looks like we're on the way to making that become a reality. The girls just got cast on a show of their own.'

'Oh.' The woman's smile dropped. 'But what does that mean for *Heartstrings*?'

Chelsea wondered what she would do if Erin gave her the truth. For years, Chelsea had been told that the actor who played her father had 'sinus issues'. It was only recently she'd realized that meant he was a raging drug addict. He had also been having an affair with his twenty-five-year-old personal assistant, and when his wife – and the mother of his children – had paid a surprise visit to set one day, she wasn't exactly thrilled when she'd walked into his dressing room to find him and the assistant half naked, fat lines of coke racked up on the coffee-table. Jason Simmons was promptly whisked away to rehab ('There's no pre-nup,' one of the hair stylists told Erin as she braided Chelsea's hair, grimacing. 'Jason is *fucked* if she divorces him') to save his marriage and his image as a wholesome family man. Luckily for the producers, the actress who played the twins' oldest sister announced she was going to pose naked for a men's magazine, which would cause enough of a scandal to warrant cancelling the show without anyone noticing Jason's absence. At least, that was what Nancy Taylor, their agent, had told Erin, promising she would use the drama to the twins' advantage. That was when she'd given their mother the *Double Trouble* script. 'This show has huge potential,' Nancy had said. 'Now, do you know where we could find a set of twins?'

'I think *Heartstrings* has run its course, don't you?' Erin said, signalling at the girls to get into the car. Maddie grabbed the passenger seat, ignoring Chelsea's protestations that it wasn't fair, why did she always have to sit in the back? 'Because I'm the oldest,' Maddie said, clicking together her seatbelt.

'By ten minutes!' Chelsea retorted.

'Chel,' her sister said, turning around, 'statistically, you're more likely to die in the front. I'm only doing this to protect you.'

'Shut up,' Chelsea said, half kicking at Maddie's back through the car seat but they were both laughing.

Fifteen minutes later, their mother pulled the steering wheel hard, screeching to a stop at Sunset Plaza. The twins jerked forward in their seats, and Maddie said, 'Whiplash, much?' rubbing at her neck.

But Erin wasn't paying attention. She was bending to the side so she could see out of the window. 'Girls! Look!' she said, pointing up. Chelsea undid her seatbelt, scooting forward so she could see what her mother was looking at and muttered, 'Oh, my God,' when she saw the enormous billboard. It was a picture of her and Maddie in matching outfits – cotton dresses with sunflower embroidery, black velvet chokers, and butterfly clips in their hair – and they stood back to back. *Double Trouble*, the name of the show, was emblazoned across the top of the poster in block pink letters, and at the bottom was the tagline. *Sugar and Spice, Naughty and Nice . . . coming to AtomicKids, Fridays at 5 p.m.!*

Erin grabbed Maddie's elbow. 'Madeline, I said look.' Their mother's voice was turning, that unnerving edge in it, but Maddie simply bent down to rifle through the backpack at her feet, pulling out a battered paperback. She put her feet on the dashboard and started to read, pointedly ignoring their mother. 'Fine,' Erin said. 'Be like that.' She got out of the car, slamming the door behind her so hard that it rattled.

'Why do you have to—'

'Because it's never enough for her,' Maddie said, before Chelsea could continue. 'It doesn't matter what you give her, Chel. It'll never be enough. The sooner you learn that, the better.'

I know, Chelsea wanted to say. *But because you give her nothing, I'm forced to over-compensate. I have to be enough for the two of us.* 'She's just excited,' she said instead because the truth was a part of her liked being the peacemaker. It was the one thing she was better at than her sister. 'It's a big moment for her . . . I mean,' she stumbled over her words, 'for us.' She went to open the door and Maddie turned around, putting her hand on Chelsea's arm. 'Don't,' she said. 'Don't give in to her.'

Chelsea looked between her sister and her mother, sitting on the hood of the car, staring up at the billboard. Erin's shoulders were tensing, inching closer and closer to her ears, and Chelsea knew what would happen if she didn't join her. Erin would drive to their new house, the air thick with tension, and she wouldn't say another word. The twins would have to lug all the stuff inside, and unpack, while their mother sulked in her bedroom, the door locked. It would be a week of slammed doors and silence until Chelsea would eventually cave, and apologize. It never seemed to bother Maddie when their mother was in one of these moods – it was like she didn't even notice – but Chelsea would barely be able to eat or sleep until things returned to normal. It was just easier to do what Erin wanted.

'I'm not *giving in to her*,' she said. 'I'm just . . .'

'Sure,' Maddie said. 'Keep telling yourself that.'

'Mads . . .' she pleaded, and her sister sighed.

'Don't worry,' Maddie said. 'I will always love you, even if you are a giant sap when it comes to Mommy Dearest.'

'Thank you. I love you too.'

'I love you the most,' Maddie countered.

'Impossible,' Chelsea said, and Maddie put a hand on her heart, pretending to swoon.

'Go on,' she said, returning to her book as Chelsea stepped out.

She approached her mother warily. Erin glanced sideways, and Chelsea could see the disappointment on her face. Of course her mother would have wanted it to be Maddie. Chelsea always did the right thing and Erin always wished it was her sister instead. 'Hey.' Chelsea leaned against the hood, next to her.

'Look at that,' Erin said, still gazing up at the billboard.

'I know,' Chelsea responded. 'It's . . .' She trailed off. It was strange, staring at a fifteen-foot poster of yourself. She glanced over her shoulder, in case anyone was watching her watching herself. Then she focused on the billboard again, looking at it with a critical eye, trying to imagine what a stranger might think. Would they say that one twin was prettier than the other, cuter, thinner? *You're identical,* Chelsea reminded herself. *If it wasn't for your scar, even Mom would have difficulty telling you apart,* but it didn't help. *Heartstrings* had been one thing: she and Maddie had been sharing the role. This was the first time the public would be introduced to them as a duo, as individuals. Of course they would compare the girls to each other, decide which one they liked the best. Chelsea had a sneaking suspicion it wasn't going to be her. Not when she was playing the 'spice' in the equation, the naughty twin.

It was her own fault: she had frozen in the meeting with Donald Tomei, the founder of AtomicKids, an elderly man with sun spots on his bald head and beady eyes that seemed to look right through her. Before they'd gone into the office, Erin and Nancy Taylor had warned them how important this meeting was – this man had the power to change their lives: they had to impress him. Chelsea had been so overwhelmed by the enormity of it all she had been rendered silent. Not Maddie, of course. It would take more than an old man in a suit to intimidate her sister. Maddie had walked into that room as if she owned the place, joking with the board of management like they were old friends, telling one man that his multicoloured tie was 'da bomb' while he preened in delight. *Well*, she'd heard Donald Tomei say, just as the door was closing behind them, *it's clear which one is the star, isn't it?*

'It really is,' Erin said. 'Wait.' She held Chelsea's bare arm out, inspecting it. 'Did you apply sunblock?'

'Um,' Chelsea wavered.

'For Pete's sake!' her mother admonished her. 'You know you can't go out in the sun without protection. What do you think they'll say if you turn up to the first day of shooting with a *tan*? You girls have to maintain your current look. It's in the contract that you—'

'It's eleven a.m., Mom, and it's not even hot yet. And I've been outside for like two seconds. I think it's gonna be okay.'

'Don't get smart with me.' Erin pulled away and Chelsea found herself leaning forward, yearning. 'I have enough on my plate with your sister. I need to be able to depend on you.'

'You *can* depend on me,' Chelsea said, stung.

'Can I?' Erin stood up straight, still facing the billboard, and she put her hands on the back of her head. 'I don't understand how you girls can be so ungrateful. My God, if I'd had the opportunities you two have, if my mother had made the sacrifices that I made for you, that I continue to make . . .' Erin was still young, only thirty-one as she kept reminding them, and she was so beautiful, with her long blonde hair and her wide-set blue eyes and her heart-shaped chin. She could have been someone, she could have made it, if it hadn't been for Ed Stone.

Do you want to hear the story of how I met your father? she used to ask the twins when they were little and she'd had one too many glasses of wine. It was the end of May, she'd tell them, and there was a hint of summer in the air. Erin had been working behind the bar at a dive joint in the small town in Nevada where she'd grown up, only a couple of miles from the Californian border. Ed had walked in and, after one look at Erin's ass in her tight little skirt, he'd taken up residence at the counter, giving larger and larger tips until Erin agreed to go on a date with him. She was pregnant within six weeks. *You stupid girl.* That was what her mother had said when Erin told her the news. *You stupid, stupid girl.*

'Why does your sister always have to be like this? It's not fair.' Erin let her hands fall to her sides. 'You girls don't understand how difficult it is to live in this town, how expensive everything is. I just want to make sure you have the best life you possibly can. This show is our ticket out.'

'I'm sorry,' Chelsea said, and she could almost hear Maddie telling her to stop, that she had nothing to apologize for, neither of them did. But she said it anyway because she knew it was what her mother wanted to hear and all she wanted was for Erin to be happy. 'We didn't mean to upset you.'

Erin sighed but when Chelsea came up to her, nestling into her side, she didn't pull away. 'I'm sorry,' Chelsea said again, and something broke in her chest when Erin put a hand on her head and said, 'I know. I know. You're such a good girl, Chelsea.'

7.

2025

She was sitting in her car, parked outside Linda's care home, but Chelsea found she couldn't move. 'Are you okay, Mrs Bennett?' her security guard asked, and she said, 'Yes, sorry, I just need a minute.' It was Monday, exactly one week since the last blog post had gone live. *What secret?* Nick kept asking her. *Do you have something you want to tell me, Chelsea?* And she kept saying no because what else was she supposed to do? She couldn't tell him the truth. She pulled up the blog on her phone again, staring at the words on the screen. *Ready to tell your secrets . . . even that one.* It felt like her brain short-circuited every time she looked at it, like for a brief moment she was free-falling in space and didn't know when it would end, if ever. Chelsea had many secrets, but only one would destroy her life. Surely this person, whoever they were, couldn't know what had happened? How could anyone except—

Her phone pinged, the screen lighting up, and she inhaled sharply when she saw the name. What were the chances that she would receive this message at this very moment?

I saw the website. Are you okay?

She read it once, twice, three times. The desire to reply was so fierce, it was almost impossible to resist. Then she deleted the text and pushed the feelings down deep inside, where no one would ever see them.

Chelsea plastered a smile on her face as she signed in at the front desk of the care home, and she went into Linda's room, closing the door behind her. 'Hi, Linda,' she said, touching her former co-star's hands, shivering at the feel of her papery skin. 'Are you okay? Do you need anything?' She knew Linda would not respond but she always asked, every time, just in case that day was different. Chelsea talked in a stream of consciousness, about Nick and his ferocious need to make Foto the number-one social-media site in the world even when it was abundantly clear it never would be, about Grayson and the latest book he was reading, and how his face lit up when he was telling her about it, and the amusing comment Ivy had made at dinner, how surprised her daughter had looked when they all laughed, asking what was funny. How innocent her children were, still. Chelsea tucked some of Linda's greying hair behind her ears and reminded herself to talk to one of the nurses about dyeing it. Linda had never been vain, like Erin, but she liked to look her best all the same. Then finally, she started to talk about the blog.

'We don't know who's behind it,' Chelsea said. 'It was Maddie's diary entries uploaded to the website first. Did you know Maddie had an eating disorder? Like, a proper one, not the crazy diets the rest of us were put on.' She paused. Linda had been in the home for more than ten years and her moments of lucidity were vanishingly rare now, but Chelsea wanted to give her the chance to speak, just in case. 'And then some childhood photos,' she continued. 'I can't remember seeing them before.' Grainy shots of Maddie and Chelsea, sitting cross-legged in the park by Cedar City, making daisy chains. Others from their pageant days, glossy lips and tight curls, barely three years old. In a few of them, Chelsea's face had been scratched out, as if with a pin but she didn't know if that had been done already, by Maddie before she died, or if the person behind the website was responsible. 'And, of course,' Chelsea said, 'the final note.' *I know everything. I know what you did. And I'm ready to tell your secrets.*

'I know you didn't believe she would kill herself.' Linda had always argued that, while Maddie had been struggling, it had never come to that stage, but Linda didn't know how bad things had been at the end. Chelsea had never been brave enough to tell the older woman about that last terrible row, what she had said to her twin. *Could that be the secret?* she wondered. And, if so, what would people think if they knew how cruel she had been to Maddie? Would they blame her for Maddie's death? 'They still can't find whoever made the site. But . . .' Chelsea's voice dropped to a whisper, the fear choking her '. . . who could know what I did? It's impossible.'

It was strange how Linda had become the only person in her life with whom she could be completely honest. Everyone else wanted something from her, demanding a performance. Nick wanted the perfect wife, her children wanted the perfect mother, Erin wanted Chelsea to pretend that her childhood had been idyllic, that Erin had never made any mistakes with the twins. Chelsea loved her friends, but Kelly was a lot of work, Hannah was her employee, and Nya lived over two thousand miles away. Even her psychoanalyst seemed to want proof that Chelsea was getting 'better', that the therapy was working. It was only Linda, poor, silent Linda, to whom Chelsea could tell her secrets.

She startled as the door opened, putting a smile on her face, ready to greet a nurse, but it was Zach, Linda's son, standing there. She got out of the chair to kiss him. Zach was thirty now, his sister Emily twenty-eight, and Chelsea had known them since they were little, since she was a child. The first table read for *Double Trouble*, the AtomicKids sitcom that had made her and Maddie famous: that was when they were introduced to Linda, the woman who would play their on-screen mother. She must have been in her early thirties then, tall and beautiful with her freckled skin and red hair, and so warm, Chelsea felt instantly at ease.

'Don't worry,' Linda had told their mother. 'I'll take good care of the girls,' and Erin had stiffened, defensive. She had been suspicious of Linda from the jump, annoyed at an interview the other woman had given in which she said she hoped neither of her kids would follow her into acting, that the industry was 'no place for children'. But Linda had been true to her word: she *had* taken care of Maddie and Chelsea, as best she could anyway. She'd checked with Julia, their tutor, to see how they were getting on with their school work, queried lines in the script she thought were inappropriate, and insisted they finish up shooting whenever they were clearly exhausted. Even after the show had ended, she took the girls out for lunch once a month to catch up, asked them to babysit Zach and Emily on the rare Saturday night she had plans, phoned and texted them regularly. Sometimes it felt like Linda was the only person in the twins' lives who didn't want anything from them, who loved them despite their fame and not because of it.

When Linda started showing symptoms of early onset dementia in her forties, Chelsea hadn't been there to see it. She was still in a fog following Maddie's death, her guilt that she was somehow to blame for her sister's decision paralysing her. So, she hid from everyone. She hadn't answered Linda's calls in more than a year when Zach and Emily came to visit her. Their mother was having trouble finding words in the middle of a conversation, they said, and she kept losing her keys, and once she'd asked why Maddie never came to see her any more. They didn't know what to do. By the time Linda was fifty-five, her condition had advanced so rapidly that there was no denying it any longer. She would need full-time help. Zach and Emily, barely adults at the time, could not afford the kind of care their mother deserved, and Linda's residuals from *Double Trouble* were not sufficient to foot the bill for the decades to come. That was when Chelsea had stepped in, promising to pay for the home, which she and Nick had done for the last ten years, as well as covering Emily and Zach's college fees. They were family, after all.

'How is she?' Zach asked, moving closer to her bedside. He took a deep breath, leaning down to kiss Linda's cheek. He visited only once a month, the staff told Chelsea. He'd always struggled with his mother's illness, hated seeing her lying in that bed, comatose.

'She's okay. Were you talking to Mayumi?' she asked, tilting her head towards the nurses' station outside.

'No. I just came in.'

'Don't worry,' Chelsea said. 'Your mom had a chest infection during the week so they put antibiotics in her drip. Mayumi said it's clearing up nicely.'

'That's good to hear.' He was still staring at Linda, and Chelsea tried to think of something that would distract him.

'How is everything at work?' she asked. 'Has that guy stopped reheating fish in the microwave?'

'No!' Zach made a face. 'It's so disgusting. It's a crime worthy of The Hague.'

'I'll get Nick's lawyers on it,' Chelsea said drily. 'Oh, I meant to ask you. What's up with Emily? I haven't heard from her all week.' The three of them had a group chat but she and Emily usually texted each other separately. Zach wasn't as interested in Real Housewife memes as they were and had made that abundantly clear.

'She's at some silent retreat,' he said, with a shrug. He thought his sister's woo-woo inclinations were bullshit.

'Damn, I forgot.' Emily had mentioned something about it during their last phone call but Chelsea had been distracted, trying to get Ivy into the bath at the same time. She should have known Emily was off grid: she would have texted Chelsea as soon as she'd heard about the website otherwise, wanting to make sure Chelsea was okay. Would Emily ask what the secret was? she wondered, with a sense of dread. And what would Chelsea say if she did? 'I'll give her a call when she's back.'

Zach took her seat as she gathered up her coat and bags, telling Linda she would be back next week to see her. Chelsea didn't know if it made a difference, if Linda could even hear her, but she kept talking anyway. It was probably more for her own benefit than anything else, throwing her stories into Linda's hands, knowing the older woman could do nothing with them. She gave Zach's shoulders a gentle squeeze, then went to leave.

'Chel,' he called after her, 'I've been meaning to text all week but work has been crazy. I hope you're doing okay. With all that . . . you know. The website stuff. It's fucked up, man. I wish those vultures would leave you guys alone.'

She paused, touched by his sincerity. No one else in her life had put it quite as bluntly as that. It was as if they had all just accepted that the invasion of privacy was inevitable rather than, as Zach said, fucked up. 'Thank you,' she said. 'You're a sweetheart, do you know that?'

He half smiled and Chelsea was struck by the similarities between him and his mother, the crooked mouth and freckled skin, those warm brown eyes. 'I think anyone with a sense of decency would think the same,' he said. 'And now this bullshit about all the prescriptions? It's fucking cruel, man. Like, that's private. That's *healthcare*.' He looked at his mother again, and Chelsea knew he was thinking about the tabloid coverage of Linda's illness, the almost gloating satisfaction they took in detailing how she had no one left to care for her except two broke kids. 'It's messed up.'

'Wait,' Chelsea said, her heart picking up pace. 'What do you mean, prescriptions?'

8.

2025

Chelsea left the care home, keeping a smile on her face as she called goodbye to the staff. It was only when she got into the car that she allowed herself to pull her cell out of her bag. She could hear her breath, unsteady, as she clicked into the website and read though the new documents, all the prescriptions, under all the fake names. The captions helpfully explained what, exactly, each drug was used for. *Oh, my God. Maddie, what did you do?*

She checked X, on her burner account in case she accidentally liked anything, and, as she had expected, Madeline Stone was trending again. The response was divided almost fifty-fifty. One half were sniggering at the thought of the once beautiful Stone sister, riddled with STIs, the incels out in full force saying it was what she deserved. They were calling Maddie a whore, a slut, sharing photos taken at a house party in the 2000s, her sister clearly drunk, a nipple falling out of her lace camisole, lines of a white powder on the kitchen table in the background. On the other hand, there were the people who were furious about the blog, who asked when poor Madeline Stone would be allowed to rest in peace. Wasn't she allowed some dignity? Either the poor woman had 'un-alived' herself, as the kids said these days, or she had made the decision to disappear from public life – either way, her desire to be left alone should be respected, they said self-righteously.

The speculation quickly turned to Chelsea. Whatever

could this secret be? The worst of the conspiracy theorists were having a field day in their attempts to guess. Chelsea and Maddie had swapped places, Chelsea had actually killed Maddie, both the twins were dead and a third sister had taken her place.

Chelsea scrolled through them all, panicking. She didn't know what to do. She tried phoning Nya, but there was no response – it was late in New York, her friend was probably getting ready for bed – and, she thought, as she sent yet another of her husband's calls to voicemail, she couldn't go home, not yet. She picked up her phone to text the one person she knew she shouldn't – *no*. She put it back into her bag. That wasn't fair. They had agreed that no contact was the best for everyone involved. It was safest. But who would she go to instead?

It had taken her almost two hours to drive to Kelly's house in Central-Alameda, and by the time she pulled up at the tiny house, the clapboard sides painted mint green, it was after ten p.m. With anyone else, she would have felt embarrassed about arriving at their front door unannounced at bedtime but she and Kelly had known each other too long for that. Besides, she had thought, as she rang the doorbell once, twice, three times, Kelly owed her.

'Your sister was always messy,' Kelly said now, shaking her head. 'And, like, that's coming from *me*.'

The two women were in Kelly's kitchen, staring at the screen of her tablet. Chelsea had pulled up the website – 'Hurry on, Grandma.' Kelly had laughed as she watched Chelsea struggle with the device. 'How are you *this* bad with technology when your husband works in the industry?' and Chelsea had thought, a little shame-faced, it was because she usually had staff to do everything for her. There was another note on the blog's homepage, saying *Welcome to Monday Madd-ness!* and promising that a new item from Maddie's storage unit would be uploaded every Monday. Chelsea's limbs went heavy at the thought of going through this on a weekly basis.

'Monday,' Kelly said thoughtfully. 'That's interesting, isn't it?' and Chelsea knew exactly what her friend meant. In the old days, when they were famous, publicists used to try to bury a news story by releasing a statement on Friday afternoon, after the weekly magazines had been put to bed, meaning they couldn't cover it in time. That was before the blogs, before social media, before the twenty-four / seven news cycle. There was something remarkably old school about choosing Monday, deliberate too. This person, whoever they were, wanted to make the biggest splash they could.

She stood there as Kelly scrolled through the images. There were numerous prescription scripts from a variety of doctors. It seemed that Maddie had used different aliases too – Maddie Ryan, their mother's maiden name, Erin Ryan. On at least two, Kelly pointed out, her eyes widening, her sister had used Chelsea Stone. 'Oh, fuck,' Chelsea heard herself say, but her voice sounded muffled, like she was underwater. '*Fuck.*' They were mostly for anti-anxiety medication and sleeping pills, Xanex and Ambien and Valium, beta blockers and an antidepressant, but what was getting the most attention online was the prescription for Valtrex and Clamelle.

'Commonly used to—'

'Treat herpes,' Chelsea said. Thankfully, her sister had used her own name for these. 'And chlamydia.'

'It happens to the best of us.' Kelly shrugged. 'Ain't no shame in this game.' She kept scrolling. 'Except for you, obviously, Miss Perfect. Was this the big secret? That you were on antidepressants?'

Chelsea stiffened but there didn't seem to be any rancour

in Kelly's words, no hidden barbs that Chelsea would have to choose, once again, between ignoring or calling out. 'I've told you a million times there is no secret.' she said, wishing Nya was there to tell Kelly to back off. 'And I'm not perfect.'

'Oh, please!' Kelly snorted. 'You're the only person I know who stayed a virgin until they got married. Even Britney admitted the purity ring was just for show. Nick must have been ecstatic when he found out you were untouched by human hand.' She paused. 'Or dick, I suppose.'

'Stop it.' Chelsea had never been comfortable talking about sex, even when they were younger, no matter how much Kelly had pushed her to 'loosen up' on the set of *Vigilante Queens*.

Kelly put the tablet flat on the counter top and swivelled on her high stool so her knees were touching Chelsea's. 'Speaking of Nick,' she said, 'what was his reaction when he saw this?'

'He's not exactly thrilled. His people keep getting the site taken down, and then another version of the blog appears and then . . .' Chelsea grabbed Kelly's glass of water, drinking some. Her husband had sent her a terse message as she was leaving the care home, telling Chelsea this was getting out of hand. *If there's something you want to tell me,* he'd said, *now is the time to do it so we can get ahead of it, Chel. You and I have been through a lot. There's nothing we can't fix.* But Nick was wrong. There would be no fixing this, if he found out what she'd done, which meant he never, ever could. 'Next year is a big deal for him. If he decides to run, that is,' she said quickly, because he hadn't officially announced his campaign, and if Kelly let it slip to anyone, Nick would know it had come from her.

'I hope he does run,' Kelly stretched her arms overhead and yawned. 'LA needs a mayor who'll get shit done. I'm, like, afraid to leave my house these days with all the crackheads on the streets.'

Chelsea waited for her friend, a recovering addict, to see

the irony in her words but Kelly never had been one for introspection. She wished she was brave enough to point this out to her, the way Maddie would have done – her sister had always hated hypocrisy – but she stayed quiet. Why was she so afraid of confrontation? It was pathetic, at her age.

'Who do you think is behind this?' Chelsea asked.

'If I was a betting woman, my money would be on Milo James. This *reeks* of him.'

'But wouldn't he want the credit?'

'He might want the clicks but not the heat,' Kelly said. 'He's on thin ice with Gen Z as it is. But the question is – does he know your secrets?'

'I told you, there are no . . .' Chelsea didn't finish her sentence because the other woman wasn't listening to her. She watched as Kelly got up, walked to the fridge and opened the door.

'Do you want something to drink?' her friend waggled her eyebrows. 'I have wine here. It's good.' She took the bottle out and looked at the label. 'I mean, it's probably not "good" by Chelsea Stone-Bennett standards but it's decent enough.'

'Should you be drinking?' Chelsea said, unable to stop herself.

Kelly's shoulders tensed and she put the bottle back in the door of the fridge. 'I'm not an alcoholic.'

'I know but . . .' Chelsea thought of the family therapy sessions at the last rehab centre, just her and Kelly and Kelly's sister, a blowsy woman with five small kids who still lived in Kelly's home town. Kelly hadn't asked Nya to be there, probably because she knew Nya would tell the truth, something no one worried about with Chelsea. Chelsea told people what they wanted to hear. She always had. Kelly's mother wasn't there either, or her father. She had been emancipated from her parents since she was fifteen and discovered they had been taking so much commission from her Nickelodeon wages that she was practically broke. *So much for the Coogan Law, so much for 'protecting kids'*, she would say bitterly, to anyone who would listen. The therapist at the rehab facility had said that, while Kelly's primary issue was drugs, she had an addictive personality and needed to be careful. 'There's always a risk of cross-addiction to other substances,' the woman had explained. Kelly was vacant, staring out of the window, and her sister appeared equally bored, as if she couldn't wait for this to be over. Chelsea had been the one taking notes in her journal, listing all the ways she might say goodbye to another person she loved.

'I just didn't think you were supposed to have any kind of—'

'It's not for me. It's for visitors,' her friend said. She leaned against the fridge door, crossing her arms over her chest. 'Or am I not allowed to have visitors, Chelsea? Please let me know.'

'Of course you're allowed . . . I mean, it's none of my business but—'

'You're right.' Kelly cut across her. 'It's none of your business.'

They didn't say anything for a few minutes, just looked at one another. Chelsea and Nick had set Kelly up in this house almost two years ago, after her last overdose. Before that, Kelly had lived in downtown LA, in a neighbourhood so sketchy that Nick begged Chelsea not to go there, even with security. Until one night when Kelly had FaceTimed Chelsea at three a.m., her eyes black, spittle in the corners of her mouth, wanting to talk about their *Vigilante Queens* days, how famous they'd been, how much everyone had loved them. *Where did it all go wrong?* Kelly had cried, as Chelsea snuck out of her bedroom, trying to be quiet so Nick didn't wake up. She'd begged her friend to please, *please*, call her sponsor – and the next morning, when Kelly had stopped responding to her messages, Chelsea had got into her car immediately and driven to the dilapidated apartment building where Kelly was living.

There was no answer at the door so Chelsea had used her spare key, putting a hand over her nose when she'd walked in. It had smelt disgusting, like rotting food and filth, and a chemical, burning smell. Her suspicions were confirmed when she saw the glass pipe on the coffee-table, an empty baggie next to it, and she'd called Kelly's name, rushing into her friend's room.

Kelly was on the floor, unconscious, her skin bleached of colour, and Chelsea had been sure she was dead. She'd fallen to her knees beside her, and when she'd felt her friend's skin, clammy but still warm, the relief had been so overpowering, Chelsea had almost screamed. That was what Kelly didn't seem to understand. She looked at Chelsea and all she could see was her wealth, her status. She couldn't see beyond the house, the husband, the kids. She never seemed to think about how much Chelsea had lost, and how afraid she was of losing Kelly too.

'I'm sorry,' she said, the way she always did when Kelly was angry with her. 'I trust you to know what's best for you.' It was a blatant lie but, to Chelsea's relief, Kelly didn't call her out on it. It was easier for both of them that way.

Her phone beeped, another message from Nick flashing up on screen.

Nick: have you left yet

Nick: Poppy put the kids to bed

Nick: Chelsea im worried. please call me

She turned the phone face down on the kitchen counter. 'You know what?' she said. 'I think I will have that glass of wine.' Anything to silence the fear rising in her, if only temporarily.

She gestured towards her friend's spare bedroom, the tiny cramped space with a single bed, covered with cheap sheets. 'Do you feel like a sleepover?'

Kelly squealed. 'We haven't done that in ages!' and Chelsea laughed, warning the other woman, 'I have to get up crazy early. I want to be back in time to get the kids ready for school.'

'The nanny will take care of that,' Kelly said dismissively, and Chelsea tried not to show her irritation. She hadn't had kids so other people could raise them. Chelsea had always been a hands-on mother. Given her own childhood, it was especially important to her and she wished Kelly would acknowledge that, just once. Kelly opened the pantry, standing up on her tippy-toes to reach the top shelf and grab a packet of popcorn. She put it in the microwave, staring through the tinted glass, and said, 'I know you said you didn't want to talk about the show but—'

'Kelly,' Chelsea's voice was a warning. 'Not now, I'm serious. I didn't want to do the reunion before,' she touched her hand on the tablet, 'all of *this*, and I have even less desire to do it now. It's too much of a heat score. This website, the blogs . . .' She rubbed the back of her neck. *The secrets this person was threatening to reveal.* 'It hasn't been like this since . . .'

Kelly turned around, the sound of popping emanating like gunfire from the microwave, and there was something on her face that Chelsea couldn't decipher. 'I don't want to put you under pressure. I know how good you and Nick have been to me.' She looked around the small kitchen. 'This house. Paying for my treatment.' Neither of them ever mentioned the stipend that was deposited in her account, weekly rather than monthly so Kelly couldn't blow it all on drugs if she relapsed. It was too awkward to acknowledge the shift in their relationship from friends to something else. Worried mother and wayward daughter, perhaps, or carer and patient. 'I can't rely on you guys for ever,' Kelly continued. 'It makes me feel like a fucking drain.' She bit her lower lip. 'I want to get back to acting. I miss it so much.'

Chelsea had never loved acting in the way Kelly and Nya did, or the way her sister had. When Maddie talked about the joy of disappearing into the character, of how she came alive on set, Chelsea had been mystified. For her, the work had been stressful, trying to remember her lines and find her mark and hoping she looked pretty enough for the cameras. The only part she had enjoyed was when the director told her she had done a good job, or when her mother smiled at her after a successful audition, saying she was proud of her. That part had felt like love and she wanted more of it – she wanted *all* of it. 'And . . .' Kelly's voice cracked '. . . people think I'm a liability now. Nancy Taylor is the only agent who returned my call and she, like, only works with kids.'

'And a few adults,' Chelsea reminded her.

'Yeah, but I'm not Chelsea fucking Stone, am I?' Kelly said bitterly. 'Nancy said she couldn't represent me anyway because no one will hire me. They can't get insurance, she said, not with my history. The only reason she's doing my deal for the reunion is because she's hoping I'll convince you to do it too.'

Chelsea couldn't disagree. Nancy Taylor didn't do any favours unless she thought they would directly benefit her. She had always been ruthless. Maddie used to say their agent was the sort of person who could run a child over, keep driving, and never think about it again. 'I'm not saying Nancy Taylor is a sociopath,' her sister had always said. 'But I'm *not not* saying that, either.'

Kelly took the bag of popcorn from the microwave, muttering, 'Shit,' as it burned her fingers. She shook it into a Perspex bowl and walked over to the couch, throwing herself down. The bowl nestled in her lap. 'Come here,' she said, and Chelsea went to join her. Chelsea knew the producers of *Vigilante Queens* had done everything in their power to protect her, their precious cash-cow, and in the process, they had thrown Kelly under the bus too many times to count. Nya, too, of course, and that had been worse, because Nya's race had been so easy to weaponize against her, the tabloids frothing at the mouth to cast her as the bitch of the trio, which was ironic given how sweet she was. Chelsea, like any former child star worth their salt, was good at *performing* niceness but Nya had been genuinely kind, always doing the right thing even when no one was watching. But, then, Nya had something neither Kelly nor Chelsea did: stable parents who didn't need their daughter's earnings to cover their mortgage, and Chelsea was convinced that was what had saved her.

Kelly might have been the family breadwinner by her fourth birthday, yet she had never been strong enough to survive what the industry did to the women they saw as disposable. Chelsea had heard such terrible stories about former It Girls falling on hard times, and having to use the only assets left to them – their bodies and their dwindling fame – to survive. Parties on yachts, standing around in bikinis as rich men pawed at them, taking whatever pills and powders were on offer to make it bearable, their only hope being that one of the men would fall in love with them, marry them, save them. If Maddie hadn't died, is that what would have happened to her sister?

'Let's take a pic,' Kelly said, reaching into the pocket of her jeans. She always did this when they hung out – photos of the Queens did well on social media. There would be at least three blog articles tomorrow detailing how strong their friendship was after all these years. Kelly held her arm out, pouting, and Chelsea kept her head on Kelly's shoulder. 'What do you think?' Kelly asked, showing her the photo. 'You good with this?'

Whatever Happened to Madeline Stone?

In it, Chelsea was beautiful, her skin taut, her hair perfectly tousled despite the long day. She looked at least ten years younger than Kelly. *Stop that*, she admonished herself. It was the sort of thing the wives of Nick's friends would say, viewing visible signs of ageing as a moral failure. It wasn't Kelly's fault, what had happened to her. She was another victim, another sacrifice on the altar of Chelsea's career. Just because Chelsea hadn't done it personally didn't mean she wasn't to blame.

'Whatever you're happy with,' she said to her friend. It might be a temporary distraction from the blog, and the secrets it threatened to reveal. 'Just post it to Foto and not Instagram, okay? Nick will kill me if you don't. Oh,' she added, 'and make sure you tag Nya. Something like we wish she was in LA right now.' Nya might live on the east coast but Chelsea felt closer to her than she did to Kelly. It was easier to be close with Nya: she was a soft space to land. Spending time with Kelly felt like walking through a field of hidden landmines – one wrong step could trigger an explosion.

Kelly uploaded the photo, applied a filter, and her face lit up as the likes and comments began to flood in. 'Kell,' Chelsea said, but her friend wasn't listening. 'Hey,' she said sharply. 'I didn't come here to watch you stare at your phone.'

Kelly's head snapped up, like she was about to argue, but she decided against it. She put the phone back into her pocket, and leaned into Chelsea, wrapping an arm around her shoulders. 'Sorry,' Chelsea said, 'I'm not myself. I just feel like . . . all this stuff on the website. The diaries and the prescriptions. It's not Maddie.'

'It sounds like her to me.'

But Kelly didn't know Maddie, not really. It had been impossible for anyone else to know the twins as well as they knew each other. Not that Chelsea had appreciated it at the time. Instead she had run from it, leaving her sister behind. That was part of the reason why she had loved filming *Vigilante Queens* so much: Chelsea could be an autonomous human being, judged on her own merits rather than constantly compared to Maddie. On the Queens set, *she* was the star, not the 'other' twin, the less talented, less interesting one. How easy it had made abandoning Maddie, that feeling.

Kelly started stroking Chelsea's hair. 'I just want you to know that you can trust me,' she said. 'If you are hiding something . . . it might make you feel better to talk about it.'

Her hand on Chelsea's head, gentle, and it made Chelsea want to close her eyes and open her mouth. She wanted to tell someone, *anyone*, yet she could see, with terrifying clarity, that as soon as she did so, her life would fall apart. She would be destroyed. 'I'm not,' she lied.

'Okay. Well, do you think there's more to come?' Kelly asked. 'From the website, I mean.'

'Yes,' Chelsea replied, something twisting in her stomach. 'For some reason, I do.'

9.

2001

'You're gonna look like a mermaid,' the stylist said, as she crimped Chelsea's hair, the steam rising off the ironing tool with a hiss. The director had said he wanted the girls to look like Christina Aguilera, except less trashy, of course. Their wholesomeness was a constant topic of conversation, these days. Mr Tomei, the head of AtomicKids, asked them to wear purity rings, declare their intention to stay virgins until they were married, and while Chelsea was willing to go along with it, Maddie had put her foot down, saying it was patriarchal bullshit. *Our little feminist*, their mother had said, with a roll of her eyes, but when Maddie said no, she meant it.

Chelsea had spent the last two hours in Hair and Makeup, watching as the team carved beauty from the bones of her face. She loved this part, being made pretty for television. It was a momentary relief from the constant thrum of *not good enough* that echoed through her brain on a daily basis. *Not thin enough, not cute enough, not talented enough.* Wardrobe had put her and Maddie in coordinating outfits, the same striped poplin shirt, except hers was rust red and Maddie's was an icy blue. 'To bring out your eyes,' the woman had said, as she dressed Maddie, hoicking up the girl's breasts so they filled out her bra, and Chelsea stared at the mirror, wondering if the red brought out *her* eyes and, if not, why hadn't they given her a blue shirt too?

'Okay,' the sound guy said, as he walked into the dressing

room. Chelsea stiffened, but no one else took any notice. 'Here we go.' He gestured at the twins to stand, and quickly mic-d Maddie.

'Thanks, Gary,' her sister said absentmindedly, sitting down in the makeup chair and returning to her book. She was reading the latest in the *Vigilante Queens* series, and it was huge, over five hundred pages.

'Maddie's the smart one!' their mother had told the hair stylist, when she commented that the girl always had her head in a book. 'Chelsea is more like me, a magazine gal. Isn't that right, Chelsea?' And even though Chelsea had wanted to deny it, wanted to say that she was smart too, she'd replied, *Yes, that's right, Mom.*

Gary turned to Chelsea, and smiled, showing a chipped front tooth. 'And now you, little lady,' he said, and he slowly slipped the mic down her back. 'Sorry,' he said. 'I hope my hands aren't cold.'

'It's fine,' she said, because that was the first rule on set. Her mother and her agent had warned her: don't cause any trouble. But she didn't like Gary. She didn't like how his hands lingered on her skin, the smell of his breath when he stood so close to her. Why was he like this with her and not Maddie? Had Chelsea done something that made him think she *wanted* this?

'Okay, Gary,' Robbie interrupted. 'I think you're needed on set.' Gary held up a hand in mock salute, walking backwards out of the room. 'You okay?' Robbie asked, winking when Chelsea nodded. Robbie was relatively young, twenty-five on his last birthday. He was the assistant director on the set of *Double Trouble*, and he was also dating Julia, the twins' tutor. The two of them had been sitting at the back of the dressing room, playing cards, and he had obviously seen that Gary was creeping Chelsea out.

'Thanks,' she said to him, and he waved it off, returning to his girlfriend and crowing when she had to pick up another two cards.

Chelsea sat up straighter when she heard her mother's voice from the corridor outside the dressing room. Erin and Linda, the actress playing the twins' on-screen mother, arrived together, both holding coffee in takeaway cups, laughing. Maddie and Chelsea made eye contact, a little quizzically – the two women weren't exactly the best of friends.

'Okay, girls!' Their mother stood in front of them. 'Are we ready for another day of work?'

'If you could take the chirpiness down by, like, ten notches, that would be awesome,' Maddie said, miming turning a radio dial.

'Enough of the sarcasm, please,' Erin said, but Maddie wasn't paying attention. She put her book down and patted the chair next to her so Linda would sit. 'What's happening in the latest book?' Linda asked.

At this Julia, their tutor, piped up and said, 'Don't encourage her, please! That series is trash.' She raised an eyebrow at Maddie. 'And Madeline's time would be much better spent on her English reading list.'

'I don't know,' Robbie chimed in, throwing down his hand of cards with relish. 'I gave the first book a try because Maddie wouldn't stop talking about it and it's not bad. What do you think, Chel?'

Chelsea was about to respond when her stomach rumbled loudly. 'Sorry,' she said, blushing. 'I'm just . . .' her stomach made the same noise again '. . . a bit hungry.'

'Oh, sweetie,' Linda said, concerned. 'Go down to Craft Services, we have time. You don't want to be—'

'The girls have already eaten,' Erin rifled in her handbag for a small Ziploc bag. 'Here,' she said, handing Chelsea two almonds. 'That should tide you over until lunch.'

Chelsea took them, chewing them slowly, and when she had swallowed, she muttered, 'Thanks, Mom.' She could see Linda's forehead creasing, and she silently begged the other woman not to say anything, not today. Her mother was only doing what she had to do to make sure the twins looked good on camera. Chelsea snuck a look at herself in the mirror, at her narrow thighs and flat chest. At this weight, she would be like a child for ever, and she and Maddie could keep playing the *Double Trouble* twins indefinitely. She would come to set every day, pretend that Linda was her mother, and that life was a series of inconsequential obstacles that could be resolved in twenty-two minutes, and nothing had to change.

'So, Linda,' her mother took the third chair down, between Linda and Maddie. She looked at herself in the mirror dotted with a semi-circle of light bulbs, and she resembled an Old Hollywood star, with her ice-blonde hair and pale skin, the enormous blue eyes. 'You were telling me about this guy's movie?'

'Oh, it's extraordinary,' Linda said. 'I was sent a screener when he signed on to direct a guest episode. And honestly, having watched it, I have no idea why he agreed to an AtomicKids show. He's a genius.'

'Are you talking about *Fooling Around*? I worked with Lee Osman on that as AD,' Robbie said, smiling proudly.

'Robbie!' Linda said. 'Well done you. I couldn't believe it was a debut film, it's so confident and self-assured and *sexy*.' She made a funny face at the twins. 'Although perhaps I shouldn't say that in front of present company.'

'Linda,' Maddie said, arching an eyebrow at her, 'we're fifteen now, not babies.'

'I know, but—' Linda started, but their mother interrupted.

'I'm not surprised his movie is sexy,' Erin said, 'because *he's* sexy, isn't he?'

Whatever Happened to Madeline Stone?

'He's twenty-four!' Linda laughed but it was the wrong thing to say.

Erin's face was darkening. 'Yes,' she said. 'And I'm only thirty.' (*Plus four, please,* Chelsea thought.) 'And I look twenty-five,' Erin continued, facing her reflection in the mirror again. She was frequently asked if she was the twins' older sister, and she would say, 'Bless your heart,' and then on the car ride home, she would ask Maddie and Chelsea if they'd heard what that man said, *He thought I was your sister, can you believe that?* and Maddie would stay silent, which meant it was up to Chelsea to say, *Yeah, Mom, it's so cool, you look so young. You're beautiful, Mom,* and hope that would keep Erin in a good mood. 'And I know you're not exactly . . .' Erin gave Linda a bright smile '. . . looking for companionship.' Linda was resolutely single; she'd conceived both her children with the help of a sperm donor, and Erin often speculated as to whether the other woman was a lesbian or just hated men. 'But I'm still a young woman,' Erin said. 'And I appreciate a sexy man.'

'No, no, *no*,' Lee Osman said, tearing off his headphones. He was sitting at the side of the sound stage, staring at the monitor as Chelsea fluffed her lines yet again. He strode onto the set, a generic approximation of a high school, where Chelsea and Maddie were leaning against a row of lockers. 'Chelsea,' he said, putting his hands on her shoulders and bending at the knees a little so he could make direct eye contact with her. He was attractive, with his aquiline nose and high cheekbones, which only made Chelsea even more nervous around him. 'This isn't good enough,' he said.

'I'm sorry,' she said, and felt faint with panic. She couldn't mess up, not in front of everyone. 'I'm doing my best. I . . .'

It was an emotional scene they were shooting: the *Double*

Trouble twins were fighting over a boy. He had chosen Maddie's character over Chelsea's ('Of course he likes you best,' Chelsea had said, when she'd read the script, although Maddie had laughed and said, 'Girl, we have the same face. What are you talking about?'), and Chelsea's character was supposed to cry when she found out about it. But no matter how much Chelsea tried, the dialogue came out wooden, stilted, like she was reciting the back of the cereal box. Again, Lee said, *again*. They had run the scene fifteen times at this stage, and Chelsea saw Linda sneak a look at her watch. She must be wondering if she would make it out on time to pick up her kids from the nanny, and Chelsea didn't want Zach and Emily missing their mom, not because of her. Why couldn't she get this right?

'Okay,' Lee said, his hands still heavy on her shoulders. 'But I need you to step it up. Maddie is so natural, she's . . .' he smiled at her sister '. . . well, it's like she's not acting at all and, unfortunately, that's making your performance look even more obvious.'

'Okay,' Robbie interrupted. 'Maybe we just need a second? Give Chelsea a chance to catch her breath.' He held out a clipboard and the director nodded, calling, 'Okay. We're gonna take a five-minute break, everyone.'

Chelsea turned into the locker, pretending to rifle through the prop books in there. *Don't cry, don't cry*, she told herself. She heard Robbie come up behind her. 'It's fine,' he said gently. 'It's a long day and you haven't eaten anything.' He handed Chelsea a chocolate granola bar. 'See if that helps.'

Chelsea took it, glancing over her shoulder to see if her mother was in eyesight, but Erin was flirting with Lee Osman, twirling a strand of hair around her finger. Chelsea opened the candy, stuffing it into her mouth, almost moaning at the taste. But as soon as she finished, she regretted it. What was wrong with her? She'd already gone up a size in the last year. *Only natural*, the wardrobe mistress had said, they were growing girls, after all, but Erin had been furious. Her mother was right – without her body, what else did Chelsea have to offer? She wasn't as good an actor as her sister. That much was clear. How could she fail to notice that Maddie's stack of fan mail was always larger than hers, that when they were out in the real world, people always seemed more excited to see Maddie than her?

It wasn't just that Maddie was the better actor. She also seemed to have more of that indefinable quality that made someone a star. It was an aura, the way Maddie walked into a room and people looked at her, the atmosphere shifting ever so slightly. Whatever it was, Chelsea did not possess it. She could feel her breath becoming shallow, even as Robbie patted her shoulder awkwardly, saying, 'You're going to be okay, Chel,' looking around for his girlfriend to come help him out. But Chelsea didn't believe him and, worse, she thought Robbie didn't either.

'Okay, people,' the director said, a few minutes later, putting his headphones back on. 'Let's make this the one!'

Maddie and Chelsea hit their marks again, and Chelsea took a deep breath. 'You gotta chill,' Maddie said, under her breath. 'It's just pretending.'

'That's easy for you to say,' she snapped, and Maddie flinched in surprise. It wasn't like Chelsea to get cranky, especially not on set. They were both too professional for that.

'Listen,' Maddie said. 'I'm not a better actor. I'm *not*,' she insisted, when Chelsea snorted. 'I'm just less afraid of failing.' She tilted her head to the side. 'Forget them. Forget the director, forget Mom. It's you and me, right? Just the two of us, talking to each other. You can do that. You've had a lifetime of that.'

'Is fifteen years a lifetime?'

'It's our lifetime, smartass,' Maddie said, poking her in the ribs and, despite herself, Chelsea smiled. 'Just keep looking at me,' Maddie whispered, as the director called for quiet on set. 'Forget everything else. I want you to think of something really sad, okay? The worst thing you can think of and then just let yourself *feel* it. Let yourself go, Chel. I know you can do this.'

Chelsea nodded, and they began the scene again. And she could immediately sense the difference, how much more grounded she felt, how natural the words sounded coming out of her mouth. She did what her sister told her to do: she thought of the worst thing she could imagine. It wasn't Erin dying, or *Double Trouble* getting cancelled with no way for the twins to continue paying the mortgage on the expensive house their mother had just bought. No, it was the thought of what life would be like after this, when the show ended. When Chelsea outgrew her cuteness, and she couldn't hide her lack of talent behind it any more, and she would have to watch as her sister became more successful and famous, even more beloved. Erin would have her golden child, and no one would even remember Chelsea's name. She would simply disappear, so easily forgotten. And with that, Chelsea burst into tears.

'Amazing!' the director said, when he called cut. 'That was perfect, Chelsea,' he said, as she wiped her eyes. 'More of that tomorrow, please.'

As they walked off set, everyone congratulating Chelsea, saying what a great job she had done, Maddie grabbed her hand. 'You were incredible!' she said. 'I knew you had it in you.'

'I couldn't have done it without you,' Chelsea replied and Maddie batted it off, as if it was a compliment. But that wasn't how Chelsea had meant it. She needed Maddie and she didn't want to. She wanted to be the star, the one dispensing advice, not the other way around. Chelsea was nothing without her sister, and no matter how hard she tried not to feel this way, she was beginning to hate Maddie for that.

10.

Got a Long List of Ex-Lovers!

Another Monday, another Madd-ness! Yes, it's another revelation about the late, great Madeline Stone. (She was always our favourite Stone Sister – what about you, RumorMillions? Sound off in the comments!) It's been just over two weeks since we were ROCKED by the contents of MaddieStoneStorage.com and we didn't think it could get any more salacious. That was until TODAY'S post went up. There are the photos, sure – but, come on, who among us hasn't sent a spicy pic or two?! NO JUDGEMENT! – but we have decided not to share them. I like to think we've all learned a thing or two since 2005 (I know I have regrets about that time. See here for more) and surely this kind of shit is unacceptable now? Revenge Porn? No Bueno, my friends!

What's faaaar more interesting to us here at RumorMill HQ is The List. It's Maddie's handwriting all right and it's a greatest hits of some of the sexiest men from the 00s!!! Justin, Colin, Ashton, Ryan, Jesse – if you crushed on a hottie during Y2K, his name is *definitely* on this list. And then, at the bottom, some dude called Christopher. Who do we think that is? And, much more importantly, is this Madeline Stone's body count?!!! That's what we're guessing here at RumorMill. What about you, guys? (And is it wrong to say we are kinda JEALOUS?!)

11.

2025

'Fucking Milo James,' Nya said, her face screwing up on the phone screen.

'I know,' Chelsea said. She could still remember where she was the first time she'd heard that name. They were in Wilmington, filming the first season of *Vigilante Queens*, and there was buzz, obviously, given what a phenomenon the novels had been. Everyone said it was going to be the next big thing. It had been Kelly who'd shown her the site, the cheap graphics drawn onto paparazzi shots, the crude nicknames given to celebrities – female celebrities, anyway, it seemed to be mostly women Milo was targeting – the blind gossip items, the 'overheard' conversations from club restrooms and trendy lunch spots, repeated word for word. He wasn't the first blogger to emerge in the early days of the internet but he quickly became the most popular, and the most dangerous. Everyone in the industry had complained about RumorMill but they'd all read it too.

'I can't believe he has the audacity to still write about you and Maddie, after everything he—' Her friend stopped, her eyes narrowing. 'What's that behind you?' she asked.

Chelsea didn't reply, she just flipped the FaceTime camera around to show her friend the set-up in the pool house. Nya let out a low whistle. 'Are you for real? It looks like a serial killer's bedroom.'

'And what does a serial killer's bedroom look like?' Chelsea asked. She sat down on the floral love seat, turning the camera off and pressing the phone between her ear and her shoulder, using her spare hand to scroll through old blog posts on RumorMill from the early noughties. Milo James had tried to delete as much as he could – his particular brand of misogyny was considered outdated today, and much less interesting than the likes of DeuxMoi – but an enterprising young person had taken it upon himself to archive it all, creating an Instagram account to document the havoc the blogger had wreaked during that time, something Chelsea was increasingly grateful for.

'Your guesthouse,' Nya said, and as Chelsea took in the stacks of printed-out notes, the large whiteboard with photographs taped on it, images of Chelsea and Maddie and their mother and all the other players in their orbit in their heyday, she knew what her friend meant. 'You're just missing the red string,' Nya said. 'Primo serial killer behaviour.'

Her friend had video-called as soon as the list had been published on RumorMill, and they had spent the last thirty minutes running through the names. Some, they'd known about, a few others were a surprise ('The youngest Hanson brother?' Nya had sputtered. 'Every middle school girl's fantasy!') but neither could figure out who the mysterious Christopher was. 'Not that we have much to go on,' Chelsea admitted. 'A list of men written by someone detoxing from pills' – what if Maddie had been hallucinating? What if it was all just a figment of her imagination? – 'and a first name. Maybe it's not important.' But it had to be. It was the only name on the list written in black pen, and it had a little skull and crossbones next to it. 'Christopher could be anyone. Where would we even begin?'

'Ask Kelly,' Nya said. 'She knows where all the bodies are buried.'

'I texted her,' Chelsea replied. 'And she said she didn't have a clue before going on a rant about Maddie sleeping with Chad Michael Murray when Kelly was dating him.' She and Nya laughed a little guiltily, like they always did when they spoke behind Kelly's back. The pact the three of them had made all those years ago, to promise to be loyal to one another, no matter what, still ran deep.

'And,' Nya's voice turned serious, and Chelsea felt herself tense, 'what about this secret, Chelsea? Is there—'

'Come on,' she cut her off. 'You know me! What secrets could I possibly have?'

'Yes,' Nya said slowly. 'I know you. And you've always been . . . private. No,' she said, as Chelsea protested. 'You have. And that's not your fault. It was how you were raised. But I just want you to know that I'm here if you want to talk about it, and I would never judge you.' There was a pause, and Chelsea could hear the click of fingers against a keyboard at the other end of the line. 'Sorry,' her friend said, 'I just wanted to pull up the website again. What are you guys doing to get this removed?'

'Nick's people have had it taken down like ten times already,' Chelsea said. 'And every time, a different one pops back up, uploading the same photos again. It's driving them nuts.' Chelsea knew Nick was wishing he could do it himself. Her husband might be revered as a god by his fan-boys but he had always been better at marketing than coding, which he did his best to keep quiet. 'What I can't understand is how they haven't traced the IP address yet.'

'Do you know what that means? Trace the IP? Because I sure as hell don't.'

'No,' Chelsea admitted. 'But it sounds good.' Nya started to laugh and so did she. It felt so good to forget her fear, if only for a few minutes. 'Nee Nee,' she said, 'I need to tell you something. I'm . . .' she lowered her voice '. . . I've decided to go meet Milo James.'

'What?' Nya said, shocked. 'Why?'

'I just have this feeling that maybe he's behind this.' The blogger had always had an unsettling insight into Maddie and Chelsea, breaking stories about the twins before they'd even had a chance to confide in their closest friends. They'd never figured out who the leak in their camp was, which made it hard for the girls to trust people. It could have been anyone, Nancy Taylor, perhaps, or even their mother, Maddie argued. But Chelsea had the sense that if anyone knew what was going on with the storage unit, it would be Milo James. 'I don't know. But I have to figure it out.'

'Wouldn't it be better to send one of Nick's guys?'

'No.' Chelsea was resolute. 'It has to be me. I don't want to get anyone else involved.'

'Why?' her friend said. 'What are you afraid they'll find out?'

Chelsea didn't answer that. She couldn't. If she told Nya the truth, she would never be able to take it back. 'Apparently Milo still writes in the same coffee house that he always did,' she said instead, 'so it should be easy to find him.' That had always been part of the lore. When Milo James set up RumorMill, it was so early on in the days of blogging that he still didn't have WiFi in his apartment. He'd had to go to the local Starbucks to use theirs.

'Good.' Nya didn't say anything for a minute but Chelsea could almost picture her face, the flash of anger across it. 'That man should be held accountable for what he did to me and Kelly.'

'He did it to us all,' Chelsea reminded her, but Nya wouldn't let that slide.

'Chel. I love you,' her friend said. 'But you were protected. First by the network and then by The Director. RumorMill barely even mentioned you, and if he did, it was usually to say what an angel you were compared to me and Kelly. And Madeline, of course.'

Whatever Happened to Madeline Stone?

'And that was my fault? Don't do that, Nya. Please,' Chelsea said. 'I didn't have any control over what was written about me in those days.'

That had been one of the hardest parts, after Maddie had disappeared and she'd told The Director she couldn't collaborate with him any more. Without his protection, Chelsea quickly realized how vulnerable she was. The tabloids could and would run any conspiracy theory about Maddie's disappearance – *why hadn't Chelsea done more to find her sister? Did you hear The Director refused to work with Chelsea any more after the Oscars? The Stone family were white-trash, they deserved everything they got. No wonder Madeline had killed herself!* Chelsea had been thrown to the wolves, too, before Nick had rescued her. His money, his power, his love, all of it had saved her.

'I know,' Nya said, her voice softer. 'But, Chel, the stuff they wrote when Kelly went to rehab. The photos from outside the facility.' The images had been splashed all over the front of the tabloids. Kelly, terrifyingly thin, her shoulder blades poking out of the back of her washed out T-shirt, and her matted hair in a high ponytail. She had been crying, begging her assistant to take her home again. MESSY QUEEN, the headlines had screamed. 'Giving the other patients money to talk about what she said in group sessions,' Nya continued. The inpatients had said Kelly had confessed to feeling envious of Chelsea's career, saying she didn't understand why Chelsea had been the star of the show when Nya was the talented one and Kelly the most charismatic. Chelsea couldn't even argue, as much as she might have liked to. She'd always known that if The Director hadn't taken a chance on her, she would never have amounted to much. Maddie was the one who was supposed to be the star, not her. Chelsea had stolen her sister's fate, her future, and made it her own.

'Anyway,' Nya said finally. 'Go meet Milo James. Tell him

what he did was wrong. Tell him that he . . .' Her friend's voice caught in her throat, as if she might cry. Even Nya, who had worked so hard to undo the damage of that time, even she was still grappling with the aftermath of what had happened to them '. . . he hurt people. Tell him he ruined their lives.'

They said their goodbyes and Chelsea walked back to the whiteboard, staring at the photos, tracing her fingers from one face to the next. *Wait.* An idea came to her, blooming fast in her mind's eye, and she couldn't believe she hadn't thought of it before. She pulled up the website on her phone again, scanning the page until she found it. A little button that said 'Contact'. Had that been there before? She couldn't recall seeing it, maybe it was just on this newest iteration of the blog. Could she . . . She almost dismissed it, telling herself that she should leave it to Nick and his people, but then she caught herself. *Why not her?* She was perfectly capable of doing this, no matter what anyone else thought. She took a breath and clicked on the contact button, typing out a message. *Hello,* she wrote. *I'm not sure who you are but it's me, Chelsea Stone.*

She was waiting for less than five minutes when she saw the email notification pop up, a message: *Hi,* the person wrote back. *I thought I might find you here. How have you been finding the Monday Madd-ness? I have some very juicy material for next week, just FYI* 😊

Quickly, another message followed. *I sent you a DM on the Foto app. Why didn't you reply?*

Chelsea followed only one person on Foto – Nick – and she never checked her direct messages. Her heart began to beat faster. This was a terrible idea and Nick would be furious with her if he found out what she had done. *Do not get involved,* he would tell her. Just pass on the details to his team, let them deal with it. But if this person knew the truth, Chelsea had to be the one to talk to them. She couldn't risk anyone at Foto finding out. Another message popped up in her inbox.

I know your secrets, Chelsea Stone.

What secrets? she replied, because maybe they were bluffing, maybe they— And then another email came in, and it was just one word, one name.

Carter.

She dropped down on her haunches, whispering, *Oh fuck, oh fuck, oh fuck*, over and over again, because here it was, the worst thing she had ever done, and if anyone found out, if Nick found out – she started to hyperventilate, imagining what would happen, what he would do. She would lose the kids, she realized. She would lose everything, and after that, what reason would she have to live?

I'm guessing you don't want this particular piece of information to leak, they wrote, and Chelsea could hear someone starting to cry, softly: it was her. She had always been a quiet crier, ever since she was a child and had come to understand that no one wanted to see her sad.

You still there?

Chelsea tapped out her reply as quickly as she could, pressing send. *What do you want?* she asked, waiting for the reply.

And then, finally: *I thought you'd never ask.*

12.

2025

A million dollars: that was what this person wanted. They hadn't given Chelsea much information besides that – they didn't mention Bitcoin or an offshore bank account or a suitcase stuffed full of unmarked bills, the way blackmailers did in movies. They had just emailed, *I want a million dollars*, and Chelsea had replied, *I need time.* Nick was astonishingly wealthy, yes, the sort of wealth that made her head hurt if she thought too much about it but even he would notice if his wife transferred a million dollars out of their joint account. He would want to know what it was for, and if she told her husband, she would also have to tell him *why* she so desperately needed to keep this person quiet, and she couldn't. It was just a name, she told herself, maybe they didn't know anything else, or at the very least, maybe they didn't have any evidence of what she had done, but she couldn't take the risk.

She checked her phone, looking at the text she had sent to Carter that morning. *You didn't tell anyone, did you?* And the response, so quick: *Of course not. I would never do that to you, Chelsea. You can trust me.* But that was the problem, she thought, as she deleted the messages. She didn't feel like she could trust anyone.

A bell tinkled as Chelsea pushed open the door of the coffee shop and she hesitated, wondering if Milo would look up at the sound. If he saw her walking in, what would he do? But the music was playing so loudly, some kind of inoffensive folk-rock, that he didn't even notice her arrival. The café was generic in design, brightly lit with white walls and industrial-style wooden tables, succulent plants hanging over the ceilings, and it was empty apart from an exhausted young mother scrolling on her phone, a baby dozing in the stroller beside her, and there *he* was, tucked into the corner, tapping on his laptop. Chelsea remembered a photoshoot he had done years ago, in a coffee shop just like this one, smirking at the camera, his bubble-gum pink computer matching a streak of pink dyed in his white-blond hair. Milo James had always been outrageously handsome, with high cheekbones and a jaw that could have cut glass, wearing his self-proclaimed 'uniform' of a tight tank top and low-slung jeans to showcase his gym-toned body. He had never confirmed his age or what state he was born in. He had never talked about his family or his hobbies or his friends. He had never even dated anyone, not publicly anyway. No one knew if he was gay or straight or asexual. For someone who had dedicated his career to dishing the dirt on other people's private lives, Milo was remarkably clandestine about his own.

'An Americano,' Chelsea gave the barista her order.

The young woman barely made eye contact, just replied, 'Sure.' She seemed not to clock who Chelsea was, which was a relief. After Chelsea had paid and left a generous tip, she took her coffee and sat next to Milo James.

'I—' He looked up, clearly about to ask why a stranger would take the seat next to him when the place was basically empty, but the sentence died in his throat when he saw who was there.

'Hi, Milo,' she said.

His eyes widened in alarm. He looked to the front door, but her security guy was standing outside, his arms folded across his chest. Milo reached for his phone, to call for help or to take a photo of her, Chelsea didn't know, but she put a hand over his and stopped him anyway. 'No,' she said, taking his cell and putting it on her side of the table. He stared at it but didn't move. 'I don't think we need our phones right now, do we? Let's just talk.'

She thought he might argue but he half slumped in his seat, giving a weak nod. She hadn't seen Milo in years – it wasn't like Nick Bennett's wife ran in the same circles as a low-rent gossip blogger – but she was surprised at the change in him all the same. He was still attractive but not the dazzling beauty he had been in his heyday, his face a little puffy, his hair wispy and thinning. RumorMill was no longer the go-to blog for celebrity gossip. There were other websites now, smarter, more nuanced, offering intelligent analyses of Hollywood's machinations. This new generation wanted critical thinking, not cruelty, and Milo James had never been much good at that.

'What are you doing here?' he asked.

'I'm here to see you,' she said.

'But – but why?' he said, shame-faced. Milo had so little cultural capital now, so little power, and they both knew it. It wasn't like in the old days, when starlets would come to him, begging him to be kind, hoping to befriend him so he would see they were human. They tried to exchange their friendship for better coverage on the site and sometimes Milo would play along, going shopping with the girl or getting lunch, and that night he would post the photos he'd taken during their day out, mocking them for how 'obvious' they had been: did they really think that Milo James could be bought so easily?

'I'm here to talk about the storage unit,' Chelsea said, taking a sip of her coffee. It was slightly bitter, as if the beans had been burned. 'And the blog.' Milo just stared at her, nonplussed, so she continued. 'Just wondering if you know who's responsible for it, I guess.'

'Wait a sec,' he said. 'Do you . . . You don't think it's me, do you?' She gave him a hard look and he half laughed. 'I barely have enough time to write my own blog, Chelsea. Are you kidding? And where would I have just *found* this storage unit?'

'I don't know,' she snapped. 'You always seemed to have pretty good sources back in the day, didn't you? Maddie and I couldn't sneeze without a story about us catching a cold appearing on RumorMill. Is it really that far-fetched?'

'It's not me,' he said simply, and for some reason, she believed him. 'And as for you and your sister,' he continued. 'I've apologized for all that.' That was true. There had been a reckoning about how women had been treated in the early noughties, and Milo was crucified online as the bully-in-chief. He'd tried to apologize multiple times, posting teary-eyed videos of him holding up his hands, saying it was a different time back then, he had been a different person, and shouldn't we all be allowed to grow and learn? 'This is such bullshit,' he continued. 'It's basically harassment and you—'

'You're talking to *me* about harassment? Are you kidding? I was twenty years of age, chased down alleyways by grown men shouting obscenities at me, and I couldn't even go to the police because apparently the fact those men had cameras in their hands meant they were just doing their job. And the reason why they were "just doing their job" was because of *you*.'

'Like I was the only blogger?' he said. 'What about Perez and Gawker? Are you stalking them too, asking if they're the ones leaking shit from your sister's storage unit?'

'You were the most powerful one,' she said simply, and Milo James had no answer to that. It was the truth. 'And you made my sister's life miserable. You *ruined* her.' She took a minute, afraid she might cry and she wasn't going to do that in front of this man. 'I don't understand why. Why Maddie? She wasn't even on TV any more. I was the famous one. I was . . .' There was that corrosive guilt again, the feeling that this was her fault. If she hadn't become *the* Chelsea Stone, who would have cared about her twin? She and Maddie would have faded into obscurity together. Maybe her sister would still be alive.

'Posts about her did well.' Milo shrugged. 'I wrote whatever got the most clicks, end of story. Everyone loves to take the moral high ground, saying it was such a "toxic" time and blaming the blogs, the magazines and the paparazzi – but who was driving all of that? The same fucking people acting like saints now. It's *bullshit*,' he said. 'If the appetite wasn't there, if the *audience* wasn't there, the site wouldn't have lasted two weeks. I gave people what they wanted. And you come in here, acting all high and mighty, as if you don't operate in the same world as I do. No,' he put out his hand to stop Chelsea when she began to protest. 'I don't wanna hear it. You were in the industry. You were part of this eco-system too. Publicists would reach out – including yours, Chelsea, so give me a fucking break – trading secrets, asking me to bury a story about one client if they gave me a bigger one about another. Every last one of you thirsty bitches.' He shook his head. 'You needed me just as much as I needed you.'

'Oh, really?' she asked. 'What about Kelly Foster? You think she *needed* you to post pics of her entering a rehab facility? You think she wanted that all over the internet, people calling her . . . What was it you said again, Milo? "A skanky crackhead"?' He had the good grace to look embarrassed. Chelsea continued: 'And to find people who had been in her NA meetings, to bribe them for private details of what she said. Have you no decency?'

'I didn't bribe anyone,' Milo muttered. She must have looked sceptical because he insisted, 'I didn't. I wasn't, like, *Page Six*. I didn't have that kind of money to throw around. People would come to me, telling me who was fighting at a club or what celebrity stiffed out on the tip at a restaurant. They'd email me anonymously. Money was never even discussed.'

'Oh. I . . .' Chelsea found this both surprising and depressing. Money, she could understand – people were desperate, they needed to pay their bills, buy groceries. But to sell someone out for – for what? A cheap thrill? 'So, you pushed my sister to suicide for clicks, is that it?'

'Jesus Christ,' he said, recoiling. 'You can't just say that to me. That's insane, that's, that's . . .' He was stuttering, unable to formulate a sentence. 'I'm out of here.' He grabbed his laptop and stuffed it into a leather tote, winding up the charger. Chelsea signalled to her security guard and he came in, closing the coffee-shop door behind him. He leaned against it, watching them intently. 'Fuck,' Milo said, under his breath, but he sat down again.

'You ruined her life,' she said. 'Do you get that? Do you even care?'

'Oh, give it a break. Madeline ruined her own life.' He was so dismissive, he was the old Milo again, the shiny veneer he had painted over the black hole where his conscience should have been momentarily disappearing. 'And, besides, I could have written a whole lot more. The shit I was told about Madeline Stone. It nearly killed me not to publish it.'

'Like what?' Chelsea asked, her heart slowing to a painful thud. What else about her sister was she about to learn? He mimed zipping his lips shut, and after a few minutes of silence, Chelsea tried again. 'Okay, then, at least tell me why you didn't write the stories. If they were as juicy as you're claiming, why—'

'Isn't it obvious? I was paid *not* to write them,' Milo said, checking his fingernails. 'And I'm gonna be real with you. I wasn't motivated by money back then. I wasn't,' he insisted, when she made a sceptical face. 'I was in my twenties. All I wanted was to be on the guest list for the coolest parties in town and have enough cash to, like, pay my rent and shop at Kitson or whatever. You think people didn't try to bribe me before? Please. I didn't want to be rich, I wanted to be—'

'Famous?' she asked, because that was all anyone in this town ever wanted. They thought that being seen was the same as being loved, and that was their first mistake. They didn't know that fame was like walking into a funhouse of mirrors, your reflection thrown back to you distorted, grotesque. If you stared in the glass for long enough, it was easy to confuse the monster for the real you.

'Maybe,' Milo said defiantly. 'What would be so wrong with that?' Chelsea didn't reply. There was no point. He didn't get it and he never would. 'I was offered stories in exchange too, some shit about Kelly Foster, which always got good traction, but *this* money?' he continued. 'This was money I couldn't refuse. It paid for my condo.'

'Maddie didn't have that kind of cash, not then,' Chelsea said. Even if her sister had had the money, Maddie would never have paid someone like Milo James to stay quiet: her principles wouldn't have allowed it. But who else would have cared enough about a former child star to silence a gossip blogger? Chelsea racked her brain but she came up blank. 'Who?' she asked again, but Milo shook his head.

'It's not worth my life to give you that name, no matter how big your security guard is,' he said. 'But I'll say this . . . If you really think I'm the one responsible for driving Madeline to suicide, I guess I'm not the only one, am I?' He pulled his phone out of his satchel, and turned it so she could see the screen. There was a photo, another journal entry, her sister's handwriting, but it was new. This hadn't gone live on the blog. She knew that for certain. As she scanned quickly through the page, reading what Maddie had written, she could hear her breathing scraping the back of her throat. Fuck. *Fuck, fuck, fuck.* She looked up at Milo, and she said, 'I thought you weren't behind the storage unit.'

'I'm not,' he said. 'But I do know where it is.'

13.

2025

The storage unit was in Glendale, a series of blue rolling doors in a grey stone building. That was all the information Milo had been given, he said. An email from an anonymous account, with the address. And the attached document, the diary entry. Maddie's words, detailing the last conversation between her and Chelsea, the vicious things Chelsea had said to her, what she had told her sister to do. *Come see for yourself*, the anonymous email said, giving Milo an address, but he couldn't, he told Chelsea. His reputation was precarious as it was. He needed to keep his hands clean. He had to wait for the storage-unit blog to run with it first before he could touch it. So, Chelsea had come here herself. She knew if she'd asked Nick to come with her, he would have, but then she would have had to tell him about confronting Milo James and Nick would ask, *Why? Why? Why?* She couldn't tell her husband she needed to shut down the blog as quickly as she could, removing any more leverage the blackmailer might have. What if there was something in the unit that linked her and Carter?

Chelsea had to clear this place out before Nick's team got their hands on it. But she didn't want to do it alone so she'd gone through the increasingly short list of people she trusted, wondering who else to ask. Emily or Zach? Too young, she decided. Even though Linda's kids were twenty-eight and thirty now, she couldn't help but still see them as children. Nya was across the country, and Chelsea still tried to spend as little time with her mother as possible. In the end, Kelly had seemed like the best option, and her friend had agreed immediately.

The guy who ran the place was a gangly white man with huge pupils and a gurning jaw, like he'd just dropped a pill twenty minutes before they'd arrived and was desperately trying to keep his shit together. Chelsea had brought cash in an envelope, the sort of money that made the man inhale sharply when he opened it. He nodded his head when Chelsea said what a shame that this particular storage unit had been broken into on the very same day the CCTV cameras were turned off, what were the chances? Her money, and all the things it could do for her. He didn't have much information besides that – the lease had run out, he said, and they'd tried to contact the person who had rented it but to no avail. *Unit number 63. Madeline Ryan,* he read out from his notes. So, Maddie had used their mother's maiden name again, like she had on the prescriptions. 'We couldn't get in touch with her,' the guy said, fidgeting, 'when the lease ran out. We tried to call the owner but the number was out of service.'

'That's because she's dead,' Chelsea said, watching to see if he recognized her, if he was piecing together that she was called Chelsea and the owner of the unit was called Madeline, that they were the Stone Sisters. She was here with Kelly Foster, one third of the *Vigilante Queens*, although Kelly looked so different now, she was rarely spotted these days. The guy didn't seem to get it, whether because he was too young or simply because he was high, she didn't know. He rolled up the blue aluminium door, and switched on the light, an exposed bulb hanging from the ceiling. It was large inside, bigger than Chelsea had imagined, and she found herself hesitating to walk in. What would she find? She glanced at her phone again, to see if the blackmailer had emailed her in the last ten minutes since she'd last checked, but there was nothing.

She could hear Kelly interrogating the attendant about how this could have happened. 'I just go with what's on the form,' he said. 'It says Madeline Ryan so I look for a Madeline Ryan. We have a thirty-day payment policy, if—'

'Was the payment made monthly?' Chelsea interrupted, an idea forming in her mind. 'Was it by card? Do you have that number on file?'

'No,' he said. 'She paid upfront for twenty years.' He paused, licking his lips. 'It's up now. If the unit isn't claimed in that time, or the lease isn't renewed . . . We can't hold on to this shit for ever. We're tryna run a business here.'

'You just sell people's personal belongings?' Kelly said. 'That's disgusting.'

The guy shrugged. 'There are folks who make a living out of this, ya know. If the stuff isn't claimed, you can buy a unit for maybe a couple thousand bucks. You never know what you might find in there, designer clothes, furniture. It's like a game for these folks.'

Kelly frowned. 'Well, who bought this one?'

'I can't say.'

Chelsea watched out of the corner of her eye as her friend reached out her hand, stuffing money into the attendant's. Another bribe. He looked at the note, and nodded. 'I don't know. They paid in cash. The only name they put down was . . .' he checked his file '. . . Christopher.'

Chelsea jolted. Christopher? The mystery name at the bottom of Maddie's list? She met Kelly's eye, and nodded, urging her friend to continue.

'So, it was a man?' Kelly asked.

'I don't know,' he said. 'I wasn't working that day. I never seen anyone come in here.'

Kelly's jaw was tight. 'Then who *was* working that day?'

'I can't say.'

Whatever Happened to Madeline Stone?

Another handshake, more money exchanged. How much was she giving him? A couple of hundred? Kelly couldn't afford more than that, surely. The only income she had was dwindling residuals and the allowance Chelsea and Nick gave her every week.

'I can't help you, lady,' the attendant said, but he took Kelly's money all the same. 'It was a guy called Luis working that day – he's Mexican. Paid under the table, ya know? No documents, no nothing. But he's gone. I don't know where he went. Now, we might have camera footage.' He looked at them shrewdly, taking in Chelsea's expensive handbag, her perfectly pressed silk trousers. 'But it'll cost you.'

Chelsea could hear the two of them arguing as she took a deep breath and stepped inside the storage unit. It smelt musty, dead air trapped within the stone walls. There were dozens of cardboard boxes and old suitcases, a fabric headboard in a delicate floral print, a yellowing mattress, an antique writing desk, a filing cabinet, two standing lamps, an old TV, five, no, six black refuse sacks knotted at the top, plastic laundry baskets full of Kodak envelopes, Polaroids spilling out of the sides.

Chelsea started to pick her way through the clutter to the back, and it was behind the upstanding mattress that she found the sofa. She stopped dead, remembering the day Maddie had bought it. It was 2001, they were sixteen, and they had just shot their last scene of *Double Trouble*, hugging Linda and Robbie and Julia and the rest of the cast and crew as they all cried. The twins had driven to a furniture store afterwards, the soft top of Maddie's Chrysler convertible down, blasting Missy Elliot. They both wore baseball caps – it was unlikely that any of the women milling around testing the firmness of the beds were *Double Trouble* fans, but some of the sulking pre-teen girls in tow likely were – and they sat on couch after couch, debating the pros and cons of each one, like it was the most important purchase of their lives. Finally, they found one that Maddie was happy with – a burnt-orange L-shaped sofa with what the salesgirl called an English arm roll. 'Where are you gonna put it?' Chelsea had asked. 'You know Mom thinks anything that isn't cream is, like, an atrocity.'

It was then Maddie had told her. She was moving out, she said. She had already signed a lease on a cute little house in the Hollywood Hills. Chelsea had taken a step back, dumbfounded. 'But we're only—' *We're only sixteen. We're only kids. Don't we have to ask for someone's permission before we do things like this?* 'I'm moving out,' Maddie said again, and Chelsea knew by the set of her chin that there was no arguing with her sister. Maddie stepped closer to her. 'It's a two-bed, Chel. You can come too,' she'd whispered. 'I don't want to go without you. You're my best friend.' *If they were best friends, why had Maddie done this without telling her?* 'Come with me,' her sister said again, and it had been dizzying, imagining the freedom of it, the independence. The yearning was so acute, Chelsea almost said, *Yes, yes,* but she knew she couldn't. Their mother would not survive alone. How would Erin even pay the mortgage by herself? It was impossible. Maddie moving out meant that Chelsea could never do the same. She was trapped in that house with Erin. There was no escape. 'I can't,' she'd said. 'You know I can't.'

Chelsea touched the arm rest of the sofa now, the feel of the brushed velvet. 'You okay?' Kelly asked, walking up behind her, and Chelsea nodded. She pushed a cardboard box to the side so she could sink down into the couch, the cushions sagging beneath her.

'That guy is useless,' Kelly said, perching on the arm rest. In the low lighting, her friend looked haggard, dark circles under her eyes. She was wearing a hot pink velour tracksuit – 'Juicy is back, baby!' she'd announced earlier, when Chelsea had picked her up. 'Y2K for ever!' – and her blonde hair was in a high ponytail. She needed to get her roots done, and her nails were chipped. Those were the small markers of wealth, Chelsea had realized over the years. What looked like health was often just money well spent. She had learned to assimilate, asked discreetly where the best place to get perfectly subtle highlights and the kind of facial that would make people think you had naturally flawless skin. It had seemed easier, fitting into Nick's world. It was the same feeling she'd had on set as a child, following the rules so she never had to think for herself. There was a certain peace in it.

'He sent the CCTV footage,' Kelly continued. 'I'll review it and see if there's anything worth following up, although I'm guessing probably not. But don't worry, I'll sort it out.'

'Can I see it?'

'The footage? What, like right now?' Kelly asked, tucking her hair behind her ears. 'Okay, okay,' she said, when Chelsea threw her an exasperated look. 'Chill.' Kelly reached into the pocket of her jeans to get her iPhone. She tapped into her email and she held the phone between her and Chelsea so they could both watch. It was dark, clearly night-time, and the person was wearing black clothes, jeans and an oversized sweater, a baseball cap pulled down low on their forehead. Chelsea couldn't see the person's face so she watched their gait carefully as they walked towards the storage unit, unrolling the door and pushing it up. 'It looks like a woman?' Chelsea said, her voice rising.

'I'm not sure,' Kelly said as she X-ed out of the video, promising to forward it to her later.

'No, it was definitely a woman.'

'Named Christopher? Seems unlikely.' Kelly picked at her cuticles. 'It's probably just some loser. Maddie was always picking up strays at the side of the road.'

'Hmm.' Kelly could hardly talk, given some of the people she'd dated over the years. Chelsea remembered one guy, a coke head who regularly wet the bed after a particularly heavy night. *But the sex is incredible*, her friend had added, with a wink, as if that was a valid excuse.

Something was sticking into the small of Chelsea's back, and when she reached into the sofa, she pulled out an old Black-Berry. 'Stop it,' she said. 'I haven't seen one of these in a while.' She tried to turn it on but it was dead. 'Damn.' She tucked it into her handbag. 'I'll tell Nick to give it to one of his guys.'

'Okay, just be careful. Who knows what's on that thing?' Kelly looked around the storage unit, wrinkling her nose. 'Fuck, there's a lot of shit in here.' She glanced at her watch, the Cartier tank that Chelsea had given her for her thirtieth birthday, hoping it would appease her friend. She'd always been annoyed when The Director had given Chelsea one during the last season of the show, after he had gifted Kelly and Nya day-passes for a local spa. 'You don't have to be back until three, right?'

'Two p.m. I like to be there when Ivy gets back from pre-K.'

'Cool.' Kelly pushed herself to standing. 'Then we'd better get started. Did you say your PA is gonna arrange for everything to be moved?'

Chelsea nodded. She trusted Hannah to be discreet, telling her that the entire contents of the storage unit needed to be sorted, documented and moved to a container in the Foto headquarters, where it would be safe. Her assistant had promised she would take care of it, and Chelsea had made a mental note to give her another bonus. She was lucky to have Hannah, and she knew it.

'That should shut this all down,' Kelly said. 'As long as the asshole behind the website hasn't taken anything out of here. Thank God Nick's PI found this place.'

Whatever Happened to Madeline Stone?

Chelsea smiled weakly. She hadn't told her friend about her conversation with Milo James, afraid it would start an uncomfortable conversation about how Kelly had been used as a sacrificial lamb to protect Chelsea. And she certainly hadn't told her about the blackmailer. She couldn't even bring herself to tell Nya, and her friend kept messaging, *What's going on, Chel?* and *Can we chat?* and *Are you okay?* but Chelsea didn't have the emotional bandwidth to reply. She knew Nya's first question would be *why* she was contemplating giving this person a million dollars and she couldn't answer that without telling her what she had done. *How did the blackmailer know Carter's name? Who had told them?* The fear, thrumming through her, was so fierce. *Who else knew?*

'Okay,' Kelly said. 'Let's focus. We need to go through all this stuff as quickly as we can and remove anything that's too . . . delicate. You don't want the movers finding anything like that.'

'For sure,' Chelsea said, standing up, a rush of blood to the head making her dizzy. She waved off Kelly's 'You good?' and said, 'I'm fine. You take that half. Everything in front of the mattress.' She climbed over two tattered suitcases lying on top of one another, cursing her decision to wear heeled boots. 'I'll start back here.'

The first box Chelsea opened was full of old CDs – there was Alanis Morissette, Lauryn Hill, Fiona Apple, Tori Amos. When they were still on *Double Trouble*, Maddie would joke in interviews that she was basically a fan of 'any artist who could conceivably play Lilith Fair', and the journalist would laugh, saying she had good taste for a girl her age, before asking Chelsea the same question. She didn't want to say, 'Whatever's playing on KIIS-FM,' because that would sound stupid, and oh, fuck, the guy was looking at her, waiting for her answer, and she panicked and said, 'The same as Madeline.' She could see the scorn in his eyes. He thought she was just a poor imitation of her sister, and her cheeks burned with shame.

'Forget that guy,' her sister had snorted afterwards. 'Good taste for a girl, my ass. What a douche.' Chelsea had tried to smile, but she was still smarting. Maddie had put her hands on Chelsea's shoulders and said, 'Just be yourself, Chel. You don't need to pretend to be anything else.' But that had been easy for Maddie, whose 'self' was interesting and smart and apparently had great taste in music too. Her sister had never understood how empty Chelsea had felt, like she was just the vase in which Maddie's flowers would be displayed.

There were multiple boxes of clothes, and she shook her head when she saw them. It was a time capsule to the new millennium. There were low-rise jeans and cargo trousers, skinny scarves and slogan Ts, tube tops and waistcoats, the oversized sunglasses and caftan dresses and ballet flats that her old stylist, Blake Logan, had made a trend. Hannah would say that she could sell it all for a fortune on eBay now. Was there anything that made you feel older than seeing the clothes of your youth repurposed as 'vintage'?

'Look at this,' Kelly called, and when Chelsea peered around the mattress, she could see her friend was holding a photograph of Maddie, one she'd never seen before. In it, Maddie was standing by the ocean – was that Pismo Beach? she wondered, taking the photo from her friend so she could look more closely – and she was staring down the lens with a serious expression on her face. 'She's wearing your necklace,' Kelly said, and it was only then Chelsea noticed what was around her sister's neck, a tiny golden compass on a thin filigree chain. The one Maddie had given her all those years ago, the necklace Chelsea had worn to the Oscars, layered with the Harry Winston jewels Blake had selected, *A perfect example of her stylist's high-low style,* a commentator had said afterwards, even though it had been Chelsea who had insisted on wearing it. She had wanted to have her sister close to her on the biggest night of her life. 'Not mine,' she said, turning away before Kelly could see her tearing up. She hadn't known that Maddie had bought two, one for each of them. 'My necklace is at home in a lock box.'

She started to dig through the filing cabinet dumped in the corner of the room. There were financial records in it, and she could see as Maddie's accounts dwindled year after year that her sister had been down to her last five hundred dollars. Why had she never asked Chelsea for anything? They had still been relatively close until that last fight – even though Chelsea wasn't rich then, not the way she was now anyway, surely Maddie knew she would have done her best to help. She closed her eyes, thinking of the way Maddie had described their fight in the diary entry Milo James had shown her, how heartbroken her sister had been. For years, everyone had told Chelsea it wasn't her fault that Maddie had taken her own life. Her sister had been sick, they said. She had been an addict, depressed. Her behaviour was not Chelsea's responsibility. But what if it had been? How was Chelsea supposed to live with that?

She crouched beside the filing cabinet where there was a stack of exercise books. Maddie's diaries, like the one Milo had shown her, but most of the pages were ripped out. There was nothing left but lists of what she had eaten that day, how many calories were in each item. There was a stack of letters too, and Chelsea grabbed them, her mouth drying when she saw the name scribbled across the front of one, of two – she looked through all the envelopes: they all had the same name on the front. It was in bubble handwriting, tiny love hearts drawn around it.

CHRISTOPHER.

Christopher. The man on The List, the man who had found the storage unit. More than likely the person who had set up that website, who was sharing all of her sister's most intimate secrets, who was sending Milo James anonymous tips. The person who was now blackmailing her. *Who was Christopher?*

'Oh, shit,' she heard Kelly say. 'Chelsea. Chel, come here. Now.'

She stood up, stuffing the envelopes into her purse to study later. She picked her way through all the detritus to where her friend was sitting cross-legged, a pile of documents in front of her. 'Look at this,' Kelly said, and Chelsea picked up the piece of paper, her eyes scanning the words. It was a medical bill, for 'Chelsea Ryan' again. The twins' birth date was on it and the address given was Cedar City, even though they hadn't lived in that apartment block for over a decade by that time. 'A miscarriage?' Chelsea said aloud, her stomach tightening.

'More like an abortion,' Kelly said, under her breath. 'What?' she said, when Chelsea looked at her, confused. 'I had to get one the summer before we started shooting *Queens*. They wrote "miscarriage" on my file too.' She took the document away. 'But that's not what I wanted to show you.' She pointed at the date on the piece of paper, and it took Chelsea a second to register. 'Oh, my God,' she whispered, when she saw it, a kick of adrenaline in her stomach. It was for 2009. The year after the Oscars, the year after Maddie had disappeared, presumed dead.

'Did you have an abortion in 2009?' Kelly asked.

'No,' Chelsea said.

'So, this means—'

'It means,' Chelsea said, an impossible certainty flooding through her, leaving her light-headed with hope, 'it means Maddie is still alive.'

14.

2001

Their mother had decorated the kitchen for the party. There were tiny twinkling lights and pink bunting hanging from the ceiling, helium balloons with *Sweet Sixteen* stamped across them, a large banner that said HAPPY BIRTHDAY MADDIE AND CHELSEA! (Shouldn't it be Chelsea and Maddie? Alphabetically, at least, even if her sister had arrived in the world a full ten minutes before she had and— *Stop*, Chelsea told herself. It wasn't Maddie's fault their mother preferred her. Everyone did.) Erin had ordered a cake too, dairy and sugar free and utterly tasteless, and after they had blown out the candles, she had cut the twins a slice each 'As a birthday treat!' Chelsea wasn't sure if it was a test – their mother never allowed them cake, even on special occasions – or if Erin was trying to seem chilled in front of the guests, but Chelsea didn't want to make a mistake, so she said, 'I'm not hungry,' and she picked at a plate of watermelon instead. But Erin didn't smile at her, the way she normally would have, she didn't whisper, *Good girl*. Their mother didn't even seem to notice, too busy flirting with her latest boyfriend, a cute but dim grip she'd met on the set of the twins' last straight-to-VHS movie.

'That watermelon looks *delicious*,' Maddie said, sidling up to her sister. She leaned against the counter top, spooning a large dollop of cake into her mouth. She winced. 'Not that this is any better. Erin couldn't get a proper cake today, of all days?'

'Sugar is poison,' Chelsea said automatically.

'Oh, shush.' Her sister looked over to where their mother was, then moved so she was hiding Chelsea from Erin's view. Maddie put her hand into her pocket, pulling out two Taffy Laffys. She handed Chelsea the caramel apple one, saying, 'Your favourite.'

Chelsea grabbed it. 'You're a bad influence,' she said, and Maddie laughed.

'You need to be led astray, Chel,' she said, unwrapping her own candy and eating it in two bites.

The party was small: a few of the cast and crew from *Double Trouble* – Linda, of course, who had brought Zach and Emily with her, the assistant director, Robbie, and their old tutor Julia. Robbie was looking for a project of his own. 'I can't be an AD for ever,' he said, wrapping his arm around his girlfriend's shoulders.

Julia looked up at him adoringly, then told the twins she had already been hired to tutor three middle-graders on a rival Nickelodeon show. 'But we'll still be your favourites?' Maddie asked, with a twinkle in her eye, and Julia had laughed and said, 'Oh, yes, I promise.'

Their agent was there too. Nancy Taylor had shown her face for less than five minutes before she air-kissed Erin and told her she'd be in touch next week, trilling, 'Busy-busy!' on her way out.

It was then Chelsea spotted two teenage girls she thought she recognized but couldn't remember where from. 'Mads,' she said, standing closer to her sister so she could lower her voice. 'Who are those girls?'

Maddie looked to where she was pointing. 'Are you tripping?' she said. 'That's Birdie. And Amber. From Cedar City.'

'No!' Chelsea tried not to stare at them. Amber had grown so tall, she must be nearly six foot now, her long legs in frayed cut-off denim shorts, and Birdie was almost unrecognizable. She was undeniably pretty with her flushed cheeks and auburn hair. When did Birdie get pretty?

'What are they . . .' Chelsea wasn't sure how to phrase this. 'I didn't know you guys kept in touch.'

'Yeah,' Maddie said, shrugging. 'We chat on AIM, you know.'

'Oh.' Why hadn't Birdie and Amber invited *her* to chat on AIM? 'That's fun.'

'Don't be weird.' Maddie always knew what Chelsea was thinking. 'It's no big deal. I've been meaning to get us all together for ages.' She turned around, calling the two girls. 'Amber! Birdie! Get over here.'

Chelsea braced herself for the worst but there were hugs and squeals, *Oh, my God! How* are *you?*, and they told Chelsea they loved her outfit, and it was so good to see her, they'd missed her. 'Well, we don't need to hear what you guys have been up to,' Amber said. 'The most famous twins in town.' She told Chelsea she had given up acting. As soon as her last growth spurt had happened, her mother had decided 'we' should pivot into modelling. 'Don't you love how the moms always say "we"?' Amber said. 'It's not "we" who are fending off photographers trying to convince the underage models to take their tops off. It's very much a me-thing then.'

Birdie was still auditioning, she said, and still failing, but she was secretly glad of it because she wanted to focus on school anyway. 'I'm hoping to go to UCLA,' Birdie said, 'major in American literature and culture.' She made a face when Chelsea asked what Birdie's mother thought of those plans. 'Oh, you know,' Birdie said, 'devastated that she can't live out her dreams through me. But I gave her my childhood, and now it's time to do what I want.' She shrugged her shoulders and Chelsea imagined what it would be like to do the same, to leave the industry and go to school. To be a normal teenager.

'Chelsea?' Birdie said, and she realized the girls were staring at her, waiting for her to say something.

'Sorry,' she said. 'I zoned out for a second. What did you say?'

Soon they were swapping stories about Cedar City, trying to remember the worst performances they'd seen at the Wednesday-night talent show the complex threw for prospective managers and agents. 'I'm sorry,' Birdie said, 'nothing could ever top my rendition of "Kiss From A Rose".' She didn't seem embarrassed, the way Chelsea would have been if she'd been so publicly humiliated. Birdie couldn't keep a straight face. 'I think a part of me hoped that Mom would put me out of my misery there and then, but of course not. She just decided I needed more classes.' Birdie grimaced. 'I swear to God, when I think of all the money my parents wasted on those freaking classes . . . They could have paid for my college tuition outright.'

Amber nodded, 'Amen to that,' and then she asked Chelsea, 'What about you guys? What are your plans for school?'

'Oh,' Chelsea said. Linda had brought up the subject once, asking if the twins had given any consideration to what they might do when *Double Trouble* ended. Maddie had said she'd love to move to New York, maybe study acting at the Tisch School of the Arts, and Chelsea had stood there, silent. College had never been suggested before, not even as an option. She had just presumed they would continue their tutoring with Julia, get their high-school diploma, and start working full-time when they didn't have to worry about child labour laws. It would be great, their mother said. A whole new chapter in their career. 'I—'

'Hey, Chel,' Robbie said, coming up behind them, a hand raised in greeting. He was wearing a white sweatshirt and sneakers, his wire-rimmed glasses pushed up his nose. 'I just wanted to say goodbye.' He gave her a quick hug. 'I have a phone call I need to take, about a new project, hopefully.' He crossed his fingers. 'Julia left already. She had to go work. Say bye to Maddie for us too, okay? Don't be a stranger.'

It was only then she realized that Maddie wasn't there any more. She had been having such a nice time with Amber and Birdie, she hadn't noticed her sister slipping away. 'Sorry,' she said. 'Do you mind if I go find Maddie? I'll be back in a few.'

Her sister wasn't with Linda, who gave Chelsea a kiss and said, 'Sixteen! I can't believe it!' Linda kept her hands on Chelsea's shoulders. 'You have the world at your feet, Chelsea. Don't . . .' a half-glance here at their mother, swaying in her vertiginous high heels as she poured herself another glass of wine '. . . don't let anyone tell you otherwise.' Linda looked like she might say something else before Emily dropped her ice-cream on the floor and started to cry. Linda turned, scooping up her five-year-old daughter, and Chelsea kept searching for her twin.

Maddie wasn't sitting on the front porch, sneaking a cigarette, and she wasn't in the garage, listening to her sad-girl music on the car radio. Chelsea was walking upstairs when she heard Maddie's voice, loud, almost angry.

'How would you know?' Maddie said. 'You didn't even give me a fucking chance. You knew how much that book meant to me. You—'

She opened the door to find Maddie by her bookshelves, her face red, shouting into her cell. 'Is . . .' Chelsea trailed off as Maddie turned to stare at her. 'Is everything okay?'

'I have to go,' Maddie said, to the person at the other end of the line.

'Mads?' Chelsea wanted to go to her sister but everything about Maddie's body language advised against it. 'Are you—'

'I'm fine,' Maddie cut across her. 'But congratulations are in order for our friend.'

'What friend?' Chelsea asked, confused.

'Who do you think? Robbie. He's just bought the rights to *Vigilante Queens*. He told me he's hoping to start shooting next year.'

'Isn't that . . .' Chelsea was trying to play catch-up '. . . isn't that the book you're into?'

'Into?' Maddie snorted. 'Yeah, I guess you could say that. Just me and forty million teenage girls around the world. It's the biggest book series since *Harry Potter* and Robbie hadn't even *heard* of it before me.'

'But why would that make you mad? Aren't you happy for R—'

'No, I'm not happy for him.' Maddie stared at her. 'Chelsea. Every actress in Hollywood is gonna audition for this. Willow Gray is the kind of role that would change your career for ever.' The energy seemed to leave her sister, her body slumping. That was when Chelsea began to worry. Maddie never gave up, never backed down from a fight. She wanted to ask if her sister was okay, but all she could think was—

'Will I be able to audition too?' Chelsea asked. She couldn't stop herself. She felt like her ribs were knitting together, tighter and tighter, making it difficult to breathe. If this was the role of a lifetime, the role that would change someone's career for ever, why did it have to be Maddie and not her?

'What?' Her sister wiped her nose with the back of her hand, her lower lip quivering. 'Chel, are you hearing me?' She sat down on the bed, putting her head into her hands. Chelsea sat next to her, pushing her thigh into her twin's, waiting for her to speak.

'I was the one who told Robbie the author was a recluse, that she'd refused to sell the rights until she found a collaborator as passionate about the books as she was.' Maddie put the heels of her hands into her eye sockets. 'I spent *hours* talking about how I thought the show should be shot, about the dynamic between the three characters, how important it was that their friendship was, like, a good example to young girls watching. And Robbie listened and he took all of that and he went to Utah to meet Amy Jenson and persuaded her to give *him* the rights. Then he tells me on the phone rather than in person, like a fucking coward! Says it's not that big of a deal, that I'm a shoo-in to play Willow anyway, that he couldn't visualize another face on screen except mine. I thought he was my friend. I thought . . .' She turned to look at Chelsea again. '*I* wanted to make it. I wanted to have some control, for once. This is gonna be the biggest show in the world and Robbie will get all the credit.'

'But it sounds like you already have the main role,' Chelsea said, trying and failing to keep the bitterness out of her voice. 'I guess that means you're about to become the most famous woman of our generation.'

'Oh, my God.' Maddie gritted her teeth. 'You sound just like Mom. I cannot talk about that bullshit prophecy again.'

'I know it's bullshit,' she replied, stung. 'But the point is – Mom doesn't. No matter how shitty you are to her, she says, "Oh, Maddie is so charismatic, she's so magnetic, she's going to be a superstar." And there's me, always doing the right thing and she doesn't give a shit. Do you know what that's like for me, Maddie? Do you even care?'

Maddie took a minute but when she spoke, her voice was cold. 'I love you, Chelsea,' she said. 'But I just told you that someone who is supposed to be a . . . he's our friend. And he's stolen my fucking dream and suddenly this has become all about you?' She took a beat. 'You're always saying how "easy" it is for me,' her sister said, 'But you never seem to give any thought to what it's like being the focus of Mom's attention. No matter how much I try and push back against it, she won't let me alone. She wants to control every aspect of our lives, what we eat, how much we weigh, who our friends are, if we go to fucking college. I wanted to go to Tisch, I wanted . . .' Maddie took an unsteady breath. 'I don't know how much more I can take.'

'Mom wants the best for us,' Chelsea said. 'Everything she does, it's for us.'

Her sister looked at her, wearily. 'Do you really believe that, Chelsea?' she said. 'Still?'

15.

2025

Maddie is alive. Maddie is alive.

Maddie is alive.

She might not be, Kelly had said, trying to get Chelsea to stay calm. It could have been a clerical error, they wrote everything in pencil back then, or maybe Maddie hid out for a year and then . . . Her friend trailed off, the words too brutal to say aloud. 'And if she was alive? Come on. You can't honestly believe *Maddie* is responsible for this.' She gestured around at the storage unit. 'Why on earth would she set up the website? Whatever her issues, your sister would never want to hurt you.'

That was easy for Kelly to say. She didn't know the truth of what had happened, what Chelsea had done to her twin, what she had said to her that night. 'Maddie's dead,' Kelly continued. 'You've got to let this go.'

'But the date on the forms? And a body was never found, she could ha—'

'She had your face.' Kelly was firm. 'You think someone with Chelsea Stone's face could have just disappeared in 2009? Maddie could have gone to, like, Siberia, and they would have recognized Willow Gray.'

But if Maddie had dyed her hair and hadn't worn makeup, if she had pulled on a baseball cap and baggy clothes, if she'd used a different accent – and she was so good at that, she had been an incredible mimic – maybe she could have gone unnoticed. No one would have expected to see Willow Gray in Siberia, or in whatever one-horse town she ended up in. In her fans' imagination, Chelsea Stone existed in Beverly Hills or Bel Air. If they saw her in a gas station or a rundown diner, they might have done a double-take but they'd tell themselves not to be stupid: what would a celebrity be doing here by herself, without security? People could still disappear back then, if they wanted to.

'And, besides,' Kelly had continued, 'why aren't you more worried? If this leaks, Chel, everyone is gonna assume it was you who had the abortion.' But Chelsea didn't care. For the first time since the website had gone live, she didn't feel as if she was choking on fear. Her sister might be alive – she might be out there, all alone. If she was, then Chelsea had to find her.

'Hi, babe.' It was Nick, coming in to find her, and she quickly hid her phone so he wouldn't see it. He might work in tech but Nick had strict rules about the use of devices, the same as all the other parents from the kids' school did. One of the mothers had confided in Chelsea that she'd had to fire her nanny for handing her daughter an iPad on the flight to Lake Tahoe, and Chelsea had wondered what she was doing in this life, with these women, who acted like the worst thing that could happen to a child was back-to-back episodes of *Paw Patrol*. She remembered the letters she and Maddie had received on the *Double Trouble* set, asking if they could send their used panties to the enclosed PO box. The late-night chat-show host asking the twins if they'd had matching boob jobs when they were only sixteen, and the website counting down to their eighteenth birthday – 'The Stone twins are finally legal and loaded!' But she had pretended to be shocked, and told the mother she'd done the right thing in firing the nanny because that was what was expected of her. Chelsea had always been good at doing what she was supposed to.

'What are you doing in here?' he asked.

She was back in her guesthouse, staring at what Nya had referred to as the serial-killer wall. The photo of her and Maddie in the centre of the spider web, all the supporting characters surrounding them – their mother, Nancy Taylor, Milo from RumorMill, Robbie, Linda. The mysterious Christopher, whoever he was. She hadn't pinned anything about the Foto account, the person looking for a million dollars to keep her secrets, in case Nick or the kids came in here and saw it. *Please be patient with me*: that was the last message she had sent. *I'm still trying to get the money together*, and an email arrived back, maybe twenty minutes later. *Time's running out, Chelsea.*

'What the fuck?' her husband said, standing in front of her whiteboard. 'Chelsea, what is this?'

'I . . . I need to tell you something.' She sat down on the low-backed armchair, gesturing at her husband to take the sofa opposite her. 'I'm going to talk for a bit,' she said, 'and I need you to listen and not say anything until I'm done.' Her husband started to protest but Chelsea raised her hand to stop him. 'Please, Nick,' she said. 'This is important.'

'Okay,' he said, and she could see him reach for the 'active listening' skills their couples' therapist had taught them. 'If it's important to you, it's important to me.'

Chelsea reached down to her feet, to the leather handbag there. She pulled out all the files – the letters, the diaries with pages missing, the prescriptions. She laid them down on the coffee-table between them.

Nick glanced at the papers, then back to Chelsea. 'What is this?' he asked.

Chelsea leaned forward, rummaging through them until she

found what she was looking for. She handed it to her husband, watching as he unfolded the document, his eyes scanning the words. 'What the fuck? Where did you get this?'

'I found the storage unit.' She winced, waiting for his reaction.

'What?'

'You said you'd let me talk!' Chelsea leaned her head back so she was staring at the ceiling, her eyes following the grains of wood. 'I went to meet Milo James,' she said flatly. 'He told me where it was.'

'The man behind that awful blog?'

They had spent a lot of time discussing RumorMill during the early years of their marriage, Chelsea veering between fury as she recounted the damage the website had done, and berating herself for continuing to read it, like everyone else. 'What . . .' For once, her husband seemed lost for words. 'What on earth did you say to him?'

'I tried to . . .' Chelsea could barely remember the words she had used with Milo. When she thought of their encounter, all she could recall was the smell of coffee, the manicured cuticles of Milo's hands, the red-eyed mother of the newborn baby at the table next to them, the hum of background music. 'It doesn't matter,' she said. 'The point is, we went to check it out. Kelly and me.'

'And you didn't think to ask me?' Her husband sounded hurt rather than angry and, somehow, that was worse. 'You didn't think I'd want to be there with you?'

'I'm sorry,' she said, and she found that she was. There had been a time when Nick would have been her first call, the only person she would have wanted by her side for a trip like that. 'I was in shock.' She had been since Kelly had handed her the document in the storage unit. Staring at it, wondering why *her* name was on the form. Chelsea Ryan. Maddie might have used their mother's maiden name, but anyone she had come into contact with in that hospital, the other patients, the doctors, the nurses, the cleaning staff, visitors, they would all have seen her face, and heard her name, and assumed it was Chelsea Stone, not Madeline. 'I can't believe she did this. If the tabloids heard about this, that Chelsea "Ryan" had had an abortion, my life could have been *ruined*.' Chelsea ran her fingers through her hair. 'I was America's teenage sweetheart, the girl next door, all that crap. I was supposed to be a role model to millions of teenagers across the country. If they thought I'd had a termination . . .' She would have been crucified in the right-wing media. They would have called for her head on a platter, and AtomicKids would have given it to them. There was a morality clause in her contract: they'd have been legally entitled to do so.

'Who else have you told about this?' her husband asked, as he read it, and she waited for him to notice the date, to have the same realization she'd had. *Maddie is alive. Maddie is alive. Maddie is alive.*

'Kelly,' she admitted, and Nick groaned. 'Hannah, because she had to get the movers down there,' she continued, 'but you know how discreet she is. She won't—'

'You mean her NDA is too terrifying,' he put in. 'What about your mom? Does she know about this?'

'No.' She was still avoiding Erin. She couldn't face the thought of having this conversation with her mother. Erin texted her every Monday when the new blog post went live, wailing about how it was so typical of Maddie to cause drama, even beyond the grave. Her mother didn't know anything about this. She thought Maddie was dead, Chelsea was sure. She rifled through the piles on the table until she came to the envelopes, torn open. 'These letters,' she said, handing one to her husband who accepted it gingerly. 'They're all written to some guy called Christopher. His name was on the List of Lovers that RumorMill published, and when we went to the storage unit, they said the person who bought it, his name was Christopher too. I never heard Maddie mention anyone with that name. And then I read all these letters and it's like Maddie is obsessed with him. It doesn't even sound like her.' She unfolded a letter so she could read it aloud. '"Christopher, Christopher. My love. I miss you so much and I cannot wait to see you again. I didn't know it was possible to feel this way but I can't live without you now."' Chelsea broke off. 'It's like a romance novel. It isn't Maddie.'

'It sounds like a typical teenage girl to me,' Nick said, leaning back in his chair.

'You don't understand. I . . .' Chelsea touched her fingers to the documents on the table. 'I need to do this, Nick,' she said. 'I let Maddie down all those years ago, I can't do that to her again. I need to find out what happened to her.'

'Darling,' Nick said, 'you're not Jessica Fletcher.' He waited for her to laugh at his joke, the way she always did. When she remained stone-faced, he became serious. 'Your sister was a drug addict,' he said. 'She was a careless individual, and when she took her own life, she left even more mess behind for other people to take care of. There's nothing to be *figured out*. It's done. My guys were getting the blog taken down every time a new version appeared, but now you found the storage unit, we don't need to worry about that any more. Well done, babe.' She didn't think he was trying to sound condescending but her jaw clenched anyway. 'We can just move on and forget all about this now, okay?'

But the problem was, she couldn't just forget about it. If she pointed out the dates to her husband as proof that Maddie had not killed herself, or at least not the night she had gone missing, Nick would insist on getting a private investigator, the best one there was. He'd tell Chelsea not to get involved. But she *had* to be involved. She couldn't tell him about the blackmailer and the million dollars – oh, fuck, where was she going to get that money? – because she would have to tell him why she needed it, what she had done. She had loved her husband once, no matter what had happened. She didn't want to hurt him. 'But, Nick, the abortion. If—'

'Stop,' he interrupted her. 'If that leaked, it wouldn't be great but it wouldn't be insurmountable. We'll just release a statement saying your sister used your name and hopefully that'll be enough. Christ, the last thing I need is questions about my stance on abortion.'

'I mean,' Chelsea could feel herself getting annoyed, 'we live in California, *darling*. I doubt saying you're pro-choice will lose you too many votes.'

Her husband went quiet, waiting for her to apologize. She tried to stay strong – she hadn't done anything wrong: why did *she* have to say sorry? – but after a few minutes of silence, she capitulated, as they'd both known she would. 'I'm sorry,' she said. 'But this is my sister we're talking about. Surely you can see why this would be important to me.'

'I guess,' he said, in a way that heavily implied that, no, he did not understand. 'But I think it's a tad . . .' he paused, trying to find the right word '. . . childish to be fixated on this. It happened almost twenty years ago, Chelsea. You're married. Me and the kids, we're your family now.' That was what he had said on their wedding night. He had put his hands on her waist, drawing her closer, and he'd told her that she was all he needed, and she had felt like her heart might explode with joy. All she had ever wanted was to be someone's favourite. 'That's what you should be focused on,' Nick continued, 'the kids. They're at such important stages, Grayson particularly. They need you more than ever.'

'I am focused on them,' she replied, stung. 'The kids are my priority, you know that.'

It hardly seemed fair of Nick to bring the children into it, when he spent so little time with them. They had meals together when he was home, which was maybe once or twice a week, and they vacationed as a family multiple times a year, but Nick was always *on*, always taking work calls, always checking in with his team at Foto. His family was the reason he worked so hard, he told Chelsea. He was building generational wealth, creating a legacy for their children, their grandchildren, but they had more money than they could ever spend in a dozen lifetimes. At this point it just felt greedy.

'Of course I know that! You're a great mom,' he said. 'But you don't want to get distracted by this, babe. Let's leave it behind us.' He patted next to him on the sofa and she reluctantly joined him. 'It's okay,' he said. 'It's all going to be okay,' and he nuzzled into her, kissing her neck, and she felt herself freeze.

Chelsea, come on. It was the first time in months that Nick had initiated anything with her. She had to encourage him. She forced herself to move towards him, straddling him. She leaned down to kiss him, both hands on his face, and she moved her hips, grinding into him, waiting for him to harden beneath her, but there was nothing. She broke away. 'Do you want me to . . .' she said, gesturing her head towards his lap. He hesitated but she began to shimmy down his body anyway, reaching under his sweatpants, and pulling out his limp dick. She licked up the shaft but nothing was happening, and she wondered how much longer she would have to—

'Just leave it.' He pushed her head away. 'I'm not in the mood.'

'I'm trying—'

'I said I'm not in the mood.'

'But when are you going to be in the mood?' she asked. 'It's been almost a year, Nick. I don't know what—'

'I'm aware of how long it's been,' he snapped at her. 'I don't need you reminding me. And I've told you, it's kinda difficult to get hard for someone who acts like giving me a blowjob is some huge fucking favour.'

'I'm sorry.' That was what he had said when they went for couple's therapy. Chelsea was damaged from her childhood, he said. Her attitude to sex was fucked up because of the purity rings and The Director's insistence she remain as wholesome as apple pie. What was Nick supposed to do? How quickly it had become Chelsea's fault in the end. She pressed her lips together to stop herself crying. 'I didn't mean to make you feel like that.'

'Well, you did. For someone who was supposed to be this great actress, you're not very good at pretending, are you?'

'I—' She could feel her eyes prick with tears. It was ironic. Everyone in the world must assume that Nick Bennett and Chelsea Stone had wild, passionate sex. They were both so attractive, and seemed to adore each other. They had the perfect marriage. No one could have imagined the truth.

'I'm going back in the house,' he said. 'I'll see you at dinner.'

She waited until he was gone, then went to use the bathroom. She stared at herself in the mirror, at how exhausted she looked, and she couldn't help but remember how she had felt with Carter. Vibrant. Sexy. For the first time in years, she had felt alive. Before then, she'd thought Nick was right about her, that she was frigid, that her time as a virginal pre-teen star had broken her. She didn't realize she could feel pleasure, desire. How sad that it had taken her so long to understand herself.

She opened the toilet lid and sat down to pee, swiping up on her cell to open the home screen. There were multiple texts from Nya, and a missed call.

Nya: Chelsea, what is going on? That's the tenth time I've tried to call you in the last two weeks.

Nya: If you don't start replying to my messages soon, I am gonna fly to LA and take up residence in that fancy guesthouse of yours 😊

Nya: Please phone me back, okay?

She swiped out of iMessage without replying. She had made Kelly swear she wouldn't tell Nya about the dates on the abortion records, about Chelsea's new-found conviction that her sister was alive. Nya would be soft, gentle, but she would be sceptical too, and Chelsea didn't want that right now. She desperately needed to believe that this was true.

She scrolled through the other apps, wondering what to do. She shouldn't look at Reddit or any of the forums. She'd never sleep if she did that, arguing in her head with anonymous trolls, telling them to fuck off and die. They didn't know her or Maddie, didn't know how much they'd loved one another. She thought about the blackmailer, about how they said they had sent her DMs, which she'd never seen, and she downloaded the Foto app instead, in case there was anything new. Chelsea rarely did this; she logged in only when she needed to post photos on special occasions, signing out immediately afterwards and deleting the app again. She would have preferred to hand over responsibility to Hannah, or a dedicated social-media manager, but she didn't want anyone else reading through her messages.

What if yet another young woman slid into her DMs with more screenshots? *Receipts*: that was what the girl had called them. Chelsea couldn't face the thought of Hannah seeing something like that, wondering if she should tell her boss or ignore it. She didn't want Hannah to lose respect for her, or maybe she would just assume this was part of the deal, that Chelsea had accepted her husband's infidelity in exchange for the house and the private jet. And the money was important – she would be lying if she said it wasn't. She and Maddie had worked their entire lives, and yet when they turned eighteen, there was so little left. Agency fees, their mother had explained, and the mortgage, of course, but no one mentioned the 20 per cent rate Erin had paid herself as their 'manager'.

Chelsea had managed to build up a nest egg from *Vigilante Queens*, but during her time off, The Director would tell her she shouldn't take that blockbuster movie, she should focus on smaller, indie films. That way she would be respected in the industry. But you couldn't eat respect or pay for gas and heating with it, and after Chelsea quit acting, she was basically broke. She'd met Nick and he was good to her and he was handsome, driven and ambitious. She wasn't attracted to him, not really, but how important was sex, in the end? Nick would take care of her and that was enough. Their relationship had felt somewhat equal then – he might have had money but Chelsea had her youth, her beauty, her fame, and there had been power in that too. Everything had shifted the day she'd found the photos and messages on his phone – *How could you do this?* she'd screamed at him. *How could you cheat on me?* And he had said, *I have not and have never cheated on you, and I never would. It was nothing. It's basically the same as porn.*

Porn wouldn't have been able to contact her. Porn wouldn't have popped up on her phone at breakfast, while she was sitting with her children as they ate their oatmeal. Porn wouldn't have made her feel stupid and small and humiliated. Porn wouldn't have felt like such a complete betrayal of her and their life together. It wouldn't have left her feeling unsafe, as if the ground was giving way beneath her. Would anything have happened with Carter if Nick hadn't cheated first?

She opened the Foto app to thousands of notifications and unread messages. She hadn't posted since the holidays – a carousel of photos of their ten-foot Christmas tree and the beautifully wrapped presents underneath, the back of Ivy and Grayson's heads as they hung their tartan stockings over the fireplace, the tiny place cards in front of the eleven types of dessert, each one written in swirling calligraphy letters – Mississippi mud pie, Belgian chocolate ganache, buttermilk pecan pralines, red velvet cake. It had over five hundred thousand likes. She clicked into the inbox, scrolling down, down. She was looking for something or someone, and she wasn't sure exactly what it was until she saw it.

The username was Maddie Ann Ryan, and the profile photo was the one Chelsea had found in the storage unit of her sister staring down the camera lens, wearing the compass necklace identical to Chelsea's. There was a green dot above the account name, unblinking: someone was on the other side, waiting for her. She opened the message.

So, the person had written, *you cleared out the storage unit.*

Chelsea's heart began to beat faster. *Yes*, she wrote, even though she knew this was a terrible idea.

Typing, typing, typing.

Do you really think that's going to help? they wrote. *I took photos of everything.* An image appearing in the chat. One of the letters to Christopher, professing Maddie's undying love for him, that she would do anything he wanted, be whatever he desired. She was his to do with as he wished. Chelsea didn't reply and the words *typing, typing* appeared again.

Besides, we both know that's not the secret you really want me to keep. Is it? So. Chelsea Stone. Where's my money?

Chelsea started tapping at the phone but the green dot disappeared, and seconds later the account disappeared too, she had either been blocked or the person had deleted it. '*Fuck,*' she said, under her breath, resisting the temptation to throw the phone onto the tiled floor and smash it to pieces. She got up and flushed the toilet, washing her hands. Then she stared at herself in the mirror again as she phoned the one person she had hoped she would never need to speak to again.

'Hi,' she said, as Nancy Taylor picked up. 'It's Chelsea. I want to talk to you about the reunion show.'

16.

2002

'Do you think—'

'The cell reception is fine,' Maddie cut Erin off.

'But maybe we should—'

'We've already checked. Your cell is working, the reception is fine.' Maddie stretched her legs out to rest on the cream-fringed ottoman. 'We just have to wait.'

Erin got to her feet, chewing the skin around her thumb. 'I have all this anxious energy,' she said, pacing back and forth. 'I don't know what to do with myself.'

Maddie and Chelsea were sitting side by side on the sofa and they made brief eye contact, a half-smirk. Chelsea looked away before she cracked up. How was it, today of all days, her sister was still able to make her laugh?

'Stop doing your twin thing,' Erin snapped at them. 'It's annoying.'

'Sorry, Mom,' Chelsea murmured, dropping her gaze to the floor, but Maddie didn't say anything. She didn't need to answer to Erin any more. She had moved out soon after their sixteenth birthday, saying she was practically an adult – she'd certainly been working like one for the last ten years, anyway. After the moving van left, Erin had followed Maddie out to her car, and Chelsea watched through the window as they had what looked like a heated exchange. Erin had stomped back into the house, slamming the door after her. 'I don't want to talk about it,' she'd said, when Chelsea tried to comfort her.

Whatever Happened to Madeline Stone?

But later that night, Chelsea had awoken to the sound of her mother creeping into her bed. There was a smell of whiskey on Erin's breath as she said, 'You'll never leave me, right?' She had pressed her arms around Chelsea so tightly, she couldn't breathe.

'No, of course not,' she'd choked out, and her mother had whispered, 'Do you promise? Do you promise you'll never leave?' waiting, waiting until Chelsea had replied, 'I promise, Mom. I'll never leave.'

Maddie hadn't come back to the house since then but she had relented today, because Chelsea had asked her to be there. 'It would mean a lot to me,' she'd told her twin, but they both knew that it was Erin who wanted both her daughters to be with her for this, the biggest moment in their careers so far, and things would be easier for Chelsea if Erin was happy. Their mother looked at her watch again, cracking each knuckle on her left hand, then her right. 'Nancy Taylor said they'd know by three,' she said. 'It's three thirty now. What's taking so long?' Erin let out a sigh, before sitting down between the twins, pushing them apart to opposite ends of the sofa. 'Whatever happens, girls,' she said, but she was only looking at Maddie, and Chelsea swallowed her frustration, 'I want you to know that I'm proud of you. We always knew this was gonna be a tough one, didn't we? Remember what Nancy Taylor said?'

Their agent had warned them that every hot young thing in town was auditioning for the role of Willow Gray: Lindsay, Mary-Kate and Ashley, Mischa, even Britney was rumoured to be interested. It would be a fight to the death, Nancy had said, even if they were friends with the director. This was Robbie's big break too: he wasn't going to squander it on misguided loyalty. The twins had taken her at her word, running lines together every day for the month until the video tapes were due. Maddie had helped her so much, talking through Willow

Gray's motivations, giving Chelsea advice on how to move her body, what mannerisms would make it feel more natural. She had felt quietly confident about her audition tape until she had watched Maddie's and she felt like she might be sick. Her sister was perfect. Stoic, sweet, a little bashful but fierce when she needed to be – Maddie *was* Willow Gray. Chelsea had watched the tape again and again, studying it, and then she had re-recorded her own audition, doing her best to embody her sister's energy.

'We've just got to—' Their mother jumped to her feet. 'Oh,' she said, staring at her phone screen. 'I thought I heard a beep.'

'It was me,' Chelsea said, holding up her cell. 'Linda messaged to say good luck.'

'Me too,' Maddie said, texting back quickly.

'For God's sake, girls, can you turn them on silent until we get the fucking phone call?' Erin said, returning to worry at her thumb.

Chelsea wasn't sure why she was being so uptight. It was clear she thought Maddie had it in the bag. Chelsea had come out of the shower yesterday, still wrapped in a towel, when she'd overheard her mother in her bedroom. Erin had been on her cell phone, talking so loudly that Chelsea couldn't help but wonder if her mother had wanted her to hear. 'Oh, that role is Madeline's to lose,' Erin had said. 'Robbie said she was *born* to play Willow Gray.'

Erin stopped pacing. Her phone was ringing and she held it up so the twins could see the name on the screen – *Nancy Taylor.* 'Nancy,' she answered. 'Hello. I'm here with the girls . . . Yes, both girls.' She paused, the muffled sound of the other woman's voice through the cell. Chelsea's palms started to sweat. She snuck a glance at her sister. Maddie was chewing her lower lip, uncharacteristically pale.

'Oh,' their mother said . . . 'Okay. Okay, I understand. I'll call you back once I've told them.' Erin spun on her heel so she was facing the twins and it was then Chelsea could see the shock on her mother's face.

'Mom?' she asked. 'What's happened? What did Nancy say?'

'She said . . .' Erin sank to her knees and she wrapped her arms around Chelsea's waist. 'Oh, baby. She said you got the part.'

'Me? But I'm . . . It's Chelsea, Mom,' she said, afraid that her mother had mixed them up, the way she used to when they were kids, but Erin only laughed. 'I know, baby,' she said. Chelsea turned to her sister, but Maddie was silent, completely still.

'It's you, baby girl.' Her mother's eyes were shining, and Chelsea realized that Erin had never looked at her like that before. It had always been reserved for Maddie, the star, the daughter who was going to fulfil all of her dreams. 'You got the part.'

Erin grabbed Chelsea's hands and raised them in the air in victory, trying to make Chelsea dance with her. But she was frozen, her eyes on Maddie, waiting for Maddie to say something, *anything*. Her twin still seemed unable to move, the blood draining from her face until she was almost grey. Maddie had seen both of their tapes too. They both knew hers had been better. 'I . . .' Maddie looked at the floor, a muscle in her jaw pulsating. 'Congratulations, Chel,' she said, overly bright. 'That's amazing.' She walked over to Chelsea, ignoring their mother, and gave her sister a brief, tight hug. 'You'll be great,' Maddie whispered into her ear, and Chelsea wanted to cry. Her sister was so gracious. Maddie had wanted that role badly – the books meant so much to her. Chelsea knew she would have been unable to be as generous if the roles were reversed, which made her feel ashamed. *I'm sorry*, she wanted to say. *I'm so sorry*.

17.

2025

The money is nearly sorted, Chelsea emailed the account. *I just need a couple of weeks but it's a done deal.*

Finally asked that husband of yours to cough up? The response was quick and there was something about it, the cadence perhaps, or maybe the over-familiarity, that niggled at Chelsea but she couldn't figure out why. *No,* she was tempted to reply. *I had to do something much worse than ask my husband.*

Nancy Taylor used to have an office in a soaring glass and steel building close to the Fox Studio lot. Chelsea and Maddie would come in with their mother when they were little, fighting over who got to press the button in the lift, their ears popping as it zoomed up to the fifty-fourth floor where the Nancy Taylor Agency had its home. They would sit in the waiting room, a light-filled space that smelt of sandalwood and musk, glossy magazines piled on the glass-topped coffee-table, avoiding eye contact with the other stage moms and child actors. In Chelsea's memory, there was always a young woman behind the front desk, answering the phone with a shaky voice – the sound of Nancy screaming at her was audible even through the handset. Those receptionists changed so often that Chelsea and Maddie stopped asking their names after a while. It was pointless.

After *Double Trouble* aired, quickly becoming one of the biggest shows on AtomicKids, they stopped going to the office.

'Nancy can come to us now,' their mother had declared, a gleam of satisfaction in her eye.

'There's my favourite client,' Nancy said, as she opened the front door. She had given up the office during the pandemic, she'd explained, when Chelsea had phoned, saying she would do the reunion show but at a price.

It was a lovely house, a single-storey bungalow that wrapped around the swimming-pool out back, typical of the pan-Mediterranean architecture popular in that part of LA. Chelsea had looked up the listing when Nancy had sent her the address – she'd bought the house for six million dollars almost five years ago, and Chelsea guessed it would sell for closer to ten today. It must have been lucrative, selling children for profit. Chelsea leaned in to give the older woman a kiss on the cheek. Nancy looked the same as she always had, the bouffant grey hair, the heavy eyeliner, the pantsuits – she was the sort of woman who had looked fifty when she was thirty, but hadn't aged a day after that – and she still wore Yves St Laurent Rive Gauche, the perfume she'd used for as long as Chelsea had known her.

'It's good to see you,' Nancy said, holding Chelsea at arm's length, her eyes narrowing a little as she took Chelsea in. She had always done this, whenever she met a client, silently assessing if they'd put on weight or grown tits, if they were still small and cute enough to be sent on auditions. *I'm not a child any more, Nancy Taylor*, Chelsea wanted to say. She hadn't seen her agent since the day she had fired her, telling Nancy she was sorry, she just couldn't work any more. Maddie was dead, she'd thought, and The Director had moved on, found a new muse. She had been twenty-three and broken, and her agent had taken one look at her, and instinctively understood there was no point in arguing.

'Aren't you going to come in?' Nancy said.

'Yes, sorry.' Chelsea stepped into the hall. It had arched frames and a terracotta tiled floor, and it smelt the same as the Century City office did, that hint of sandalwood. 'You have a beautiful home,' she said.

'Oh,' Nancy said, with a wave of her hand, 'I'm sure it's paltry compared to what you're used to, these days, but it does the job.' She stopped outside a small, cramped room, peeking in at the three grey filing cabinets, one half open, and dozens of archive boxes on the floor, piled on top of one another. 'My office,' she said, by way of explanation. 'It's a mess. We can go into the living room, if you prefer?'

'That might be better,' Chelsea said.

In the living room, there were two deep couches upholstered in threaded linen, cushions in vintage textiles, and a deep shag rug. The artwork on the walls was impressive: a neon light fixture she guessed was a Tracey Emin, two tapestry panels, and an oversized oil painting. She sat on one couch, Nancy on the other. There was a yellow legal pad and a pen on the table between them and her agent picked them up, resting the pad on her lap. She wore a pair of reading glasses on a pearl string around her neck and she perched them on her nose now. 'I'm thrilled you've agreed to do the show,' Nancy said, scribbling something on the paper. 'I'd begun to think we'd never manage to convince you.'

'Yes,' Chelsea said, scratching the side of her neck. 'Well, we have to agree on our terms first.'

'Of course,' the agent said. 'But if you don't mind me asking, Chelsea, what changed your mind? You were so adamant before.'

Chelsea hesitated. She couldn't tell Nancy the truth, that she was being blackmailed and this was the only way she could get the money, but neither could she mention the new thought that kept coming to her since she'd found the storage unit.

Whatever Happened to Madeline Stone?

Maddie is alive. If Chelsea did the show, would her sister watch? Could this be the thing that made her sister finally reach out? 'I'm doing it for the fans,' she lied. 'They've been so loyal. Look, Nancy, I need you to keep this quiet, just for a few days. Okay? Until I can talk to Nick properly.'

'Husbands,' Nancy said, with an eye-roll. 'More trouble than they're worth.' She had never married or had children. What need had she? she always said. She had a hundred kids to take care of as it was.

'I'm serious,' Chelsea said, leaning towards her.

'Have you ever known me to tell tales?' Nancy mimed zipping up her lips and throwing away the key.

'Funnily enough, I wanted to ask you about that.' She waited a beat. 'I went to see Milo James.'

'Why on earth would you want to see him?' Nancy asked, frowning.

'I had a few questions to ask him.'

'Oh, really?' Nancy wrinkled her nose. 'And what did Mr RumorMill have to say for himself?'

'Quite a lot, actually. He said that people used to sell him stories about me and Maddie all the time, which we knew, of course. But he also said someone was paying him to run negative stories about Maddie.' Chelsea watched her agent carefully. It had been bad in those days. She remembered sitting in the hair salon, flicking through a magazine, and she would stumble upon a photo of herself. Usually, all she paid attention to was how thin she was – her stylist would be pleased – and the accompanying story would be so nonsensical Chelsea could almost enjoy them. But other times, there was a kernel of truth at the core of the article – a conversation she'd had with a friend, a disagreement she'd had with Nancy Taylor over a script, something she had said to Maddie or her mother, a throwaway comment now twisted into something salacious, more 'newsworthy'. She would put down the magazine, her throat closing, wondering which friend was selling her out, who had betrayed her. 'Do you have any idea who that could be?' she asked.

'Wait.' Horror dawned on the other woman's face. 'You're not seriously implying . . . Chelsea, you hardly think *I* was doing that?'

'I don't know what to think,' Chelsea said. 'Milo said agents and publicists used to reach out to him, giving him stories so he would bury others.'

'Well, obviously,' Nancy dismissed this. 'but I told him stupid stuff, like how Kelly Foster's new boyfriend had stolen cash from her wallet and never called her again,' poor Kelly had been so humiliated when that story ran, 'not stories about Madeline. Why would I have done that anyway? Your sister did a great job of ruining her own reputation. She didn't need my help.' Nancy looked up at the ceiling, as if gathering her strength.' My God, that *GQ* interview. I still have nightmares about it.'

'I don't want to talk about the interview,' Chelsea said. 'I want to know about the last time you spoke to Maddie. What did she say to you?'

'Goodness, I don't know – it was ages before she died. Months, at least.' Nancy made a note on her legal pad. 'Now. Back to business. I'm still working on the contract for the reunion. You said in your initial phone call you wanted a million dollars so—'

'A million into my bank account,' Chelsea interrupted. 'After your fee has been deducted and the lawyers and tax, et cetera.'

'Yes.' Nancy nodded. 'I got it. The network tried playing hardball but they rolled over in like five seconds. They need you a lot more than you need them, which is always my favourite negotiating position.' She smiled. 'I'm just finessing the smaller details – you have your own glam squad you work with, right?'

'Yeah, and I—' She stopped herself. 'That's not why I'm here today. I'm here to talk about Maddie. I presume you've seen the website.'

The agent put her pen and pad on the arm rest, and an eerie blankness slid over her features. How good this woman was at pretending. 'Yes,' she said. 'Terrible business.' She stood up, walked into the kitchen. Chelsea strained her neck so she could see in there – it had teal cabinets and a marble splash-back, teak stools around an island of a dark-painted wood. 'I'm making tea,' Nancy called over her shoulder. 'D'you want some?'

She followed Nancy, and sat on a stool made of what looked like reclaimed wood, accepting a cup. 'Oolong,' the older woman said. 'It keeps the brain alert.' She sat on the other side of the island, watching Chelsea as she took a sip.

'Delicious,' Chelsea said, placing the mug back on the counter. 'Now.' She was determined her agent wasn't going to fob her off this easily. 'Back to Maddie. I found the storage unit. Me and Kelly, we went down there. There was all this other stuff, these medical reports.' She kept her gaze trained on her agent's face but Nancy didn't move a muscle. If Chelsea mentioned the date, the fact it was a year after Maddie had supposedly died, what would her agent say? 'She had an abortion.'

'Twenty-five per cent of American women will have had one by the end of their childbearing years. I've had two,' Nancy said, with a shrug. 'Most women I know have. This isn't exactly shocking news.'

'It's not the abortion,' Chelsea cried. 'It's the fact I didn't know about it. It's the fact that my twin sister had one under *my fucking name* and I—'

'Hold on, she used—'

'Yes, she used Chelsea on the admissions form, which I didn't know about, obviously. And I guess I'm wondering, who did know?' She paused, waiting for the other woman to say anything, but Nancy remained resolute. 'Did you?'

'If you're suggesting I would have allowed your reputation to be put at risk like that, you've lost your mind. You were my most profitable client! Of course I didn't know.' Nancy crossed her arms. 'Madeline wasn't even on my books by then. I couldn't work with her when she was still using. She was too unpredictable and—'

'You mean she wasn't making you enough money. If that had been me, at the height of *Vigilante Queens*, and you were still getting your cut . . .' Chelsea stared her down '. . . would you have fired me too?'

'That's a false equivalency and you know it. You never caused any trouble – you wouldn't know how to. Your sister might have been talented but she was so . . . opinionated, Jesus, she just always had to have her say, no matter what the consequences. That fucking interview was proof enough of that. You were an angel in comparison.'

'That's not what I asked you.' Chelsea was tired of being compared to Maddie. The two of them had been pitted against one another since they were children. It was as if one could not exist without the context of the other. One had to be more talented or better-looking or easier to manage. It was exhausting, and it was only now that Chelsea understood how much she had played into it too. She had believed only one could win and it had made her afraid, and in her fear she had seen her sister, the person who had loved her most, as her enemy.

'This isn't fair. I've known both of you since you were babies. I wanted the best for you. When Madeline died—' Hurt skittered across her face. 'I'm not a monster, Chelsea.'

'I'm not saying that.' Chelsea tried to find the right words. 'Ever since they found that storage unit, I've been so confused. We were always so close, Maddie and I. You saw it, right?' She needed someone to confirm her memories, to reassure her that it had been special, what she and Maddie had shared. That they had loved each other fiercely. She waited until her agent nodded before continuing. 'I know things were weird with us at the end . . .' A lump formed in her throat as she thought of the diary entry on Milo James's phone, the pain her sister had been in, and it was all her fault. 'I'm not an idiot. But for Maddie to have had this entire other life? It doesn't make sense. Something else was going on and I need to figure it out. I need to do this for Maddie.'

'I understand,' Nancy said, turning away and rinsing her mug in the sink. 'I do. And I wish I could help you but I can't.'

'Fine.' Chelsea reached down to grab her purse, pulling the strap over her shoulder. 'In that case, maybe we shouldn't worry about the contracts. I'll get one of Nick's people to deal with it.'

Her agent spun on her heel. 'What? Chelsea, don't be—'

'No, no, it's fine.' She pretended to smile at her agent. There was a feeling of expansion in her chest, wings spreading, something about to take flight. The sudden understanding that Nancy needed her far more than the reverse and – what was it her agent had said? That was her favourite negotiating position to be in. 'It was silly of me to come here. You're just a children's agent, anyway. You said you can't help me. I'll find someone who can.'

'Oh, for the—' Nancy took a deep breath. 'Okay. What do you want to know?'

Chelsea sat on the stool again, doing her best to conceal her satisfaction. Was this what power tasted like? She had forgotten, or maybe she had never really known, but either way, she found that she liked it. 'After I got the part,' she said. 'Willow Gray, I mean,' and Nancy gestured at her impatiently, as if to say, *What other part would we be talking about?* It was *the* role, the one that had changed all their lives for ever, 'what kind of conversations did you have with Maddie?'

'She was . . .' Nancy was careful with her words. 'She was upset, naturally. Your sister knew the books inside out. She was desperate to play Willow and then . . . Well, she said her tape was perfect. I told her, "You don't have the part until you have the part," but Madeline was adamant. She said it was magic.' *And she was right,* Chelsea thought, as she remembered the video audition. Her sister had been pure magic.

'She was confused,' Nancy continued. 'She wanted feedback and I said I didn't think that was a good idea. We argued about it.' The agent would have been protecting her own relationship with the casting director, Chelsea guessed, and Maddie wouldn't have given a fuck about that. 'I couldn't see the point, but your sister wanted to know where she had gone wrong,' Nancy said. 'Why they had chosen you over her.'

'That's what she said?' That was always how it had felt to Chelsea, that she was competing with Maddie for everything – to be the prettiest, the most successful, for their mother's love and attention – but it had never seemed as if Maddie had felt the same. Her poor sister. She didn't deserve what Chelsea had done to her.

Nancy tilted her head, holding Chelsea's gaze. 'I told her that was ridiculous. Half of Hollywood had auditioned. Everyone wanted to play Willow Gray. It wasn't like it was just the Stone sisters who went out for it. But I guess it's harder to square away when the person who gets the role you desperately want has the same face as you.' Chelsea reared back. She could still hear herself screaming those words, the last night, the last time she saw her sister alive. *Oh, Maddie. I'm sorry. I'm so sorry.*

'And, look, I did my best,' Nancy continued. 'I told her we'd find a different part for her, one that would make her name as an adult actor. I really thought *Mixed Signals* was going to be it. We all did. It had everything – a great director, a good script . . .' She trailed off. 'After the *GQ* interview came out . . . that was that. She blamed me for that too. She claimed I'd pushed her into signing on to *Mixed Signals*, that she had never wanted to do it.'

'Was that true?' Chelsea asked.

'Maybe,' the other woman admitted. 'But only because I wanted to help her. I know you think I'm a megalomaniac but I do care about the kids I represent. I saw Madeline was floundering and that movie seemed a sure-fire hit. It could have made her name as an adult actress if she hadn't . . .' She shook her head. 'This industry, it's tough. You have to be able to roll with the punches, and get back on your feet and –' she clicked her fingers on both hands '– keep it moving. I told Maddie to apologize. I told her to—' Nancy turned away from Chelsea and looked out of the window again.

'What did you tell her?'

There were a few moments of silence before Nancy spoke. 'I wanted her to go to rehab, then do a media blitz saying she had learned her lesson. I told her I couldn't represent her any more if she didn't publicly apologize to the guys at Punch Media.'

'You fired her?'

'I just wanted to shake her out of her complacency.' Nancy still didn't turn, her shoulders squeezing up towards her ears. 'She couldn't live off her *Double Trouble* residuals for ever, not if she was using them to buy drugs.' She sat down opposite Chelsea but she still didn't meet her eye. 'I've lost too many clients to that.'

'Yes.' Chelsea thought of the documentary that had aired two years ago, *Whatever Happened to the Child Star?* She had been contacted by the filmmakers to participate, an easy no, but she had watched it as soon as it had dropped on Hulu. All those familiar faces from her childhood, some from Cedar City, others from waiting rooms, a few co-stars from the straight-to-VHS *Double Trouble* movies she and Maddie had made as kids. Adorable faces turning plump and awkward, all braces and acne, and there was no use for them any more – what was a child star worth without their prettiness? More and more auditions, but never booking anything, thrown on the scrap heap before they were old enough to vote. They began to drink, and they began to smoke and snort and stick needles into veins and then they were dead, and the photos the press used were always from when they were in their prime, when they were still beautiful. How sad, they said. How very, very sad it was. 'And yet you kept signing new kids,' Chelsea said. 'Were we that easy to replace?'

'I know this might be difficult for you to understand, given your current circumstances, but I did have a mortgage to pay,' Nancy said, and Chelsea started. It was so similar to the excuse Milo James had given. Her agent placed her hands on the counter. 'If it wasn't me representing you, it would have been someone else. It's not like movies would have suddenly stopped needing kid actors. It was a job. Just like any other—'

'It was *children*.'

'Yes,' Nancy said, like she was talking to an idiot. 'Children who had parents. Mothers and fathers who were supposed to keep them safe. My job was to get the best deal, that's all. Perhaps Erin is the one you should be talking to right now.'

Chelsea could feel her eyes stinging with tears. She couldn't talk to Erin or, to be more precise, she didn't want to. If she did that, she would drown in her mother's needs, her mother's wants, like she had before. She wouldn't survive it again.

Nancy softened. 'I'm sorry,' she said. 'I'm sorry your mom didn't . . .' She sighed. 'It's funny,' she said. 'I can always tell the kids who'll be okay, and it's the ones whose parents aren't excited by any of it. The ones who insist their kids go to high school and prom and apply for college. The parents who don't uproot their entire families to try to make this crazy dream come true. Because it doesn't for most of them, you know? I've had some amazing kids on my book, talented and cute and hardworking, kids who seemed destined to make it, and it still doesn't work out. If you have parents who are depending on that kid to pay their bills,' Nancy let out a low whistle, 'it's a recipe for disaster.'

'What did you think when you met my mother for the first time?' Chelsea asked.

Her agent's mouth thinned. 'I thought you and Madeline were great. And I really hoped you guys would make it out okay.' She leaned across the counter to grab Chelsea's hands. 'I'm glad you did,' she said. 'But you were always a survivor. You were always the strong one.'

But that had been Maddie, everyone knew that, Chelsea thought, as she followed the older woman to the front door. She looked at the black-and-white photos lining the walls in the hall, the headshots of the kids Nancy had represented over the years. This one had been molested by her stunt double; that girl had been signed by a rap mogul when she was fourteen, then trafficked at his infamous sex parties, passed around his friends, and when she tried to speak out, she was called a gold-digging liar, hounded by the press until she was found dead in her apartment at the age of seventeen. This boy had dated his tutor when he was thirteen and the teacher was twenty-two and everyone said he was 'lucky': what teenage boy wouldn't want that? All the photos, all the ways they had been ruined. *Dead, dead, suicide, drowned in a pool off his head on pills, accidental overdose, rehab, dead.* Two had become superstars, and they were given pride of place at the end of the wall, closest to the door. The girl who had transitioned from movies about teenage vampires to Oscar bait indies, and the actor who had starred in the trilogy about a school for black magic and was now considered the greatest stage performer of his generation. And there she was, Chelsea saw, in a photo taken on Oscars night, tiny and delicate in her silk gown and the compass necklace. The night Maddie had disappeared.

'Such lovely memories,' Nancy said. Her hand was on the small of Chelsea's back, nudging her closer and closer to the door. She leaned in to air-kiss Chelsea once she was on the front porch. 'I'll be in touch about the show,' she said. 'I'll get everything sorted at my end, don't worry.' Nancy smiled at her. 'It's good you're doing it,' she said. 'It will mean so much to the fans.'

She went to close the door but Chelsea put her hand on the wood, holding it open. 'Is everything okay?' Nancy asked, but Chelsea could see the edge to it, the way her agent was trying to hide her irritation.

'Yes,' Chelsea said, and her mind went blank. The problem was she didn't even know what questions she should be asking in the first place, or of whom she should be asking them. Who was the person blackmailing her? And how was she going to find Maddie?

Nancy reached out to touch Chelsea's face. 'You mustn't feel guilty, you know,' she said. 'You did what you had to do. All my best kids were ruthless, underneath it all. You had to be if you wanted to succeed. Madeline was a wonderful actor but you were hungrier. That's more important, in the end.'

'I don't know what you're talking about,' Chelsea said weakly.

Her agent quirked an eyebrow at her. 'Don't you?'

18.

2004

'I know what we should do,' Kelly said, tying her hair in a high ponytail, a mischievous expression on her face. 'We should play Truth or Dare.'

'Girl.' Nya threw a cushion at her. Kelly ducked, laughing. 'How old are you again?'

It was a Friday night in Wilmington and they had the weekend off so the three of them, Chelsea, Kelly and Nya, were thrown on the sofa, in flannel pyjamas and clay facemasks, as they watched an episode of The OC. 'Do you think *Vigilante Queens* will be as big as this?' Kelly had piped up at one point. Chelsea and Nya looked at one another, neither able to answer. There was so much buzz building around the show already that their success seemed both inevitable and impossible. *Your entire lives are about to change*, everyone kept saying, but even for Chelsea, who'd known a certain amount of fame as a child star, this next level of notoriety seemed beyond the realms of imagination.

'Come on, it'll be fun!' Kelly said, sitting up straight. As she smiled, little cracks appeared in the green clay at the side of her mouth. 'Gotta wash this off,' she said, walking over to the sink and running a facecloth under the faucet.

They'd been on set in North Carolina for almost a month but it felt like they'd known each other for much longer. Robbie had insisted the Queens live together for the duration of the shoot – he wanted them to bond, he said. It would give an authenticity to their relationships on the show – so Production had rented an adorable clapboard house for them, right on the beach. Chelsea had only ever lived with her mother and her sister so she was nervous before she arrived. What if Kelly or Nya were messy, leaving dishes piled in the sink and their hair clogging the shower drain? What if they took her stuff without asking, or they played loud music late at night and she couldn't sleep? What if the two of them became best friends and excluded her? She'd never needed to make friends before. She'd always had Maddie to protect her, to stand up for her. She wanted to phone her sister and talk it through but she couldn't. This was Maddie's dream role, the one she'd always wanted, and Chelsea had taken it from her. Asking for her advice would be rubbing salt in the wound.

However, within days of moving in, Chelsea knew she had nothing to worry about. Soon they were borrowing clothes and talking about boys they had crushes on and showing each other photos of their friends and family back home. Some nights they would sit out on the porch, Kelly smoking weed and swapping stories with Chelsea about the perviest crew members they'd encountered on set as kids – 'The boss kept insisting Wardrobe put me in shorter and shorter skirts,' Kelly said, putting a hand on her thigh to demonstrate how high the hemlines were. 'Because I was *soooo sexy*, he said. I was twelve' – while Nya read her book, occasionally chiming in with horror at what the other two had been through and, worse, how jaded they seemed about it all. 'You just get used to it,' Kelly had said, with a shrug.

Kelly flopped back on the couch. She reached for the Perspex bowl of popcorn resting precariously on a striped footstool and grabbed a fistful. She must have eaten at least half of the bowl already. Chelsea had counted out twenty pieces for herself, listing the calories in her head, and put them into a smaller bowl, eating each one slowly. During their costume fitting earlier, the wardrobe mistress had frowned, staring at Kelly's body, pointing out the girl's 'problem areas'. As she was measuring Kelly's bust, she'd said, 'I guess I'm just used to Chelsea. Chelsea is *so* disciplined. She watches her diet, and she goes to the gym every day, which means she can wear anything. It makes my life a hell of a lot easier.' Kelly had flushed, staring at herself in the mirror, and Chelsea, who was maybe twenty feet away for her own fitting, pretended she hadn't heard anything.

'I'll go first,' Kelly said, still chewing popcorn. 'Nya, truth or dare.'

'Are you actually making me do this?' The other girl groaned. At twenty-two, Nya was a little older than the two of them, but she looked seventeen. She had trained at Juilliard, and took her 'craft' very seriously, always searching for her character's motivation in the most surface level of scripts, trying to book in sessions with Robbie to get his help in doing so. She was from Manhattan, and an only child; her father was a surgeon and her mother an English lit professor at NYU, and she was the most elegant person Chelsea had ever met, with her slender limbs, her fine-boned face and feline eyes. 'Fine,' Nya said. 'Truth.'

'Boring,' Kelly said, flicking a piece of popcorn at Nya's face, but she was laughing too. 'Hmm,' she said, pretending to tap her finger against her chin. 'What question shall I ask Ms Nya?'

They were so different, these two. Kelly was one of six daughters raised in a trailer park by their alcoholic mother after their father had been caught for armed robbery, a childhood very far away from Nya's, and yet somehow, here, on set, none of that mattered. They were just girls, just the Queens.

'I've got it!' Kelly said. 'I want to know what's been your

favourite part of the last three weeks and what's been the worst.' She preened. 'I know the best part is meeting me, obviously.'

'Oh, obviously,' Nya replied, taking a second. It was something Chelsea had noticed about her, how Nya never rushed, even if everyone around her wanted her to. 'Well,' Nya said, 'for me, the best part of this experience has been the work. I feel so grateful just to have the opportunity to *act*. Opportunities like this, they're relatively rare for Black actors, especially one straight out of college. I know the scripts aren't exactly Shakespeare—'

'What?' Kelly pretended to be shocked. '*People will die, Frank. That means they'll be dead,*' she quoted one of her character's lines. 'You don't think that's genius?'

'Guys,' Chelsea said, 'it's not his fault. He's a brilliant writer, he's just—'

'We know,' Kelly said. They had talked at length about how hamstrung Robbie was by the author of the book series. She vetoed every creative choice he made, insisting he stick to the novels verbatim, and the scripts were suffering as a result. 'We didn't mean to insult the chairperson of the Robbie Myers Fan Club.'

'Oh, shut up.' Chelsea coloured in embarrassment.

'Leave her alone,' Nya said, rescuing her. 'But seriously, even if the dialogue is a little . . . underwhelming at times –'

'You mean dumb?' Kelly said.

'– I do think the show itself has something,' Nya continued. 'There's an energy to it. And the three of us,' she smiled at Chelsea and Kelly, 'I think we're doing a great job with what we've got. We're elevating the material.'

Chelsea smiled back. She agreed: filming had felt electric so far and she had surprised herself by how well she was doing. Robbie had helped – she had known him since she was a child, and there was a friendship, a familiarity that put her at ease. When she asked him to run lines with her, to give her the instruction that Nya was craving, Robbie always said yes and Chelsea knew how lucky she was. This was her opportunity to claw her way out of Maddie's shadow, to prove she was a viable entity in her own right. She had to succeed.

Nya reached out and grabbed Chelsea's hand with her right, Kelly's with her left, and squeezed hard. 'It's exciting.' The smile on her face faded and she let go as she said, 'And the worst part, obviously, is Geneen.' Geneen was the hair stylist, inherited from a WB network show that used to film on location in Wilmington. She was in her fifties with ass-length black hair and no eyebrows, and she was tiny, maybe five foot tall. She adored Chelsea, winking at her in the mirror as she filled her in on all the local gossip, and she tolerated Kelly, but it was clear from the very first day of shooting that she had an issue with Nya. 'I don't know what I'm supposed to do with . . . this,' the older woman had said, touching Nya's hair with her fingertips, then tried to comb it out.

Nya had stopped her. 'No,' she'd said, jerking her head away from Geneen. 'You can't brush 3B curls. You should know that.' At this, Geneen had welled up and walked out of the makeup room. Nya had been reprimanded later. The show runner said that Geneen felt Nya was hostile and confrontational. Nya was forced to apologize to the older woman, and now she did her own hair before she got to set.

'And then for that blind item to appear on RumorMill.' Nya got up and walked over to the sink, taking two facecloths, and dampening them with hot water. Returning to the couch, she kept one for herself, handing the other to Chelsea. '*What exotic beauty is causing havoc on set in North Carolina with her diva behaviour? Looks like someone thinks she's the Queen Bee when she's only a sidekick!*' Nya quoted the piece in a sing-song voice as she wiped off the facemask. 'Exotic beauty? Like, what the fuck? It's so . . .' She stopped herself, her eyes darting to Kelly first, then Chelsea. 'It's nonsense,' she said instead, carefully.

'I know,' Chelsea said. 'But with people like Geneen, you have to do things their way. She's never gonna change. You learn that when you're on set as a child. You have to keep everyone happy.'

Nya looked at her a little strangely. 'That's not how my parents raised me. I was taught to be polite but clear, which is exactly what I did with that woman. It should have been enough.'

Chelsea wanted to argue – she was only trying to help Nya, after all – but she could tell by the set of the other girl's jaw that it wasn't a good idea. She made comforting noises, then cut her eyes at Kelly, silently pleading with her in jump in. 'Okay,' Kelly said, clapping her hands together. 'Chelsea, you're up, babe. Truth or dare.'

'Truth,' Chelsea said, instantly regretting it. Kelly would probably ask about Maddie: that was what everyone always wanted to know about, what it was like being one of the most famous twins in America. And what could she say? This was the longest she and her sister had gone without seeing each other and Chelsea missed her, although they still texted every day. Maddie was on set too, filming a gross-out comedy called *Mixed Signals* in San Francisco and she sounded miserable – the atmosphere was toxic, she said, and the revised scripts were sexist to the point of being offensive. I'm sorry, Chelsea wanted to say to her. This is all my fault. Maddie should have been here, in Wilmington, with Nya and Kelly. Would they have preferred her to Chelsea? Would Maddie have done a better job?

Her mother phoned too but she never wanted to talk about Maddie or *Mixed Signals*. Erin only ever asked for gossip from set, if Kelly had managed to get her eating under control, or if Robbie was still seeing 'that actress'. After the news broke that he was adapting the *Vigilante Queens* series for screen, Robbie had broken up with the twins' old tutor, Julia, and quickly met Diana Dawson, Hollywood's hottest rom-com queen. In photos, Diana was tiny and yoga-toned, with sun-kissed limbs and honey-streaked hair, but she'd never come to Wilmington as far as Chelsea was aware. Robbie had insisted that the set was just for cast and crew: no stage parents, no agents, no managers, he said. And though Erin had been sure he would make an exception for her – they were practically family, after all – Robbie had remained true to his word. Chelsea would never tell her mother this, but she was secretly relieved. This way, she could be independent. She could stand on her own two feet. She didn't have to deal with people mixing her and Maddie up, the slight hesitation before they addressed her, afraid they would say the wrong name. She loved her sister but she didn't want to be Maddie-and-Chelsea for ever. It was time to just be Chelsea.

'Truth, truth, truth,' Kelly chanted. She lay down on the couch, her feet on Nya's lap. 'What do I want to know about the mysterious Chelsea Stone?'

'I'm not mysterious,' Chelsea protested. 'What?' she said, when Nya and Kelly both threw sceptical glances at her.

'Be for real,' Kelly said, and Chelsea bristled.

'You're private,' Nya said quickly, before Kelly could say anything else. 'And that's fine. It's healthy! You're entitled to privacy. God knows, you haven't been given much of it over the years.'

'Sure, sure,' Kelly said. In three short weeks, their dynamic was established already: Kelly was the troublemaker, Nya the truth-teller, and Chelsea the peace-keeper, as she had always been between her mother and her sister. 'But you have to answer me when it's Truth or Dare. I don't make the rules.' She clicked her fingers. 'I have it!' she cried. 'Who did you lose your virginity to? Was it Nathan Warner?'

Nathan had been their co-star in *Roman Switch*, one of the many straight-to-VHS movies she and Maddie had made for AtomicKids during the off-season. The films were formulaic and clichéd, capers in which the twins travelled to various European cities and high jinks ensued. Nathan had played the handsome son of the American president whom the twins met while on vacation in Italy, a gender reversal of *Roman Holiday*, and while he and Maddie had hooked up multiple times, for some reason, the stories online had said it was Chelsea he had fallen for.

'Of course it wasn't Nathan Warner,' she said. 'He was dating my sister.'

'But I read on RumorMill that—'

'We should know better to believe what we read online, shouldn't we?' Chelsea said.

'Okay, okay,' Kelly held up her hands in mock surrender. 'It wasn't Nathan Warner. He's *so* cute, though.' She pretended to pant, fanning her face, and Chelsea couldn't help but laugh. That was the thing she'd learned about Kelly: it was impossible to stay mad at her. She always had a quip to get her out of trouble. 'But if it wasn't him, then who was it?' Kelly asked.

'I . . .' Chelsea trailed off. She didn't know quite what to say, how to explain this to her new friends. Kelly was always talking about the men she fucked, which ones went down on her, who made her come and who did not, and usually, Chelsea just nodded along, hoping Kelly wouldn't expect her to chime in. She could feel her face getting hot as her cheeks burned.

'Oh,' Nya said, understanding dawning. 'Oh, Chel, don't even think about it. You're still just a baby, you're only eighteen. You have loads of time to meet the right guy.'

What if I don't want to? Every time she imagined herself getting naked in front of a boy, Chelsea had this vision of the CEO of AtomicKids, bursting into the room, and telling her she was a whore and, worse, that she was fired. She rubbed the back of her finger with her thumb. It had been a while since she'd worn her purity ring. Robbie had told her it wasn't the right image for *Vigilante Queens*, but she could almost feel it there, a shiver of metal, a ghost. Kelly flipped over, shuffling down the couch until her face was almost in Chelsea's. 'Listen,' she said, with sincerity in her eyes, 'don't worry about it, babe. When this show comes out,' Kelly shimmied her shoulders, 'every boy in Hollywood is gonna want you.' She blew a kiss at Nya. 'They're going to want all of us. Don't waste your virginity on some loser before then.'

Nya burst out laughing, saying, 'You are the worst, Foster,' and Chelsea made herself laugh too.

'You're right,' she said. 'I just have to wait for the right guy.'

19.

2025

Kelly: YESSSSS BITCH. I knew ud do it!! DA QUEENS R BACK! 👑👑🎉🎉

Chelsea saw the message pop up in the Queens group chat immediately – her phone was constantly in her hand, these days, refreshing her email. She had messaged the blackmailer three hours earlier, telling them she had made a deal and would get the money as soon as the reunion show was filmed, but they'd have to wait until then.

Tick tock, they had replied, before going silent. But now it was Monday and there wasn't any new post on the storage-unit blog, no sign of Maddie's diary, so maybe Chelsea was safe. She was about to reply to Kelly – *Wait, how do you know about that?* – when the door was flung open, and it was Nick, his face flushed red. 'What the fuck, Chel?' he said.

She was with the kids and Elena, the night nanny, in their home theatre, with its large screen, cosy armchairs, and a popcorn machine the housekeeper restocked weekly. Chelsea tried to keep up this ritual with the kids every Monday night, even though it was becoming difficult to find a movie that kept them both entertained. Ivy was engrossed in the latest Pixar release, Chelsea and the night nanny laughing at the occasional joke thrown in for the grown-ups, but Grayson was curled up on his chair and reading a book, just like Maddie used to do. His head snapped up as he watched his father stride into the room. 'Nick,'

Chelsea said in warning – *Not in front of the kids*, she wanted to say. She was always trying to shield them, to ensure they had the kind of childhood that had been denied to her – but Nick either didn't understand what she was saying or chose to ignore it. He stood in front of her, waving his cell phone at her. 'Do you want to tell me what this is about?' he asked. She squinted at the screen, her stomach sinking when she saw what it was.

'Nick, I—' she tried but her husband raised his voice, speaking over her.

'"The much-anticipated *Vigilante Queens* reunion show will debut on March the first,"' he read aloud from his phone. '"Nya Williams and Kelly Foster will return to the iconic teen drama's original soundstage in Wilmington, North Carolina, and in a stunning coup for the network, the reclusive Chelsea Stone is set to come out of retirement to join her former co-stars – as well as the man who made her name, the director, Robbie My—"'

'Okay.' Chelsea got up, turning to smile at Ivy and Grayson, whose eyes were darting between her and their father. 'I think it's time for bed,' she said, and the night nanny jumped to her feet.

'Yes,' Elena said, in her thick accent, a beguiling mix of Polish and Californian after fifteen years in the city. 'I agree. Come on, kids.' She took Ivy by the hand, and nodded at Grayson to follow them. 'Now,' Chelsea heard the nanny say, as she led Ivy out of the door, 'what book would you like me to read to you, little . . .' and her voice faded away.

Grayson hadn't moved, still sitting in the armchair with his feet curled up underneath him. 'Mom,' he said, his face worried, 'are you okay?'

Her heart melted looking at him. Her children, how young they were. She needed to protect them, to make sure that her stories were dead and buried for ever. She had to get that million dollars into her bank account no matter what. 'It's okay, G,' she said. 'Your dad and I just need to talk.'

Whatever Happened to Madeline Stone?

'You need to fight,' Grayson said.

'Yes.' Chelsea decided honesty was the best option. She remembered how annoyed Maddie used to get when their mother or Nancy Taylor withheld information from them, saying they were too young. *If we're old enough to work*, her sister would say, *we're old enough to know why the stunt double got fired.* 'We need to fight,' she said. 'Adults disagree sometimes. That's normal. Healthy, even.' She took Grayson's book out of his hands, and walked to the door, holding it up as an incentive for him to follow her. Grayson looked to his dad first, and when Nick nodded, he walked after his mother. 'But it's also private between your father and I.' She gave him the book. 'Now, go to your room and I'll come in to you later for a chat, okay?' She waited until she heard Grayson's footsteps walking away before turning back to Nick, trying not to show apprehension on her face. 'I meant to tell you,' she said.

'You meant to tell me.' He narrowed his eyes. 'What is that supposed to mean? We talked about the show. We decided that it wasn't the right decision, given my—'

'You decided,' Chelsea said. 'I didn't have much say in the matter, did I?'

'That's not fair, Chel. We're a team. Everything I do is to benefit the team. Can you say the same thing?'

'I am not a member of your team. I'm not an employee. We're married. We're . . . I've tried to explain this to you but it feels like you never listen to me.'

'Oh, I'm sorry,' he said. 'I know your life is *so* difficult. I can't tell you how sorry I feel for you, living in one of the nicest houses in California, spending money – *my* money – like it's fucking going out of fashion on clothes and spa treatments and whatever the fuck you put on your face to make it look like that.' He gestured at her poreless, taut skin as if it offended him. As if he hadn't spent the car journey home from his last college reunion talking about how much younger she looked than all the other wives, how much hotter she was, how he could see all his old friends staring at her. He had sounded so excited about it that Chelsea had smiled, pretending it didn't bother her that her husband still knew so little about her. How did he not understand, after all these years of fame, that Chelsea was tired of people looking at her? She wanted someone to *see* her instead. Like Carter had done, she thought, and started guiltily. She couldn't think about that, about him, not now. It wasn't fair to Nick.

'You don't get to sneak around behind my back,' he continued. 'And make huge decisions like this, decisions that impact *both* of us, without my say. This is so messed up.'

'You want to talk about decisions that impact both of us?' Chelsea knew she was being hypocritical, given what she had done, but she couldn't help herself. 'What about messaging that girl? That impacted me, didn't it?' She held his gaze. 'I didn't see you running that one past me, Nick.'

'Oh, for—' He stopped himself. Nick could be defensive, he had admitted as much in couples' therapy, but he was *trying*, he'd said. He wanted their marriage to work. Did Chelsea? 'I said I was sorry, what more do you want from me?'

Had he actually apologized? She couldn't remember.

'And this isn't about some dumb mistake I made years ago,' he continued. 'This is about you. How could you let me find out from a fucking *Variety* article?'

She sat down, leaning forward so her elbows were on her knees, her head in her hands. 'I know,' she said. Nick was right. That wasn't the way he should have found out the news. He would never have done this to her. She had signed the documents that morning, and as soon as she lifted the pen from the paper, she'd had a sudden rush of fear. What was she doing? What if she sent the million dollars to the blackmailer and they double-crossed her, selling the story elsewhere? No one would care that she had only said yes to Carter because Nick had betrayed her first. If this came out, she would lose everything. She rang Nancy Taylor in a panic and her agent had sworn that she would keep it quiet for a few days, give Chelsea time to tell her husband. She should have known the network would want to make as much of a fuss of this as possible, celebrate Chelsea Stone's triumphant return to television after two decades. 'I'm sorry, Nick.'

'You can't do this, babe.' He took the seat next to her, and she could smell the woody musk of his aftershave. 'It's too much attention on you. On our family.'

'I've signed the contract,' she said weakly.

'Did you get someone from Cohen and Ashforth to look at it?'

'Nick,' she said, exasperated, 'come on. If I'd done that, you would have heard within two minutes. Why else do you think I went with Nancy Taylor, of all people?' Nancy might be a snake but she was Chelsea's snake, not her husband's. 'And I—' She cleared her throat. 'I need to do this.'

'Why?' He looked baffled. 'Why on earth would you need this? You have *everything*.' She knew Nick meant she had money, and what more could she want? To him, that would always be enough. 'I . . .' She scrambled to come up with an excuse that would satisfy him. 'The kids,' she tried. 'They see you working, Nick, and they respect you. Grayson especially. They've watched some old episodes of *Double Trouble* but they're not old enough to watch *Vigilante Queens* yet, or *The List of Second Chances* and –' she could see her husband's mouth twist. He would never want the kids to watch that movie, not with the amount of sex scenes in it, no matter how tastefully shot '– and I want them to see me as a person,' she finished.

'What are you talking about?' he snapped. 'You're *not* a

person to them. You're their mother. You think they're gonna respect you more because you're working? That's not how it'll go down. My mom worked – she never stopped working. She was always complaining about this client or this case, and I'll tell you this for nothing, it did not make my childhood any better realizing that she was a "person". I don't want that for my kids, and you always said you didn't want it either. I don't underst—'

A floorboard creaked, cutting Nick off mid-rant, and he looked towards the door. Hannah was standing there, awkwardly, an iPad in her hands. 'I'm sorry,' the assistant said with a half-grimace. 'Chelsea and I said we'd talk through the week's schedule this evening but I can—'

'There is never any fucking privacy in this fucking house,' Nick spat, ignoring Hannah's flinch of surprise as he stormed past her.

Chelsea dropped her head but she could hear Hannah walk towards her, sinking into the seat next to her. The steady inhale and exhale of the younger woman's breath, then, tentatively, a hand on Chelsea's shoulder. 'Are you all right?' she asked, and Chelsea let out a shuddering breath. Hannah squeezed a little harder. 'It's not right,' her assistant said, 'the way he treats you sometimes. He's not a bad man but—'

'Hannah,' Chelsea warned her. They were friends, she liked to think, but she couldn't allow her to criticize Nick, not in his own home. It wasn't appropriate. And, besides, her assistant was right. Nick wasn't a bad man and he certainly wasn't the only one who had made mistakes.

'Okay.' Hannah held up her hands. 'I just . . . Sometimes I feel like you don't realize how much power you have. You seem scared, almost, and I don't understand why. Nick is rich, yeah, but you're Chelsea fucking Stone. You're an icon. Don't you get that?'

Chelsea attempted a watery smile but she didn't answer.

Whatever Happened to Madeline Stone?

She could feel her phone buzzing in the pocket of her jeans, and when she pulled it out, the screen was flashing: dozens of notifications, text messages, emails and missed calls.

Nya: I just saw the announcement. Phone me when you get this. I love you xo

Mom: Oh. sweetie . . . I am delighted at this news ! You are making the right choice !!

She could see there were messages from Zach and Emily, an email from Nancy Taylor too, the subject line *I have no idea how* . . . but she didn't have the energy to deal with her agent right now. She put her phone on airplane mode and tossed it onto the seat next to her.

'For what it's worth,' Hannah said, 'I think you've made the right choice, doing the show. The online hype . . . it's next level, Chelsea. People are psyched for this. You and Robbie Myers, in the same room again!' Hannah put a hand over her mouth, and she looked so young in that moment, like a pre-teen girl again. 'Everyone is obsessed.'

They had never been together, no matter what anyone thought. That wasn't what he had wanted from her – he and Diana Dawson were still together back then: they weren't married yet but it was clear that was the direction things were going in. Sex, romance, none of it had featured in Chelsea's connection with The Director. It was too strange, too symbiotic for that. Too fucked up, she realized now. Chelsea needed Robbie to draw her performance out of her. He would skin the character, strip it to its skeleton, then help Chelsea step inside its bones. And, for some reason, he needed her too. The words he wrote on the page, they only came alive when he heard them in Chelsea's voice, and because of that, he said she had to take care of herself. She had to eat right, she had to get enough sleep, she couldn't drink, couldn't take drugs. He hated it when Chelsea wore anything that was too revealing, or when she had a crush on a boy. He said it was all a distraction from the most important thing of all: their art, their craft. *Our fortunes are tied now*, he would say. *We fall or we rise together.* Their work would stand the test of time. What could be more meaningful than that?

'Did you watch *Double Trouble* too?' she asked, and Hannah shook her head.

'No,' she said. 'But I've seen clips online and it was cute. It was nice seeing you and your sister together.' She paused. 'Everyone always talks about that interview Madeline did with *GQ* so I googled it recently. She came across as really smart, and funny. Was she funny?' Chelsea nodded, a lump in her throat, and Hannah continued, 'Yeah, she seemed it. It's wild to think that it ruined her career. Nothing she said was even controversial. She was right. That movie was garbage.'

She was ahead of her time. That was what they said about Maddie now. She had seen *Mixed Signals* for what it was but Punch Media had destroyed Madeline Stone for telling the truth about the rot of misogyny in their movies. Did Maddie know that? If she was alive (she is, Chelsea told herself, she is alive, *Maddie is alive*), did she search for her name online, wherever she was? Chelsea should have done more to stand up for her sister but she had felt so powerless back then, so afraid that it would all be taken away from her if she made one mistake. It was terrifyingly plausible: she had seen it happen to Maddie in real time. But things were different now. She couldn't use that as an excuse any more. She was a grown woman, with access to wealth and resources beyond her wildest dreams. Hannah was right – she was Chelsea fucking Stone. It was about time she started acting like it.

20.

EXCLUSIVE INTERVIEW: MADELINE STONE ON MIXED SIGNALS, HOLLYWOOD SEXISM, AND WHY SHE'S DONE PLAYING 'THE GIRL'

MADELINE STONE HAS NEVER BEEN ONE to mince words. One half of the Stone Sisters, who shot to fame as the mischievous twins in the hit AtomicKids sitcom *Double Trouble*, she has had to watch over the last year while her other half, Chelsea Stone, rocketed to stardom as the heroine in the hottest teen drama of the decade, *Vigilante Queens*. Madeline spent months trying to find the perfect vehicle to launch her own adult career but the movie she chose to do that, *Mixed Signals*, produced by Punch Media, has her questioning everything.

When we meet in a quiet café in Silver Lake, Madeline is dressed casually in jeans, an oversized sweater and no makeup, but her eyes are sharp, her voice firm. She's here to talk, and she doesn't hold back.

INTERVIEWER: I saw *Mixed Signals* and I loved it. You must be proud to be part of such a huge hit.

MADELINE STONE: Not really.

INTERVIEWER: What? (Silence) Are you saying you're not a fan of the film?

MADELINE STONE: Where do I even begin? (Laughs) Look, I signed on because I thought it was going to be a clever, modern rom-com.

The script I read had an edge to it, like it was trying to subvert the genre a little. But by the time we got to shooting, it had turned into this . . . I don't know. This *thing*. Just another movie where the guy gets to be complex and flawed, and the woman is there to be hot and kind of exasperated with him.

INTERVIEWER: Wow, okay. That's what you took from it?

MADELINE STONE: Come on! The whole movie is basically, *Oh, no, men are such lovable idiots!* They can't help themselves! And the women roll their eyes and put up with it. I play this character who is supposed to be strong and independent, but all she does is nag the guy. And then, spoiler alert, she falls in love with him anyway, despite him being objectively terrible. And it's played like, oh, isn't this soooo romantic? No, it's not. It's stupid and sexist. I find this shit so depressing.

INTERVIEWER: You read the script. You presumably watched some of Punch Media's oeuvre, right?

MADELINE: And?

INTERVIEWER: I'm just wondering how . . . Are you saying you didn't know what it would be like until you were on set?

MADELINE STONE: The initial script was nothing like that – it was sharp. But it seemed like every day there were revisions thrown at me. I was trying to learn the new lines as quickly as I could, and when I pushed back on certain things, they'd say, 'Lighten up, it's just a joke.' But I'd say, 'Okay, why are the jokes always at the expense of the female characters? Why are all the women portrayed as self-obsessed mean girls? Why does my character have to be the one who has no sense of humour? Why does she have to be the one to "fix" this man child?' And they'd be like, 'Because that's what women do.'

Whatever Happened to Madeline Stone?

INTERVIEWER: Wow.

MADELINE STONE: Yeah. And don't even get me started on the way they shot my scenes. I get, what? A slow-motion hair flip and a close-up shot of my ass as I walk away? Like, great. (She slow-claps) Groundbreaking.

INTERVIEWER: Some people might argue, well, you signed up for it?

MADELINE STONE: Sure. Ultimately it was my decision and I own that. But I'm also allowed to say I regret it because I do. And that's why I'm talking about it now. Otherwise, they'll just keep making movies like this, and actresses will keep getting cast in these awful, one-dimensional roles. And nothing changes.

INTERVIEWER: So, no *Mixed Signals* 2?

MADELINE STONE: (Laughs) Over my dead body.

21.

2005

The industry is still in SHOCK after Madeline Stone's outrageous interview with *GQ* where she TRASHED everyone involved in *Mixed Signals*, the year's most successful R-rated comedy. When asked if she was proud to be a part of it being such a huge hit, the former child star said, 'Not really', telling the magazine the movie was 'stupid and sexist' and that all the female characters were portrayed as 'self-obsessed mean girls'. Punch Media, the crew behind *Mixed Signals*, shot back that Madeline was a nightmare on set, constantly complaining and demanding multiple script rewrites, trying to get her role expanded. 'She knew what this movie was when she signed on,' a source at Punch Media told me. 'And she was desperate to take the role. It's not like Madeline Stone has people knocking down her door with offers. And now that she's a part of the biggest movie of the year, she's talking shit?'

They have a point!! What do you guys reckon? Do you think Madeline is being ungrateful? Comment below xo

'Chelsea?'

She looked up when she heard her name, and it was the publicist standing at the door of the dressing room, the journalist behind her. 'Are you ready?' her publicist asked, and Chelsea smiled her yes, shoving her BlackBerry into her bag. Maddie had emailed her the latest RumorMill blog, the subject line simply *When is this going to end?* but Chelsea couldn't respond to her sister until after the interview. She couldn't afford to fuck up now.

The woman from the teen magazine took a seat next to her, switching on her recorder. 'Chelsea Stone,' she said. 'What a whirlwind the last few months have been for you!'

She was in her late thirties, Chelsea guessed, maybe early forties. It was hard to tell: her skin was flawless, her hair smoothed into a tight ponytail, and she had a small black recorder placed on the table between her and Chelsea, so discreet that you would almost miss it. *Never, ever forget that everything is taped,* she could almost hear the PR remind her. *These people are not your friends.* That same publicist was sitting on the sofa next to Chelsea, pretending to answer emails on her BlackBerry, but they both knew she was listening to every word, ready to pounce in case of emergency. Every publicist in LA was on high alert after what had happened to Madeline Stone.

'Yeah,' Chelsea said brightly. 'It's been, like, crazy.'

She could feel a droplet of sweat beading at the nape of her neck, dripping down her spine. The car had picked her up from the hotel at eight a.m., driven her to the building on the Hudson River. The studio was hot and bustling with people, the photographer's assistant fixing the lights, the interns unpacking the racks of clothing, Craft Services setting up their stalls. Since Chelsea had flown in from LA especially for the shoot, the magazine suggested doing the interview on set. It would take just forty-five minutes, they said, it would be so much easier. Chelsea hadn't been able to sleep the night before – 'The time difference,' she had told the makeup artist when she'd hopped into the chair that morning, grimacing at the dark circles under her eyes, although the truth was that she had been awake until three a.m. trying to talk Maddie off the ledge, as she had done every day this week. Their agent wanted Maddie to apologize publicly, to say she had been misquoted, or that she was suffering from 'exhaustion', something, anything, to make this go away, but Maddie refused. 'I was just being honest,' her sister had kept saying. 'Why should I apologize?'

That was when things would take a strange turn, and Maddie would become paranoid, talking about conspiracy theories, someone trying to destroy her, someone who wanted to see her career finished. Chelsea would tell her that she needed to be calm, that was ludicrous, no one would do that to Maddie. *Just apologize,* she said to her sister. *Just say you're sorry and then—* Then be a good girl. Do as they tell you. Smile and say how grateful you are for every opportunity they give you. It's easy, when you know how. 'It was just a stupid interview and now it's everywhere,' Maddie would continue, as if Chelsea hadn't spoken. 'It doesn't make any sense. They're saying I'll never get another job, that—' Chelsea had said that wasn't true, and Maddie had said quietly, 'Then why does it feel like it is?' There was silence then, the sound of their breathing, ever so slightly out of sync. 'All I wanted was to act,' Maddie had said finally. 'This is all I know how to do.'

But Chelsea had to put it out of her mind now. She had to appear peppy and friendly so that this woman would tell her readers Chelsea Stone was an utter sweetheart. *It's important the fans think you're the sort of girl they could be friends with,* Nancy Taylor had told her. *They need to believe you're just like Willow Gray.*

'It's been three months since *Vigilante Queens* aired,' the interviewer continued. 'And it's safe to say that your life will never be the same again.' She looked down at her notes, reading aloud. '"The pilot episode attracted a record nine point seven eight million viewers, and those numbers have only increased, week on week, with the season finale attracting thirteen point four million viewers, second only to *American Idol*. It was the highest rated new drama of 2005 among adults aged eighteen to thirty-four, and averaged ten million viewers an episode.'" The woman glanced up at her. 'Those are staggering numbers. And you're still only nineteen! It's a lot to process at your age. How do you think the sudden fame has changed you?'

The publicist coughed gently, and Chelsea felt like telling her to calm down, she wasn't an amateur. She didn't need to be reminded that the magazine's demographic would be unhappy to think that their darling Willow Gray had been affected by the show's success in any way. Which was ridiculous: no one could experience fame on this level and remain unchanged but Chelsea had to pretend otherwise. 'Oh, it hasn't,' she said. 'I mean, of course I feel so grateful to have been given this opportunity. I know how lucky I am that Robbie Myers took a chance on me. I count my blessings every day.' She tucked her hair behind her ears, bashfully, like she'd practised. 'But I try not to read any of that stuff. I just loved the books so much. We both did. Our main aim was to make sure we did the story justice and the fans are happy, you know?' The interviewer didn't look convinced, so Chelsea kept going. 'And,' she said, 'I'm super lucky to have my family to keep me grounded, and the other girls on set too. We're like sisters, at this stage. I mean,' she said, warming to her topic, 'that's the message of the show, isn't it? *Vigilante Queens* is all about sisterhood and looking out for each other. Kelly, Nya and me have that in real life too.'

'Speaking of sisterhood,' the interviewer said, and Chelsea wanted to kick herself for how stupid she was: she had handed this question to her on a fucking platter. 'There's been a lot in the media about your own sister after her recent rather, uh, contentious interview with *GQ*. I know many of our readers were big fans of the Stone Twins, and they'd want to know if Madeline is—'

'We're not answering questions about Madeline,' the publicist barked. 'I told you that on the phone yesterday.'

There was a moment of hesitation. Then the woman nodded. 'Sure,' she said. 'Got it.'

When the interview was finished, Chelsea posed for a photo with her, then scribbled an autograph – 'For my niece,' the journalist said. 'She's a huge fan of the show.' She laughed. 'But who isn't?' – before Chelsea loaded a paper plate with a slice of frittata and a handful of berries at Craft Services and headed back to the makeup chair for a quick top-up.

'Darling!' Hands on her shoulders, squeezing tightly. Chelsea looked up to see Blake Logan making eye contact with her in the mirror. Blake was the most famous stylist in Hollywood, the only famous stylist, really, given she was the one who had a reality show on E!, which followed Blake and her partner, an equally beautiful woman called Billie, their two yappy Chihuahuas, Princess and Pickles, and their long-suffering assistant, Wyatt. Every actress in town was desperate to work with Blake Logan but she worked only with people whose style she could 'elevate', which, as far as Chelsea could tell, was to dress all her girls in identical outfits to her own, caftan dresses and strappy sandals and oversized sunglasses. Blake was a former model, the tallest woman Chelsea had ever met, around six foot one, and she was thin to the point of emaciation. She'd never seen the stylist eat; Blake seemed to subsist on Diet Coke and cigarettes. 'Doll, you look stunning!' Blake said. She glanced at Chelsea's breakfast plate, and her lip curled for half a second, so quickly Chelsea thought she might have imagined it. She leaned down to whisper in Chelsea's ear. 'And I heard about *Saturday Night Live*! That is *so* exciting.'

'I know.' Chelsea hadn't been able to believe it when Nancy

Whatever Happened to Madeline Stone?

Taylor had phoned her with the good news. *SNL* wants you to host, her agent said, waiting until Chelsea had stopped screaming before filling in the rest of the details. It would be December, the final show before the holidays, and Shakira would be the musical guest. Just you, Nancy confirmed. No mention of Maddie. None of the other *Vigilante Queens* either. Just Chelsea Stone.

'It's a big deal,' Blake said. 'Major. We're gonna have to plan your outfits, like, super carefully.'

'But won't *SNL* have their own wardrobe? The costumes and stuff, I mean.'

'Not for the monologue,' Blake said. 'And there'll be photos of you coming and going to the studio all week. We need to make sure you look perfect.' The stylist steered her towards the racks. There were two interns, both white and around the same age as Chelsea. They were dressed in skinny jeans and cheap ballet flats, and were hard at work, one steaming a cobalt blue gown, the other photographing the first look and scribbling down the credit details in a notebook. 'Okay,' Blake said, flicking through the hangers with ruthless precision. 'Let's try this Dolce dress.' It was strapless, red lace with a rosette on the belt, and as soon as Chelsea tried to pull it on over her head, she knew it wasn't going to fit. 'I . . .' She stopped, glancing at the two interns, then at Blake, wondering what they should do. 'It doesn't—'

'Give us a minute, girls,' Blake said to the interns. 'Allison, can you phone Giulia at Fendi? I want that cream scalloped dress, the sleeveless one, and I don't see it. Get it couriered here ASAP.' As the two girls scurried off, Blake led Chelsea to a makeshift dressing room behind the racks, and yanked the dress down. They got it over her hips but there was no way it was going to zip up. 'It'll be fine,' Blake reassured her. 'We'll shoot it from the front, no one will know.'

I'll know. Her ass was hanging out and she already felt uncomfortable with the photographer, a hipster with seventies-style glasses and a porn-star moustache. He'd leered at her when she walked in, saying he'd been a big fan of *Double Trouble*, that he'd always had a thing for twins, were she and her sister still . . . He'd paused there, cutting his eyes to one of his assistants, who stifled a laugh. 'Are you still close?' he'd finished, smirking.

Chelsea had laughed too, hating herself. Maddie wouldn't have laughed: she would have told him to fuck off, but then again, that attitude was what had led to the *GQ* interview, and the deluge of negative publicity her sister was dealing with right now. Chelsea could handle a little teasing. She had to, if she wanted to succeed.

'Is there anything else I can wear?' she asked, but Blake shook her head.

'I'm sorry, doll,' she said. 'But the magazine has to answer to advertisers and they want their latest collection on the cover. That means sample size, I'm afraid.'

'Right,' Chelsea said. 'I'm sorry.' Tears pricked her eyes and she half turned away, embarrassed.

'Oh, sweetie.' The stylist gingerly patted her on the back. 'Please don't cry. You are gorgeous, look at that face! But, I'm not going to lie to you, it does make things easier when the girls can fit sample. Luckily,' she took a step back, checking around her to make sure no one could overhear, 'I can probably help you out. With,' she gestured at Chelsea's body with a limp wave, 'that.'

'What do you mean?' Chelsea wrapped her arms around her waist. She'd always been slim – her mother would not have allowed anything else from her or from Maddie – and she had never received any negative feedback on her body before. If anything, Wardrobe was always telling her how amazing she looked, how perfect she was, using her as a yardstick for Nya and Kelly to compare themselves to. 'I'm a size four.'

'Which is fabulous, of course. I'm not implying it's not. You're so . . . healthy!' Blake said. 'But sample size is a zero, two at most. Look,' she said conspiratorially, 'you're not the only girl I work with who's had this problem. Look at Jamie and Kayla.' Two of Blake's other clients, the stars of a hit WB drama about rival cheerleaders who became stepsisters and decided to work together to split up their mom and dad in a reverse *Parent Trap*. Chelsea had seen photos of them recently on RumorMill, walking out of a Starbucks together, holding matching Frappuccinos. 'PRO ANA', Milo James had scrawled above the pic in hot pink letters, and they *had* lost a considerable amount of weight, their clavicles exposed in loose maxi dresses, their arms the same width at the wrist as they were at the shoulders. 'They look major, don't they?' Blake said. 'And, more importantly, they're *everywhere* right now.' This was true. Jamie and Kayla were on the cover of all the gossip magazines, headlines screaming that they were anorexic, they were on drugs, they were a bad influence on the teenagers of America. Chelsea hesitated, just for a second, and the stylist pulled back. 'Don't worry about it,' she said. 'I just thought it might be cool for *SNL* to dress you in the latest collections but we can find some cute options from like, Alice + Olivia.' She returned to flicking through the rails. 'It's a pity,' she said. 'Because I had a call from Karl and he—'

'Karl? As in *Karl*—'

'Yeah,' Blake replied. 'He's always looking for new girls to invite to the shows, and if he likes you, he might make you an ambassador. Maybe even . . .' she paused for emphasis '. . . a face for one of the campaigns. But he has to like you, and Karl, well . . . Let's just say he's really into Jamie and Kayla's look right now.'

Chelsea's cell rang and she held a finger up at her stylist in apology: she would have to take it if it was her sister – Maddie was way too fragile to be put to voicemail right now – but it was only Kelly. She put it on silent, making a mental note to call her co-star back as soon as the shoot was over. She hadn't spoken to her or Nya in a couple of weeks. She had been so busy with promo and all the events she was being invited to and the dozens of scripts her agent was sending her to read, not to mention trying to keep Maddie sane in the middle of the shitshow her sister found herself in. Things would calm down when they returned to Wilmington for season two, she promised herself.

'Sorry,' she said to the stylist, tucking the cell into her purse. 'So, what are you saying? I should go on a diet?' Chelsea was constantly hungry as it was. She wasn't sure how much less she could possibly eat. She wasn't like Maddie, able to eat all the candy and ice-cream and fries she wanted, and never gain a pound. Chelsea had to work hard to maintain her figure.

'Not necessarily,' Blake dropped her voice so Chelsea leaned in closer to hear her. 'There are these pills you can take. They were initially designed for, like, horses or something but in some countries you can use them for asthma.'

'Some countries?' Chelsea repeated. 'But not the US?'

Blake waved that away. 'Don't worry. Bodybuilders take them before competitions – it shreds body fat. And fast. *SNL* is in six weeks, right?'

'Yeah.'

'Okay, perfect. I'll get you some today and we—'

'Do you use it?' Chelsea interrupted.

The stylist gave a tinkling laugh. 'Absolutely not, darling,' she replied. 'I'm blessed with good genes. Now, my girls who are on it tell me there can be a *tiny* bit of jitteriness and I know Jamie said her heart was racing at first but nothing, like, unmanageable. It's *so* worth it.' Blake reached out and grabbed both her hands. 'But you mustn't do it if you don't feel it's right,' she said. 'You know I think you look amazing. Your curves are to die for! But the fashion industry . . .' Blake turned to the racks of clothing and grabbed a mini-skirt so small, it looked like something she and Maddie would have worn during the first season of *Double Trouble*. 'It's tough. I just want to make sure that you have the best chance you can at success.'

But wasn't Chelsea successful already? She was the star of the biggest show on network television; she was in every magazine; she could barely leave the house without being mobbed by fans or paparazzi, calling her name. She was about to remind the stylist of this when, suddenly, Chelsea remembered *those* photos, the ones taken during the summer. She had been on the beach, leaning over to grab sunblock from her canvas bag, and she hadn't realized a photographer was hiding behind the lifeguard's station. The images were everywhere the next day, red circles drawn around the small rolls of fat on Chelsea's tummy. RumorMill had posted them too, captioned 'BEACHED WHALE?????' and the comments had been equally brutal. *Ewwww, who let Shamu out?* and *Maybe she's pregnant??* and *I don't know why she got the part of Willow. Madeline would have been sooooooo much better.*

That was the comment that had needled Chelsea, the one that came to her when she was just about to fall asleep, jolting her awake. She was aware her sister would have made a better Willow Gray – she had seen both audition tapes. She just didn't want anyone else thinking the same thing.

Chelsea knew it was just a bad angle, but that hadn't stopped the shame burning through her as she wondered who had seen the photos – her old friends from Cedar City, the cute guy she'd been flirting with at the gym? Or, worse, the executive producer of the movie she was reading for? Would those photos hurt her chances of getting the role, she asked her agent, and Nancy Taylor's silence didn't do much to assuage Chelsea's fears. Hollywood liked its girls small and well behaved. She'd been told that since she was a child.

'Okay,' she said. 'I'll do it.'

'Are you sure?' Blake said. 'I don't want you to feel under any pressure, doll. This has to be your decision.'

'No, I want to do it.'

The stylist walked behind the rack to where her personal bags were, unzipping a secret compartment in the large suitcase, and she pulled out a small cardboard box. She popped a pill out of the foil packet and gave it to Chelsea, handing her a Diet Coke to wash it down. 'Start with twenty micrograms a day,' Blake said, slipping the rest of the pills into Chelsea's purse. 'And we can adjust it afterwards. Oh, this is going to be so much fun.' She clapped her hands together. 'I'll compile a mood board of all the looks I wanna pull for *SNL*. We'll have so many options now!' She walked away, calling for one of the interns, and Chelsea was left alone.

She stood in front of the full-length mirror, turning around to where the dress was gaping open. She kept staring at the mirror as everyone whizzed around her, *busy busy busy*, and she had this overwhelming urge to talk to her twin. Maddie had always been so definite with her opinions, so clear on what she would or would not do, unlike Chelsea, who only ever wanted to make everyone else happy. But she couldn't text her sister about this, not with everything Maddie was going through right now. No. Chelsea had to figure this out on her own. She would be fine. Everything was fine.

22.

2025

'Where's Poppy?' Ivy asked, when her mother got into the driver's seat of the SUV. It was Tuesday, the morning after she and Nick had argued about the *Variety* article, and nothing had gone up on the blog the day before. What about Monday Madd-ness? a couple of fans said online, tagging @MaddieStorageUnit, but there was no reply. The noise around Chelsea's decision to take part in the reunion show was so oversized it was drowning everything else out. Now all she had to do was hope that the blackmailer would keep their side of the bargain until Chelsea could pay them. 'Don't worry,' Nancy Taylor had said when she asked about the money, 'it will land in your account the day after the show', as if Chelsea could do anything but worry right now.

'Poppy is running late today but she'll pick you up later, okay, honey?' Chelsea said, as she clicked her seatbelt together, adjusting the seat. 'I thought it might be nice if I did the drop-off.' Chelsea waited for one of the kids to say yes, it was nice, how lovely of their mother to drive them to school instead of the day nanny, but Ivy just looked at her tremulously, while Grayson stared out of the window. She had gone to his room after the altercation with Nick the night before, tried to reassure her son that everything would be okay, but he had been quiet, taking refuge in his books, the same way Maddie had always done. Chelsea wanted to stop the car and reach out, take her son's head between her hands and stare at him, let her eyes roam all over his face to find some trace of her twin. But maybe Chelsea was so desperate to remember her sister she would find her anywhere she could. When one of the kids asked for pancakes Chelsea would think about breakfasts on the set of *Double Trouble*, the days Erin wasn't there to police what they ate, and the twins would order chocolate-chip pancakes from Craft Services, so many they were almost sick. Or the days when a big news story would break – a missing submarine, a doctored photo of the royal family – and Chelsea would have the urge to phone her sister and she would remember, all over again, that she couldn't phone Maddie because she was dead.

But now . . . Chelsea saw the abortion record in her mind's eye, seared into her consciousness, and she zoomed in on the date again. 2009. Paid for in cash. She didn't care what Kelly had said about a clerical error, she had a deep knowing that it had been her sister, still alive. *Maddie is alive.* All Chelsea had to do was find her.

She pulled out of the drive, and as they crawled along in the morning traffic, her thoughts turned to Nick. He preferred Grayson and Ivy to be driven to school separately: he said it was too much of a security risk them being in the one car. But then she thought about the reunion show, the million dollars for the blackmailer, her attempts to track down her sister, long presumed dead, and she almost laughed. She was doing a lot of things that her husband didn't like these days.

'When will Dad be home from his trip?' Grayson piped up, as if he had read her mind. Chelsea tried to remember the official line they had given the kids. Last night, she had followed him upstairs to their bedroom, and watched as he had rung the airfield, told the person at the other end of the line to have the jet ready: he would be there in half an hour. 'I'm gonna go to Maui,' he'd said. Nick had bought a hundred-acre estate there about ten years ago – it was where he had built his luxury underground bunker, in preparation for Doomsday – but he rarely used it, preferring the climate at the ranch in Montana. 'I need to clear my head,' he'd said. 'I'll be back when I'm ready to talk.' For all his faults, Nick had never given her the silent treatment before and it was unnerving.

'Soon!' Chelsea's voice was bright as she pulled up to Ivy and Grayson's school. 'Now, out you get. Have a good day, you two.' The children hopped out of the SUV, Ivy the only one to wave back at her. 'Sergei,' she said, looking at the security guard, his thin, dark face inscrutable, 'I'm gonna go see my mother.'

She could feel her palms beginning to sweat the closer she got to Calabasas, the same way they always did when she knew she needed a serious conversation with her mother. She had been avoiding this for too long, hoping she could figure things out without involving Erin, but it was time for her to show some courage. What would Maddie do? she found herself thinking, but then she stopped, and asked instead, *What would Maddie want me to do?* That distinction felt important now. She was a grown woman: she needed to be strong. She owed her sister that much.

Chelsea drove into the gated community, and asked the guard to either stay in the car, or in front of the door if need be. 'I want to be alone with my mom,' she said, and he nodded. She checked her reflection in the mirror, wishing she had brought some makeup with her, even a lipstick: Erin would invariably comment on how 'washed-out' she looked. Well, she thought, this was just her face. Her mother would have to deal with it.

'Darling!' Erin's hair was perfectly blow-dried, her makeup done, and she was wearing cropped white trousers with an off-the-shoulder cashmere sweater in a buttery beige. Did she ever take a day off and wear sweats? 'Oh, hello.' She kept the front door half closed, and her smile was tight. 'I wasn't expecting you.'

'I just thought I'd drop by.' Chelsea raised an eyebrow. Now that she was here, she realized that, besides the text after the news about Chelsea joining the reunion show, she hadn't heard from Erin in weeks. Usually her mother was blowing up Chelsea's phone on a daily basis, asking if she should buy these boots or that shirt, did Chelsea think she needed a deep plane facelift, if Chelsea had seen the photos in the *Daily Mail* online of a former co-star, *He looks so old these days*. 'Is that okay?'

'Well, I have company arriving in—' Erin stopped when she saw the expression on Chelsea's face. 'Of course it's okay.' Erin stepped back reluctantly. She took her phone out of her pocket, tapping at the screen, the whoosh sound of a text sent. 'Come in.' She looked Chelsea up and down. 'Have you lost weight?'

'I don't think so,' Chelsea said, as she followed Erin into the kitchen.

'You have.' Her mother opened the fridge door and grabbed a bottle of Pellegrino. She filled two glasses with ice from the dispenser, and poured in the water, handing one to Chelsea. 'And what perfect timing, with the show coming up! You know the camera adds ten pounds and you—'

'I don't want to talk about the show,' she said tersely, and her mother's face fell. 'Okay,' Erin said. 'I didn't mean to upset you.'

She watched as Erin went back to the fridge to grab a lemon, cutting it into slices on a wooden chopping board, one from her ill-fated lifestyle brand, Stone & Sage. Their mother had never quite managed to parlay a career out of the twins' success, as much as she had tried. Her chat show, *Stone Speaks*, was a disaster straight out of the gate. Erin's blonde prettiness was rendered bland in front of the camera, and she had a tendency to monologue at guests, speaking over them to tell an anecdote of her own. Poor ratings and abysmal reviews ensued, and the show was cancelled after five episodes.

Erin had been determined to put on a brave face so she hit the town, going out with Maddie and her socialite friends, and was routinely mocked by RumorMill for acting in a way unbecoming for a forty-year-old woman. Milo James would post photos of Erin and Maddie falling out of clubs together, arm in arm in matching mini-skirts and tank tops. He'd draw white lines coming out of their noses, the words COKE WHORES scribbled across the top. It had been a mess, and Chelsea and The Director had had to strategize carefully to ensure that it wouldn't impact her reputation. He and her stylist decided that Chelsea needed to invest in an exclusively white and cream wardrobe to suggest innocence, and he persuaded Chelsea not to take a big role she'd been offered, one that would have paid her millions of dollars, because there was nudity involved. There were sex scenes in his films too, of course, but that was tasteful, that was *art*, Robbie said. She couldn't be guaranteed that another director would take the same approach.

'Do you want a slice of lemon?' Erin asked, as she dropped one into her own glass. 'Are you allowed citrus fruits, these days? I can never keep track. I read something about the acid being bad for your teeth. And with the reunion show coming up, you have to be careful. It's a real pity you didn't agree to do it earlier. You could have stepped up your sessions with your aesthetician, although I know you keep—'

'I said, I don't want to talk about the show,' Chelsea interrupted. 'I have to ask you about something.'

Her mother went very still, and she looked pale underneath her makeup. 'What . . .' she swallowed '. . . what do you have to talk to me about?'

'I want to talk about Maddie.'

Her mother sat down heavily, and it was strange, she almost looked relieved. 'What is there to talk about?' she said. 'There was nothing new on the blog yesterday. All anyone wants to talk about is the reunion show. It's so exciting. I—'

'I don't care about that.' Chelsea cut her off. 'We found the storage unit, me and Kelly. We went down there, Mom. We found all of Maddie's –' she broke off, her voice thick with grief '– all her things,' she choked out. 'Her clothes and her CDs and her books and her diaries and her couch and her—'

'Chelsea.' Erin stared at the countertop. 'I can't do this. You have children of your own now. You have to understand that it's too much for me to talk about it. About her. It's too painful.'

'I need to talk about her.' Her mother had built a wall of silence around herself that night, using her grief as a way of deflecting any criticism that she might have failed Maddie, failed both of them, and it wasn't fair. 'We found medical records, Mom. Maddie, she—' Chelsea faltered, for some reason she didn't want to tell her mother what the procedure had been. 'The date on the paperwork was for February 2009.' She looked Erin straight in the eye, wanting to make sure her mother understood what she was saying. '2009,' she repeated. 'A year after—'

'No,' Erin whimpered. 'Stop it. I can't . . . Your sister is dead.'

'She might not be, Mom. Don't you get that? Maddie used my name but the date, it was after she disappeared, after—'

'Stop it!' her mother screamed, and her voice was like a howl, so loud that Chelsea was afraid the neighbours would hear and call the cops. 'Stop, stop. STOP.' Erin began to cry, tears rolling down her cheeks. 'You have no idea,' she said, 'no idea what it's like to lose a child. It took me so long to come to terms with this, to accept that Maddie was dead, and now you come in here and you try . . . And with nothing to show for it except an old piece of paper with the wrong date on it? Chelsea, you can't do this to me, you can't, you can't, you . . .'

Chelsea recoiled in shock, her stomach dropping, and, for a second, she wanted to scream back at her mother, see how she liked it. Why did Erin get to dictate the terms of Chelsea's grief, to mould the shape it was allowed to take? But instead she did what she always did when faced with Erin's resistance. She gave up. 'I'm sorry,' she said. 'I didn't mean to upset you.'

She wondered what it would be like to have a mother who would take care of her rather than expecting it to be the other way around. A mother to whom she could tell the truth – about Carter, and the mysterious Christopher, *Who was Christopher?*, and the person attempting to extort a million dollars from her, and how badly Chelsea needed to get that money so she could make it all go away. All her secrets, all of her dirty little deeds. What would Erin think if she knew what Chelsea had done?

'Well, you did.' Erin reached for her handbag, rummaging through it for tissues. She blew her nose loudly. 'You have no idea how hard things have been for me, Chelsea. I had dreams too, you know. Things could have been so different, if my mother had had even an *ounce* of ambition for me. People used to literally stop her in the street when I was a child, and tell her I was so beautiful, I should be a model, or an actress.' Erin's voice became bitter. 'If she had been brave enough to do what I did for you girls, who knows what I could have achieved?'

Erin's parents had been poor. Her father was a farmhand, her mother stayed at home, babysitting neighbours' kids for a few dollars a day so she would have some money of her own. Not that there was ever enough: her father drank too much and when he drank, he got mean. They fought a lot, and after her father left the house, screaming and shouting, her mother would take out her anger on the kids, but especially Erin. She had ideas above her station, that was what her mother said, and Erin agreed, she *did* have ambitions these people would never understand. She wanted to get out of their small town. She wanted to move to LA. She wanted to be rich because, even as a teenager, she knew that money wasn't just an escape route, it meant safety too. If you had money, you couldn't get trapped in a marriage with a man who slapped you after too much whiskey. Erin had plotted and planned and saved every dollar she earned working in that shitty bar, until the night she met Ed Stone. Cute, she had thought, but not husband material. That didn't mean she couldn't have some fun though . . . Ten weeks later, when she couldn't remember the last time she'd had her period, Erin learned that fun was not for girls like her.

'So,' Erin continued, wrapping her fingers around her glass of water tightly, 'when the psychic told me that you girls were destined to be famous, it felt like Fate. Like a do-over.'

'We were children,' Chelsea said quietly. She had never believed in the prophecy, and neither had her sister, yet somehow it had come true. Chelsea had been the most famous woman of her generation, and Maddie had disappeared, presumed dead, well before her thirtieth birthday. Would Chelsea have been so determined to secure the role of Willow Gray if she'd known what would become of her sister? She still didn't know and that frightened her, the depths of her own hunger. 'We weren't props for you to live out your own dreams, Mom.'

'Give me a break.' Her mother brushed her off. 'You loved it. You both did. From the moment I took you to that first pageant, I've never seen kids hamming for the camera like that. And then, when you started going to auditions, you said it was your dream to become a movie star. You begged me to move to LA to help with your career.'

'I don't remember that.' And even if it was true, hadn't it been Erin's job to say no? To say that the twins had to wait until they'd finished school, when they'd had a chance to have a proper childhood? What did a kid know about such things?

'It was Maddie,' Erin said quickly. 'She was always the more natural performer.'

Chelsea stayed still, wondering how that had the power to hurt her, even after all this time.

'But you loved it too, in your own way. You always said you felt happiest on set.'

She couldn't imagine ever saying such a thing. She had found the work exhausting and overwhelming, and every day she felt like she was being compared to her twin sister and found lacking. That the constant monitoring of her diet had left her so underweight that she hadn't started her period until she was fifteen. She was only thirteen when Jared had given her the photo of himself, naked, his dick in hand, with a note saying *Thinking of you*. Erin had torn it up and said to forget about it, there was no point in making a fuss. Jared was the show runner's nephew, they were never going to take Chelsea's side. It was only a joke. Chelsea could take a joke, couldn't she? And so she had learned to dismiss such things, to make an amusing anecdote out of them. It was only as an adult, when she'd recounted the experiences in therapy and she had seen Dr Ursula's horrified reaction, that Chelsea had realized it wasn't that funny after all.

'It's strange,' Erin said. 'I really did think it would be Maddie who'd be the famous one. I never would have imagined . . .' She trailed off. All the things that had happened to Madeline. The interview, the reaction afterwards. Her sister's attempts to claw back a career until it became clear the industry would not allow such a thing, that Madeline Stone's head would be placed on a spike as a warning to all the other young actresses out there. The drinking that followed, the drugs, the upskirt photos taken by paparazzi lying on the kerb as she stumbled into a taxi. All the stories on RumorMill, which Chelsea now knew had been paid for, but by whom? Who had been so determined to ruin her sister? And if Maddie was still alive – she had to be, *she had to be* – where was she now? Her mother stood up, and put her hands on Chelsea's face, tracing her fingertips up into her hairline. 'I miss your scar,' she said. 'It was the only way I could tell you girls apart.'

'Robbie said I needed to get it removed. He said that scars have memories, and as long as I had this one, I would never move on from Chelsea.' She had thought it was a reasonable thing for him to say at the time but now it struck her as odd. What had he meant by that?

'I suppose he wanted you to look perfect for the camera.' Her mother began to stroke her hair. 'My beautiful girls.' She half laughed. 'I wonder where that fortune teller is now,' she said. 'Madame Destiny.'

Chelsea jolted. Was that the psychic's name? Her mother had never mentioned it before, always saying she couldn't remember.

'I often wondered if she recognized you,' Erin continued. 'If she knew that you were the girl she said would be the most famous woman of her generation. Incredible, really.'

'She also said one twin would die before her thirtieth birthday,' Chelsea muttered, under her breath. Erin always ignored that part of the prophecy. 'Did you ever think about that?'

'No,' her mother said simply. 'I don't think it does any good to dwell on the past. You should know that by now, Chelsea.'

23.

2006

When had The Director become the most important person in Chelsea's life? Was it when she had first stepped onto the *Vigilante Queens* set? Watching Robbie in full control, his eyes narrowed as he stared at the monitor, moving the actors around like chess pieces, bending them to his will. She had always liked him but their relationship had shifted since their *Double Trouble* days, slowly in the beginning, then all at once. The first night she'd arrived in Wilmington, he had taken her for burgers and milkshakes in the small, slightly run-down diner, where no one had looked twice at her – he'd said that would change once the show hit the airwaves, everything would change then. He told her that they were a team now. This was a big break for both of them, their chance to show the industry what they were truly capable of. 'We have to prove ourselves,' he'd said, his eye contact so intense that Chelsea had found herself blushing. 'We have to make this show a success, no matter what happens. It's you and me, kid.'

After that, it didn't matter how tired Chelsea was, or how sick she was of repeating the same lines over and over again: if Robbie wanted another take, if he wanted sixty more takes, she smiled and said, *Yes, of course*, because they were a team. He even asked for her advice – what did she think of the script? Was this how kids spoke? Was it authentic? – and she helped him shape the words as much as they could without freaking out the author. He trusted her, and she couldn't let him down.

He had been the first person she'd phoned to tell about getting *SNL* and he was delighted, telling her she deserved it. 'I can't do it without you,' she said. 'Will you help me?' Thankfully, he said yes, and she told Nancy Taylor to let *SNL* know that they were a package deal, she and Robbie, and he would be coming to all the meetings with her. They booked adjoining rooms in the same hotel that week, meeting one another for breakfast before walking to the Rockefeller Center together. He sat next to Chelsea as the writing team pitched sketches, saying which ones he thought would play to Chelsea's strengths, immediately vetoing any he thought were too sexy, or anything even remotely critical of *Vigilante Queens*. He asked Blake Logan to send him photos of all the outfits she was pulling for Chelsea, telling the stylist Chelsea would look best in a simple silhouette, something timeless, rather than all these low-rise jeans she kept sending over. He instructed the costume designers to raise necklines and make skirt lengths more modest. He cut in if he thought any of the cast members were monopolizing Chelsea's time – they could afford to goof around, he reminded her, they were used to live television, but she was not. She had to focus if she wanted to do her best. They rehearsed and rehearsed and rehearsed, Robbie making her go over the lines until her intonation was exactly right. It would be worth it, he said, when she was the best debut host *Saturday Night Live* had ever seen.

There were a few rumours rumbling that not everyone was happy with his involvement. Nancy Taylor had asked if his presence on set was strictly necessary. She'd had a phone call from Lorne Michaels, saying the writers were annoyed when Robbie had reworked a sketch without their permission. A story had run in *Page Six* saying the cast members thought Chelsea was too reliant on The Director, she couldn't make any creative decision without his say-so, but most of the blogs had stayed quiet, even RumorMill had nothing to say.

On the night of the show, Chelsea did her best to stay in the moment – she was hosting *SNL*, this was a once-in-a-lifetime opportunity, something she would tell her grandkids about when she was old – but even as she said her lines, as she responded to the audience's laughter, she could hear it still, like a second heartbeat: *Is he happy with me? Does he think I'm doing a good job?*

At the after-party, there were hugs and kisses and Nancy Taylor saying, 'You were amazing, sweetie, this is going to open so many doors for you!' and Chelsea wanted to ask what doors had been closed before now, when Chelsea Stone was, as the *SNL* promos had said, the most famous teen star of her generation. Linda hadn't been able to make it – *A cross-country flight would be too much for the kids,* her former screen mom had texted Chelsea, *but I'll be watching and cheering you on!!* and she'd sent a huge bunch of flowers, with a card signed from her and Zach and Emily. Nya and Kelly were there, of course, Nya glowing with pride, Kelly making a couple of comments about how it was a pity it couldn't have been the three of them as presenters, *That would have been so cool.* Her mother had come in a strappy bandage dress, telling everyone who would listen how young she'd been when she'd had the twins, how she was more like their older sister than anything else, but there was no sign of Maddie.

They'd had lunch together before Chelsea left for New York, a sushi place in a West Hollywood strip mall, both wearing baseball caps to cover their hair, and sitting facing the wall so no one could see their faces. '*SNL*,' her sister had said wistfully. It was Maddie's favourite show – she had idolized Molly Shannon and Will Ferrell when Chelsea was still taping posters of the Backstreet Boys on her walls. 'This is the big time.' Maddie had smiled, but she couldn't hide how exhausted she looked. She wasn't sleeping, she said. She could barely eat. She was afraid to go anywhere by herself, in case the photographers would be there, screaming at her, telling her that *Mixed Signals* was a great movie and she was an ungrateful bitch, just so they could get a good reaction shot. 'It's amazing,' Maddie continued, and Chelsea had shrugged it off, saying, 'I'll probably fuck it up, I've never done live television and—' Maddie had stopped her, reaching across to grab her sister's hands. 'You'll be awesome,' she'd said fiercely. 'Do you hear me?'

She'd promised Chelsea she would come tonight. Why wasn't she here? Chelsea hadn't been able to take her calls this week but surely her sister could understand how busy it was, with rehearsals and fittings and trying to learn her lines. She took out her phone, texting Maddie again. *Where are you, Mads?*

It was Robbie who'd noticed that Chelsea was standing by the bar, a glass of wine in hand, staring at the door. How she would straighten up every time it opened, hopeful, and slump again when someone walked in and it wasn't her twin. He had come over to her and asked, 'Who are you waiting for?'

Chelsea had laughed, said, 'Oh, no one,' but he'd known her and Maddie for too long to be fooled.

'It's a shame she's not here,' he'd said, and with that, Chelsea's face had crumpled and she could feel the tears coming, treacherous.

'I'm sorry,' she'd said, but he had grabbed her hand, pulling her into a quiet corner where they wouldn't be seen.

'Don't apologize,' he'd said. 'And don't let Maddie ruin this for you.' He looked her dead in the eye. 'Tonight was a triumph, Chelsea. And it's only the beginning.'

That had been six weeks ago, and she had spent every day with him since. Robbie was working on a new script, something he said was going to change his career, and having read an early draft, Chelsea had a feeling he was right. She was helping him rework some of the dialogue, coming up with ideas to shape the plot, make it tighter, more emotionally impactful. *You should be credited for that*, she could hear Maddie say, but she pushed it away. What did it matter, in the end? She would star in the project, Robbie said, and every other project he made after that. *What about Diana Dawson?* she'd asked, curious. Wouldn't his girlfriend be jealous?

He had laughed. *Diana makes romance movies*, he said. *She's not a serious actress. Not like you, Chelsea.* He'd smiled at her. *We're gonna be like Hitchcock and Grace Kelly, David Lynch and Laura Dern, Pedro Almodóvar and Penélope Cruz. We rise together,* he reminded her.

And now here they were, sitting in his car, parked on the hillside outside her mother's house. 'I don't want to go in,' she said.

'I know,' he said. He knew how mercurial her mother was, how unpredictable she could be. 'But the sooner we get this done, the better.' He wanted Chelsea to move into the guesthouse on his property – 'You're my muse,' he'd said. 'I don't want to have to wait for you to drive across town if inspiration strikes. I need you nearby at all times.' Now he added, 'But I'm surprised you haven't told Maddie yet. The two of you have always been so close.'

'I didn't want to tell her by text,' Chelsea said. 'But she'll be fine about it.' He made a face, one she couldn't interpret, so she said, 'What? She will.'

'Just be careful. You two have always done everything together and now, all of a sudden, your career is taking off and hers is in the toilet.' He sucked his teeth. 'It's only natural for her to be jealous.'

'Maddie's not like that.'

'You said yourself she's been down the last few months. Ever since the interview came out . . .' He grimaced. 'I don't know what she was thinking, saying all that shit to a journalist. She came across as a spoiled brat and no one wants to work with someone like that. I mean, look at you.' He gestured at her. 'You always make a point of saying how grateful you are in interviews. You're always polite to the suits at the network. You know how to play the game.' He leaned across her to open the car door. 'Maddie should be able to do the same.'

'Hey, it's me,' she called, as she stepped into the hall of her mother's house. It smelt of vanilla, a white candle burning on a side table. Chelsea instinctively blew it out: she didn't trust her mother to remember to do so. 'Mom?' she said, and she could hear a rhythmic thud coming from the den.

'Oh, hi,' her mother said, when Chelsea walked into the room. The television was on, Jane Fonda in a leotard and leg warmers on screen doing deep squats. Erin paused the video, turning to hug her daughter hello. She was in a vest top and leggings, her long blonde hair tied up in a bouncy ponytail. 'Sweetie,' she held Chelsea at arm's length, 'you look amazing.'

Her mother said this to her all the time now, ever since the stylist had put Chelsea on the pills, and she'd dropped fifteen pounds within weeks. It didn't seem to matter that, just like Blake Logan's other clients, there were now paparazzi photos of Chelsea on the cover of US Weekly, her chest bones like a xylophone, saying she was too skinny, she must be starving herself. But, then, Erin had always wanted the twins to be as slim as possible. *I know it's awful,* she'd said once, when Chelsea had a stomach flu and had spent three days crouched over a toilet, vomiting, *but think how good you'll look when it's over.*

'Thanks,' Chelsea said. 'Where's—'

Whatever Happened to Madeline Stone?

'Did you see the email I forwarded you?' Erin interrupted her. 'The one from Nancy Taylor.'

'I . . .' Chelsea tried to remember. All of her emails went through an assistant now. Robbie's assistant, to be exact. He said it made more sense. That way he could vet any offers to make sure the scripts aligned with his vision for her career or, indeed, if there was anything that might be suitable for him to direct. He wasn't so precious that he would only use his own material, he said, as long as it was a good fit for them both. 'Which one, Mom?'

Her mother's face dropped. 'The one about the show?' She waited for Chelsea to show any sign of recognition, and when she didn't, Erin continued, 'They want me to host a chat show! Don't you think I'd be great at that? I'm such a people person – that's what everyone says. I'd be, like, the new Oprah Winfrey. And, of course, you'd be my first guest. How cute would that be?'

Chelsea could feel a headache coming on. 'Is this official? Have you signed a contract?'

'No, not yet!' Erin said, her eyes darting to the left. 'I have to sort out a few things first.'

Like getting your daughter to agree to appear as your first guest? 'Where's Maddie?' Chelsea asked instead, checking her watch. It was a Cartier tank, a present from The Director at Christmas. He had given all the cast members gifts but had wanted to get something extra special for her. *Don't tell Nya and Kelly*, he'd warned her. *We don't want them to be jealous but you're practically family.* 'I told her to be here at two p.m.'

Maddie was always punctual. They both were: it had been drilled into them since they were children. Chelsea walked over to the window and, sure enough, there was her sister in jeans and ballet flats, a boat-neck sweater in blue stripes. She was leaning down into the car, talking to Robbie – no, it looked like she was yelling at him. Surely she wasn't still angry with him about the *Vigilante Queens* rights? That was so long ago now. Chelsea was about to go out there to smooth things over when Maddie turned and stumbled up the driveway. A few seconds later, Chelsea heard the door crashing open.

'We're in here,' her mother called. 'In the den.'

'Mad—' The words died on Chelsea's tongue when she saw her sister up close. They hadn't seen each other since that sushi date before she'd left for New York – ever since Chelsea had been back in LA, she'd been working with Robbie on his script. Maddie looked dishevelled. She wore no makeup, and her eyes were bloodshot. Her twin was staring at her, and Chelsea realized she had to say something. 'Hey.' Chelsea was freaking out internally but didn't want to say too much in front of their mother. They had always tried to protect one another from Erin. 'Are you – you good?'

'Yeah,' Maddie replied flatly. She threw herself onto the sofa, as if she was too exhausted to hold herself upright any longer. 'Why have we been summoned here? And why is that dickhead outside?'

'Hey, come on. I know you've had your issues with Robbie but he's a family friend. He—' Chelsea stopped. Her sister had lain down fully, her head on the arm rest, and her eyes were closing. 'I'm talking to you,' she said, sharper than she'd intended. 'Are you actually falling asleep right now?'

Maddie put a hand over her head, covering her face. 'I'm tired.' Her voice was slightly muffled. 'It was a rough night.'

'I'm sure it was.' Chelsea had seen photos on RumorMill that morning of Maddie and a blonde heiress stumbling out of the front door of Les Deux, eyes glittering black, their jaws clenched. The blog had been posting a lot about Maddie since the interview had gone viral, but there was always shit on there, and most of the time it wasn't true, or it wasn't entirely true at least. But there was no arguing with Milo's captions saying Madeline was on drugs, it was undeniable that her sister was high. 'I saw the stuff online.'

'What stuff?' Maddie looked up at her. 'There's so much on there now, it's hard for me to keep straight. What did it say? I'm a coke head, I'm a whore, I'm an ungrateful piece of shit. And it's not just online, is it? I can't get a job – Nancy Taylor says I'm basically un-hireable. Isn't that nice? And all because of a one-hour interview where I told the fucking truth. Who'd have thunk it?' Her sister gave a humourless smile. 'I guess if I can't work, I may as well have fun, right?'

'This doesn't look like fun,' Chelsea said.

'Yeah, well . . . I'm not sure what else I'm supposed to do with my time. It's not like you've been blowing up my phone to hang out, Chel.' There was no admonition in her tone. Maddie was just being honest. 'It's been, like, nearly two months since I've seen you.'

'What?' their mother interjected, surprised. Usually, the twins couldn't bear to be apart, they had never gone that long before without seeing one another, but Robbie said Chelsea needed to stay focused. He didn't go running home to Portland every weekend to hang out with his family because he was an adult and his work was the priority and it should be the same for Chelsea. *But Maddie is my—* She'd tried to argue and he had cut her off. *Maddie is a distraction,* he'd said.

'I'm sorry,' Chelsea said. 'It's just been crazy since *SNL* and we're working on this script together that Robbie wants me to star in. Oh, God, it's phenomenal. I've never read anything like it.'

'That's exciting,' their mother said. 'Is there a part for Maddie in it?' Chelsea curled her hands into fists at her sides. Why did Erin always have to centre everything on Maddie's needs, even now? But there was no time to discuss it. Her sister was pushing herself up to sitting, her face even paler than it had been before.

'What do you mean, you're working on it together?' Maddie said. 'No. Chelsea, don't do this. He'll just steal it from you and take all the credit, like he always does.'

'Oh, for . . .' Chelsea stopped herself. 'You're being ridiculous.'

'I'm not,' her sister said. 'If you want to write a script, do it yourself. Or you and me, we can try working together – we could do something amazing, I know we could. But Robbie, he's a fucking thief. He's—'

'He's a genius,' Chelsea said coldly. 'Do you know how lucky I am that he's taking a chance on me for this movie? He could have anyone in this role.'

'What are you talking about?' Maddie said. 'You're awesome in *Vigilante Queens*, everyone says so. And you smashed it on *SNL*, you—'

'Because he helped me,' Chelsea interrupted. 'He's the only one who can make me give a half-decent performance. Remember what I was like on *Double Trouble*?'

'This is crap,' her sister insisted. 'You were a kid then, and it wasn't like anyone at the network cared about us being the next Meryl Streep. They just wanted us to look cute and hit our marks. But you always had it in you. Robbie doesn't have magical abilities, no matter what he's managed to convince you of. He can see how good you are and he just wants to capitalize on it. You have to cut him off, Chel.'

'Well, that's going to be tricky,' Chelsea said, getting up again. 'Since I'm about to move into his house.' She paused. 'The guesthouse, anyway.' Erin made a *moue* of shock and Chelsea said snarkily, 'Don't worry, Mom, I'll still cover the mortgage,' and her mother didn't even have the decency to look ashamed.

Whatever Happened to Madeline Stone?

'Chelsea,' Erin said, a hand to her chest, 'are you sleeping with that man?'

'Oh, my God—'

'Jesus Christ, Mom!'

Chelsea and Maddie responded at the same time, with identical horrified expressions on their faces.

'Robbie is with Diana Dawson. Anyway, he's almost . . .' *sexless*, Chelsea wanted to say, but maybe that was just how people were around her. She didn't give off the kind of energy that made men attracted to her, not like Kelly or Maddie. Robbie said it was a good thing – Chelsea was pure, an unsullied instrument through which he could tell his stories – but she worried about it all the same. 'It's work,' she said instead.

'Yeah,' Maddie said. 'Robbie just sees Chelsea as a kid. He doesn't want to fuck her. He wants to mine her for all she's worth.'

'I'm not a child.' Chelsea could feel the tears beginning to build. 'I should have known you'd be like this,' she whispered. 'You can't let me have anything, can you?'

'What are you talking about?' Maddie stood up now so she and Chelsea were eye level, and Chelsea fought the urge to back away, to run, to hide.

Robbie had been right: Maddie *was* jealous. She was still furious about losing the role of Willow Gray, and now that she had torpedoed her own career with the interview? She couldn't stand to see Chelsea succeed instead of her. No wonder she never returned Chelsea's phone calls or texts, Robbie said. Chelsea wasn't sure if that was quite accurate – if she scrolled through their messages, she could see that it was *her* who had gone quiet, not Maddie – but his story tasted better in her mouth, so she told that one instead. 'I . . .' Chelsea tried to remember what he had told her. 'You're just jealous,' she said, spitting out the words. 'You wanted to play Willow

Gray. That's understandable, it's a great role. But you need to get over it now and stop trying to . . .' she paused '. . . trying to *sabotage* me.'

Maddie shrank back, as if Chelsea had hit her. 'You don't believe that,' she said, and her face was so sad it hurt Chelsea to look at her. 'Yeah, I wanted the part. I loved those books. Robbie wouldn't even have *heard* of them if it wasn't for me, and he never once gave me any credit. He didn't even give me a small part in the show. But you're my sister. My *twin* sister. I know you don't believe that I would try to sabotage you.'

'Don't I?' Chelsea was tired, she realized. Tired of being known inside out by Maddie. Tired, too, of always being the lesser twin. Less talented, less magnetic. It had felt so good being seen by Robbie as her own person. She couldn't lose that now. 'You didn't even come to watch *SNL*,' she said. 'I bought a plane ticket for you, Maddie, booked a hotel. That was one of the biggest moments of my career. If you had been on it, I would have—'

'You would have what?' Maddie said, losing patience. 'Why can't you just be honest? If I'd won the role of Willow and I'd been the one hosting *SNL*, you would have killed yourself already.'

Erin gasped, but then there was silence, no one saying anything. The words smashing into the ground beneath them, shattering into a thousand pieces, but they could never be unsaid now. She could never unhear it. 'Chel.' Maddie sat down again, as if her legs were too weak to hold her. 'I'm sorry,' she said. 'I didn't mean that. I'm so proud of you, I am. I'm just . . .' Maddie put a hand over her mouth to cover a sob. 'It's been really hard. You don't know what it's like for me right now. The paps won't . . . they won't stop, Chelsea. Every time I leave my house, they're there, yelling at me and taking photos, and sometimes I get so scared, I feel like I'm having a heart attack. I'm fighting and fighting to catch my breath and I can't, I can't, and . . . I feel so alone.'

Chelsea looked at her mother, who had walked to the window, staring out to the driveway where Robbie's car was parked, pretending that Maddie wasn't having a breakdown right in front of them. Chelsea wanted to move towards her sister, to wrap her arm around Maddie's shoulders, but for some reason, she found she couldn't. She stood there, rooted to the ground, watching Maddie cry.

'And then one of those girls texts me,' her sister continued. 'And they say they're going out for drinks, do I want to come too? And I don't want to go, not really. But I'm so lonely, and I don't want to stay at home either so I go. I go and, for a few hours, I'm out of my body. I'm out of my head. I can forget about *Vigilante Queens* and how I would have shot it differently, the stories I would have told with it. I can forget about the *GQ* interview and how much I miss acting and how scared I am that I'll never get a job again. And it's nice, you know? To have some quiet, even if only for a few hours. But the next day I look online and there are all these photos and people are saying I'm trash, that they hate me, that I deserve to have my life ruined. That I should just fucking die already. And I start to think maybe they're right.' She looked up, all the light gone from her eyes. 'I needed you, Chel. You got the role. You won. Fine! I don't care any more. I just want my sister back.'

'I'm right here,' Chelsea said.

'No,' Maddie replied. 'You're not.'

24.

2025

Chelsea woke in a sweat, the same way she had all week, her dreams dissolving before she could make sense of them. All she was left with was an image of Maddie's face, her sister mouthing something at her, but Chelsea couldn't hear her voice. She didn't know what Maddie was trying to tell her. It was the sixteenth of February. Two weeks to the reunion show, two weeks until she could pay off the blackmailer, and she was no closer to finding out where her sister was. She showered and dressed and went to her guesthouse, staring at the faces pinned on the whiteboard, and the Post-it note she had added, the words MADAME DESTINY written on it in capital letters. She had spent the last couple of days since her visit to her mother's house searching for the psychic online, but there were literally thousands of results on Google. How would Chelsea find her?

She checked her phone again. Nothing from Erin, which bothered her. It reminded Chelsea of when the kids were little and playing in another room – it was usually when they went quiet that they were wreaking the most damage. There was nothing from Nick either, and as she scrolled through his monosyllabic texts, her stomach tightened. She imagined the RumorMill blog post, *Chelsea Stone and the Explosive Secret!*, as if her life was a book series for young adults, and the fallout afterwards. Nick would leave her, of course. He wouldn't care that he had broken their marriage first. He would take the children, or maybe he would only take Grayson – his son was the favourite, after all. Was Chelsea destined to repeat her mother's patterns – abandoned, with no money, and a daughter to feed?

She touched her fingers to the photo of her and Maddie on the whiteboard. If she had told her sister the truth about what she had done to get the part, would Maddie have forgiven her? Maddie had said she would always love Chelsea, but that was before Chelsea had betrayed her, and so spectacularly too. She heard the door open and she turned, expecting to see her assistant, or one of the kids, but instead, it was—

'So, you are alive?' Nya was standing there in jeans and a cashmere cardigan, dumping a Louis Vuitton holdall at her feet. She looked beautiful, as ever, her skin glowing and her curly hair loose around her face. 'I had presumed you must be dead, given you haven't replied to any of my texts or picked up my calls.'

'Oh, my God.' Chelsea rushed over to her, hugging her friend. 'What are you doing here?'

'Hannah let me in. And I had to come,' Nya said, hugging her back fiercely. 'I've been so worried about you, Chel. Did I do something? Are you pissed at me?'

'No. No, I . . . I'm sorry. I've just been busy and—'

'Please don't.' Nya's voice softened. 'You always do this when things get bad. You isolate yourself and you shut everyone out and it's not healthy.'

When Maddie had died (disappeared, she reminded herself, her sister could still be alive, she *was* still alive), Chelsea had ignored her phone, buried herself under her duvet and refused to leave her apartment. Until one day when the doorbell rang, a finger on the buzzer, and it wouldn't stop until Chelsea dragged herself to the front door. There had been Nya, a backpack hanging off her shoulder. She'd moved in for the next six weeks, appearing at the foot of Chelsea's bed every morning with a cup of coffee, nudging her into the shower, cooking easy, comforting meals, like chicken soup and scrambled eggs, telling Chelsea to *take just one more bite, good girl*. It was only when she was certain that Chelsea could manage without her that Nya had left again.

'Then why haven't you texted me back?' Nya asked. She allowed Chelsea to lead her to the sofa, sitting down beside her. 'You and Kelly, it's like you've both fallen off the face of the planet.'

'I'm fine,' Chelsea said, trying to hide her surprise. She knew her own reasons for avoiding Nya's calls, but why was Kelly doing the same? 'It's just a lot right now. The storage unit and RumorMill and the reunion show . . . all of it.'

'That's understandable,' Nya said, her tone changing into what Chelsea assumed was her therapist voice. 'There's so much trauma from that time that hasn't been fully processed, let alone integrated. It makes sense that it would be resurfacing now.'

'Hmm.' Chelsea tried to change the subject. 'How are the girls doing? And Marcus?'

'Marcus is good.' Nya kicked off her sneakers, curling her feet under her. She still looked so young, even without Botox or lasers. *Melanin*, she would say, whenever Chelsea asked what she was doing to her face. *It's our revenge for white supremacy.* 'Some big work deal at the moment so he's stressing, but mostly good. Simone and Elise are always asking about Auntie Chelsea. They miss you. You should come to the city to see us for a few days.' Her friend paused, a little playfully. 'If only to use the famous gym.'

'Oh, my God.' Chelsea groaned. When Nick had bought their townhouse in the West Village, he'd considered converting the basement into a home gym but decided against it when he learned that the apartment building next door had one of the best fitness centres in Manhattan. It was strictly for residents' use, so he bought a condo to circumnavigate the issue. 'I should never have told you about that. I know it's bad but—'

'Bad doesn't even begin to cover it. Your husband paid seven million dollars for an apartment he's never used just so he could avoid walking three blocks to the nearest gym,' her friend said, but she was laughing, and Chelsea couldn't help but laugh too. 'And this is the same guy who refused to pay sixteen bucks for a carton of raspberries at the farmers' market in East Hampton because he said it was a rip-off.'

'My husband is a man of many opinions, you know that.'

It was then Nya spotted the whiteboard and got up, walking closer to peer at it. She didn't say anything for a minute, just stood there, staring at the photos pinned to it, all the familiar faces. Chelsea went to join her. 'Madame Destiny?' Nya asked, gesturing at the Post-it note.

'It's a long story,' Chelsea said.

'Okay, then. Tell me,' Nya said. 'Did you go see Milo James?'

'Yes. Still a piece of shit.'

'And what about him?' Nya touched the photo of The Director.

'No. Not yet.'

'Good.' Nya said, and when Chelsea turned to look at her in surprise, her friend continued, 'I know you and Maddie were friends with Robbie since you were kids but there was always something about this that gave me the creeps. Like the way he insisted you get rid of your scar. It was weird. You could barely see it on screen, and he was so fixated on it.' Nya shuddered. 'And I felt . . . I don't know. I felt like he was messing with me, in some way. He used to change the script without telling me, like he would make a tweak to a line and then he'd yell cut when I said it the old way. I thought maybe it was just a mistake but it kept happening and finally he admitted he wanted to see how I adapted under pressure. He said it made my performance more "real".'

'Why didn't you tell me?'

Nya gave her a side-eye. 'Chelsea,' she said, returning to sit next to her, 'you adored him. Would you have believed me?'

Chelsea couldn't answer that, and Nya sighed. 'We were all very young,' she said, taking Chelsea's hand in hers. 'Where's Nick, by the way? Hannah said he's not at home.'

'He's travelling with work,' Chelsea tried to sound breezy, 'so I have to be here with the kids. It's not great timing, with the reunion and all.'

Hannah was fielding the emails and phone calls from Nancy Taylor, the woman from the network and the producer of the reunion show who wanted to go over the questions, it would take only a minute, and was Chelsea available to hop on a quick call to talk through a few things? No matter how efficient Hannah was, Chelsea still had to sign off on everything, which required daily meetings at which her assistant went through the notes, waiting for Chelsea's yes or no or maybe or let me think about it. She was trying to stay offline but whenever she had fittings with her stylist (her outfit had to be dignified yet sexy, couldn't wrinkle or ride up when she sat down) or a session with her dermatologist (she needed to have enough movement in her face that anyone watching the show would assume she was 'ageing gracefully', which meant, of course, she had enough work done to look the exact same as she always did but not so much that anyone could tell), and this meant meeting people who would say, *You must be so excited about the show! It's all anyone is talking about!* Chelsea would have to smile even as her stomach dropped with fear. The noise around the reunion was getting louder and louder, and as much as she tried to ignore it, it was becoming impossible to do so. The higher she rose, the greater the fall would be in the end. She had learned that much as a teenager.

'I can't even imagine how intense it must be for you,' Nya said. 'My phone won't stop blowing up and I'm a nobody, these days.'

'Don't say that about yourself.'

'I don't care,' Nya said, amused. 'I like my life the way it is.'

'Of course.' Chelsea was embarrassed. She, of all people, should know that not everyone wanted to be famous. 'I just—'

'It's okay,' Nya cut in. That was one of Chelsea's favourite things about their friendship: they always gave each other the grace of good intentions. 'But I've got to ask.' She scrutinized Chelsea. 'Why are you doing this?'

'You signed on too! Why are *you* doing it?'

'Because I thought it might be fun,' Nya said, and leaned back into her seat. She had left the industry after *Vigilante Queens* had finished. She still loved acting, she'd said, but she couldn't take the bullshit that came with it – the stylists who complained about her hair or didn't have makeup to match her skin tone, the fans who always asked Kelly and Chelsea for photos first, ignoring her, the casting directors who said they loved her but they weren't going 'ethnic' with this role. Nya had to work ten times as hard for half the pay, and it wasn't worth it to her any more. She went back to school, retraining as a psychotherapist, and moved into the beautiful brownstone in Park Slope her parents bought her as a wedding present. Whenever Chelsea asked if she missed acting, Nya would say she didn't believe in regrets. Chelsea wondered what that must feel like, to be so sure of your life decisions that regret wasn't a part of your vocabulary.

'As soon as Simone and Elise hit middle school, they decided I was the biggest loser imaginable,' Nya continued. '*Nowhere* near as cool as Auntie Chelsea, of course. I knew I shouldn't have allowed you to take them to Paris on the jet. You've ruined those girls for life.' She snorted. 'The reunion might make them think otherwise, although I'm sure it'll somehow be the most embarrassing thing any mother has ever done in the history of the world. But, Chel . . .' a beat '. . . this show is just a trip down Memory Lane for me. There'll be a flutter of excitement and the other school moms will ask me tons of questions, mostly about you and Madeline.' She hesitated. Even Nya knew not to talk about Chelsea's sister. 'Then it'll all die down and go back to normal because my life *is* normal now. But you're the most private person I know. Ever since you and Nick got together, you've done everything in your power to protect your image, to make sure no one looks beyond the bland mask you've created for yourself. What's changed?'

'Don't psychoanalyse me, Nya. You know I hate when you do that.'

'I'm not,' she protested. 'You're my best friend and I'm worried about you. Doing this show, especially on the back of the storage unit and the website . . . I just don't get it. Besides, Nick must hate it . . .' she paused, waiting for Chelsea to agree '. . . which, honestly, I'm not mad at. You need to stand up to him more. But this? You were so distressed about all the attention last year with the trial and that didn't even directly involve you.'

Nick had tried to get her out of it, pulling every string he could, but Chelsea had to testify, the lawyers said. She'd been subpoenaed. She had worn a beautiful suit from The Row, her hair held back with a simple black band, and she'd spoken softly about how she had never seen The Director display any kind of abusive behaviour in all the time she had worked with him, avoiding eye contact with his ex-wife, sitting with her legal team, staring up at her. It was the truth, she reminded herself. Robbie might have been obsessive and even controlling at times but that was because he was an artist: he had to stay true to his vision and it was the actors' job to help him fulfil it. But he had never screamed or shouted, never lashed out and had never raised a hand to anyone on set. He had only ever wanted the best for Chelsea, and for Maddie, she had no doubt about that.

'A *Vigilante Queens* reunion was always going to be enormous,' Nya continued. 'I was worried that Kelly had guilt-tripped you into this and, God knows, she's capable of that and more. But when I phoned her, she said this was your idea.' She held Chelsea's gaze. 'Please, help me understand. Why put yourself through this?'

In a moment of madness, Chelsea had the compulsion to confess. *Nick and I haven't had sex in over a year and he blames me. He says my attitude to sex is messed up because of my childhood, and the purity rings, and he says that every time we fuck, he feels as if I'm doing it under duress, and it's made him feel less virile, less like a man. So he won't stop asking strangers for nude photos on social media and I'm so humiliated. Oh, and did I mention that I'm being blackmailed for one million dollars and I can't tell anyone about it because then I'd have to admit to the worst thing I've ever done and my whole life will fall apart. Maybe I'm just losing my mind, maybe I lost it a long time. What do you think, Nya?*

'Did Kelly tell you what we found in the storage unit?' she asked instead, and Nya nodded, as Chelsea had known she would. Kelly had never been good at keeping her mouth shut.

'The abortion?' Nya asked.

'Yeah. But did she tell you about the dates?'

Nya looked confused so Chelsea rummaged through the files on the coffee-table until she found what she was looking for. She handed the piece of paper to her friend, watching as Nya speed-read it. 'The date,' she said.

The other woman's eyes flicked to the top of the page and

widened in shock. 'Fuck,' she said. She looked up at Chelsea. 'But it's—'

'I know.' Chelsea swallowed. 'That's why I'm doing the show, Nee Nee. If there's even a chance that Maddie is still alive . . . Maybe she'll watch. Maybe this will be the thing that makes her reach out.'

'Oh, Chel.' Nya sounded so sad. 'Sweetheart, I—'

She started talking about grief and magical thinking but Chelsea wasn't listening because Hannah had knocked at the guesthouse, opening the door before Chelsea had a chance to respond. She could tell by her assistant's face that whatever news she was about to impart wasn't good. 'There's a story . . .' Hannah said.

'What kind of story?' Chelsea asked, her mouth dry. Had the blackmailer gone rogue? Had they told RumorMill about Carter? She unlocked her own phone, typing her name into Google.

The secret Prophecy that drove the Stone Sisters apart, the *Page Six* headline screamed.

> A psychic predicted that one twin would be the most famous woman of her generation and the other would die young in tragic circumstances . . . It was 1988 and Erin Stone's husband, Ed, had just left her. A friend recommended a local psychic, Madame Destiny, or Destiny de Divine. as she prefers to go by these days as she works above the Enchanted Emporium, a Wiccan store on Venice Beach, and . . .

'Destiny de Divine,' Chelsea said aloud. She handed the phone to Nya so her friend could read, her eyes scanning the screen.

'This had to have come from your—'

'My mom?' Chelsea finished her friend's sentence. 'Yes.'
'But why?'
'I don't know,' Chelsea said grimly. Who knew why Erin did the things she did? She took her phone back, and tried to phone her mother but it went straight to voicemail. 'But I'm going to see this psychic right now.' She bent to put her shoes back on. 'Hannah, will you sort out the guesthouse for Nya? Stock the kitchen, et cetera. And a flight home on the jet in the morning, please.'

'Chel,' Nya tried, but Chelsea put up her hand to stop her friend. 'Thank you for coming,' she said, 'but I have to do this. If this woman has any kind of powers— No,' she said, speaking over Nya as her friend protested. 'Her prophecy came true, didn't it? In a way? If she can tell the future, maybe she knows where Maddie is. Maybe she . . .' Maybe she could tell Chelsea that everything would be okay and she could breathe easy again. 'I have to go. I love you, okay?'

'I love you too,' Nya said sadly. 'But I don't know if any of this is going to give you what you're looking for.'

25.

2025

Just as *Page Six* had reported, the psychic was working on Venice Beach, in one of the small shops on the waterfront that sold intention candles, bath salts and incense. The clientele seemed to be primarily female, giggling teenage girls and a pale-faced woman in her late thirties who was lingering at the love potions, looking at the glass bottles with an air of sadness about her.

There was a blackboard sign at the stairwell, the words *Destiny de Divine* written in red chalk and an arrow pointing upwards. Chelsea climbed the steps, past a dingy restroom and what looked like a broom cupboard, until she came to an open door. It was dark in there, the walls painted black, a handful of spindly candles spilling wax onto every available surface. There was a floor lamp, the shade made of yellow fringe, and ochre velvet drapes covering the one poky window. It was quiet too, save for the occasional car horn from outside or a high-pitched laugh from one of the girls downstairs.

And there *she* was, Destiny de Divine, sitting at a round table covered with a lace cloth, a deck of tarot cards and a crystal ball in front of her. The psychic's eyebrows were over-tweezed and drawn back in with dark pencil, a thatch of grey hair growing out of her hairline. She appeared to be in her early seventies, and looked her age, a rarity in this town where everyone had Instagram Face, as Hannah called it – the inflated lips, frozen forehead, and overly filled cheeks that often made it impossible to guess if a woman was twenty-five or forty-five.

'Come on, come in,' she said. It was only when Chelsea was sitting in front of the woman that she realized the psychic must be partially blind now: her eyes were a strange milky white. 'Do you want the tarot or the crystal ball?' Destiny de Divine asked, placing one hand on each. 'The tarot is twenty and the crystal ball is fifteen but I can do both for thirty bucks.'

'No, I . . .' Chelsea tried to gather herself. 'Do you know who I am?' she asked.

The psychic squinted at her. 'I don't think so,' she said. 'Have you come to me before, child?'

At thirty-nine years of age, it had been a long time since anyone had referred to Chelsea as a child and, despite herself, she had the urge to smile. 'No,' she said. 'Well, I was at one of your readings but I don't remember it.' The psychic looked confused. 'My mother came to you in the late eighties,' Chelsea explained, 'when you were living in Nevada. Big Valley? She brought me and my sister with her. My twin. We were maybe two at the time.'

'I've seen many women over the years,' the psychic said. 'Thousands. It would be impossible to remember them all.'

Chelsea leaned forward, her voice urgent. 'You gave my mother a prediction about me and my sister. You said one of us would be the most famous woman in the world and the other would die young. Do you remember?'

She and Maddie had never believed in the prophecy, seeing it as a big joke. They were famous because they were cute and there were two of them and because their mother had done everything in her power to ensure their success. But the prophecy had still come true, hadn't it? Whether because it was a self-fulfilling story, she and her sister acting out the fate their mother had decided upon years ago, or because the woman in front of her had genuine powers, Chelsea did not know. But if it was the latter, maybe the psychic could tell her where Maddie was, and what Chelsea needed to do to bring her home.

The woman looked at her with those cloudy eyes and she shook her head. 'I'm sorry,' she said. 'As I said, I've seen so many people over the years . . . And I'm getting older, too. My memory isn't what it used to be.' She touched Chelsea's hand. 'Would you like a reading now? It's a good deal.'

'Fine,' Chelsea said, ignoring the twinge of anxiety in her chest. Why she was asking a fortune-teller rather than the highly skilled private investigator Nick had ready to go, she didn't know, but she found she couldn't resist. *Where is Maddie?* It was the same question that had been reverberating in her mind for weeks – she was afraid she might go mad with it. Had it been easier when she'd thought her sister was dead?

'Excellent.' The psychic sat in silence, tilting her head to the ceiling. She let out a strange hum, then picked up the tarot cards, knocking on them three times and began to shuffle. Once she had laid down her spread, she opened her eyes again, gazing into the crystal ball. 'I see . . .' she began, then started to cough. 'Sorry,' she gasped, reaching down to grab the bottle of water at her feet. She took a gulp, then stared at the ball again. 'I can see that you'll never be rich but you will be happy,' she said. Chelsea looked down at what she was wearing, the Loro Piana linen cardigan, the wide-leg pants from The Row, and her Céline Triomphe bag. The woman was definitely half blind, that was for sure. 'And I can see a man, he isn't very handsome but he is kind. He'll take care of you. I can see that you've been worried about your ability to have children, but the cards are telling me you'll be able to conceive naturally. I see a little girl. And someone has passed over recently. I'm seeing an E name. Elizabeth? Emma?' Chelsea kept saying no, no, no, and the psychic continued. 'Evelyn? Everley?'

'No,' Chelsea said. 'No one has died recently, and no one with an E name.' Shit. *Erin.* She would have to phone her mother after this to make sure she was okay.

'I also see you getting a promotion at work soon,' the psychic went on. 'Do you work on a computer? I see you tap-tapping on a laptop.'

Chelsea stared at her without saying anything. She got to her feet, pulling the strap of her handbag over her shoulder. 'I'm going now,' she said. 'But I'm gonna ask you one more time. Are you sure you don't remember my mother? Erin—'

'Erin!' the woman cried. 'See! An E name.'

'Yes, but she's not dead.' Chelsea gritted her teeth. 'Please listen to me. Erin Stone came to you in 1988 when you were working out of Nevada. She was young at the time, blonde, pretty. She had two girls with her, twins. And you said that one of the twins would become—'

'Wait,' the psychic cut across her, lighting up. 'I do remember now. The woman's husband had died – he was in a trucking accident. She had two little girls, they looked like Snow White, with dark hair and alabaster skin. I said that one would become a star and the other would die young. Oh, she did not like that. Not one bit.' The psychic let out a low whistle. 'She got up and stormed out. She didn't even pay.' She glanced at Chelsea again. 'I don't suppose you feel like settling the bill today?'

Chelsea took a fifty-dollar bill from her wallet and stuffed it into the older woman's hand. When she got to the stairs outside, she was too dizzy to go any further so she sat down on the top step. It was filthy but she couldn't move. The psychic was a crook. She wanted to tell Maddie, for she knew her sister was the only person who would understand how both hilarious and tragic this was. Destiny de Divine had given the same prophecy to another family, another single mother of twin girls, and that woman hadn't done what Erin had.

She hadn't taken the fortune as gospel, moving her family to Los Angeles to live out her dreams vicariously through her children. Chelsea would have bet good money that the other woman never even told her daughters about it, allowing them to grow up without the spectre of death hanging over them, wondering which would be the chosen one. They were probably happy, those girls, with no idea of what fate could have befallen them if they had been born to a different mother.

Her phone beeped and she reached into her handbag to grab it. There was a message from Nya. *I love you, Chel*, it said, *and I'm here when you need me. Always xx* But there was another message too, from Emily, Linda's daughter:

Emily: Mom is sitting up and talking?!!! We haven't seen her like this in months!!!

Emily: She's looking for you. She says she wants to talk to you.

Emily: Can you get here as soon as you can? xo

26.

2006

Chelsea smiled at the young man behind the front desk at the inn. 'Is it okay if I make my phone call?' she asked him, and he blushed furiously, his face so red it almost turned purple. 'Sure,' he managed to choke out in his Canadian accent, gesturing at her to follow him into the small, windowless office tucked behind Reception. Inside, there was a filing cabinet, a desk and chair, and the precious phone. The moment she had arrived in this tiny town near Moraine Lake in Alberta to film *The List of Second Chances*, The Director had taken Chelsea's BlackBerry from her, locked it in a safe box in his room and informed her that she could make one phone call a week from the hotel's landline. It was only for three months, and it wasn't just Chelsea: her two co-stars, Owen and Finn, had to follow the same rules. Robbie thought it would help them get into character, improve their performances. Chelsea wanted to give the best performance she could, didn't she?

She waited until the receptionist left and she stared at the phone. Pressing it between her shoulder and her ear, she tapped in Maddie's number. As she listened to the dial tone, she could feel herself getting nervous and she hated that. It wasn't how she should feel about her sister. They had made up after that argument they'd had when she'd told her sister she was moving into Robbie's house. There had been a stilted phone conversation, which ended in Maddie asking tersely if Chelsea was still making the movie with him. 'Yes,' Chelsea said, 'of course I am,' and that had been that. They didn't see each other as much afterwards – they texted, of course: Chelsea hadn't abandoned her completely, still checked in. She was just *busy*. But she read the blogs, like everyone else, saw the covers of the gossip magazines. Every week, there was another story, more photos, and Maddie was increasingly frail in each one, her eyes a little wilder. Her sister was clearly veering out of control, she needed help, but Robbie reminded her it wasn't her job to do that. She wasn't Maddie's mother. Besides, he said, Chelsea had to keep a clean image. It was more essential than ever now if she was going to make the jump from TV to movies. The industry was so sexist. Chelsea needed to be well-behaved if she wanted to be successful. It wasn't fair, he said, but that was just the way it was.

When the call went to voicemail – 'This is Maddie, you know what to do' – Chelsea was both relieved and disappointed. Was her sister deliberately avoiding her call? 'Hey,' she said. 'It's me. I know I haven't phoned in a while but I just . . . um. I was thinking about you today. For some reason, I remembered the day we had a house party. Well, not a party exactly – who would we even have invited? It was just you, me, Robbie and Julia.' How sad, looking back, that the only friends they had at fourteen years of age were their tutor and her boyfriend. 'And I was messing around,' Chelsea continued. 'Do you remember? I knocked over that vase.' Robbie and Julia had left immediately – they knew enough of Erin's temper to do that. Chelsea had cleared up the debris as best she could. Maybe it could be saved, maybe it could be glued back together, she kept saying, but she knew it was hopeless. Erin had come home later that night from a date, and when she saw the shattered pieces of the lamp, she had started screaming, *This was Murano glass, it was so expensive, why can't you just be careful, why do I have to do everything myself?* Then she had stood up, her face furious, and she'd looked between the two girls. *Which one of you did this?* 'I thought I was gonna puke, I was so scared,' Chelsea said. 'But you stepped in front of me, looked Mom straight in the eye and you took the blame.'

Erin had shouted at Maddie, told her to go to her bedroom, and to stay there until the following morning. Later that night, when she was sure their mother was asleep, Chelsea snuck into her sister's room, climbed into the bed beside her and curled her body around Maddie's. 'What is it?' her sister had said, and Chelsea had thanked her.

'You saved me,' she'd said, and Maddie had said, still half asleep, 'I've got your back. It's you and me, Chel.'

'Anyway,' Chelsea said, a little awkwardly, 'I don't have my phone on set. I'm not sure if Mom told you? That's why I haven't been texting. We're not allowed to go on the internet either so I . . . Um. But I wanted you to know I was thinking about you, I guess. I hope you're well. I hope . . .' She didn't know what to say. 'Okay, see ya,' she said, hanging up. 'Fuck,' she half said to herself. That couldn't count as her phone call, surely? She took a small Filofax out of her purse, flicking through the pages, wondering who else she could call. She had phoned Nya last week; they had talked about the production of *Cat on a Hot Tin Roof* that Nya was doing in New York, before moving on to Kelly. They seemed to spend a lot of their time these days discussing the problem of Kelly. 'That's all very well,' Chelsea had said, after Nya gave an impassioned speech about how Kelly was an addict and she needed compassion and support rather than judgement. 'But the bottom line is, she's not just hurting her own reputation now. She's hurting *Vigilante Queens* too.'

There had been a pause, and then Nya had said, 'Wow. You sound more and more like The Director every day.'

But what was Chelsea supposed to say? Every time she spoke

to Kelly, her friend would either be high or coming down, making sly digs but denying it if Chelsea called her out on it, saying Chelsea was 'too sensitive'. She knew Kelly thought *she* should have the role on *Second Chances*, it was much closer to Kelly's own lived experience after all, a small-town girl from the wrong side of the tracks, one alcoholic parent, the other in jail. Chelsea had thought the same when she'd first read the script, wondering if Robbie had mined Kelly's life as inspiration. *You mean stolen*, she could almost hear Maddie say, but even if he had, was that so bad? That was what artists did. They borrowed from the world around them, every conversation overheard, every story told in confidence was material. At least, the brilliant ones did. And Robbie was a genius, everyone knew that. It would be a privilege to have your life story taken by him and shaped into something new, into *art*.

She continued flicking through the pages of her Filofax, frowning. She didn't want to talk to Erin – she and Robbie had decided the best policy was for Chelsea to disengage as much as possible. *It's called individuation*, he had explained to her, *and it's something you should have done as a toddler if your mother hadn't had such poor boundaries*. It was only right that Chelsea would want her own life, separate to Erin. It was natural. But who was left on her list? Linda? Nancy Taylor? She didn't want to talk to either of them, not today.

She left the office, smiling at the receptionist. 'That was fast,' he stammered, taking his binder out to make a note.

'There was no reply,' she said quickly. She didn't want to waste her one phone call: she might need it again later. 'I'll be back.'

She walked through the foyer, calling hello to the grip and the Best Boy, sitting in the lounge playing chess. They were supposed to be shooting an outdoor scene today but there had been an unexpected thunderstorm so Robbie had given everyone the rest of the day off. 'Who's winning?' she asked, laughing when they both claimed they were. Ever since she was a child, she'd always made friends with the crew but it had been especially easy on this shoot because there were so few of them.

The movie was being made on a shoestring budget: she and her two co-stars, Finn and Owen, were being paid the minimum Screen Actors Guild rate, as were the crew, and they were happy to do it because the script was that good. 'We're gonna get nominated for Oscars,' Owen had said, the first night on set, as the two men had smoked weed in Finn's bedroom, blowing smoke out of the open window, Chelsea sitting cross-legged on the bed, watching them. 'All of us.'

'Where's Robbie? I want to talk to him about tomorrow's scene,' she said, and thought she saw an uneasy glance between the two men.

'Not sure.' The grip shrugged, turning back to the chess board. 'Maybe in his trailer.'

The Director was the only person on set who had a trailer, and it was really more of a makeshift caravan, somewhere he could go through the day's rushes. She didn't bother to knock, just opened the door and bounded up the steps. 'Hey, I—' She stopped when she saw Robbie there, standing with his arms folded across his chest. Sitting on the two-person sofa was one of the production assistants, a cheaply bound script in her hands. She was a local girl, hired straight out of high school so she wouldn't cost as much as someone from LA. She couldn't have been more than seventeen. The girl looked up at Chelsea, and it was clear she had been crying, her eyes red and bloodshot. 'Oh,' Chelsea said. 'I'm sorry, I didn't mean to interrupt.'

'Aimee was just—' The Director started, but the girl jumped up, rubbing at her eyes.

'I'm sorry,' she said. 'I'll leave. I was going anyway.'

She brushed past Chelsea as she walked out, and Chelsea waited until the door closed before saying, 'What was that about?'

'How do you mean?'

'The girl. She was—'

'Oh, God,' Robbie stretched his arms overhead. 'I made the mistake of saying I would read a script she had written. It was terrible, of course. The formatting was all over the place, and she can't understand structure to save her life. I told her to read some Syd Field and get back to me. But then . . .' He trailed off, and there was a flicker of something. He was bothered, Chelsea could tell that much. 'She's claiming I took a couple of lines from it,' he said, under his breath.

'What?'

'I know.' He gestured at the couch, telling her to sit down. 'It's bullshit, obviously, I barely skimmed her script, and *as if* I would need to plagiarize a seventeen-year-old kid who's barely finished high school. It's insulting.' He rolled his eyes. 'Anyway, it's sorted now.'

'Right.' For some reason, Chelsea was afraid to ask what he had done to ensure it was 'sorted'. 'I'm relieved,' she said instead. 'When I walked in here, I thought—'

'What did you think?' he asked, his eyes narrowing.

'I don't know.' She felt stupid. It was so out of character. She knew Robbie would never do anything like that and yet . . . 'I wondered if maybe something happened with the two of you?'

'Chelsea.' He looked disgusted. 'Diana and I have literally just got engaged.' It was a huge story, America's Sweetheart and the Next Big Thing in directing, tying the knot. 'You think I'd cheat on my fiancée with some random kid? What the fuck is wrong with you? I'm here, trying to make the best film that I can so I'm not stuck making shitty teen dramas for the rest of my life, and I gave you a chance to be a serious actress and now you—'

'I'm sorry, I didn't mean—'

'You know how important this film is to me.' He spoke over her. 'You, of all people, know how hard I've worked on this, and how much it means to me. And you think I'd hook up with an *intern*?' He walked over to his desk and yanked open the top drawer. He pulled out a magazine and slammed it down in front of her. Chelsea exhaled slowly when she saw that she was on the cover. The main photo was one of her at a party back in LA. She was wearing flared jeans over wedge heels, a silk top with ribbon shot through it, and she had a glass of soda water in her hands. But the inset was a grainy shot of her with her two co-stars from the film, Finn and Owen. She recognized it immediately: it was a booth in the local dive bar in town. She was sitting in the middle, a boy on either side of her, and there was a bottle of Jack Daniel's on the table. Her face was flushed, her hair tousled, and the two boys were gazing at her with what looked like adoration. THREE'S COMPANY, the headline screamed, and when she rifled through the magazine to find the article, she found that 'allegedly' she was toying with the boys' affections, playing off Finn and Owen against one another, and the set was in disarray as a result. 'This is bullshit,' she said. 'You know that, right? You're the one who wanted the three of us to bond! You said it would be good for the film, for our chemistry and stuff.'

'Let me get this straight. You're fucking around, making it look like I have no control over my own set, and now it's my fault?'

'No, of course not. I didn't mean it like that. But there's nothing going on, as you know.' She bit her lip so she didn't start to cry. 'I haven't . . . I've never . . .'

Chelsea had tested with dozens of young male actors, trying

to find the perfect pair to play the Calahan boys, the two brothers who would fall in love with her character, Sissy. Owen and Finn had been the immediate standouts. Owen was a heartthrob from a soap opera who regularly posed topless for teen magazines, saying he was single because he was waiting for 'the right girl'. She had recognized Finn as soon as he auditioned: he was a fellow Cedar City child star, although he had never booked anything beyond commercials.

Robbie had insisted upon six weeks of rehearsal time before they started shooting, and he'd spent hours doing 'trust exercises' with the three of them, encouraging them to open up, to confess their deepest, darkest secrets to one another – how else were they going to access the vulnerability this script demanded? Owen had confessed that he was secretly gay, living in constant fear that RumorMill would out him – Milo James seemed to think it was his moral prerogative to eject queer stars from the closet – and he would never book another job if that happened.

Finn had gone very still, and when he did speak, his voice was so quiet, Chelsea strained to hear him. He told a story about a party he had gone to when he was a kid, and his mom had said it was important he was on his best behaviour and did whatever was asked of him. The men at this event were important, powerful, she said. They could make his career. And then . . . His voice became laboured, as if the words cost him something. 'You did great.' That was what his mother had told him when he came home in a limousine, crying. *You did great, sweetie.* Chelsea couldn't move, but Owen had wrapped an arm around Finn's shoulders, for nothing else needed to be said. The Director had thanked both men for their bravery, then turned to Chelsea, and he asked what she wanted to share with the group. 'I'm still a virgin,' she'd blurted out. Both Owen and Finn had looked surprised but Robbie had smiled at her, and she could tell he was pleased.

Whatever Happened to Madeline Stone?

'Come on,' she said now, turning the magazine face down. 'You know I'm not like this. And, besides, all Finn cares about is acting and Owen is gay. This is ridiculous.'

'You've embarrassed me,' Robbie said, his voice cold. 'And, more importantly, you've embarrassed yourself. I warned you about this, Chelsea. The studio doesn't want any scandal, and your reputation is hardly unassailable right now given your sister and your mother and—'

'None of that has anything to do with me,' she argued.

'Think about how this makes me look. I *begged* them to hire you. I said you were reliable, unlike your sister, and there wouldn't be any drama. And this is how you repay me?'

Chelsea began to panic. Would he fire her from the film? The budget was small, yes, but they still had time for reshoots. He could get Kelly up here in a day. Despite her issues, her friend could play Sissy with her eyes closed and still win every award going. 'Please,' she begged. 'I'm doing my best. And the dailies are good, right? You said the studio was happy with them.'

'They are,' he said, slightly mollified.

'Of course they are,' she said. 'You're a genius. Me and the boys,' he clenched his jaw at this so she rushed on, 'I'm always saying how brilliant you are, what a phenomenal script this is. You're going to be the next Spielberg, everyone knows that. I was just . . .' She trailed off. *I was just having fun*, was what she was about to say. *I'm twenty and Owen and Finn are the only other people here my age.* But, like her mother before her, she needed to understand that fun wasn't for girls like her, not when everything she had worked for could be lost so easily. 'I'm sorry,' she said again. She walked over to him, wrapping her arms around his waist, and pressed her head into his chest. She waited until he relaxed, putting his arms around her, like he used to when she was a child, and she let out a deep sigh.

Everything would be okay. She would just have to be careful going forward. She didn't want to disappoint him again. 'I'll do better,' she whispered. Robbie didn't reply but that was okay: she hadn't expected him to. Not when she'd let him down so badly. 'You can rely on me.'

27.

2025

'Hi,' Chelsea said, as she rushed into the care home. It was stiflingly warm in there, so she took off her jacket and folded it over her arm. 'Where's Emily? She said she'd be waiting for me.'

'She just had to take a work call,' the nurse said, a woman from the Philippines.

'But Linda?' Chelsea asked urgently. 'She's awake, she was asking for me?'

'She was,' the nurse said. 'But she's asleep again, I'm afraid.'

Chelsea slumped. It had taken her twice as long to get there from Venice Beach than it would have if she'd been at home in Montecito. Why had she wasted her time going to see the psychic? She was an idiot. 'Okay,' she said. 'I'll wait for Emily inside.'

Chelsea made her way into Linda's room. The older woman was dozing, her breath slow and steady, and the television was on, playing *The Price Is Right*. Chelsea drew the plastic seat closer to the bed and watched a few minutes of the show before she began to talk. 'Hi, Linda,' she said. 'How are you feeling today?' She waited a moment but there was nothing. Until a few years ago, there had been days when Linda would recognize Chelsea, and she would be so happy to see her, but then she would ask for Maddie. *Maddie, Maddie, where's Maddie?* Maybe it was easier when Linda didn't remember and Chelsea didn't have to explain to her, yet again, that her sister was dead. *But what if Maddie was alive?*

She reached down to grab the woman's hand. 'Linda,' she said. 'I don't know what to do. You're the only person I can talk to.' She wondered at that, that the only person in her life she trusted to be discreet was a woman with dementia, rotting away in a hospital bed. 'Nick hasn't come home in weeks. The kids are worried – they keep asking where he is. I don't want my children coming from a broken home, not after what Maddie and I went through. I don't want that for them. But,' she gripped the woman's hand ever tighter, 'if Nick finds out about Carter, about . . . It's not fair. I only did it because I was lonely and because I wanted, just for once, to feel like I was making my own choices. But Nick won't understand that, or if he does, he won't care. He'll divorce me and I'll lose the kids. He'll take them, I know he will.' The thought of losing Grayson and Ivy made her brain freeze, until there was only a terrifying emptiness. She would have nothing to live for, if that happened.

She had tried so hard to be the antithesis of Erin, to be a good mother when she had never known one, yet she had still fucked it all up so spectacularly. 'Maddie had an abortion, Linda. But the date on the paperwork, it's a year after she went missing. Which means there's a chance she's still alive. Maddie could still be alive,' she said, and her voice broke in half at the thought of it, the hope. 'You always said there was something strange about the whole thing, didn't you?' *I've been in this industry a long time and I don't think I've ever seen a campaign this vicious*, Linda had said over lunch in some bougie restaurant, back at the height of Chelsea's fame. *It's like they want her dead.* Linda had thought Maddie's downfall was too swift, too thorough to be organic, and if Milo James was anything to go by, maybe that had been the truth. 'Do you remember?'

When Maddie had been gone for two years, Erin had broached the subject of having her declared legally dead, but

Chelsea couldn't bear the thought. Instead, Erin had insisted on throwing a memorial service. They had tried to keep it as private as possible, but somehow, the media had found out where it was. Chelsea would wonder about that afterwards, wonder who had sold out her family for their thirty pieces of silver. The paparazzi were outside, snapping photos of any celebrities they could see – Chelsea, Robbie and his then-wife, Diana Dawson, walking hand in hand, Kelly and Nya, Finn and Owen, her two co-stars from *The List of Second Chances*. RumorMill had run a poll, asking readers which black dress was the chicest, and, unbelievably, Chelsea found she was irritated when she didn't win.

Linda had been there too, cornering Erin and asking why the hell she hadn't taken Linda's advice. She had told Erin that Maddie had a problem. She'd *told* Erin that Maddie needed an intervention, that she was using again, that she was in danger. Why hadn't Erin done anything? Her mother had simply turned on her heel and walked away. Linda was left there, in the hall, weeping, and she'd spotted Chelsea then. Linda had hugged her, ignoring The Director. 'Come find me when you're ready,' Linda had said, 'I have something I want to talk to you about.'

'Don't worry,' Chelsea had said. 'I have Robbie. He'll take care of me.'

And Linda had said, 'That's what I'm afraid of.'

Chelsea didn't know what the woman had meant by that. She avoided Linda for such a long time after Maddie had disappeared, the same way she avoided Nya. She didn't want to be around anyone who would expect her to be honest. That was until Zach and Emily had come to her and said they were worried about their mother, something wasn't quite right, and they needed Chelsea's help.

'I just don't understand,' she continued. 'How does someone

go from being your best friend to a complete stranger? I've been talking to all these people – Nancy Taylor and Milo James, and even the fucking psychic. *I found the psychic*, Linda. And she's a charlatan, can you believe that? Well, of course you can. Anyone with half a brain would know it was bullshit. But Mom believed it, and it was so obvious she thought it was going to be Maddie who would be the star. Oh, God, I wanted to prove her wrong so badly. I wanted to be the famous one so that she would love me more, the way she loved Maddie. But the worst part of it was, she didn't love either of us, not really. I don't think she's capable of it. Not like how you loved Zach and Emily, or even how you loved me and Maddie. And I lost my sister because I was so determined to save myself. And now all I can think is what if I could have saved us both?' Chelsea started to cry, tears streaming down her face, and it was then she heard the door open. She wiped at her eyes, turning, expecting to see Emily there, but it wasn't either of Linda's children. 'Oh,' she said, the shock rendering her inarticulate. 'Oh, it's you.'

'Hi, Chelsea.'

It was Robbie standing in the open-door frame. In the flesh, rather than in her dreams, her memories. He was in dark-blue jeans and a grey T-shirt, and as he smiled at her, she saw that he'd had veneers, papering over the snaggle tooth she had always thought suited him. Why did everyone do it, these days? Were she, Kelly and Nya the last generation of women allowed on screen with their real teeth? 'It's good to see you,' he said, gesturing at her to return to her one-sided conversation with Linda. He was holding a small camera, pointing it in their direction. 'Just pretend I'm not here,' he said.

'What are you doing with that?'

'The camera? It's just some shots for the reunion show.'

'What?' she said, louder than she had intended. 'What do you mean? Linda wasn't even in *Vigilante Queens*. Why would you—'

'She worked with both of us on *Double Trouble*,' he cut across her smoothly. 'She's part of the legend, you feel me?'

'I . . .' Once Robbie had secured the *Vigilante Queens* gig, he had changed almost overnight. No longer the sweet, quiet AD they had known as children, he was suddenly sharp, his mind like a steel trap, whereas she would go blank as she searched for the right words, the right sentence that would make her more interesting to him. *Don't worry*, he had told her once when she'd admitted this. *I don't need you to be interesting. That's not what a muse does. Your job is to inspire me.* 'I don't know,' she said, telling herself to be strong. Her instinct had always been to fold, to show him how malleable she was. She was a doll whose limbs he could manipulate to his own ends. But it was more than fifteen years since they had worked together. She was a mother of two now and married to one of the richest men in the States. She could stand up for herself. 'That feels inappropriate, Robbie. I don't think Linda would have wanted that.'

'Don't worry.' He walked to the opposite side of the bed from her and continued filming. What was it he had always said to her? *It was better to ask for forgiveness than permission?* 'It'll be tasteful.'

'Well,' she said, turning her head away from him, 'tasteful or not, I haven't signed off on this.' The only makeup she was wearing was tinted moisturizer and some mascara, and the lighting was terrible in there. Chelsea knew she still looked good but she was far from camera ready. 'Put that away, please,' she said, and Robbie stiffened. He wasn't used to her issuing demands: that wasn't how their dynamic functioned. He had talked and Chelsea had listened. He made decisions and she did what she was told. That was how it had worked for them until, of course, it didn't.

'Fine,' he said, powering it off and placing it on a side table, and Chelsea felt a rush running through her, that same feeling she'd been having these last few weeks. Power or something akin to it. She was almost getting used to it. 'It's so sad what happened to Linda, isn't it?' he continued. 'I always liked her. The nurses tell me you visit every week.' He pulled up a plastic seat and sat at the opposite side of Linda's bed. 'They say you never miss a day.'

'Yeah, well. You know how important Linda was to me. To Maddie, too. She was like our second mother.'

'Yes.' The Director had been there. He'd witnessed the Stone family up close from an early age. 'Although Erin seems to be doing well, these days.'

'How do you know that?' Chelsea asked, surprised. She didn't know her mother and Robbie had kept in touch. Erin had never mentioned it to her anyway. He coughed, clearing his throat. 'Just what I see on social media,' he said quickly. 'You don't have as much to do with her these days, do you?'

Erin wouldn't like that observation. She had always wanted to maintain the perfect family image even after Maddie had disappeared. 'No,' Chelsea admitted. 'Not really.'

'I was always trying to tell you that, wasn't I? That you needed separation from your mother. From . . .' He stumbled. Neither of them would want to talk about Madeline. 'And how is the great Nick Bennett?' He changed the subject. 'And those kids of yours?'

'The kids are great,' she replied, avoiding the subject of her husband. 'Growing up so fast but I'm sure you feel the same about your own.'

'Yeah.' His face darkened. 'Not that I get to see them much these days, not if Ruby has anything to do with it.'

He had cast Ruby Grainger, an actress from the UK, in the last film he and Chelsea had been slated to work on together, the one she had pulled out of after Maddie disappeared. He had still been married to Diana then but there had been rumours of an on-set romance for months before. Finally, photos of him kissing Ruby on a deserted beach in Ireland had been published all around the world. He and Diana were divorced within the year, and after that, all anyone cared about was him and Ruby, with their identically sharp bone structure and penchant for French-kissing on the red carpet. Ruby had been even younger than Chelsea, and somewhat of a wild child, famous for interviews in which she confessed to being high on coke or telling stories about how she'd fucked both of her co-stars at the after-party of their première. The Director had made her change her ways, Ruby said, and for the next ten years, she was a paragon of virtue. She stayed at home to raise their four children, sharing videos of herself making sourdough bread from scratch, arranging wildflowers the kids had picked in their garden, demonstrating how she had used her babies' old knitted sweaters to craft a memory quilt. When they'd broken up, it had been a shock – they had seemed the perfect couple – but it turned messy so quickly, with Ruby claiming that The Director was controlling and emotionally abusive. Five years later, they were still not divorced, their lawyers unable to agree to terms. The children did not want to see their father – Ruby said they were afraid of him – but Robbie's team called this a deliberate and calculated act of parental alienation.

'It's devastating,' he said to Chelsea. 'I miss the little ones so much. But I have to trust that they'll come back to me eventually, once they realize that all of this is just a figment of their mother's imagination.'

'The public are on your side, anyway,' Chelsea said, which Robbie batted away, as if it didn't matter, when he and Chelsea both knew it was *all* that mattered in this town. Nya had sent her an article a few months ago, investigating claims that Robbie's team had hired bots to spread misinformation about his ex-wife, saying she was a liar, it was #MeToo gone too far: it was a witch hunt. But even though the evidence was credible – there was a tape of Robbie screaming at Ruby that she was 'a fucking cunt', which his fans promptly called a deep-fake – none of it seemed to stick. People loved The Director's work too much to be willing to believe that he was capable of such cruelty – it was easier to call Ruby a psycho. She'd always been crazy, they said, and she had stolen Robbie from Diana Dawson in the first place, remember?

'Did I hear something about a different lawsuit?' she asked. 'I hope I won't get another email from your team.'

'Yes.' Robbie screwed up his face. 'I'm sorry about that. I know how private you are. I can't tell you how much I appreciated you doing that for me.' He had sent Chelsea an Hermès blanket and a gift card for Shutters on the Beach to say thank you, which she had given to Hannah, telling her assistant to take her latest girlfriend there for the weekend. 'I hate having to sue, I really do,' he said, 'but I missed out on a couple of opportunities after her allegations and I lost a considerable amount of money. I had to protect my reputation.'

What about Ruby's reputation? Robbie's cartel had quickly circled the wagons: Hollywood was like high school and he was Prom King. No one would hire Ruby now, not if it risked pissing him off. It reminded Chelsea of what had happened to Maddie, how her sister had been thrown upon the pyre and they'd all watched her burn. So little had changed in the last twenty years, no matter what anyone said.

'You look great, Chel,' he said, and she hated that she was pleased to hear it. His eye had always been exacting, a compliment from him meant something.

'Thanks,' she said. 'So do you.' He smiled and she tried not to cringe at the veneers. 'What are you working on these days?' she asked, changing the subject.

'I'm adapting a novel about a pirate queen,' he said. 'Very feminist, very moving. I really wanted to make something my girls would be inspired by, if they ever get the chance to watch their old man's work.'

'Is it about Grace O'Malley?' she asked.

'No.' He leaned back in his seat, raising an eyebrow at her. 'But aren't you clever to guess that?'

Oh, fuck off. Had he always been this paternalistic? 'Yes,' she said drily. 'I'm very smart.'

'We're in the middle of casting right now.' He tilted his head to the side. 'We already have our queen – Scarlett is playing her, she's phenomenal – but there is a role I think you'd be perfect for. It's small but, still, a pivotal part. Would you be interested?'

A role in his new film? Starring alongside Scarlett Johansson? Chelsea allowed herself, just for a moment, to imagine what it would be like to be back at work. The early starts and hair and makeup, the hours spent in her trailer, running lines with her co-stars or knitting or reading to fill the time before she was called on set. But then she remembered Grayson and Ivy. Nick, of course. And, finally, she thought about publicity junkets and all the questions, questions about her sister, *whatever happened to Madeline Stone?* Nancy Taylor had had any such questions banned from the reunion show – it was written into Chelsea's contract. There would be severe repercussions if the agreement was breached, even if it was live TV, but her agent couldn't get that promise from every journalist in town. 'No,' she said quietly. 'I don't think that would work.'

He shifted in his seat. 'You know, when you said you were gonna quit acting, I thought it might last six months, a year tops. I didn't think it would be permanent. It's a shame.'

'I'm happier this way,' she said, wishing it didn't sound like a lie. 'Everything got so difficult after Maddie disappeared.'

He didn't reply. What could he say? He had been there. He had watched as Chelsea had fallen apart in slow motion. The nights she couldn't sleep, when he would go out to his guesthouse to check on her and find her sitting on the couch, red-eyed, watching yet another rerun of *Double Trouble*, staring at her sister's face on the screen. She wasn't taking her diet pills but she still couldn't eat. She had lost an alarming amount of weight and her thinness had come to fascinate her, in a strange way, the bones rising to the surface. She didn't want to leave the house – she couldn't bear it, all the paparazzi yelling at her, asking if she was sad, did she miss her twin, did she think Madeline had killed herself, like everyone was saying? Robbie had tried his best, pushing Chelsea to get back on set, telling her that the best way to get over her sister's disappearance was to throw herself into work. She took his advice, signing on to every project she was offered, each one worse than the last, but she didn't care. She just wanted to be so busy she couldn't think any more. And then finally, after a year of back-to-back films, Chelsea was so burned out that she'd collapsed. Nervous exhaustion was what they'd called it in the hospital, which Chelsea had always assumed was a euphemism for a drug overdose. When she'd been discharged, she had gone to Robbie and then to Nancy Taylor, and she had told them she couldn't do it any more. She had to quit. She was done.

'And all this mess with the storage unit?' The Director gave a low whistle. 'How are you doing?'

'I mean . . .'

'Yeah.' He was sympathetic. 'That's rough. I hope you're able to put it behind you and focus on what's important. All of that was so long ago. You can't let it derail you, Chelsea.' His tone was so sympathetic, it was almost nauseating. 'You have to keep moving forward.'

'Hmm,' she said, trying not to bristle. She was about to

speak again when Linda stirred, her arms flailing, like she was having a bad dream. Chelsea got to her feet, bending over the bed. One hand on Linda's shoulder, the other holding her wrist. 'Linda,' she said gently. 'Linda, you're okay. I'm here. It's me, Chelsea.'

The older woman opened her eyes, blinking. She murmured something, and her throat sounded dry. Chelsea grabbed at a plastic cup and filled it with water, putting a straw into it and bringing it to Linda's mouth. The woman gulped at it gratefully. When she had finished, Chelsea put the cup away and brushed Linda's hair back from her face. She heard a cough, and when she looked up, Robbie had picked up his camera again, pointing it at them.

'Robbie . . .' she said.

'I'm sorry,' he said, although he didn't look it. 'It was such a beautiful moment, I couldn't resist. I just wanted to capture it on film. We don't have to use it but it'll be nice for you to have anyway, right? When she . . .'

She ignored him, returning to Linda, but the older woman was staring at Robbie, her expression somewhere between anger and fear. She was muttering words that Chelsea couldn't quite make out so she leaned in even closer. And then she heard it.

'Christopher,' Linda was whispering, still staring at him. '*Christopher.*'

28.

2008

'I'm not sure,' Chelsea said, making a face at her reflection in the mirror. Blake Logan had come to The Director's house that morning with racks of clothes, shoes and jewellery. Fab place, her stylist had said, when she had arrived at Robbie's mid-century modern home in the Hollywood Hills, and Chelsea had accepted the compliment graciously, although she was only living in the guesthouse, still afraid to move anything in case she disrupted the 'flow' of the place, as Robbie called it. 'It just feels a bit . . .' Chelsea smoothed down the full satin skirt of the gown. 'A bit dated, maybe?' She peered at herself in the mirror again. The dress might not be right, but the woman in it certainly was. She had never looked more like a star, her hair dyed the blondest it had ever been, her body whittled as thin as possible without a diagnosis of anorexia. Not that it stopped the magazines, and RumorMill, of course, publishing photos of her from angles where she looked particularly frail, the straps of her dress hanging off her razor-sharp collarbones. Yet another starlet fallen prey to the size 00 trend, they said. *They're just jealous*, Blake Logan told her, as she handed over another package of the magic pills. *You look amazing, doll.*

'Dated?' Blake drew herself up to her full six feet, one inch, visibly insulted that Chelsea would imply she would ever pull anything that wasn't high fashion. 'This was shown at Paris in September. It's new. It's *fresh*. But . . .' She shrugged, unzipping the gown and yanking it down over Chelsea's hips, leaving her naked from the waist up. She rushed to cover her breasts, and Blake said, 'I've seen it all before, don't worry.' She flung the gown at her assistant and returned to the racks, frowning. 'It does have to be Couyer,' her stylist said, 'which limits our options slightly.'

Just before *The List of Second Chances* was released, Blake had managed to score Chelsea a contract with Couyer, one of the most prestigious fashion houses in France, for three million dollars. Even Robbie had approved – it was a legacy brand, he said, elegant, timeless, perfect for the image he was creating for her. Chelsea was the new face of their perfume, and she was contractually obliged to wear the brand for every major public appearance she attended over the next four years. It had seemed like a lot of money when she had signed, but now Chelsea wished she had waited. She should have known from the reaction at Cannes that the movie was going to be big – it had received one of the longest standing ovations ever recorded at the festival, as well as winning the Palme d'Or for best film – but Robbie had told her they couldn't take anything for granted. So much would depend on the domestic box office.

But within a few days of its release at the end of November, it was clear they had a smash hit on their hands. Movie theatres were sold out, audiences adored it, the reviews were ecstatic. It was being heralded as a modern classic, something that would cement The Director's place in movie-making history. He was a genius, critics were saying, he was an *auteur*, he had the potential to become an icon of film one day, if he continued to make movies of this calibre. *He even managed to do the impossible,* the review in the *LA Times* said, *and that was to coax a career-defining performance out of Chelsea Stone, a child actor who has been wooden in every other vehicle she's starred in to date. She has never been more luminous on screen than she is as Sissy Miller, the down-on-her-luck girl from the wrong side of town with whom both Calahan brothers fall in love. A star is born, indeed.*

'Okay, what about this one?' Blake held up a gown that was practically identical to the one Chelsea had just tried on, except it was black with beading on the bodice.

'Fine,' Chelsea said, stepping into the dress. She had been nominated for everything this season – the Globes, the Emmys, the SAG awards, the BAFTAs – and at each ceremony, there she had stood on the red carpet, in yet another dowdy Couyer ensemble. *Boring!* That was what Joan Rivers had said about her on *Fashion Police* and Chelsea had had to agree.

The door to the living room swung open and Nancy Taylor walked in, her cell phone pressed between her ear and her shoulder. Chelsea's agent had come to the house that morning, saying she could just as easily answer emails from there as from the office, but that wasn't the real reason and they both knew it. 'Any news?' Chelsea mouthed at her, and Nancy shook her head. *Not yet.*

'Awesome, thanks, Grant,' Nancy said. 'I'll shoot you an email later.' She hung up, and looked Chelsea up and down. 'Nice dress. What's that for?'

'The SAG awards,' Blake piped up. She had pins in her mouth and was taking the dress in around the waistline – even the sample size was a little big for Chelsea now. 'What do you think?' Her tone was sardonic. She had made her disdain for Nancy's style perfectly clear, saying Hillary Clinton had called and she wanted her pantsuits back. Nancy tolerated the stylist – she might not know much about fashion but she knew that Blake was the best in the business – and although Nancy pretended to be ignorant of the pills Blake slipped into Chelsea's bag at the end of every fitting, Chelsea knew her agent preferred her at this size too. It made her more hireable and, ultimately, that was all Nancy Taylor cared about.

Whatever Happened to Madeline Stone?

Nancy's phone rang again and Chelsea froze. She stared at her agent as she answered. 'Yes, this is she . . .' Nancy said, turning away to talk to whoever was on the other end of the line. Nancy wasn't giving anything away, her tone neutral and controlled. 'I see . . . Yes, of course. That makes sense . . . Okay, great.' She spun on her heel to face Chelsea and Blake, both of whom were staring at her. 'I have some news,' Nancy said. 'The Oscar nominations have just been announced and—'

'We know that!' Chelsea interrupted. 'Get to the point.'

Nancy raised an eyebrow but she continued. 'You'll be pleased to hear *The List of Second Chances* has been nominated in several categories. Hair and makeup, costume. Best Picture and, of course, a Best Director nom for Robbie Myers.'

Chelsea heard herself gasp. The relief was so sharp. She hadn't realized until this moment how nervous she'd been at the prospect that Robbie might not get the nomination, and how he would react if that happened.

'My God.' Her agent chuckled. 'What a coup! From assistant director on *Double Trouble* to an Academy Award nomination in under ten years. And one in the Best Original Screenplay category, which we had been expecting,' Nancy said. 'Finn and Owen both got nominated for Best Supporting Actor and—' she broke off here and Chelsea saw that her eyes were welling up. Nancy Taylor, famous hard-ass. Who would have thought she was capable of it? 'And a Best Actress nomination for the one and only Chelsea Stone.'

Nancy barely got the words out before Blake started screaming and Chelsea couldn't help it: she burst into tears, crouching on her haunches so she could touch the floor to steady herself. She felt Nancy bend down beside her, whispering into her ear, 'We did it, we fucking did it.' When Chelsea's breath steadied, she barked at Blake, 'Where's my phone?' and the stylist ran to grab it from Chelsea's purse. Already, Chelsea had dozens of missed calls and text messages, and the screen lit up with her mother's name. She sent that call to voicemail – she had to talk to Robbie first: she had to congratulate him and to thank him too, of course. No matter what happened, for the rest of her life, she would be referred to as Academy Award nominee Chelsea Stone, and it was all because of him.

'Hi, Erin,' she heard her agent say, and she looked up quickly, mouthing *I don't want to talk to her.* Nancy nodded. 'She's just on a call with Robbie,' the older woman lied smoothly. Chelsea could hear her mother's voice at the other end of the phone. Even from that distance, Erin sounded elated, screaming with joy.

'OMG.' Blake grabbed at Chelsea's hands. 'What are we going to dress you in? These pictures will last for ever. It has to be a knockout.' She frowned. 'I don't know about the current Couyer collection. Is there anything major enough for the *Oscars*? Maybe they'll let us pull from the archives, a little vintage moment. What do you . . .'

Chelsea zoned out, allowing the stylist to ramble on. She dialled Robbie's number but it went straight to voicemail. She tried again and this time it rang once, twice, three times, then went to voicemail again. It was probably nothing, she told herself. Everyone would be phoning him now to congratulate him but really to ingratiate themselves, to make sure he remembered them when he was working on his next project. She knew that made sense – her own phone was blowing up, what must his be like? – but, still, she couldn't help feeling anxious that he was angry with her about what had happened the night before.

They'd hosted yet another screening of *Second Chances*. It was too late for Oscar nominations, but it was still no harm to get some face time with potential voters, Robbie had said. Afterwards, they had worked the room, together then separately, and Chelsea had been cornered by the legendary producer Jeffrey Green. He was a heavy-set man whose breath smelt of cigarettes and he had stood so close to her, his hand lingering too low on her hip for comfort. He kept making jokes about the sex scenes in the movie, asking if Chelsea had enjoyed filming them as much as he'd enjoyed watching them, and she laughed too, hating herself for doing so. Maddie wouldn't have done that. Maddie would have told him to go fuck himself and to read some Andrea Dworkin for good measure.

She had been relieved when Robbie joined them, clapping the man on the back with a hearty 'Jeffrey, it's good to see you!' They'd talked about the film for a while, Jeffrey telling Robbie how brilliant he was, and Robbie lapped it up because, no matter how gross he was, Jeffrey was still the most powerful producer in Hollywood, he was a kingmaker. Then Robbie had gestured at Chelsea and said, 'The biggest challenge was trying to get this one to stop emoting like she was auditioning for *Annie*. Child actors!'

'What's up with you?' he'd said, on the car journey home, when he noticed how quiet she was, and when Chelsea had tried to explain how insulting she had found his comments, not to mention how damaging they could be to her own campaign, Robbie had gone mute. He didn't say anything as they pulled into the driveway of the house, or as he slammed the car door behind him, walking up the steps and through the front door. It was only there that he turned to her, pointing his finger in her face. 'What is wrong with you?' he'd asked. 'You know what a big deal this is for me. I thought I was going to be an AD for kids' shows for ever. You know how hard I had to work to get here, the sacrifices I had to make. You know how stressful this is for me, how much fucking pressure I'm under right now. And I brought you with me, Chelsea. I'm out here, trying my best to make sure this movie is a huge hit for both of us, and you can't cut me some slack over a stupid joke.' He'd walked away from her then, ignoring her calling after him, saying she was sorry, she was being too sensitive. When she followed him upstairs to his bedroom, she found the door locked, and no matter how many times she knocked, pleading with him to talk to her, Robbie refused to answer. She'd gone out to the guesthouse to sleep, and when she'd woken that morning, he had already gone.

Chelsea tried calling him one last time, and yet again it went to voicemail. She stood there, staring at her BlackBerry, and she realized there was only one person she wanted to talk to about this. Maddie. They used to stay up every year to watch the awards, eating junk food and sighing over the beautiful dresses. 'Who would you thank if you won?' Maddie had asked, throwing a chip at the TV in disgust after Kate Winslet lost for *Titanic*.

Chelsea's mind had gone completely blank. She was incapable of even imagining such a fate. 'I don't know,' she said. 'What about you?'

And with that, Maddie had jumped to her feet, holding her can of Coke as if it was the statuette. 'I'd like to thank the Academy, and the Lord Jesus Christ, of course,' she'd said in a silly voice before turning serious. 'But mostly I would like to dedicate this award to my best friend in the whole world, my sister.'

Chelsea smiled at her agent as Nancy rushed back into the room with a bottle of champagne and three crystal flutes, the stylist beside her singing, 'Celebrate! And have a good time!' off-tune. But Maddie wouldn't answer the phone, even if she did ring her. Her sister never answered the phone to Chelsea any more.

29.

2025

Chelsea half stood up, her eyes on Linda, then Robbie. 'What did she just call you?' she asked, but he just shrugged.

'I don't know.'

Chelsea turned to Linda again but the older woman had slipped back into unconsciousness, as if the effort of saying that one name had worn her out. Her head slumped to the side, her mouth open, and she began to snore. 'What . . .' Chelsea tried.

'I don't know,' Robbie said again. 'I couldn't hear her. Her speech isn't very clear these days, is it?'

'She called you "Christopher".' Chelsea took a half-step away from him, the metal side rails biting into her back. *Christopher*, the name on Maddie's love letters, the name of the person who had paid for the storage unit. Was Robbie behind all of it? Had he been blackmailing her? Had he and her sister— At this thought, her stomach clenched, and she could taste bile in her throat.

'Okay,' he said slowly. 'My name isn't Christopher. It's Robbie.'

'But why would she say—'

'Chelsea.' He gestured at the room around him. 'We're in a nursing home. Linda has dementia. She obviously mixed me up with someone else or she just didn't recognize me. I wasn't as close to her on *Double Trouble* as you guys were. She was at least ten years older than me and Julia. It's not like we had much in common.' But there had been ten years between him and the twins too, did Robbie ever think of that? 'It's been years since I've seen her. God, it must be . . .' It must have been Madeline's memorial service. That was what Robbie was about to say, but he stopped himself. 'You look like you've seen a ghost. Do you need to sit down?'

'But Christopher is—'

'I don't know who Christopher is,' he said. He leaned against the wall, crossing his arms over his body. He looked utterly nonchalant. No one else would have spotted the way his eyes half darted to Linda, as if checking to see that she was asleep. Maybe no one else would have noticed the tiny vein at the base of his throat, either, and how it pulsed. But Chelsea knew this man. She knew him because she had studied him for years. She had thought if she understood The Director like no other actor did, if she could interpret his every sigh, his every facial tic, he would feel so seen that he would need her for ever. That had been a mistake, she realized later. He hadn't wanted to be seen for his true self. He didn't want to be remembered as Robbie, the assistant director on an AtomicKids show. He'd wanted to edit his image as carefully as he did his movies, fine-tuning each still until he was satisfied. Nevertheless, Chelsea knew him. She knew him well enough to see when he was lying.

And he was lying now.

'Are you okay?' he asked. 'You're not going to faint, are you? I'll get you a glass of water. You stay right there.' He walked out of the room and she could hear him talking to the nurses, their high-pitched laughter as he charmed them, the way he did with everyone. 'Yes,' she heard him say. 'A pirate-queen movie. Very feminist, very moving. You know, I just wanted to make something my daughters would—'

Chelsea looked at Linda, then at the table, where Robbie had laid down his camera. He had a camera bag with him, and a leather briefcase, and before she knew what she was doing, Chelsea was crossing the room in quick strides, crouching so she could rummage through it. If he came back in and saw her, rooting around in his things, she would die of shame, but she kept going. A pair of reading glasses, a water bottle, a Moleskine notebook, a fountain pen with his name engraved upon it, a couple of scripts. *The Pirate Queen* was the first and then— Chelsea's hands began to shake so badly she almost dropped it.

Double the Trouble, was written on the cover. And there, underneath – *An original screenplay by Erin Stone.*

'I'd better get back in there,' Chelsea heard Robbie say and she stuffed the items back into his briefcase, getting to her feet and pretending to fix Linda's hair when he walked into the room, a glass in his hands. 'Here,' he said, giving it to her. 'Drink that.' He waited until she had taken a sip. 'Feel better?'

Chelsea forced some words out. 'I have to . . .' she tried, her white-knuckled grip on the side of Linda's bed. 'I have to go.'

Robbie nodded, watching as she walked away. Just before she left the room, he called after her, 'I'm happy you're doing the reunion show, by the way. It wouldn't be the same without you.'

30.

2025

'Mom.' Chelsea burst through her mother's front door. 'Erin!' she screamed, when there was no response. 'Where the fuck are you?'

She ran into the kitchen but her mother wasn't there. Neither was she in the living room. She went back to the hall and she found Erin, walking down the stairs, rubbing her eyes. She had obviously been napping. There were creases from the pillow on her face, and her hair was mussed. 'What's wrong?' Erin said. She picked up her pace when she saw Chelsea, racing down the last few steps. 'What's happened? Is it the kids?' She skidded to a stop, and Chelsea didn't know if it was the lighting or that Erin had just woken up, but her mother looked old to her for the first time, her crow's feet visible, a slackening around her jaw. 'Are the kids okay?' she asked again, grabbing hold of Chelsea's forearm.

'They're fine.' Chelsea had texted Hannah on the drive there, telling her assistant that she wouldn't be home until late and to make sure Ivy and Grayson got a nutritious dinner and that the nanny put them to bed on time. *I'm on it,* Hannah had replied. *But, Chelsea, are you okay? I'm worried. Please let me help.* Chelsea didn't respond. At this stage, she wouldn't know where to begin. 'I just came from the care home. Visiting Linda. And do you know who arrived while I was there?' She paused. 'Robbie Myers. Isn't that a funny coincidence?'

'Oh.' Erin let go of her grip. 'How is Robbie doing these days?'

'Oh, great,' Chelsea said. 'Super. He's doing a pirate-queen movie – *very* feminist, apparently – oh, and a little something called *Double the Trouble*. Have you heard about it?'

Her mother's skin paled and she turned away, about to walk into the kitchen. 'I don't know— Ow.' She winced as Chelsea grabbed her elbow and pulled her back, hard.

'Don't walk away from me,' Chelsea hissed. '*Double the fucking Trouble?* That's what you're calling it, Mom? This is why you've been acting so weird the last few weeks?'

Erin faced her and, for a second, Chelsea wondered if her mother was going to lie. Would she pretend she didn't know what Chelsea was talking about? But Erin squared her shoulders, like she was preparing for a fight, and when her voice came out, it was firmer than Chelsea had expected. 'And?' she said. 'What have you got to say about it?'

'You . . .' Chelsea hadn't been anticipating this. 'Go get the script for me,' she said. Erin hesitated until Chelsea said, 'Now,' in a tone that brooked no argument. She stood there, in the house her husband had paid for, and she waited.

Erin shuffled back in less than two minutes, a bound script in her hands. Chelsea grabbed it and sat on the bottom stair as she speed-read it. It was surprisingly good, was her first thought, and loosely based on *Faust*, fame working as a stand-in for the Devil. Two sisters, twins. Carrie and Melanie. Carrie sold out Melanie in order to be famous, and while there was a mother, she was gentle and retiring, nothing at all like Erin, and there was no involvement of a handsome young director. When she got to the final scene, where the Devil asked Carrie to kill Melanie in order to win an Academy Award, she gasped. Erin had the good grace to look ashamed as Chelsea said, 'No. No, you didn't. *Mom.*'

'Robbie thought it was a more dramatic ending.' Erin said, twirling a strand of hair around her finger nervously. 'No one is going to think you *literally* killed your sister. And, besides, it's my story too. I have a right to—'

'If it's your story too, why aren't you in it?' Her mother had no response to that. 'You don't have the right to take what happened to Maddie and spin it into this farce,' Chelsea cried. 'You *know* there are people out there who think I had something to do with her disappearance. And now my own mother has written a script saying I killed her? Are you insane?' She tried to think. 'Nick will stop this. You signed that NDA. He'll sue you into oblivion if I ask him to.'

'It's fiction,' Erin replied petulantly. 'It doesn't break the NDA. Robbie got his lawyers to look over it and they—'

'Of course he did. What is wrong with you? *Robbie*, of all people?'

'He's a genius.' Erin lifted her chin in defiance. 'And he's been a family friend for decades. He knew you and your sister when you were kids. Who better to tell this story?'

She stared at her mother. 'Mom,' she said, 'I'm gonna ask you something now and I need you to be honest with me. Can you do that?' She waited until her mother nodded. 'Did Maddie and Robbie . . . did they . . .' Chelsea had no idea how to phrase this. Date? Fuck? It seemed utterly impossible. Robbie had been so protective of them both. He'd always said he had seen them as little sisters, akin to the cousins he had back home. 'Were they . . . together when we were shooting *Double Trouble?*'

'I have no idea,' Erin said, but she sounded unnatural, as if she was reciting lines. 'I didn't know at the time,' she amended, when she saw the scepticism on Chelsea's face. 'Linda did come to me once and said she had her suspicions. She had seen a letter stuffed into one of Maddie's books but it was addressed to a Christopher – Linda kept saying something about a nickname or a kids' book or something, but how would I know who that was? It was probably just some boy she'd met at Cedar City, knowing Maddie. Linda wanted me to step in, to ask if there was anything going on, as if your sister would have told me anything.'

'Why didn't she tell me?'

'Linda?' Erin scoffed. 'For Pete's sake, you know what Linda was like. She didn't want to say anything to you because she said you were too young.' That was typical of Linda, the only adult in the room who had ever tried to protect them. 'After Maddie died, I imagine she didn't want to upset you and then . . .' Erin didn't need to say any more. They had all witnessed Linda's devastating decline first-hand. 'And what could she say, anyway? She thought Maddie and Robbie seemed too close, but she didn't know anything for definite, didn't have any proof. I was hardly going to go around accusing him of – of *that*. And you weren't children, you were young women. Who was I to tell you who you could and could not date?'

'We were fifteen years of age,' Chelsea said quietly. 'And you told us everything else – you told us what to eat and what to wear and who we should be friends with. You told us that going to college was a waste of time. You wouldn't let us cut our hair or get our ears pierced. You insisted on picking out my clothes for me until I left for Wilmington to film the first season of *Vigilante Queens*. But you couldn't tell Maddie not to fall for a twenty-five-year-old man?' Chelsea rubbed a hand over her chest. It was physically aching as she thought about Maddie, and all the ways they had failed her. 'Wait.' She stopped. 'What do you mean, you didn't know *at the time*? Does that mean you knew later?' Her mother looked away, and Chelsea continued, stricken, 'You did, didn't you?'

'I just didn't think it was worth making a big deal over some teenage crush gone wrong . . . Your sister was fine. It's not like she was traumatized. If anything, she hated Robbie so much over the *Vigilante* rights fiasco, he was the one who needed protection, not her.' She rushed on after seeing the expression on Chelsea's face: 'That was a joke! Chelsea, come on. What else could I do? Robbie was a powerful man at that point, and he was doing so much for your career. You were on *fire*. You wouldn't have been able to keep working with him if it came out that he'd been involved with your sister, and you and Robbie, the films you were making together were so beautiful. I didn't want anything to ruin that for you. I did this for you, Chelsea. Everything I did was for you.'

'No. It wasn't. It was for *you*. And now you're going to sell our story to him? You're going to allow Robbie to rewrite history? How could you do this to Maddie?' If her sister was still alive, would the news of this film make her stay away? More proof that she had done the right thing in leaving her family behind? With a sinking feeling, Chelsea asked, 'What did he promise you, Mom? I know it can't be about the money – you could have asked me and Nick for that.' Erin's mouth tightened so Chelsea said again, 'What did that man promise to get you to sign the rights to him?'

Conflicting emotions waged a war on her mother's face before she finally said, 'Well, there's the role of the twins' mother, Ellen. He did say that maybe I'd be the right person to play her.'

Chelsea wanted to throw her head back and howl at the ceiling in frustration. 'Are you joking?'

'You don't understand,' Erin said. 'I sacrificed everything for you girls and I had to stand back and watch as your sister screwed it up. And then you went and quit. You just quit, Chelsea! I would have *killed* to have your career. You had everything and you didn't appreciate it.' She clenched her fists at her sides. 'It's my turn now. Why can't you be happy for me?'

'You're a fool,' Chelsea said. 'There's no way Robbie's gonna let you play the mother of teenage girls. Are you kidding? It says in the script she's in her late thirties! You're too old, no matter how much plastic surgery you get. That man was manipulating you and you fell for it.'

Erin's eyes went blank, the way they always did when she was confronted with something she didn't want to deal with. 'It's my time,' she said again. 'It's my time.'

'It's your time to do what, Mom?' Chelsea pushed herself up to standing, still clutching the script. She prodded her mother's shoulder with her right index finger, pushing Erin back into the wall. 'It's your time to be selfish? To put yourself first? Because you've been doing that for as long as I can remember. It's not exactly new.'

'That's not true,' Erin said. 'I did my best. I was a good mother. I—'

'A good mother?' Chelsea started to laugh, a tinge of hysteria to it now. 'You were a *terrible* mother. You're a narcissist. Maddie knew that – she had your number long before I did. She said I needed to get out of the house, that you'd suck us both dry if you had the chance. And I defended you for so long! I took your side over hers all the time. I stayed. *I stayed with you.* I should have left with Maddie, but I didn't because all I wanted was for you to love me the most, Mom. I thought if I was the best girl I could possibly be, you would . . .' Her voice cracked with the sadness. 'But all you've ever done is sell me out. Sell *us* out. You never protected us, not once. Maddie is God knows where, but if there's even the slightest chance she's alive, I'm going to do whatever it takes to find her. And if this movie gets made, we might never see her again. Do you get that? Do you even care? *Fuck.* You're as bad as Dad.' She could see Erin was about to defend herself, and Chelsea put up a hand to stop her. 'No,' she said. 'You're worse than he is. Because at least Dad didn't pretend like he gave a fuck about us.'

She strode away from her mother, opening the front door. She could still hear the other woman behind her, talking, and Chelsea spun on her heel. 'I never want to see you again,' she said, and her voice was preternaturally calm. Erin could sense it too, her eyes widening in shock. She'd been used to this kind of defiance from Maddie, she had come to expect it, but never from Chelsea. Chelsea was supposed to be the compliant one, the easy daughter, but no more. She clutched the script tightly in her fingers. 'You and me,' Chelsea gestured between herself and her mother, 'we're done, Erin. We're through.'

31.

2025

When she got outside to where her car was parked, Chelsea's hands were trembling so badly that she dropped her keys. Her security guy reached to pick them up, asking if she was okay. 'I don't know,' she admitted, and he insisted on driving: she was not in a fit state to do so. 'Home?' he asked, adjusting the seat to accommodate his long legs. 'No,' she said. 'Not yet.'

By the time they arrived at Kelly's house, Chelsea was still unsteady on her feet as she got out of the car. 'Wait here,' she told the security guard. 'And will you call Hannah and tell her I'll be a little late? Thanks.'

She could hear Kelly on the phone as she rang the doorbell. Her friend sounded irritated, saying, 'I'm not sure what you expect me to do, I—' She broke off when she opened the door and saw Chelsea. 'I've gotta go,' she said, hanging up. 'Hey,' she said, but she didn't stand back to let Chelsea through. 'I can't hang out right now, Chel.'

Chelsea didn't listen. She just walked past her into the house. It was messy, Kelly's unfolded laundry strewn on the armchair, an empty chips bag on the coffee-table, and the room smelt stale, as if the windows hadn't been opened in a few days. 'Okay then,' she heard Kelly say, with a sigh. 'I'm supposed to be going on a date.'

Her friend was wearing sweatpants and an oversized T-shirt, her hair was in a topknot, and she had no makeup on. Kelly's face coloured a little, and she looked down, saying, 'I mean, I have to get ready for a date.'

Chelsea couldn't trust herself to speak. Her hands hadn't stopped shaking since she had left the nursing home, and she still felt queasy, as if she might vomit at any moment. She realized that Kelly was staring at her: her friend had asked her a question. 'Sorry,' she said. 'What did you say?'

'I asked if Nancy Taylor had been in touch.'

'Oh, for—' Nancy had been trying to convince her to sign off on sponsored content for social media, a J. Crew campaign starring the three Queens. The money was good but she couldn't do it, obviously. Nick would lose his mind if she was advertising on platforms other than Foto. 'She has. But I'm not doing it. I don't know why Nancy can't get the message.'

'Well,' Kelly gave her a hard stare, 'maybe because Nancy understands that this is a huge opportunity for some of us.'

'Please don't start with this.'

'What?' her friend snapped. 'I'm sorry that this is important to me. Not everyone married rich, babes. I actually need this, you know.'

'I'm doing the reunion. Isn't that enough for you?' Chelsea's voice was harder than she had used with Kelly in years, if ever. But she was tired of trying to placate her friend, tired of feeling guilty that she had been the star of the show, the one to survive. She had married a rich man, yes, a man who loved her and who had been good to her, but one who used sex as a bargaining chip, withholding intimacy to punish her. She had made sacrifices too, not that Kelly would ever acknowledge it. 'I'm not sure how much more money you need, Kelly. This house is yours.' She met her friend's eye, *And I paid for it* left unsaid. 'You don't have any debt. We've covered every single one of your rehab stays. What else do you want from me?' She put a hand over her mouth, as if she was trying to stop herself talking. A breath, two breaths, and still, neither of them said anything. 'I'm sorry, Kell, I didn't mean that. I'm just rattled. I can't tell you what kind of day I've had.'

Kelly didn't respond. She stood there, leaning against the counter top, her arms folded across her chest. Where could Chelsea even begin? 'I went to the nursing home to see Linda,' she said. 'And while I was there, The Director came in. He was filming. He said he wanted to use the footage for the reunion show but how would that make sense? Linda wasn't even on *Vigilante Queens*. And then . . .' her mouth went dry, remembering it '. . . Linda called him Christopher. *Robbie*. Robbie was Christopher all along.'

'Yeah,' Kelly replied, and she sounded almost bored, checking her nails and picking at one of her cuticles. 'That tracks.'

'What?' The room felt like it was spinning, like Chelsea was on a merry-go-round, faster and faster, and she couldn't get off. 'What do you mean, that tracks?'

'For fuck's sake.' Kelly exploded. 'Like, of course Robbie was Christopher. He's been saying in interviews that his favourite kids' book was *Winnie the Pooh* for years. Christopher Robin?' She rolled her eyes. 'It's not even a good nickname. It's exactly what a teenage girl would think was clever. They weren't exactly subtle, either. As soon as I saw Maddie and Robbie in the same room, I knew they'd fucked. She could barely keep her eyes off him, no matter how much she protested that she hated him.' Kelly made a face. 'He really screwed her over, didn't he? First, he took her virginity and then he signed those TV rights, right under her nose. And he cast her twin sister in her dream role? Oof.' She pretended to stab a dagger into her heart. 'Ice fucking cold.'

'Oh, my God,' Chelsea whispered, and she remembered Milo James, how he had said someone was paying him to write terrible stories about Maddie. 'The RumorMill stuff, the—'

'Gee.' Kelly tapped a finger against her bottom lip. 'I wonder who would have benefited from Madeline Stone's reputation being ruined. That way, if she ever came forward and told her story, who would believe her? God, he's so smart, you'd nearly have to admire it if he wasn't so evil. And you know he was friends with the Punch Media guys too – they were in film school together. You think Robbie didn't help them annihilate your sister after the *GQ* interview?' Kelly gave a humourless laugh. 'I half thought it might come out during #MeToo. It did look like there was some momentum building, a few whispers here and there about Robbie's liking for young girls during all the drama with the ex-wife. But I should have known better. The only men in this town allowed to go down for their crimes were the ones not making a profit any more.'

'But why would Robbie set up the blog? He didn't need the money and how would he have known about . . .' Chelsea stared at her friend as she thought back to the messages from the blackmailer, the oddly familiar tone they had taken. Dread twisted in her gut as a seed of suspicion took hold. 'No.'

'You should have changed the password,' Kelly said. 'DoubleTrouble123, like, any idiot could have cracked it.'

Chelsea felt a sudden chill, remembering a day, such a long time ago now, when she and Nya and Kelly were hanging out at Kelly's house. Drinking frozen margaritas and talking shit, laughing so hard she was afraid she might pee herself. Her BlackBerry had died and she'd asked to use Kelly's laptop to check her Hotmail. *Thanks*, she'd said, to which Kelly had replied, *Don't worry about it, babe! What are friends for?* 'Kelly, you didn't.' she said. 'Not my fucking email.'

'It wasn't my fault you forgot to sign out on my computer, was it?' Kelly was defiant. 'I only looked because I wanted to check if you really had messaged Robbie about a part for me in his new movie, like I'd asked you to – which you didn't, by the way, so thanks for that. And then . . . I don't know. It became this weird habit, checking it. Like, it was my reading material over morning coffee, you know? And then you switched to gmail and nothing good came in for years, it was always, like, some mailing list you signed up to in 2010. That was until the email from the storage-unit place. Apparently, Maddie had left you on file as a backup.'

'You . . .'

'Yes,' Kelly said. 'I went down to check it out. I didn't mean—' Her friend was getting defensive. 'I just wanted to save you the trouble of having to deal with it yourself. You were always so upset when anything to do with Madeline came up. I thought it would just be furniture and clothes there. I didn't know it was gonna be so personal. Like the diaries and the hospital records and stuff . . .'

'*You* set up the website?' Chelsea asked. The world felt like it was melting at the edges, like she was trapped in a horror movie and couldn't escape. Who was this person standing before her? She was wearing Kelly's face but she couldn't be the woman Chelsea had known and loved for twenty years. It was impossible. Her friend wouldn't do this to her, surely.

'Yeah, but nothing I posted on there was that bad, was it?' Kelly argued. 'Like, who cares if Madeline had herpes? *Everyone* in LA has herpes. I didn't post about the abortion, did I?'

'Was that because my name was on the record?' she asked, almost hopeful, wanting to believe that her friend had tried to protect her in some small way. But when Kelly chewed on her lower lip, the nausea hit again. 'What did you do?' she whispered.

'I changed the name to Chelsea,' Kelly admitted, and at this, she at least had the decency to look shamefaced. 'They did everything in pencil back then. It was—' She stopped as Chelsea reared back in revulsion. 'I didn't change the date, though, I swear. It really did happen in 2009. I know this sounds crazy but I wasn't . . . I didn't put any of that stuff online. Chel, you have to understand. You wouldn't listen to me, you were refusing to do the reunion, even though you knew it was the only way I had any shot at a career. I love acting. I love . . .' She paused, and Chelsea knew she was thinking of when *Vigilante Queens* had first aired, when they were famous and beautiful and everyone had adored them, and the yearning that flickered on her face made Chelsea want to cry. Fame, and the things people would do to get it, to keep it. It was a sickness. 'And I asked you to help me, to do this one little thing for me, and you wouldn't. You had everything and you threw it all away! Why couldn't you do this for me?'

'So you decided to blackmail me to get your own way? Do you know how scared I've been over the last month, Kelly? How could you do this?'

'I wasn't going to take a million dollars from you, was I? I'm not a literal con artist.'

Chelsea tried to stand up, but her legs were so shaky, she had to sit down again. 'You were supposed to be my friend,' she said. 'I loved you, Kelly.'

'I *am* your friend. You're the one who wouldn't help me.'

'You think that my refusing to do the reunion show is on a par with you blackmailing me? What's wrong with you?' Chelsea said. She stood up, pulling the strap of her handbag over her shoulder. 'I'm going,' she said. 'And I'm gonna phone—' She stopped. 'Nya didn't know about Robbie and Maddie, did she?'

'Of course she didn't. If I'd told her, she would have told you, and that would have ruined the show. We needed Robbie,' Kelly said. 'We needed him for the Queens to work. And besides,' she shrugged her shoulders, 'was it really that bad? Maddie was fifteen. She wasn't a kid and Robbie wasn't exactly some gross old man – he was cute. Not like what I . . .' Blankness melted over Kelly's features, turning it to a mask. 'There are worse things that happen in this town,' she said quietly. 'I should know.'

'Kelly,' Chelsea whispered, but she couldn't continue. She walked away, reaching into her handbag to grab her phone. She had to ring Nya – she had to talk to someone about this.

'I wouldn't do that if I was you,' Kelly called after her. 'Not if you want me to keep your secret.'

Chelsea spun on her heel to face her old friend, her throat closing. 'What secret?' she asked, even though she knew it was useless playing dumb.

'I'm talking about Carter, of course.' Kelly looked at her with a triumphant glint in her eye. 'You do remember Carter, don't you?'

32.

2025

'Carter?' Chelsea asked, but her voice was suspiciously high-pitched and she watched as Kelly swallowed a smirk. Her friend flopped onto the couch, taking her hair down from its ponytail and shaking it out, but Chelsea remained standing. 'Who's Carter?'

'I think we both know exactly who Carter is, don't we?' Kelly looked up at her. 'Honestly, Chel. He was way too young.'

'He was twenty-five,' Chelsea said, then winced, cursing herself silently for opening her mouth.

'And you were, what, thirty-four?' Kelly smoothed her hair with her fingers. 'He was hot, though, I'll give you that.'

'I don't know what you're talking about.'

'I saw you,' Kelly said simply. 'I was staying in the pool house at the time and I couldn't sleep – I could never sleep without the pills. I went outside for some fresh air and I saw the two of you.' She half laughed. 'Fucking in the outside shower! Chelsea Stone, I didn't think you had it in you.'

It had been a risk, that night, or maybe all of it had been, no matter how hard she'd tried to be careful. She had found out about the young women her husband had been messaging, and there were so many of them, it seemed, all the lewd texts and photos they had sent one another, and she and Nick were in therapy, they were making it work, but Chelsea couldn't help it: a part of her had come to hate her husband. She had married him because he had promised to keep her safe, and not only had he failed, but it was he who had brought the vampire to the door, inviting it across the threshold.

They had gone to dinner with friends of his, a hedge-fund manager named Jeremy and his simpering second wife, 'Brandi with an *i*,' she kept saying. God, she was insipid. Not that these men ever seemed to care, as long as they had a woman young enough to be their daughter on their arm. Nick's friends were dating chirpy Pilates instructors and models, beautiful young women who asked to be flown privately to Turks and Caicos and bought Van Cleef jewels in exchange for the pleasure of their company. It was grotesque, Chelsea said, and Nick had argued that as both parties were using the other, why were the women any less complicit? Although, her husband had said with a chuckle, at least money doesn't depreciate in value.

'Ah, here he is,' Jeremy had said, after dessert had been served, which she and Brandi-with-an-*i* had refused, patting their flat tummies as if to check they were still thin. 'The man himself!' They had all turned to see who was at the door. It was a young man, Jeremy's eldest son from his first marriage, and he was tall – six foot five, his father said proudly – and his arms were huge in his fitted T-shirt. He smiled, showing even white teeth, and Chelsea had felt a flicker of something go through her. It wasn't until later that she would recognize it as desire.

'I always wondered who he was,' Kelly continued, 'or where you had met him. Was he a tennis coach? One of the kids' tutors? He was *fine*, anyway, wherever you picked him up.' Her friend slow-clapped. 'Nice work, babes.'

Chelsea hadn't picked him up anywhere. Jeremy had asked his son to sit down, to have coffee with them, and the only available seat had been next to Chelsea. They had talked – about what, she could not remember now. Nothing consequential, anyway. He hadn't even touched her, but she remembered his hazel eyes behind his tortoiseshell glasses, his lovely skin.

Later that night, during the silent car ride home with Nick, she downloaded the Foto app, and somehow she had known even before she opened her DMs that there would a message from him. *It was so nice to meet you tonight, Chelsea*, it said. *I'd love to hang out some other time if you're free?*

'This is –' her voice caught in her throat '– this is nonsense. You're just trying to deflect from what you did, Kelly, and I won't allow you to – to just say this kind of thing. I'm married. I love Nick and—'

Her friend snorted. 'Sure,' she said. 'So it's just a coincidence that I saw you fucking some man in the middle of the night after four months of you looking the happiest I've ever seen you? You were glowing, Chel, and believe me, I know that sex glow. I'd just never seen it on you before and I certainly never saw it afterwards. I'm surprised Nick didn't notice.'

But that was the problem. Nick never noticed anything about her, not the way Carter did. Carter noticed that she switched from oat milk to almond milk when she was on her period and felt a little bloated. He noticed that she tugged at her sleeves when she was nervous, and that when she liked a song, she closed her eyes for a second during the chorus. Once, when Nick was in Tokyo with work, they had met in a gelato shop by Miramar Beach, pretending they were old friends who had accidentally run into each other. The woman behind the counter had smiled when she saw Chelsea, chatting to her a little, and then she'd said, 'Gosh, you are still just like Willow Gray aren't you?' Chelsea's laugh had caught in her throat, the way it always did when people said things like this to her – would she never be allowed to change, she wondered? Would they always make assumptions about who she was based on a character she had played when she was just a teenager herself – but before she could say anything, Carter had cut in. 'She's not Willow,' he said. 'She's Chelsea Stone.'

And he noticed Chelsea in other ways too. He noticed when her breathing changed as he touched her, when she threw her head back and gasped, and he didn't move his fingers, he kept going, over and over, until she was crying out, a wave of something exquisite moving through her, her toes curling with bliss, and afterwards, Carter had looked at her and said, 'That wasn't your first orgasm, was it?'

'When he was gone,' Kelly continued, 'you looked so miserable, Chel. And then . . . ' her friend glanced at her out of the corner of her eye '. . . well, then you were pregnant, weren't you?'

'I don't know what you're trying to imply, but—'

'Don't worry,' Kelly cut her off. 'Your secret is safe with me. I wouldn't do that to you. Or to Ivy, really. She doesn't deserve that kind of . . . speculation.'

'I don't have to stand here and listen to your bullshit.' Chelsea clutched her handbag to her tightly. 'You're a liar and a fantasist. After everything I've done for you, this is how you repay me?'

'Give me a fucking break,' Kelly said. She walked closer to Chelsea, and when Chelsea tried to back away, she grabbed her wrist, her grip firm, her gaze unwavering. 'I was never going to tell anyone about Carter but it was fun to make you squirm, just for a bit. Little Miss Perfect. You *loved* the fact that I was a mess, didn't you? The same way you loved it when Maddie fucked up. You pretended to be so worried about her, but we both know the truth. Her falling apart made you look better in comparison and that was all you cared about.'

'That's not true,' Chelsea said but even to her own ears, it sounded weak.

'It is, though,' Kelly said. 'And Maddie knew it too. What was it she wrote in her diary? That you said you wished you didn't have a sister any more? Well . . .' Kelly stared her straight in the eye '. . . looks like you got what you wanted.'

33.

2008

When Chelsea heard the front door open, she presumed it was her personal trainer. 'Gina,' she called. 'Did you forget som—' She stopped as soon as she walked into the hall and she saw who was there. 'Oh,' she said. She came to a standstill in her workout clothes, sweat dripping down her spine, and stared at her sister. 'What are you doing here?' she asked Maddie. 'How did you get in?'

The Director's home was gated, with high walls surrounding the property, and only a few people had the access code. Chelsea hadn't even given it to her mother, as much as Erin had asked. She'd said it was because it was Robbie's house and she didn't feel comfortable giving out the code but it also allowed her to keep a certain amount of distance from her mother, which was important. 'You're a grown woman,' Robbie kept reminding her. 'It's time you acted like one.'

'Did you sneak in after Gina?' Chelsea asked. 'My trainer, she was just here,' she continued, when Maddie looked confused.

'No,' Maddie said, but she didn't elaborate.

Chelsea dabbed at her face with a towel, wishing she was showered and dressed, had some makeup on. She felt like she needed armour right now. But it wasn't as if Maddie was at her best either. In fact, her sister looked genuinely unwell. Her jeans were falling low on her hips, her teeth were too prominent in her face, and it appeared that she hadn't showered in a while. As she walked closer, Chelsea almost recoiled – it was evident her sister *hadn't* washed recently: she smelt ripe, like stale sweat and rot. 'Maddie,' she said, and she realized she was scared for some reason. 'Are you okay?'

'I just wanted to . . .' Her sister trailed off, as if she had forgotten what she was about to say. She looked around the hallway in a daze, then at Chelsea. 'I . . .' She sat heavily on the bottom stair, her hands pressed into her knees to keep herself upright, taking deep breaths.

'Mads,' Chelsea cried. She picked up her cell, then realized she didn't know who she should ring. Erin? Robbie? An ambulance? 'Fuck,' she said. 'What should I do?'

'Nothing.' Maddie waved at her to put the phone down. 'Just talk to me for a minute.'

Chelsea hesitated, fear squeezing her chest so tight that it hurt to breathe. She had seen stuff online about Maddie, Linda had tried to tell her too, but somehow she had managed to convince herself things weren't that bad until her sister was sitting in front of her and the extent of the situation was impossible to ignore. She didn't know what to do – she was so used to other people taking care of her, these days – so she did as Maddie told her and sat down on the wooden floor, crossed legs, facing her twin.

'I wanted to say congratulations,' Maddie said, after a few minutes of silence. 'An Oscar nomination! Chelsea, it's a dream come true.'

'Thank you.' Chelsea adopted the modest expression Robbie had told her would make her seem more relatable. He said she had to act like she didn't really want to win, that it was all about the art. Like she wasn't dreaming of holding that statue in her hand, confirmation of her talent that no one could ever take away from her. The ceremony was two weeks away and she was tired – she was barely eating anything, both from nerves and from worry about what her stylist would say if she gained a single pound. Chelsea was doing a two-hour work-out every morning, and there were the facials and peels and colonics and cellulite treatments and she had to go to events every day and every night, smiling and shaking hands and being so charming that it made her teeth hurt, and she was still on the diet pills, and her heart was beating so fast sometimes, Chelsea was afraid it would explode in her chest, but it was worth it. *It was worth it.* When she thought of all the sacrifices she had made, not least her relationship with her twin, it had to be worth it.

'Chel,' her sister said, and she waited until Chelsea looked her in the eye. 'I saw the movie,' she said. 'It was extraordinary. And you, you were perfect.' Maddie smiled. She was proud of Chelsea, despite everything. 'You looked . . .' Maddie paused, trying to find the right words '. . . like you were falling in love with the camera,' she finished. 'Or with the audience. And we fell in love with you right back. You were irresistible.'

That was because of him. Robbie had believed in Chelsea when no one else had. He had fought so hard to cast her, and then he had managed to wrangle that performance out of her, just like the *LA Times* reviewer had said. She would never be able to replicate it without him.

'No,' Maddie said, and Chelsea wondered if she had spoken aloud. 'Don't,' her sister continued, because of course she knew what Chelsea was thinking: Maddie had always been able to read her mind. 'Don't let him get in your head like that. That performance, it was *you*. Robbie didn't . . .' Maddie looked down at the floor. 'He didn't give it to you. And he can't take it away from you either. Remember that, okay?' Her sister cleared her throat. 'I wanted to give you a present,' she said, 'just so you would know how proud I am of you.' She reached into her pocket, pulling out a small cloth bag.

In it, Chelsea found a golden compass on a thin filigree chain, engraved with the words – *Wherever you go, I'll always be with you.* 'Oh,' she said, turning around so Maddie could fasten it around her neck. 'It's so beautiful, I love it. Thank you.'

'I'm glad,' her sister said. Then, 'Chel? You're happy, right?' There was an urgency to Maddie's voice that surprised Chelsea but she tried to answer honestly. 'Sure,' she said, hearing her own hesitancy. 'It's just been super busy,' she rushed on, before Maddie could say anything. 'It's a lot right now and it's kind of overwhelming, you know? But it won't be like this for ever. It'll settle down.'

'Are you gonna take a break?' Maddie asked. 'After the awards, you should go on vacation.' She looked a little shy. 'I could come with you? It would be nice to spend some time together.'

'Where would we go?' Chelsea said, and she couldn't help herself, she was excited at the idea. They had never gone on vacation when they were kids. In the beginning, it was because there was never enough money and then, after they'd booked *Heartstrings* and *Double Trouble*, their mother always said there wasn't enough time. Once, Erin had agreed to bring the twins to Atomic Kingdom, the theme park owned by AtomicKids. Maddie and Chelsea had been thrilled, arguing over which rides they would go on first, the Atom Twister or the A-Bomb Rapids, they couldn't decide. It wasn't until they arrived at the park that they realized their mother had arranged for a meet-and-greet with *Double Trouble* fans, and they were surrounded by hundreds of hysterical pre-teens, clamouring for a photo. 'I don't see what the problem is,' Erin had said, on the drive home. 'It was a great opportunity for you girls. You don't know how lucky you are.'

'We could go to Pismo Beach,' Maddie said, and the words were coming out of her mouth so quickly, Chelsea knew her sister must have been thinking about this for a while. 'Get a room at a shitty motel and eat candy and watch reruns of old movies. It won't exactly be beach weather but we . . . We could be together for a little while?'

She looked so hopeful, and Chelsea was about to say, *Yes, yes, Maddie.* She wanted to go to the beach with her sister and walk along the shore and skim stones against the surface of the water, and they would talk and talk, and slowly, they would find their way back to one another. She would make sure that Maddie didn't drink or take anything while they were on vacation, she could help her sister get sober and— And then Chelsea thought of her desk diary, all the emails from her agent, and the multiple scripts she was reading, the schedule that seemed to be getting more packed with every week. 'I don't know if it's possible,' she admitted. 'It's crazy right now. Nancy Taylor wants me to strike while things are good. I won't be this hot for ever, she said. And Robbie.' Maddie made a face at the mention of his name but Chelsea didn't comment on it. 'He's writing a new script,' she continued. 'It's almost ready, and there's an incredible part for a young woman in it and I'm hoping that maybe I will—'

'What do you mean "hoping"?'

'I can't just expect that the part is mine. He's an artist and I can't . . .' Chelsea was stumbling over her words. 'I mean, I want him to pick who he thinks is best for the part and just because I'm the same age as the character and I helped him with the dialogue—'

'You helped him?' Maddie's face darkened. 'You mean he's still stealing material?'

'That's not – that's not what I said,' she stuttered. 'I don't want to put him under any pressure, you know? There are lots of actresses out there who are way more talented than me, and—'

'How many of them are nominated for Best Actress?' Maddie was staring at her like she was crazy. 'You can't let him walk all over you like this.'

'I'm not letting him walk all over me! I respect his process. He's an artist and he—'

'Yeah, you keep saying that. Does he respect the fact that you're an artist too?' her sister asked, and Chelsea laughed.

'I'm not "an artist",' she said. 'I'm a former child star turned teen-soap actress. I'm like . . .' she tried to remember how Robbie had described it to a friend of his over cocktails '. . . furniture you move around set,' she said. 'Functional. That's not art.'

'Did he say that to you?' Maddie asked, furious. 'He did, didn't he?' she continued when Chelsea didn't deny it. 'What a douche-bag. How *dare* he say that to you?'

'Don't talk about Robbie like that,' she said sharply. 'And, anyway, he's not wrong, is he?'

'Yes,' Maddie said. 'Of course, he's wrong. Anyone who's seen your movie would know that. You're astounding in it. This is what he does. He stole my ideas, and he used them to make the show, and then he used *you* to build himself a legend. I could hear your voice in every line of that fucking script, Chelsea. It was you. It was all you. And you're acting like he did you some big favour? I hate that you live here in his guest-house. It's all wrong, all of it. He's not who you think he is.' Her sister pressed her lips together. 'Chelsea. I—'

'I can't do this right now.' The way Maddie was looking at her, her eyes glistening with unshed tears, she knew her sister was going to tell her something she would never be able to come back from and Chelsea didn't have time for that: she had to stay focused. She could almost feel the weight of the Oscar in her hand, and when she won, she would be able to relax. She could ask questions, she would have more power. She could help her sister then but not yet. 'Whatever you think it is you have to tell me, just don't, okay? I don't want to hear it.'

'What?' Maddie said, something between anger and

devastation playing out in her eyes. She had always been so expressive – no wonder the camera had loved her so much. 'I've come here to tell you that you're not safe in this house, or with that man, and you're telling me you're too busy to talk about it?' She shook her head. 'I can't believe you. I've spent our whole lives protecting you, Chelsea, and you've always acted so fucking helpless, like you're a deer caught in headlights. But it's bullshit, isn't it? We both know what you're capable of when you want something, the lengths you're willing to go to.'

'What are you talking about?' A shiver ran down her spine. No, her sister couldn't know about that, she couldn't . . .

'I do know,' Maddie said, as if she was reading Chelsea's mind. 'I know what you did. Do you think I'm an idiot? I watched the audition tapes.' Her sister touched her hand to Chelsea's forehead, where her scar had once been, and Chelsea almost cried out. 'You switched them, didn't you? When you went to mail them, you changed the names so they thought my audition was yours.' Chelsea heard herself whimper but she didn't say anything, she couldn't. The worst thing she had ever done, and Maddie had known all along.

'And Robbie must have realized too,' Maddie continued. 'He always said that scar was the only way he could tell us apart. No wonder he made you get rid of it. He didn't want any evidence, did he?'

'When did you—' Chelsea made herself shut up. She wasn't going to admit to anything. She didn't have time for this: she was nominated for a goddamn Oscar. 'This is ridiculous,' she said instead. 'I don't know what you're talking about.'

'I asked Nancy to get my audition tape back, just so I could review it. And when the camera zoomed in, I saw your scar and I knew. And I didn't say anything, Chel, because you were so good. Don't you realize that? Your audition, it was brilliant.

You didn't need to switch our tapes. You could have won that part on your own.'

'Then why . . .' Chelsea held back a sob '. . . why didn't you say anything?'

Her sister rubbed the back of her nose with her hand. 'I don't know. I thought I'd be fine – another role would come along and I'd have my own career. But then . . .' She looked up at Chelsea, and she was so gaunt, she was a shadow of herself. 'Where have you been when *I* needed *you*? I needed you! And you just disappeared.'

'I've been busy,' Chelsea protested. 'I've been filming and I . . .' Chelsea was going to say that she had been giving Maddie space, or that it was important for them to be independent of one another or that she was waiting for Maddie to hit her rock bottom before intervening. All the excuses had sounded so legitimate when she was reciting them to The Director, to Linda, to their mother, but now the words turned to ash in her mouth when she was faced with the reality of what the past year had done to her sister.

'I would have never have done this to you,' Maddie said. 'Especially not for *him*. Please,' she put her hands over her mouth, the words muffled, 'just tell me. Since you moved in here, have things changed?'

'Has what changed?' Chelsea asked, confused.

Maddie looked miserable. 'You know.' she said. 'Have the two of you . . . Are you sleeping with him now?'

She physically recoiled, as if Maddie had slapped her face. 'What happened to *You could have won that part by yourself*?' This was how little her sister thought of her. She assumed there was no way Chelsea would have been cast in those roles on her own merit: she had to be fucking The Director. She read the comments on RumorMill, and the blind items in the magazines, the insinuations that she had lain down on the proverbial casting couch, spreading her legs willingly. She knew that people in the industry, men like Jeffrey Green, assumed she would do it for them, if they dangled a good enough role in front of her, but she never imagined her own sister would think the same. 'No,' she said, and her voice had turned to ice. 'I'm not sleeping with him. But thank you for the vote of confidence, Maddie.'

'It's not about you,' her sister cried. 'It's him. You can't trust him. I'm so worried about you.'

Chelsea gave a harsh laugh. 'You're worried about me? You?' She bent down to grab her sister by the shoulders, her nose wrinkling at the smell. She dragged Maddie to her feet and pushed her towards the large antique mirror hanging over a nearby table, and made her sister look at her reflection. 'I've been nominated for an Academy Award,' Chelsea said, and it was like she was having an out-of-body experience, stepping out of her skin and watching the scene unfold. The two young women, one shrivelled, grey, the other gleaming, beautiful. 'Look at yourself,' she said. 'You're just wasting away, doing coke and going to parties with . . .' she tried to think what The Director had said '. . . airheads and all those gross old men. And you have the nerve to accuse me of sleeping with Robbie? It's embarrassing. You're embarrassing me and more importantly, you're embarrassing yourself.' Her sister's face fell, her mouth beginning to quiver, but Chelsea didn't stop: she found that she couldn't. She had to bury Maddie and her story about the switched audition tapes before her sister told anyone else. 'And the worst thing is,' she spat, 'that you have *my face*. Whenever you behave like a pathetic loser, getting fucked up at clubs, people associate you with me. You're ruining my brand, and you don't even care because you're such a mess, Maddie. Sometimes I wish that I had never had a sister! It would be easier that way. You're nothing but a crackhead, you're a—' She remembered what Robbie had said about her sister when photos of Maddie falling out of a nightclub with two men in tow were published on RumorMill. 'You look like a cheap whore,' she said, and she realized, as the words came out, her voice didn't sound like her, it sounded like him.

There was silence then. Maddie looked confused, as if Chelsea was speaking a different language and it was taking her brain a moment to compute what had been said. Then, as what her sister had said hit her, Maddie's face crumpled and she started to cry, no, she was wailing, the sobs cracking her ribs, and she wept, 'I'm sorry, I'm sorry. I'm ruining everything, I know I am.'

'No,' Chelsea said, shocked at her own cruelty. 'I didn't mean that, I swear I didn't. I'm the one who should be sorry. Please, Mads.'

Maddie stood up again, and Chelsea could see that her hands were shaking, but her sister's voice was calm when she spoke. 'I'm sorry I'm such an embarrassment to you,' she said quietly. 'Maybe you're right. Maybe it would be easier if I weren't around any more.'

'Don't say that.' Chelsea reached out to hug her, but Maddie slipped out of her embrace, and then her sister was running, running away from her, out of the front door, and Chelsea tried to go after her. 'Maddie,' she yelled. 'Maddie, I'm sorry, I—' She wanted to say, I'm tired, I'm so tired, and I'm hungry, and these pills make me feel like I'm going crazy, and I didn't mean any of it. I love you, *I love you, Maddie*. But her sister was gone before she could even open her mouth.

34.

2025

The security guard had tried to talk to Chelsea on the drive home, the sort of idle chit-chat she was usually happy to engage in, dissecting the latest episode of *Housewives* – he and his girlfriend were big fans – but she'd snapped, telling him to be quiet. First he looked shocked, then hurt, and the rest of the journey had been spent in awkward silence. She wanted to apologize but didn't trust herself to speak: she was afraid that if she opened her mouth, she might cry instead. When he finally pulled up to the driveway, she got out without saying a word to him, and let herself into the house.

She found Hannah sitting at the kitchen counter, picking at a plate of cheese and olives. 'Hey,' her assistant said. 'You okay? I've been worried about you.'

'I'm fine,' Chelsea replied. 'The kids?'

'They're in bed. Ivy was acting up a bit, but she fell asleep in, like, five minutes.'

Chelsea waited to feel guilty, the way she normally did at the thought of one of the kids asking for her when she wasn't there, but there was nothing. She felt nothing.

'Poppy went home and the night nanny is all set up.' Hannah said, picking up her cell phone. 'So why don't you and I just quickly—'

'You can go home too.'

'But . . .' Hannah was confused '. . . tomorrow's schedule? And there are all these emails I need to—'

'Just go home.' Chelsea turned away from her assistant, pretending to go through her bag so the other woman wouldn't see she was holding back tears.

'Okay.' Hannah sounded bewildered but she gathered her things anyway. 'I'll see you in the morning, I guess?' Footsteps, then Hannah again, 'Oh, and by the way, Nick is back. He got in about half an hour ago and went straight to bed.' Chelsea didn't reply so Hannah half stuttered, 'Erm, okay. I guess I'll see you tomorrow.'

She waited until she heard the door close behind her assistant and then Chelsea collapsed onto one of the kitchen stools. She tried to focus on her breathing and tried not to think about her mother and the script and how Kelly had betrayed her and Carter, *oh, Carter*, and The Director and the ways he had hurt Maddie, and nausea burned up her throat, searing hot, and she ran to the sink, vomiting into it.

She turned on the faucet, waiting for her stomach to settle, then reached for her phone. She texted her husband, asking him to come downstairs, and as soon as she sent it, she saw a light flash out of the corner of her eye. It was Nick's cell, charging by the stove. She unplugged it, about to bring it up to him, when she decided to do something else. She slid to the floor, her back pressed against the cabinet, and she pulled her knees into her chest. She unlocked Nick's phone, keying in the passcode their couples' therapist had insisted her husband give her. 'It's important that Chelsea feels *safe*,' the man had said. 'It's important that she feels she can *trust* you again.'

Nick's emails were clean, as were his texts. They were mostly one-word answers to his assistant or a Foto employee. He didn't believe in niceties when it came to digital communication. Chelsea looked at his Google calendar – he really had spent the last two weeks in Maui, she saw, and he'd scheduled nothing except a few Teams meetings and a Zoom session with his shaman. Her finger hovered over the Foto app button for just a second, and she wondered at her own hesitation. It wasn't like she didn't already know what she would find. She clicked into his inbox, and there it was, multiple message threads with different women, all young, very young, she thought, as she opened one girl's profile – she couldn't be more than eighteen. Nick would have checked it out, surely? He wouldn't be so stupid as to DM a minor? She scrolled through the messages, and couldn't understand how emotionless she felt, how resigned she was to her husband's predilection for sexting beautiful women, all of whom looked eerily similar to how she had when they had first met. He used the same language with each of them, like he copied and pasted his responses, and he let them do the rest of the work. *Tell me how you like it*, and *Are you touching yourself?* and *What would you do if I were there with you?* The poor, stupid girls, falling over themselves to be as explicit as they possibly could be, as if that was going to make Nick divorce Chelsea Stone and marry them instead. They didn't know how much Nick cared about what other people thought of him, and those people wouldn't think very much if he left his beautiful wife for a social-media 'model' shilling waist binders for a 15 per cent discount with their special code.

She stood up, plugging Nick's phone back in. She remembered the first time she'd found messages like that on his phone, how she had raced into his home office, throwing the cell at him in fury. But, really, there had been a sense of relief underneath her anger, a strange kind of peace. Things had been too good for too long and it hadn't felt entirely comfortable, she realized, but this? This chaos? It had felt familiar. She was used to the people she loved betraying her. In a strange way, it had felt like home.

Chelsea went into the pantry, and grabbed a bottle of vodka.

She filled a glass with some ice and then she opened the patio door and went out to the pool area. She shivered. The sun had long set and it was chilly out there, but she sat on one of the loungers anyway, drawing her cardigan around her. She poured a generous glass of the vodka, and took a gulp. It was delicious, so smooth it tasted of nothing.

Chelsea rarely drank, citing her health and her skin as an excuse, but the truth was, she was afraid of the wildness inside her. That was what Carter had helped her discover, that passion, and he couldn't understand why it frightened her so much. For the first time in her life, she was doing something because she wanted to and not because she should, and it felt so good. *I love you*, he had told her and she had said it back. She had meant it – she had wanted to shout it to the heavens so the stars could hear it and be glad for her, but love for Carter would mean walking out into the daylight, telling everyone about what they had done. People might understand it of Nick: he was a man after all, a powerful one at that. What else could she expect? For Chelsea to admit she had cheated, even if it was only after her husband had done the same, was to be ruined.

She couldn't leave Nick – she couldn't do that to Grayson. She was determined her child would not struggle the way she and Maddie had. Carter had said he didn't want to lie and sneak around any more, he loved her too much for that, so he said goodbye and left her, like everyone she had ever loved had done. It was weeks before Chelsea realized she'd missed her period, and by then, it was too late to do anything about it. She didn't know who the father was – she and Nick still occasionally had sex back then, as long as she initiated it – so she decided the baby was his, and Nick's face when she told him, the way it lit up, the way he held her close and whispered in her ear, *This is a new start for us*, had made it almost worthwhile.

That had been five years ago and she had kept it so contained, the rough edges she had sanded down, the truths she had buried under her tongue – she couldn't risk letting loose any of it. Would Kelly tell her story? she wondered. Would anyone believe her? The vodka muted the fear so Chelsea finished the glass, pouring herself another, throwing that back too. She stretched out her legs, enjoying the warmth spreading through her limbs. It was beautiful out there, the hiss of the water sprinkler and the lapping of the pool, and the night sky above her. She couldn't see any stars but she imagined them there, behind the clouds, and she poured another glass, and another.

She thought about Robbie, about how he had always been there, since they were children, and how much she had trusted him. Her sister had tried to tell Chelsea, she had tried to warn her, and Chelsea had ignored Maddie because it was easier for *her*. Chelsea had avoided her sister in those final months because she hadn't wanted to hear anything that would necessitate difficult decisions, ones that might impact the trajectory of her own career, not when she was finally experiencing the kind of critical success she had long craved. She had lost her sister because of it and now, despite her best efforts, Chelsea was still no closer to finding out what had happened to Maddie, let alone getting any kind of justice for her. Oh, how she yearned to see her sister again, to hear her voice. Did Maddie know how much Chelsea missed her, wherever she was?

Chelsea stood up, hissing, *Fuck*, under her breath when she stumbled. She looked at the bottle in her hand. It was half empty already. She was so light-headed, and she thought she might get sick again. Everything was spinning, but she wanted to sit by the pool, dangle her legs in the water. Maybe if she looked into it, she would see her twin again, find her reflection there. Chelsea walked closer to the pool's edge until suddenly she was falling or she was flying, she couldn't tell which, and then everything went dark.

35.

2025

Her eyes fluttered open and, for a second, Chelsea thought she was still dreaming. She wasn't in her bedroom, she didn't know where she was, but there was a machine next to her, a steady beeping, and Nick was sitting in the corner, on his phone. She moaned, the sheets rustling around her, and her husband got up quickly, coming to her side. 'You're awake,' he said.

'Where am I?'

'Hospital.' He didn't elaborate.

'What?' There was a sour taste at the back of Chelsea's throat and she tried to swallow. 'I don't—'

'You fell into the pool,' Nick said. 'Last night. José had to fish you out. If he hadn't been there . . .' He allowed her to fill in the blanks as to what her fate would have been. 'He called me, and I called an ambulance and they brought you here. Chelsea, your blood alcohol levels were through the roof. Did you . . .' He looked haunted. 'Were you trying—'

'I'm sorry.' She tried to remember what had happened the night before but she couldn't. 'Are the kids okay?'

'Ivy doesn't know anything – I told her you had a stomach bug – but Grayson saw the ambulance. He's upset, as you can imagine.' He touched her hand gently. 'We all are. Babe. You haven't been yourself since the storage-locker stuff started and I'm so worried about you. I don't know what's going on with you. And now this? It's too much. I'm just wondering if . . .'

'Tell me, Nick.' She could feel her jaw tightening. 'What are you wondering?'

'I'm wondering if you might need to go somewhere.' He rushed on when he saw her face: 'Just for a little while. Until you're feeling better.'

Was this how it was going to happen? He would check her into some rehabilitation centre – the best in the world, of course, as luxurious as people in their circle would expect – and there would be mutterings about Chelsea's 'nerves', and he would wait for enough time to pass until he could divorce her and no one would judge him for it. What was a man like him supposed to do with a crazy wife?

'Nick, I—' she started, but she was interrupted by the door opening, and there was Erin, dark circles under her eyes as if she hadn't slept in weeks. She let out a wail when she saw Chelsea awake and she rushed to the bed. Nick stepped back, but it was as if Erin couldn't even see him: her focus was solely on her daughter. 'Thank God, thank God,' she sobbed, as she grabbed Chelsea's face and leaned down to kiss her cheek.

Chelsea could feel the neck of the hospital gown getting damp. Nick backed out of the room. Either he couldn't see Chelsea's mouthed, *Stay, please*, or he was ignoring it, and she was left with her mother, weeping on her shoulder. 'Mom,' she said. 'Mom, stop. You're hurting me.'

Her mother jerked back, saying, 'Are you all right? Should I get the nurse?'

'Just leave it,' Chelsea snapped. 'What are you doing here? I told you I didn't want to see you again.' She couldn't recall much from the night before but she remembered that, at least.

'I know,' she said. 'But when Nick told me what had happened, that you had almost drowned, I thought, I thought . . .' They both knew what she had thought. Once you had lost someone, the fear that it could happen again never fully went away. You understood how fragile life was, how easily things could fall apart. 'I was so afraid,' Erin whispered. 'I wouldn't survive losing you as well. I know you think I'm a bad mother and I—' She held up a hand to stop Chelsea talking. 'Please,' she said. 'Let me finish. I know you think I was a bad mother and . . .' she bit her lower lip '. . . I was,' she admitted. 'But I was so young.' It was the first time Erin had said that and it hadn't sounded like an excuse. She could hear the remnants of terror in her mother's voice, splintering her words. 'I didn't have any money – I didn't even have my high-school diploma. Your father had left and my parents had made it very clear they had no interest in helping me. The things I had to do, in those early days, just to get food.' Erin blanched. 'I can't – I can't talk about that. I don't know if I'll ever be able to talk about it. You don't know what it's like to be that desperate, Chelsea, and I hope you never will. And when the psychic said you'd be famous, I thought it could save us. You and Maddie, everyone said you were the prettiest babies they'd ever seen. Beauty, for women like me, it's the only power we'll ever get.' She made a wounded sound. 'I should have used mine better. I should have married some rich guy who would have taken care of us but I was afraid to be dependent on a man again. I'd trusted your father and . . . I wanted to make sure you and your sister never had to make the same kind of choices I did.'

'Mom.' Chelsea didn't know what else to say.

'It's not an excuse,' her mother said again. 'I know it's not. I fucked up. I was so selfish. And then Maddie, she just fell apart and I didn't . . . I should have done something. It felt like everything started to go wrong after you were cast as Willow Gray.'

'That was my fault,' Chelsea whispered. 'I'm the reason she didn't get the role. I . . .'

'I know you swapped the tapes.' Her mother brushed her hair back from her face. 'Oh, sweetheart. I saw your audition, Chelsea. You were both great. But you could have delivered your lines like a wooden plank and Robbie still wouldn't have given it to Maddie. I should never have allowed him anywhere near either of you. I should have taken better care of you. But I'm gonna try.' Her mother started to cry again. 'I'll do better. I promise you.' Erin reached into her handbag. 'Starting with this.'

She handed Chelsea a piece of foolscap paper, folded in two. Chelsea opened it out, inhaling when she saw Maddie's handwriting. She read it quickly, her heart beating fast, and when she'd finished, she could hear someone gasping, struggling for air, and then she discovered it was her. Erin was telling her to breathe, to stay calm, that it would all be okay, that it would be—

'Where did you get this?' Chelsea asked.

'I found it in her safety box the night she disappeared,' Erin said. 'I spent ages trying to figure out the code and then I cracked it.' Her mouth started to quiver. 'Six thirty-five. The time you were born, Chelsea. Ten minutes after Maddie. And when I read the letter, I didn't know what to do, so I kept it. I was afraid it would ruin your career, Robbie's too, and—'

'You think I give a fuck about his career?' Chelsea's voice was a howl but Erin didn't flinch.

'I know,' she said. 'I panicked. And then it was too late and you were so busy working and I thought it would make things worse if I . . . There's something else, too,' she said. She rifled in her purse until she found it, holding it out for Chelsea to grab.

It was a photograph. 'Oh, my God,' she said, when she saw it. 'It's—'

'Proof.' Erin finished her sentence for her.

36.

2009

'Chelsea! Chelsea!'

The screams began as soon as she climbed out of the limo, her stylist rushing to her side to fix the train of her dress. She heard Robbie behind her but she couldn't see him. She tensed. She wondered if she should say something to him – *It's your name they should be calling,* she wanted to whisper. *It's your movie. None of us would be here if it weren't for you* – but she wasn't sure how he would react and she couldn't take the risk of him recoiling from her in front of the world. She smiled at the fans, squashed behind a metal railing, and she signed autographs and posed for photos. 'That's all we have time for today,' the publicist barked, pushing Chelsea towards the red carpet.

She hurried to catch up with Robbie, who was walking ahead with Diana Dawson, both dressed in black velvet suits. It was major, Blake Logan admitted when she'd seen them, and Chelsea had felt even more like a baby in her poufy gown. 'Robbie,' she called, but it was Diana who looked over her shoulder, who told Robbie to stop and wait, and it was Diana, again, who gracefully stepped out of shot so the photographers could focus on The Director and Chelsea. They stood there, facing the cameras in the way they had practised the night before, Robbie moving Chelsea's limbs as if they were separate from her body, adjusting the angle of her face until he was satisfied. Chelsea would be happy to be manoeuvred like this for the rest of her life, if he was the one doing it. He knew her face and body better than she did. He knew how to manipulate it to its best advantage, how a single patch of light could illuminate her to beauty. *It's the Oscars*, he reminded her. *If we win, these are the photos they're gonna use for the rest of our lives. Everything has to be perfect.* She tilted her chin slightly down, giving a close-lipped smile. She couldn't be too sexy, he'd said. No one wanted that from their former child stars.

'Who are you wearing?' a TV host asked, as Chelsea continued up the carpet, trying not to step on any other guest's train or walk in front of their interviews.

'Couyer, of course,' she replied, smoothing the column dress in forest green. 'And Harry Winston,' she added. The dress was boring, she and Blake had agreed on that, but she was dripping in emeralds so they could pretend they'd kept the gown simple to showcase the jewels.

'That's not Harry Winston,' the presenter said, pointing at the tiny compass on its gold chain.

Chelsea touched it, and said, 'No, this was a present. From my sister.'

'Oh, how fabulous,' the woman said. 'And—'

'We'd better get going, Chelsea,' The Director interrupted. He didn't like all this fashion talk. It was beneath her, he said, if she wanted to be a proper actress.

Chelsea wasn't sure if she agreed but she'd nodded anyway. 'Yes,' she said now, smiling apologetically at the woman from E!, hoping Blake wouldn't murder her when she saw the footage. 'Good to see you,' Chelsea called over her shoulder, crossing her fingers when the woman said, 'Good luck tonight!'

Inside the Kodak Theater, dozens of people were milling about, air-kissing and admiring each other's outfits, refusing canapés, accepting flutes of champagne. Chelsea took her purse from the publicist and then she squeezed Robbie's hand until he turned around, his face softening when he looked at her. 'Is my little bird nervous?' he asked, and she nodded, *Yes, yes*. He pulled her to him, crushing her into his chest, and although she was worried that he might smudge her makeup, Chelsea decided it was worth it. 'Don't be,' he murmured into the top of her head. 'I have a good feeling about tonight.'

Later, as Martin Scorsese paused to open the envelope, Robbie was holding Chelsea's hand on his left and his wife's on his right. Scorsese smiled. 'The winner of Best Director is . . .' and he said Robbie's name, and he was on his feet, hugging Diana and telling her he loved her, and then he turned to Chelsea. He pulled her in for a hug and whispered in her ear, 'I told you I had a good feeling.' Chelsea hadn't won in her category earlier, making herself smile and clap as the other actress went to collect her award. Strange, how she didn't feel too disappointed. *The List of Second Chances* had lost for best original screenplay and when the names in her category had been called, she'd been gripped with fear that she might win and Robbie would not. He would feel outshone and resent her, and he might decide he didn't want to work with her any more. Better to lose than to risk that.

She pulled back to tell him how brilliant he was, she was so proud of him, but he was already gone, bounding up the steps to the stage, so handsome as he took the statue from Scorsese with a wink. He began the speech that Chelsea knew he'd been practising for the last month, but which sounded casual and off-the-cuff. He thanked his beautiful wife, Diana, and then Chelsea, before quickly acknowledging her two co-stars, Finn and Owen, neither of whom had won in their category either. All the glory had been given to The Director, just as it should.

'Can you believe it?' he said, when she found him afterwards, battling through the throngs of hangers-on, all desperate to kiss the ring of the newly crowned king. He showed her the golden statue, his name already engraved on it.

'Of course I can believe it,' she said, giving him another hug. 'You deserve it,' she said but Robbie wasn't listening, he was walking away from her, talking intently to a producer Chelsea vaguely recognized.

'You can do whatever you want now,' the squat, balding man told him. 'And as for budget? Don't even worry ab—' and then they were out of earshot, and Chelsea was left alone, smoothing her dress again, hoping she didn't look as awkward as she felt. She went to find Finn and Owen, who had brought their mothers as their dates, both women overexcited at the proximity to celebrities. They kept pointing them out, speaking too loudly.

'Is that Brad Pitt?'

'Oh, my gosh, it is. And Angelina Jolie! I never liked her, not after what she did to poor Jennifer, and—'

'Mom.' Owen's face coloured as the actress looked in their direction. 'Quieter, okay?'

Chelsea changed the subject, commiserating with the two men, and reassuring their mothers that they'd be back, their boys would win another year. That was the thing about being an actor, the belief that your next big role could be just around the corner, the one that would change everything for you. It was like playing the slot machines in Vegas, enough small, unpredictable wins to keep you hooked, to make sure you would never leave. The house always won.

'And where's your mom?' one of the women asked her, and Chelsea said that Erin would be here soon: she was coming to the after-parties. Her mother would never miss an opportunity to be charming in front of powerful men.

She heard a buzzing sound from her bag. 'That's probably her now,' she said, taking her cell out of her purse. But when she looked at the screen it wasn't Erin who was phoning her, it was Nya. 'Hey,' she said, as she answered, moving away from the others with an apologetic smile, but she'd been too late: there was no one at the other end. When she looked at the phone again, Chelsea saw she had missed five phone calls from her friend, and there were three voicemails. Her stomach tightened and she rang Nya back. 'Is everything okay?' she said, but her friend wasn't making any sense. Her voice was rising and rising, and she was so loud, she was practically shouting into the phone, and Chelsea could see people turn towards her, curious. She backed away, finding an empty restroom, and locking the door after her.

'Nya,' she said again. 'You're scaring me. What's wrong?'

'I got a text message from Madeline,' Nya said.

'I didn't know you two were in touch,' Chelsea said, surprised.

'We're not. I only met her once, that time I visited you during the off season and we hung out at her house. But the message was weird. She asked me to take care of you, to make sure you were okay. And she said to keep you away from Robbie. I didn't even know who it was from, initially. I didn't have her number saved. I rang it and it went straight to her voicemail and that's when I realized it was Madeline.'

'I don't understand. Why would she ask you to take care of me?'

'I don't know. But I remembered where her house was – I've always had a good sense of direction. I just had this strange feeling so I drove over there. Her car was gone and there was no answer when I rang the bell. So I tried the door again, the handle this time, and it was open. I went in and –' her friend took a breath '– there were pill bottles and empty wine bottles but everything else, it's gone. Her couch, her dining table, her mattress. In her room, all of her clothes were gone. In the bathroom, all of her shit, her toothbrush, her shampoo, was gone too. There's nothing left in the apartment, Chel, except a black safe in the middle of the living room. It's like the *Mary Celeste*. Did she tell you she was going out of town?'

'No.' Chelsea watched herself in the mirror as she listened to her friend, a high-pitched ringing in her ears. 'You haven't called anyone else?'

'No.'

'Good.' Chelsea tried to think. 'It's probably nothing. She did say something about a vacation.'

'But why would she take everything she owned if she was just—'

'I don't know,' she snapped. 'Maybe she's sold her house and she's moving. Maddie doesn't have to tell me everything she does.'

'Babe.' Nya's voice went serious. 'You know I wouldn't do this to you, not tonight. But I've got a bad feeling about this.'

Chelsea hung up without saying another word. She put away her phone, checked her makeup. She walked back into the room, waving at an old friend who called her name, mouthing, *I'll be right back*, and she kept walking towards the entrance, but she was stopped by too many people, all of whom wanted to talk about The Director, how brilliant he was, and could she mention their name to him, they'd love to work with him, they'd love to show him a script, they'd love to have a meeting, something casual, just to go over some ideas, you know. She tried to smile but all she could hear was Nya's voice, *I've got a bad feeling about this*, and for a second, she thought she was going to scream, to tell them all to fuck off, to move out of her way. She had to get out of there.

'There you are, darling.' It was her mother, resplendent in a black slinky evening gown, a slit up to her crotch.

'Mom,' she said, and when Erin saw her face, she took Chelsea by the hand, pulling her through the crowd, until they were nearly at the entrance. 'It's Maddie,' she said, and she told Erin everything Nya had said.

'Mom,' she said again. 'Did you hear what I—'

'Yes, I heard.' Erin grabbed both of her hands. 'I'm sure it's nothing. You stay here,' she said. 'I want you to have the best night of your life, okay? You stay with Robbie and Diana. Don't say anything to anyone, do you understand?'

Chelsea nodded. She wasn't sure what else she could do. 'What are you gonna do?'

'I'll go to Maddie's house,' Erin said, her mouth set in a grim line. 'I'll take care of this.'

37.

2025

When her mother left the hospital, Nick came back in, crunching an apple so loudly it made her teeth grit. 'You okay, baby?' he asked. 'You need me to get the nurse?'

'I'm still gonna do the reunion show,' she said, and he lost it.

'Chelsea. You're lying in a hospital bed after a suicide—'

'It wasn't a suicide attempt.'

'Fine. But you're still in hospital, you're sick. You're not in any condition to do a live TV special. How can you even think about the show at a time like this?' He stared at her like she'd lost her mind and maybe she had. 'This is the perfect get-out-of-jail-free card with your contract,' he said. 'You're not well enough to do this. Think of the kids, I beg you.'

'Oh, really? Were you thinking of the kids when you were sexting random girls on the Foto app again?' It wasn't fair of her to use that against him, not after what she had done with Carter. Was it better that it had been with someone she had actually loved? She didn't know and, right now, she didn't care. She needed to do the show for Maddie.

Nick paled slightly. 'I didn't. I . . .' She reached out her hand, asking him to hand over his phone so she could look at his account. He took a moment, then his whole body slumped. 'I'm sorry,' he said instead.

Chelsea looked at her husband. Would she tell him? No, she decided. Ivy was his daughter. She could see that every time she looked at their little girl. She had Nick's fingers, the same way of laughing, the same burst of air, as if it had taken them by surprise. Chelsea and Nick had hurt each other enough. It was time to let the past go. 'Don't apologize,' she replied. A plan was forming in her mind and she would need her husband's assistance if she wanted to execute it. This was her opportunity to set the record straight, to get justice for Maddie, and Chelsea wasn't going to stop now. 'I want you to help me instead.'

A flurry of calls followed, to Nancy Taylor and the network, reassuring them that Chelsea's little 'accident' wouldn't affect the show, that she would be there, as promised. She'd avoided calls from Nya and Kelly – she couldn't risk talking to Nya: her friend would be able to sniff out immediately that something was going on, and as for Kelly, she would never talk to that woman again. Chelsea didn't want to be in the same room as her, or The Director for that matter. But as she sat in front of the mirror on the morning of the show, fresh from the shower, she told herself that she needed to be brave. She needed to do this for Maddie. It was the least her sister deserved.

'Chelsea, you're here!' The producer clapped her hands as Chelsea walked into the dressing room, and everyone else followed suit. They had all heard about the incident, as Nick was calling it now.

'Thanks,' she said, as she sat in the makeup chair, ignoring Kelly sitting beside her.

'Chel,' Kelly said, and she was glad to see the other woman looked exhausted, like she hadn't slept since their confrontation. 'Chelsea, please, let me—' but Chelsea put her hand up to stop her saying another word.

'No,' she said. 'Just no.'

The makeup artist said something to her, and Chelsea apologized, she was busy texting Zach and Emily in their group chat.

Knock 'em dead, Zach had written. *Mom would be so proud of you, I hope you know that.* Emily had texted, *She really would!!!! We love you so much, Chel!!* She had people in her life who loved her, she thought as she swiped out of iMessage, who truly cared about her. She was luckier than most. She needed to remember that. 'No worries!' the cheery young man said. He hadn't stopped chatting since she arrived, recounting his entire life story. He was only twenty-five, he said, but was obviously already getting Botox, his forehead a waxy sheen, and his eyebrows were tweezed into oblivion. That was cool again, she'd read somewhere, and she wanted to tell him how much he would regret that choice in ten years when they wouldn't grow back, but she knew there was no point. Young people had to make their own mistakes. 'I was just admiring your necklace. Is it the same one you wore on Oscar night? That look was iconic.'

'Well spotted,' she said. 'It was a present. From my sister.' Chelsea fingered the gold compass. *Wherever you go, I'll always be with you.* She'd kept it hidden in a lock box for years, but she knew she had to wear it tonight, just in case Maddie was watching. A secret message of sorts. *Come back to me. I can't do this without you for much longer.*

The makeup artist leaned closer to apply a few false eyelashes to the outer corners of her eyes. 'My mom is super excited about this show,' he said. Then, lowering his voice so Kelly wouldn't hear him. 'She said you were her favourite queen.'

'That's so nice,' she said. The door flung open and Nancy Taylor strode into the room. She nodded at Kelly, then stood in front of Chelsea, squinting at her face. 'A little more blush,' she barked at the makeup artist. Her agent had always wanted her clients to wear more blush; she said it made them look younger. Well, Chelsea was nearly forty years of age and she could do whatever the fuck she wanted. 'I don't want any more,' she said. 'It looks great the way it is.'

The makeup artist raised his eyebrows but he didn't say anything, and Nancy floundered. She wasn't used to Chelsea talking back. 'Sure,' she said. 'As long are you're happy.' She pointed at the two men in the corner with a camera and sound equipment. 'Who are these guys?'

'They're from Foto,' Chelsea explained. 'Nick said I could do the show if I agreed to live-stream it on the app.'

'And the network agreed to that?' Nancy frowned. 'How come I didn't hear about it?'

'I don't know.'

Nancy looked around the room. 'Where's Nya?'

'She's with her own makeup and hair people,' Kelly piped up. 'In a salon nearby. I'm just texting her. She'll be here in twenty minutes.'

Chelsea threw her a look – she hadn't told Nya what Kelly had done, not yet, because she knew that once she did, the friendship between her two friends would completely implode. Nya had always found Kelly's ravenous ambition off-putting but she would never have imagined Kelly was capable of that level of duplicity. Chelsea had been the linchpin, keeping their trio together. Once she cut Kelly out, everything would fall apart and Kelly would be alone.

'Why are you worried about Nya?' Chelsea asked her agent, taking a sip from her bottle of water. It was glass, the increment times of the day marked into the side in cursive script, accompanied with cheerful affirmations. *You can do it! Keep going! No excuses!* 'It's not like she's your client any more.'

'I know that,' Nancy said, somewhat stiffly. 'I was just being polite. I—'

She was interrupted by a rush of activity. The door opened and an entire entourage entered, talking loudly. It was Robbie, Chelsea saw, her mouth drying. He was accompanied by his agent, his assistant, and a younger woman whom she didn't recognize. They were dressed in smart clothes, blazers and slacks. Perhaps they were from the network. He paused, his eyes going from person to person, smiling broadly.

'Hey,' Kelly called. She looked like she wanted to get up and hug him but the hairdresser was dealing with a particularly unruly section of hair so she was trapped. 'It's so good to see you, Robbie!'

He barely acknowledged her, sitting next to Chelsea instead, and she pretended not to notice Kelly's face falling. He leaned in so he could murmur in her ear and she resisted the urge to shiver. *I hate you*, she wanted to scream at him. *I hate you for what you did to my sister, you fucking monster.* But she forced herself to stay calm, like she didn't know the truth. She was an actor, after all, and an excellent one, no matter what he had tried to make her believe.

'You look great,' he said. He continued, when Chelsea remained silent, 'I heard that you found out about the *Double the Trouble* script. I'm sorry.' He sighed, as if it pained him to discuss this. 'I did tell Erin she should talk to you about it. I've been uncomfortable with this level of secrecy all along.' He sounded so sincere, she almost believed him. Fuck, this guy was good. 'But you know what your mother's like.' He took her hand in his. 'But now that you're aware . . . well . . .' he dropped his voice even lower '. . . I was wondering if you might be interested in playing the twins' mother?'

She pulled away, unable to disguise her shock. 'Mom said she—'

'No. I always intended that role for you. You were my muse, Chelsea. And besides . . .' he gave a little laugh '. . . it would be meta having you play that part, wouldn't it?'

She opened her mouth to reply but was interrupted by the director of the reunion show, a wiry woman in her mid-thirties with a buzz cut and a Betty Boop tattoo on her left biceps, as she knocked on the door. 'Okay, guys,' she said. 'We need you all on set in thirty minutes. Are we ready?'

Kelly kept smiling in her direction during the interview, making inside jokes, but Chelsea was giving her nothing. She knew that the viewers would notice – they were probably tweeting about it right now. *What's going on with Chelsea and Kelly? I thought they were besties. I don't know but the vibes are off for sure!!!!* The child star in her felt anxious – she wanted to turn it on, to be professional – but Chelsea couldn't seem to bring herself to do it. Let them say what they wanted about her. The slightest crinkle of the piece of paper tucked inside her shirt reminded her of why she was there, what she'd come to do.

She licked her lower lip, then made accidental eye contact with Nya. Her friend was frowning, ever so slightly, and Chelsea knew Nya wanted to ask if she was okay but she couldn't, not when they were live. She wished she could have told Nya the truth before the broadcast, about Kelly, about Robbie and Maddie, about what she was planning to do, but Nya had always had a terrible poker face. She couldn't risk it.

'So, tell me, Robbie,' the interviewer turned to him, smiling. She was a seasoned broadcaster in her fifties, in a fitted red suit and high heels, heavy makeup shellacked onto her face. 'What made you say yes to doing *Vigilante Queens* in the first place? It seems obvious in hindsight, given what a cultural phenomenon it went on to be, but that wasn't the case in 2003, was it?'

'Absolutely not,' he said. 'I'd worked on a few other projects as assistant director, as well as some sitcoms and network shows.' He half gestured at Chelsea. 'That's where I came across Chelsea. My girlfriend at the time was her tutor and we all hung out on set.'

Chelsea waited for the interviewer to comment on this, to

say how strange it was for two adults to want to hang around with teenage girls, but the woman said nothing.

'I could tell from the first moment I met her that she had the potential to be a once-in-a-lifetime talent.'

'Really?' the host said, then flushed slightly. 'My apologies, Chelsea. I didn't—'

'No offence taken,' Chelsea said. 'I doubt anyone who watched *Double Trouble* thought I'd be nominated for an Oscar one day!'

'I did,' The Director insisted. 'I could see it there, that magic you need. Chelsea had something, even then.'

'You wanted to work with her again?' the host prompted.

'Oh, absolutely,' he said. 'Now, I have to be honest, I was a pretentious young man who had very serious ideas about the kind of films I wanted to make. I wanted to make art, not teen dramas. I'd never even heard of the *Vigilante Queens* books but I went home for Christmas in 2001, I think, and one of my cousins was obsessed with the series and she told me I had to buy the—'

'That's not true,' Chelsea interrupted him, and everyone turned to look at her.

The interviewer was surprised but Chelsea could see something else there, a gleam of something in her eyes. 'How do you mean, Chelsea?' the woman asked, for this story was well known. Robbie Myers returning to his modest family home for Christmas, to the single mother who had raised him, and the three younger cousins she had adopted when her sister died in a car crash. One of the cousins had been a huge *Vigilante Queens* fan and she had spent the entirety of the holidays badgering Robbie until he gave up and read the first book. *I finished it in six hours*, he'd said hundreds of times in the years since. *And I knew it could be the biggest thing since* Dawson's Creek, *if made by the right person.* He would shrug then, dipping his head, bashful. *I really wanted to be that person.*

'I said,' Chelsea said slowly, 'that's not true. Is it, Robbie?' He widened his eyes but he didn't reply. 'It was Madeline who told you about the books. She told you that *she* wanted to buy the rights. She told you in confidence but you fucked her over and—'

'Okay,' the interviewer stepped in smoothly. 'We apologize to anyone watching at home for that language. We do hope it didn't cause any offence. But now—'

'No, I've not finished,' Chelsea said. 'I want to hear you admit it, Robbie. Stop lying for once.'

'I'm not—' he started, but Chelsea reached into her shirt pocket and pulled out the letter.

'Do you know what this is?' she asked. Kelly and Nya were frozen, unsure of what to do, and she could hear someone yelling in the interviewer's earpiece, giving instructions, trying to wrestle back control of the situation.

'No,' Robbie replied weakly. His eyes darted off set to where his manager was standing, but they couldn't help him now, not on a live broadcast.

'Let me read it out for you,' Chelsea said. She unfolded it, then looked straight down the camera lens and, with her left hand, she reached up to touch her compass. A message for her sister, if she was watching. *Wherever you go, I'll always be with you.* 'This is the note my twin sister left behind the night she disappeared,' she said, and she could hear gasps, heard Nya say, 'Chelsea, what are you—' and Kelly muttering, *Fuck*, under her breath, and Robbie saying, 'This is totally inappropriate,' then the interviewer saying, 'Okay, maybe we should go to commercial break,' but Chelsea kept talking, reminding viewers to watch on the Foto app. Who cared about the network? This was being live-streamed, right to their phones.

Nick had been hesitant at first, it was dodgy territory, legally, but then she had said that a divorce would probably cost him more, pre-nup or no pre-nup, and he immediately capitulated at the mention of money. Why had she been afraid of her husband for such a long time? Why had she been afraid of all these men? She was Chelsea fucking Stone, and she was afraid of no one.

'"I loved Robbie,"' she read Maddie's words aloud from the page. Her voice started to wobble and she forced herself to stay steady. '"I loved him from the first moment I saw him but I made myself pretend that I didn't. There was no point. I was only a kid, there was no way he would look at me like that, and I wasn't going to humiliate myself. But he kept seeking me out. He would find me in my dressing room or after tutoring, when I was getting my hair and makeup done, and he would sit and talk with me. He would ask me what I was reading and what music I was listening to, what—"'

'This is ridiculous,' Robbie shouted over her, but he was rattled – you didn't have to know him as well as Chelsea did to see that. 'We have . . .' He looked off set to where the producer was standing. 'We have only a minute or so left before we have to come back from break and she's still talking. Can't someone get rid of her?'

'You'd like that, wouldn't you?' Nya muttered, and before he could turn on her, Chelsea kept going.

'"I couldn't believe it the first day we kissed,"' she read aloud. '"I was only fifteen but he told me how mature I was. I didn't look my age, he said, I was an old soul. I was different. That was what he said to me the first time we had sex too. It was three months before my sixteenth birthday and—"' Robbie started shouting again but Chelsea refused to be silenced, not now, not by him. '"Afterwards, as we lay there together,"' she read, '"he told me he loved me. And he was going to help me buy the rights to *Vigilante Queens*, and we would co-direct it and I would star in it but ultimately, it would be my project, I would be in control. It would be perfect, he said. We'd be on set somewhere in North Carolina, no one would bother us. And the legal age of consent was sixteen there. We would be free to be together, properly together."' Chelsea's voice split in two as she read the next line. "'But then he gave the role to my sister. He said it was because she did a better audition but I know he chose her because she was untainted. She had my face but she was still pure in his eyes. This way, I could remain his dirty little secret.'"

Chaos was breaking out in the room. Robbie was shouting, 'This is bullshit. What the fuck is this? What the fuck?' and his manager was on set now, saying, 'Is this some kind of ambush?' and asking how much of that was caught on camera, that The Director would sue, he would sue every fucking person on set, and the producers of the show were talking in quick, urgent voices, but Chelsea could see they didn't have a clue what to do.

'Please,' the youngest of them kept saying weakly, 'Please, if you could just stay where you are, please—' and now Nancy was running towards her, but her agent couldn't seem to get her words out, she just stood in front of Chelsea, mouthing furiously. Robbie's manager grabbed Nancy's shoulder, spinning her around until she faced him, and Nancy hissed at him, 'Get your hands off me,' and he told her to get her fucking client under control, that they were gonna sue her too. Chelsea kept her focus on the Foto live cam, checking with the camera man that he was still rolling, that he was getting everything, and he nodded at her. He hadn't hesitated, not for a minute.

'Chel,' Nya was out of her chair and she was by Chelsea's side. Her face was tight with concern. 'Are you okay? Where did you get this letter?'

She took Chelsea's hand in hers and Chelsea said, 'I'm fine, I just . . . I have to do this.' She looked over her shoulder at where Kelly was still sitting in her chair, shell-shocked, staring into empty space.

'What the fuck is wrong with you?' Robbie was marching towards them. Nya stood between them, trying to protect her, like Maddie would have done, but Chelsea didn't need someone else to take care of her any more.

'I can deal with this,' she told Nya, and for the first time in her life, she knew it was true.

'What are you playing at?' Robbie said.

She held out the letter so he could read it and she watched him skim the words, his lips turning up in a snarl. 'What the fuck is this?' he said. 'Some bullshit piece of paper? It's forged. And if it's not forged, if your sister did actually write this, who's gonna believe the ravings of a junkie?'

Chelsea shrank at that, and she could see Robbie regretted saying it. 'Chel,' he said, softening, 'I'm sorry. But you know me. You know I would never do anything like this, right? How do you think I could do this to Maddie? She was just a kid.'

'I know she was,' Chelsea said, and she reached into the pocket of her skirt. She pulled out the photograph that had been hidden there, and she showed it to him. He paled and tried to grab it from her, but she stepped out of reach, walking over to the camera man. She held it up to the Foto live-stream, allowing it to be seen by the tens of millions of people watching. It was a Polaroid of Madeline, wearing only a pair of white and pink polka-dot panties, sitting cross-legged on a crumpled bed, holding the camera out in front of her. She was breathtakingly young with her barely budding breasts and her rosy cheeks. And behind her, naked, with his legs wrapped around hers and his right arm holding Maddie's stomach, was Robbie.

'I . . .' He was at a loss for words. He looked to his manager, whose face had gone equally pale, and the older man said, 'Come on,' and hustled Robbie out of the room, muttering, 'Don't say another word.'

Whatever Happened to Madeline Stone?

A hush had descended now. Some of the crew were on their own phones, clearly watching the live-stream, whispering at each other, 'She's so young,' and 'Jesus Christ,' until their bosses yelled at them to get the fuck back in the game, they had to run another minute of adverts before going live again.

Chelsea sat down in her seat, still holding up the photo, and she tilted her head, a signal to the camera man to come closer to her. 'The truth is,' she said, once he was in position, 'I don't blame Robbie Myers for what happened to my sister, not entirely anyway. He was just a part of the problem. He was . . .' She tried to remember what Milo James had said to her that day in the coffee shop. 'There was an eco-system, you see,' she said. 'And we were part of it, Madeline and me. We had to play our role because all that mattered was getting the shot. That's what we were told. But we were just kids. We shouldn't have been there in the first place. We shouldn't have been *working*. Why were we working so hard at that age? How is that even legal? Our mother shouldn't have been allowed to use us like that. And everyone around us – our agent and the head of the studio and the producers and the cast and crew – why did they allow it to happen? Why did they stand by and watch as we were sold to the highest bidder? And when we were older, the bloggers and the magazines and the late-night-show hosts making fun of us, and the websites with their countdown until it was our eighteenth birthday, and the paparazzi were pointing their cameras up our skirts . . . and you.' She pointed at the camera. 'All of you watching. You were complicit too. You bought those magazines. You read those blogs. You *laughed* at us. You said we were bad role models when all we wanted was to be girls.' She caught Kelly's eye and she could see her friend was crying, and while Chelsea knew she wouldn't forgive Kelly, she could never trust her after what she had done, she felt sorry for her too. She had been a victim just as much as Chelsea had, and as Maddie had been too.

'And I'm not blameless either,' she said, straight down the camera, as she had rehearsed the night before. 'I wanted to be famous. I thought that if everyone loved me, maybe that would mean I would finally feel good enough.' Her gaze zipped to Kelly again, then back to the camera. 'There are probably people watching this right now who feel the same. Or maybe your kids do – maybe they want to be singers or actors. Maybe they have YouTube channels where they play with toys for subscribers and you think it's cute, and the money doesn't hurt, does it? But you don't understand what it's like to be treated like a commodity. You don't know what it does to you, how corrosive it is. You become an object, a thing, something not quite human and then . . . Well. You've seen so many of us fall apart, haven't you? I don't have to list all the names. You've seen them self-destruct in front of the cameras. Another kid and another kid and another kid. And every time this happens, every time we watch a former child star overdose outside a nightclub or shave their head and smash in a car window or fall off a hotel balcony to their death or go to prison, we say how sad it is, how tragic, as if there's nothing we can do to stop it. We know that fame will kill these kids if they're not strong enough, and how many of us are, at that age? I thought Maddie was strong but I didn't know what Robbie Myers had done to her, and then what the industry did to her in turn. They used her up and they tried to throw her away, like she was trash. But she was a person. She was a real person and I don't know where she is now. I don't know if she's alive or dead and I miss her so much.' Chelsea brushed away a tear. 'Maddie, if you're watching this, I'm sorry. I'm so sorry. You were the love of my life and I'm sorry for everything I did.'

38.

2025

Chelsea walked out of the TV studio, ignoring Nancy Taylor calling after her. The paparazzi were outside, jostling to get closer, asking her what she was going to do about The Director. 'He's already denied it,' one particularly eager man said, his teeth bared. She didn't dignify that with a response. Robbie was finished. They all knew that. No matter how hard he tried to come back from this, it would take only one call from her husband to bury him. She sent pics of the letter and the photo to her assistant, and the log-in details for her Foto account, and she told Hannah to post them immediately. She put on her sunglasses to protect her eyes from the glare of the camera flashes and waited until her team pushed the photographers back, protecting her as they bundled her into a waiting SUV, and she wished, as she always did, that she'd been able to afford security like this at the height of her fame. The difference it would have made to her, and to Maddie. It could have saved her.

Chelsea buckled her seatbelt, taking her cell out of her purse. There were multiple missed calls and then the screen lit up. It was Nick calling. She sighed. She'd have to deal with that later. She let it go to voicemail and said to Afi, 'Drive. Please.'

They sat in silence as he wove in and out of the traffic. 'I think we've lost them,' he said, looking at her in the rear-view mirror. The way he was staring at her, as if he was half in awe of her, half afraid, made her want to laugh, if only she had the energy. She shook herself out of her stupor. 'Great,' she said.

They continued driving and he turned on the radio. 'And in today's news, the entertainment industry is in shock at Chelsea Stone's claims that—'

He slammed his hand against the dial immediately, turning it to a classical-music station. 'I'm sorry about that,' he said quickly.

'Don't worry. I'll have to get used to it, I reckon.' Chelsea stared out of the window, at the beautiful people in their tight workout clothes jogging on the spot at the traffic lights, a group of girlfriends sitting outside a popular brunch spot, eating their egg-white omelettes, tiny dogs dozing at their feet, a suited businessman sweating in the midday sun as he waited at his hotel entrance for his Uber to arrive. 'Am I taking you home?' the driver asked, and the thought of all that awaited at the house in Montecito – Nick and his questions, the kids, the staff – all of it wearied her.

'No, Afi,' she said. 'Could we go to the beach?'

'Which one?'

'Pismo Beach,' she said, for where else could she go? And he nodded, indicating left at the next set of traffic lights.

When they arrived, she got out of the car. The roar of the ocean and the tang of salt on the air. She could feel her carefully blown-out hair curling already. She took her shoes off and held them in one hand, moving along the boardwalk until she was closer to the shore. She sat on the sand, feeling its grains beneath her bare feet, and she stared out at the horizon. There would be phone calls to make, conversations to be had. She had thrown a grenade into her carefully ordered life and the clean-up would be considerable, she knew that, but there was nothing else she could have done. She wondered if Carter had seen the show, if he would contact her again, but she couldn't bring herself to care. She had loved him and he had loved her but that wasn't enough sometimes. She wasn't sure what would happen with her and Nick but, in the end, he was her husband. They had chosen one another and they had two children together and that mattered. It meant something. She touched her hand to the sand and she remembered a day, such a long time ago now, when they had smelt summer in the air, and Maddie had wanted to go to the beach. 'Not today,' their mother had snapped. 'You have to do re-shoots.' They'd filmed a *Double Trouble* movie earlier that year – *Eiffel for Two* was supposedly set in Paris but shot on location in Canada, and the network executives weren't happy with the ending: they said it wouldn't play well with audiences. It meant a full week of re-shoots when they were supposed to be on vacation – 'You do realize,' Maddie had said, 'we've had less than five days off this year?' and Erin had told her to be grateful, there were a million girls who would kill for these opportunities – but Maddie had had enough.

She'd snuck into Chelsea's room that morning, before their mother was awake. 'Get up,' she'd whispered, shaking her twin's shoulder.

'Is the car here?' Chelsea had said sleepily.

'No,' Maddie had replied. She and Chelsea had tiptoed downstairs and out of the front door. Their bikes were waiting, and Maddie had a backpack with their swimsuits and bottled water and some snacks, too, and they had cycled to the beach, just the two of them. When Chelsea had started fretting, wondering how much trouble they were in, Maddie had told her to stop. 'They can't do anything when it's the two of us,' she'd said. 'That's the only time we have any real power. It's me and you, against the world.'

Chelsea felt a lump in her throat. There was so much she wished she could say to her sister, but perhaps that was the thing she was most sorry for. That she had permitted everyone around them to come between her and Maddie when really, as her sister had said, they were more powerful together. They could have protected each other, if only she had allowed it.

She stood up, shaking sand off her skirt. She kept watching the sea, the tide coming in and out, and she pictured her sister, Maddie, with her bright blue eyes, throwing her head back as she laughed. How beautiful she had been, how free. Chelsea was about to turn when her phone rang. It was her old number, the BlackBerry she never used any more but had brought with her today, just in case. She pulled it out of her pocket and stared at the screen. It was a private number, but as she put her cell to her ear she knew who it was going to be. It was like she had been waiting for this call for the last seventeen years. 'Hello,' she said, as she answered, and she touched her necklace again. There was an inhalation of breath at the other end of the phone, the one she always heard in her dreams, and then that voice, still so similar to her own.

'Hey,' the voice said. 'It's me. Can you hear me?'

'Maddie.' Tears were streaming down her face. Chelsea could taste the salt on her lips but she didn't brush them away. She couldn't move. *'Maddie.'*

Acknowledgements

Firstly, as ever, I must thank my incredible agent, Juliet Mushens. Your sharp instincts, guidance and tireless support – not to mention your seemingly never-ending reserve of memes – makes you a joy to know. I admire you so much, and am in constant awe of your work ethic and drive. I'm very fortunate to have you in my corner! With thanks, too, to Emma Dawson at Mushens Entertainment, and Emily Hayward-Whitlock at The Artists Partnership.

Thank you to my editor, Imogen Nelson, for being such a steady hand, and for seeing what this story could be from the very beginning. I'm so grateful for your careful attention and the clear-eyed edits which shaped this book. With thanks to the rest of the excellent team at Transworld – Viv Thompson, Anna Nightingale, Irene Martínez, Lucy Upton, Isabella Ghaffari-Parker, Sophie Dwyer, Deirdre O'Connor and Lorna Browne. I must also thank Frankie Gray for her kindness, and for encouraging me to take a different route with my fiction.

To my three early readers, Catherine Doyle, Marian Keyes and Sophie White. How lucky am I to have such talented friends? Thank you for reading rough drafts, for giving thoughtful feedback, and for being so loving and reassuring in general.

Thanks to Jackie Emerson for introducing me to Laura Marano, and thank you, Laura, for reading the manuscript and giving such incisive notes. I was blown away by your generosity, and how willingly you gave of your time and expertise. (Any errors are most definitely my own.) You are a wonder.

Thank you to the very kind man I met in New York who gave me an insight into the world of American billionaires. Again, all mistakes are my own.

Thank you to MT for brainstorming with me while I was in copy-edit hell, and to Ciara, for turning up with a candle and a handwritten note just when I needed it. And as always, eternal gratitude to my amazing friends and family, but especially my parents. Mike and Marie, you gave me stories before I could read them, and more love than most people get in a dozen lifetimes. None of this would be possible without the two of you.

Reading Group Questions

1. The psychic's prophecy hangs over the story like a curse. Do you think it shaped what happened, or did the characters give it power through their choices? How did it affect Erin and Chelsea in different ways?

2. Child stardom is shown as both an opportunity and a form of exploitation. How did growing up in the public eye shape the women Chelsea and Maddie become? Do you think either of them ever had real agency as children?

3. Chelsea often tries to keep the peace in her family. How does being 'the responsible one' affect her relationships with the other characters? In what other ways does the novel explore the line between protection and control?

4. The novel uses diaries, blog posts and interviews alongside the main narrative. How did these different voices inform your experience as a reader? In what ways has the media landscape changed since the early 2000s, and in what ways has it stayed the same?

5. Although Chelsea and Maddie are twins, their lives take very different paths. In what ways do they still reflect each other, and where do their differences matter most?

6. The book explores complicity alongside victimhood, with many characters who are both harmed by the system and a part of it. Were there moments when your sympathy for any of the characters felt challenged? Why?

7. Motherhood is shown through both Erin and Chelsea. How does Chelsea try to parent differently from her own mother, and where does she struggle to escape the past?

8. The ending leaves some questions unresolved. How did you feel about that? What does the novel suggest about forgiveness, healing and hope?

About the Author

Louise O'Neill is a bestselling author from Clonakilty, West Cork. Her debut novel, *Only Ever Yours*, won multiple awards including the Sunday Independent Newcomer of the Year and the inaugural YA Book Prize. Her second novel, *Asking For It*, spent fifty-two consecutive weeks in the Irish top 10 and was awarded the Michael L. Printz honour by the American Library Association.

She has since published *The Surface Breaks*, a feminist retelling of 'The Little Mermaid', which was shortlisted for the Specsavers National Book Awards, and three novels for adults: *Almost Love*, *After the Silence* – named Crime Novel of the Year at the Irish Book Awards 2020 – and *Idol*, which went straight into the Irish book charts at No. 1. Her memoir, *A Bigger Life*, is coming in autumn 2026. *Whatever Happened to Madeline Stone?* is her latest novel.